Praise for Sarah Smit.. s Crimes and Survivors

§ The *Titanic* still cruises our imaginations... And she has secrets. Sarah Smith knows them and knows how to tell them in this **riveting, page-turning** novel, a tale unraveling from out of the ignorant past, through that terrible moment of truth on the *Titanic*, and on toward a hopeful future. **Read it and be enthralled.—** WILLIAM MARTIN, *New York Times* bestselling author of *Cape Cod* and *Bound for Gold*:

§ You may think you know everything there is to know about Titanic, but Sarah Smith's *Crimes and Survivors* carves out a space of its own—while, in the same breath, demarcating a huge swath of America's history and painting a resonant vision of its future. The result is **suspenseful, insightful, moving and highly recommended.—**LOUIS BAYARD, bestselling author of *Courting Mr. Lincoln*

§ A **thrilling and romantic literary mystery that unflinchingly examines issues of race and identity, love and family, and the danger and beauty of uncovering long-hidden truths. —** SARAH STEWART TAYLOR, author of the Sweeney St. George mysteries and *The Mountains Wild*

§ Come for the rich prose, meticulous research, and vibrant characters. Stay for the **heart-stopping mystery.** Sarah Smith's **fresh take on the doomed *Titanic* sailing is filled with twists and turns** and will enthrall both new readers and longtime fans of the *Vanished Child* series!"
Edwin Hill, Edgar- and Agatha-nominated author of *Little Comfort* and *The Missing Ones*

...and for Sarah Smith's other books

§ "Stunning...Tells a grim tale of murder and duplicity in stately prose that subtly enhances the psychological horrors...."

The New York Times **(Notable Book of the Year)**
on *The Vanished Child*

§ "A stunning tale of love, amnesia, child abuse, Victorian sexual repression and murder most foul....The satisfying denouement is a shocker."

Publishers Weekly **(starred review) on** *The Vanished Child*

§ "A lushly erotic, feminist study of artists and lovers and killers swept up in their obsessive passions. An exquisite stylist, [Smith] observes her characters in...intimate detail, defining them with witty precision and placing them in a rain-drenched portrait of Edwardian Paris that could hang in the Louvre."

The New York Times **(Notable Book of the Year)**
on *The Knowledge of Water*

§ "Intellectual stimulation of the highest order...a ripping yarn with provocative and substantial things to say."

Kirkus Reviews **(starred review) on** *The Knowledge of Water*

§ "As satisfying a mystery as the Mona Lisa's smile."

USA Today **on** *The Knowledge of Water*

§ "A virtuosic fusion of speculative history, boldly stylized character drawing, and intricately plotted rousing melodrama...Fiction just doesn't get any more entertaining and satisfying than this. A bloody triumph."

Kirkus Reviews **(starred review) on** *A Citizen of the Country*

§ "[Smith] fills the third installment with endlessly satisfying plot twists, historical verisimilitude, and character development--and still manages to keep her eye on the overarching question: ..."Where do I belong?"...*A Citizen of the Country* illuminates a society on the brink, a way of life about to be lost forever...and one man's journey, by the hardest roads, home to his family."

Detroit Free Press **(four stars) on** *A Citizen of the Country*

§ "Stunning...Sarah Smith skillfully takes readers into the dark world of the human psyche and spirit."

Romantic Times **on** *A Citizen of the Country*

CRIMES
and
SURVIVORS

SARAH SMITH

max light books

Also by Sarah Smith
The Vanished Child
The Knowledge of Water
A Citizen of the Country

Chasing Shakespeares
The Other Side of Dark

For more about the *Titanic* and Sarah Smith's other books,
including book club questions, and to contact her, visit:
https://www.sarahsmith.com
Facebook sarahwriter, Sarah Smith's Books
Twitter, Instagram sarahwriter
Pinterest swrs

Man with his burning soul
has but an hour of breath
to build a ship of truth
in which his soul may sail.
For death takes toll
of beauty, courage, youth;
of all but truth.
  —John Masefield

They that go down to the sea in ships
and occupy their business in great waters,
these see the works of the Lord,
and His wonders in the deep.
—Psalm 107; inscription on the grave of Bruce Ismay

For the survivors.

                              O.M.D.D.

ARE YOU GOING to survive *Titanic?*

There's a game people play at *Titanic* exhibitions and dinner parties. When you arrive, you get a ticket with a name on it. You are Dorothy Gibson, or John Jacob Astor, or Bruce Ismay. At the end of the evening you find out whether you survived or died.

They don't tell you what surviving means. What happens the next morning, and for the rest of your life. How you change. What you learn.

Here you are, somewhere in the North Atlantic, a hundred years ago. It's 11:44 P.M. ship's time, two minutes until the iceberg. You're standing on the deck. *Titanic's* the largest moving thing on earth or sea, the most beautiful ship, the safest. Look up at her Marconi antenna, that long wire from the bow past her funnels all the way to the stern, four New York city blocks long, the biggest telegraph antenna in the world. *Titanic's* wireless blasts across the ocean; you can hear her for five hundred miles. The millionaires show off, sending expensive telegrams: "Greetings from *Titanic.*" "Arrive New York Wednesday morning. Meet me in New York."

Ninety seconds.

Titanic has two telegraph operators, Jack Phillips and Harold Bride. Most ships have one. On the only ship near *Titanic,* the "Marconi man" has just taken off his headset and fallen exhausted into bed, and when Jack Phillips sends CQD, Come Quick Distress, and then SOS, SOS, SOS, no one close enough to help will hear.

Outside each other's safe islands of wireless, each ship in its darkness sails alone. There is no one to watch but God. And tonight God wants to play a game, about the greatest ship ever built and what happened to her, about love and death, heroism and cowardice and survival.

Seventy-five seconds.

In the first-class lounge, the bridge players are complaining. They know this route so well it bores them. *Titanic* is magnificent, of course, but it's the same bridge games; the same cooking one is used to in London or New York or Paris; the same faces at the same tables, the same music in the background. Tomorrow there'll be a dog show in first class, Astor's Airedale against some Poms and chows. One even knows the dogs.

Sixty-five seconds.

In the first-class lounge, an American girl is improvising ragtime on a piano and thinking about her family. She's a baroness, although she still jumps and looks around when anyone calls her that. Her name is Perdita. Her husband is Alexander Reisden, the owner of the famous Jouvet Medical Analyses. They have a son, Toby. Perdita's going to America to play at Carnegie Hall, her first big chance as a pianist. But she's on *Titanic* to solve a mystery that may keep her from playing Carnegie Hall or anywhere else, ever again. She's thinking about that.

In their cabin, Isidor and Ida Straus are looking at pictures of their grandchildren. In his suite, John Jacob Astor, richest man in America, is planning how to reconcile his family to his new young wife.

They're planning for a future they'll never see.

In her first-class cabin, the actress Dorothy Gibson is reading about herself in *Photoplay*. Tomorrow she and the cinematographer Billy Harbeck will shoot scenes aboard *Titanic*. Back in New Jersey, they'll make it into a movie, *Her Shipboard Romance*, "filmed aboard *Titanic*." Dorothy can see the posters.

Forty seconds.

In third class Polish and Swedish and Irish teenagers are awake, flirting. In three days they'll be American. They say America gives you new names. They say the streets are paved with gold and the cobblestones are smooth as lovers' lips. All they know is they are traveling to a new country. All they know, they will be changed.

Twenty seconds.

The dogs are curled up in their kennels on the boat deck. In their sleep they smell the cold and sigh. The electric lights are dimmed along the white corridors in first class. In second and third, the oil lamps—yes, *Titanic* still has oil lamps—are turned down, there's a man who does it, Samuel Heming, lamp trimmer; he's turning a lamp key now. From the kitchens on D Deck rises that essence of the familiar and secure, the smell of breakfast rolls.

And the iceberg is off the bow.

A telegraph operator touches his key. A child is sleeping; a man is baking; a man is dimming lamps. A woman touches piano keys. A woman plans a movie. People think of their families.

Ten seconds.

God is watching.

No one is ready to die, no one to survive; this can't be the end of *Titanic*, not yet, not yet—

Part 1: *Titanic*

Autumn 1911, Paris: Alexander Reisden

FOR SEVEN DAYS, SEVEN UNREPEATABLE DAYS, he thought they'd have each other forever. They were his family, Gilbert and Perdita and Toby. His father, more or less. His wife. His son. They went to the beach, they walked on the sand, they had picnics. Their story was over and it had ended happily.

And then the letters started arriving from Boston, two or three of them a day, Gilbert's lawyers writing, Harry writing, and he realized they couldn't be a family after all.

So here they are.

Toby's throwing a ball, and Gilbert's beagle Elphinstone is skittering after it, chasing it into the corners of the room, through the door, down the hall, and limping back triumphantly with it. "Ahhh!" Toby laughs and throws it again.

"He and Elphinstone were at it all this afternoon," Perdita says, brushing a harried curl off her face.

"We shouldn't have left you so long."

She looks up at him, hesitating a moment before she dares to ask. "Have you decided?"

She ought to know there was only one possible decision. "We can't keep Gilbert. He's going back to America."

"No!" she says; "oh *no*." Toby looks up at her tone and bursts into tears. Reisden kneels down and gathers up his son.

"It's all right, dear boy. It's all right." It's not all right. Toby hiccups against his shoulder. Reisden smooths his little boy's dark curls. "Shh. There."

"It's not all right." Perdita goes to the door and calls. "Aline! It's time for Toby's bath." It's not, but Toby's nursemaid appears. Toby struggles, not wanting to leave. "There, baby," Perdita says. "You can have Elphinstone again as soon as you're clean."

"Eff in bath!" Toby demands.

"Eff *not* in bath." She gives him a kiss and hands him over, closes the door, and leans against it. *"Why?"*

"Did you think it could be different?" He puts the ball back in Toby's box of toys and sits down on the sofa, gathering himself to justify what he and Gilbert have done. Elphinstone sniffs at the door and whines. "Let him out," Reisden says. Having Gilbert Knight's beagle there is too much like having Gilbert.

"No, stay, Elphinstone." The little beagle whines once and then obediently, sadly, thumps himself down by the fireplace. Perdita sits down on the sofa too, at the other end: a strip of uncertainty between them.

"How can you send him back?"

"He's decided to go back. There's a difference."

"Harry was *mistreating* him in Boston. Harry was stealing his letters, ignoring him—He left with nothing but his dog and the clothes he was wearing. And you're sending him back?"

"He decided. Himself."

"No. He's going back for your sake."

"For all our sakes. For Toby's."

"Not for *my* sake."

Do you think I want him to go? "We'll find ways to keep in touch. We'll write letters. Send photographs."

"Harry will tear up photographs from us. What shall I do when Uncle Gilbert writes back and *doesn't* say how Harry's treating him?"

Reisden already knows how Harry will treat Gilbert. Harry has never recovered from being adopted. Nothing is ever enough for Harry.

"How will *you* feel?" she asks.

"I'll feel we're all being responsible."

"We are not! This is because of Richard," she says.

"Of course it is." Richard Knight. Gilbert Knight's nephew. Who should have been Gilbert's safely dead nephew. The boy Harry replaced.

He half-changes the subject. "I went to see Richard's grave," he says. "When I was in Boston. Did I tell you that?"

"You went to see your own grave?"

"Gilbert had just had the name and dates engraved on the stone." He'd wanted to see. Richard Knight, 1879-1887. Richard dead and gone.

"And what was it like? Did you like yourself being dead?"

That was why he'd gone there. To find out what it was like to survive Richard. "I thanked him. For being dead and leaving me alive."

He'd brought flowers. Half in sarcasm.

But he'd put one of them in his buttonhole and walked away a free man. Not innocent. Not happy. But free of Richard.

"And I'm thanking Gilbert now. I'm sorry. I don't want him gone. But when I married you," he continues, "I could think 'at least she's not marrying Richard.' And when Toby was born, 'he's not Richard's son.'" He hesitates and says it. "He's not a murderer's son. And I don't want him to be."

"It wasn't murder," she says.

Richard Knight. Supposedly a victim. Kidnapped, killed, the body never found. Actually a murderer, at eight years old. Richard's grandfather had been outright insane. After Richard's parents drowned, orphaned Richard had ended up in William Knight's care. William had beaten Richard, with a lead-weighted cane, with a fireplace poker. Then, the summer Richard had been eight,

William had gone on a business trip. Richard had found a stray puppy. When William had returned, he'd broken the dog's back and made Richard shoot it.

And that night, when William was going to punish his grandson for having the dog—

"It *wasn't* murder," Perdita says.

"When you shoot a man and he dies, love." Even when you're eight. Especially then. Jouvet has treated a few child murderers. Even the staff, who are calloused, are spooked by them.

"Uncle Gilbert says it was self-defense."

"Can you imagine, my love, just how I feel about you and Gilbert having that conversation?"

Her cheeks redden. "That's no excuse to send Uncle Gilbert home."

"That's not why. If we kept him here—"

"Which we should!"

"Sooner or later I'd have to explain why Richard ran away."

I would have to be a murderer.

"And I'd have to be *Richard*. Richard owned the Knight Companies; he'd have to be in charge of them. Harry wants the Knight Companies, let him have them. I want to stay me, only me, so there will be no murderers in this house, and no murderers' children."

"And so you're sending Uncle Gilbert back for Harry to mistreat."

"I am sending him back to advocate for himself. He can do it. We've both agreed. Will you?"

"I hate this."

Do you think I like it?

"We'll have Gilbert for a while," he says. "He won't go back to Boston immediately."

That isn't enough and they both know it. They sit in silence, she at one end of the sofa, he at the other. Finally she reaches out her hand; he takes it. This is as close to consent as she'll give.

"Only for your sake. And I wish you wouldn't."

"Thank you."

He wants to stay, holding her hand, in this fragile truce; but she takes it back and sits with her hands folded together on her lap. She presses her wide lips together and shakes her head. She's never been able to hide what she's thinking.

"What kind of flowers did you bring?" she asks finally, a little too brightly.

"Why on earth do you ask that?"

"Just thinking of you doing it."

"Chrysanthemums." Flowers for the safely dead.

"What made you think of it?"

"Oh, sentiment. Is it that odd?" *I was thinking, because I know who I am and it isn't Richard, I was going to lose Gilbert and you.* It had been a hook in his soul, wanting to stay with them. But he wasn't Richard. So he'd put a flower in his buttonhole and walked away.

He had lost both of them. And got them back, by miracle.

He won't get Gilbert back twice.

And when they lose Gilbert, when Harry does the inevitable and mistreats Gilbert again, what will Perdita feel?

Will he lose her too?

He hasn't been good at keeping people.

"Will you promise me—" she says. She breaks off a moment, then leans forward. "Promise me we won't regret it? We won't say we should have done something to help now, when we could?"

"I promise," he says.

She wants it. He hopes it.

But he doesn't believe it and he doubts she does.

❧❧❧

HOW LONG will they have with Gilbert?

Not enough time.

Reisden tries to give Gilbert something to take back with him, something to hold on to, when he must go.

Gilbert and he, and Elphinstone, meet for breakfast at a café. Gilbert orders breakfast to suit Elphinstone's liking for sausage. Gilbert polishes the café silverware nervously with the napkin, then with his own clean handkerchief. Gilbert is anxious about many things: the cleanliness of café silverware, the French drains... And he is going back to Boston, where Harry will take advantage of—

Where Gilbert will advocate for himself.

"It works out well that you'll be Jouvet's investor," Reisden tells him.

"It is my money," Gilbert says as if he's reminding himself.

"After you go back to Boston, I'll inform you of any major actions we take. I'll ask you to confirm you've seen our reports. Jouvet will send Christmas cards and the occasional chatty letter."

His uncle smiles genuinely. "Then I shall still hear from you."

"Yes." As much as I possibly can. "Getting a post-office box was a good suggestion. Perdita wants to write you too, and send photos of Toby."

"I can keep them in a safe deposit box."

Oh L—d.

"Is there not a difficulty, though? Simply with my being an investor in Jouvet? Harry and Mr. Pelham write they are *shocked* I am investing in—" Gilbert gestures vaguely, a polite way of not saying *you.* Elphinstone, patient under the café table, looks up, hoping for sausage. "Their feelings toward you are *not kind?* Harry will want to sell my investment? And if Harry did not sell, but became *involved* in your company? You know Harry is rather— controlling." Gilbert leaves the rest up to their imaginations.

"There's no question of control." Reisden sketches their business arrangements on a page of his notebook and passes it to Gilbert. "We'll make your stock preferred non-voting, which means you get income but no say in running Jouvet, and you'll be restricted from selling for—"

"My lifetime," Gilbert says, pleased.

"Five years. We'll be solidly profitable by then."

"My lifetime," his uncle says. "So that I shall always be able to hear from you. And when I die," Gilbert adds earnestly, "I'll leave the shares to you, Alexander. They shall not go to Harry."

"You can't do that; that's not what an investor would do. We'll write it so that, if you die, I shall have the right to buy them back. We'll set up a pricing schedule. Don't die, though."

Don't ever die.

In France, business transactions proceed at a mature, stately pace, but Gilbert and he do the deed as if they were sixteen: Gilbert's investment in Jouvet is certified, stamped, and sealed within the week. At the American Embassy, a pale, balding notary public makes them right with American law, blinks at the amount of money involved, raises his eyebrows at the dates, but wishes them a good day.

And so he and his uncle have an excuse to keep in touch with each other.

❧❧❧

"Give us a couple of days before you see what you've bought into," Reisden tells Gilbert. Gilbert has seen Jouvet the building, but not Jouvet the company, not the staff, not in any organized way.

He calls the staff together and tells them to clean up the labs. "Do something with the anatomical specimens. No crime scene photos. Whatever wouldn't suit your maiden aunt, take it down."

"What do we put up, *patron,* postcards of kittens? We're *Jouvet.*"

"Gilbert Knight scares easily and he's just invested a lot of money with us."

"Do we hide the patients too?" one of the techs scoffs. "*Monsieur le docteur,* you're like a new bride having the priest to dinner."

In his own office, Reisden stares grimly at the skull, the Vesalius woodcuts of flayed men, the shelves of books titled *Criminal Insanity* and *Murder in Families,* all of which will mean too much to Gilbert.

Jouvet treats madmen. No way around it.

But madmen don't like early mornings any more than you or I, so it's early Monday morning when Reisden brings Gilbert to Jouvet. All the staff, consulting psychiatrists, testers, nurses, lab techs, clerks, guards, even the Marconi coder and telegraphist, have all come in early to meet their new American millionaire. Gilbert hangs back, smiling uncertainly.

The technicians whisper behind their hands. "Monsieur le Docteur? The American looks like you."

"I've heard that before. I don't see it." If you can't get away with lying, bluff.

He makes introductions. He takes Gilbert on a quick tour of the labs (no slices of mad brain under the microscopes, no lab specimens floating in jars, good enough). They spend more time in the assessment area, which has nothing but amusing machines and shelves of intelligence tests. "Most of our profit is in tests. We do testing for the Army." Setups for measuring blindness and deafness; a little cheerful room with little wooden testing-trays for babies. ("Do babies go mad?" Gilbert asks, appalled. "No, no, we test for neurological problems," Reisden says quickly. They know children go mad. Children kill. Children run away.) The interview rooms. The Marconi station. The locked area that holds patient records. "We're careful about privacy." Thousands of files; hundreds of records of mad families like the Knights.

What do you think of what I've made? Is it good enough?

"Are there patients?" Gilbert asks.

From a darkened spy-closet off the lab, they look down at the Jouvet patients. In the principal waiting room—bright, reassuring—a man shudders with uncontrollable terror, a woman draws her shawl up over her head. In the room on the other side—

padded, guarded—a burly man with yesterday's slashes across his face shouts that he doesn't belong here in this *fucking place for mad people*. Gilbert goes pale.

"Jouvet can help," Reisden says. "Not all of them. But the families at least."

Jouvet might have helped you. Or me. We might have been able to stay a family. We wouldn't have made the mistakes we did. We'd have survived.

We have survived. But—

"It is about fixing, isn't it?" Gilbert says. "Making things better?"

"As much as one can. Yes," Reisden says. "Something I'm glad to give my life to."

"My dear boy," Gilbert says, "then I am so glad you have involved me."

❧❧❧

"WHERE IS UNCLE GILBERT going to live while he's here?" Perdita asks.

"He's in a hotel."

"I know he's in a hotel. Why isn't he staying with us?"

Because we're going to lose him soon. Don't make things worse.

"If this is all the time we have—" she says fiercely.

The next Saturday, she invites Gilbert to lunch. She tidies too, Reisden notes. The apartment is mirror-clean; flowers riot in vases everywhere.

She chats with Gilbert at lunch, catching up with Boston gossip. In Boston, Perdita had lived with her uncle, Buckingham Pelham, who was Gilbert's lawyer. The Pelhams and Gilbert Knight lived only a couple of blocks apart. She had always been at Gilbert's house, learning to play piano on his big unused Steinway. She had been the loving child to Gilbert that Harry had never been.

She calls Gilbert "Uncle."

Gilbert should have adopted her, not Harry.

After lunch she gives Cook and Aline the afternoon off and says she's taking Toby to play with the Bullard children. "Alexander, why don't you show Uncle Gilbert round?"

Then she leaves him, to invite Gilbert to stay with them, or not.

"This is our family room." His work desk in a corner; Perdita's piano in the next room. Toby's playpen, given him by a behaviorist consultant, together with a notebook in which the family is supposed to note Toby's progress on the consultant's standard scales. Elphinstone sniffs at it disdainfully. Quite right, dog.

"And the dining room," filled with afternoon sunlight. Over the sideboard hangs Mallais's *View of the Seine*.

"What a splendid picture."

"My cousin gave it to me. Here's the kitchen. We have refrigeration without ice," Reisden says, a little proud of this. "It runs off the vapor-compression system downstairs in the lab."

"Why, that is very clever! Is it dangerous?"

"No, not at all."

Photographs crowd the hall. Perdita loves photographs of their friends. She can hardly see them but she knows they're there.

"You have made such a good place," Gilbert says. "It is so," he looks for a word. "It is a home."

Yes. We are a normal family. We have a dining room with a view out the windows to the Eiffel Tower. There are pictures on the walls, not mad Biblical verses screaming repentance. In the hall we hang photos of people we like. We'll hang your photo among them, as if you were simply another friend.

"And this is Toby's room," Reisden says. Toby's favorite toy, his stuffed dog Puppy Lumpkin, has fallen on the floor; Reisden tucks it into Toby's crib. Look, Gilbert, Toby has stuffed animals. Toby's room is always warm in winter. He will never be in fear of his life. He has two parents and they love him. My son's life is better than Richard's was.

Look, Gilbert. We've survived. Almost any price is worth that.

Toby's room, Perdita's and his bedroom, the servants' sitting-room. Beyond them stretches a long dark hall, closed doors on either side. "We won't go there. That's our terrible secret."

Gilbert is more alarmed than he was at the mad patients. "If it is a secret, Alexander, you must not tell me—"

He laughs and shakes his head. "Not that kind." Not the kind that makes normality a triumph. "Only a painful housekeeping dilemma. I told you that, before I bought the company, the Jouvets owned it? Five generations of Dr. Jouvets. They all lived here, they all collected books, Egyptiana, they simply *accumulated,* and they never threw anything away. There's a roomful of ushabtis. Egyptian funerary statues. One I can understand, but a roomful? And the *books.* Since Perdita's lived here, they're all stuffed in the extra rooms. But if Perdita and I have more children, we shall have to colonize Darkest Sixth Floor."

"Books?" says his uncle. Gilbert was a used-book dealer before he became a millionaire.

Am I telling him he would like to live here and explore? He can't. We are going to lose him. We can't break our hearts over each other. "It's very dusty, I'm afraid."

"If you like, though, we might look at them," Gilbert inquires hesitantly.

They arm themselves with flashlights. The rooms closest to civilization are piled with packages of books still unopened, furred with dust; it's worse than Reisden remembered. "The last Dr. Jouvet was over ninety when he died," he says, blaming the mess callously on Jules Jouvet. He hopes he was exaggerating about the roomful of ushabtis, but he's not; his flashlight picks out rows of little faience mummies with scowling green faces. A Napoleonic sphinx stares aristocratically from under cobwebs. In another room, ancient ballgowns pose on stands, a crowd of headless çi-devants.

"Alexander, it's a museum."

"My dear man. It's a slum."

Gilbert picks up a book, reads a moment, puts it respectfully back down. Gilbert had expected to be poor all his life. His father had disinherited him. Richard had been William's heir, which had caused endless trouble when William was murdered and Richard disappeared. Then, not so long ago, when Richard had finally been declared dead, Gilbert had inherited from Richard.

Richard's money. Of course Harry says it's about the money.

Without it, perhaps Harry might not have cared so much about Gilbert.

Except us. We'd have cared, and we could have kept him. If only Harry had the money and we had Gilbert.

At the end of the hall there's a room he's not seen before: dust-covered but miraculously uncluttered, almost bare. The shutters are folded open, letting in rich light. "Oh—" Gilbert steps forward into the light, then back, as if he's trespassing.

"No," Reisden says, suddenly nervous; "go in, look round."

It's a workroom, the corner every large library develops where books are sorted and bindings are repaired. Gilbert picks up a bookbinder's punch and peers at it. Gilbert has a room like this in Boston, with tools and leather and gold leaf.

"If Dr. Jouvet needed a punch like this," Gilbert says, "he may have some quite interesting books."

Who is Gilbert? Not his uncle. Gilbert can't be his uncle. Only an investor. But for this instant he's someone else, a book-lover holding a leather-punch. A kind old man, who keeps a dog and repairs books. *This is all the time we have.* "I suppose one should find out what the Jouvets left here." I shouldn't do this, he thinks. Who are we to each other? Who can we be? We can't be anyone. We have to give this up.

"I might come over from time to time," Gilbert suggests, "as long as I am here in Paris, and look through the books, if you like. Just to be useful, you know."

"That would be a great help." He is overcome with his own feeling of trespass. "And— You should stay here. I mean, unless you have someplace you'd prefer; the apartment's ridiculously large, we simply must tidy a bit—"

He is only ensuring it'll hurt more when Gilbert leaves.

"I would not impose on you," Gilbert says.

"Please. Stay."

Perdita

My dearest niece—

Perdita's Aunt Louisa Church writes her from New York enclosing a big package of piano music.

My dear, such wonderful news I have! We are having a big rally for Women's Rights in the spring, the first weekend in May. NAWSA is doing a fund-raising concert in Carnegie Hall—aren't we grand!— and Ethel Smyth is giving us one of her pieces. Charlotte Alden will write you, but she and I have already agreed that the very best pianist for it would be you.

"Very best pianist" is ridiculous flattery; Aunt Louisa must have cornered Miss Alden at a NAWSA meeting. Still—doing her bit for women getting the vote! And at Carnegie Hall! And a piece by Ethel Smyth! *And at Carnegie Hall!* Perdita whips out her magnifying glass and works her way through the music. It's a fugue, the pianist and violinist throwing the theme back and forth super-fast; interesting and hard and lovely. Who would her violinist be? She could visit her agent. He might be able to put together a tour.

She lays the music aside reluctantly; she has just time to finish Aunt Louisa's letter before Toby wakes from his nap.

I've heard from my brother that Gilbert Knight is with you. I'm glad; I do think the poor man deserves some happiness at last. I should warn you, though, Brother Bucky is in a complete tizzy over it.

(Aunt Louisa's brother is Uncle Gilbert's lawyer.) *He seems to think that the Knight Companies will fall apart unless Gilbert returns to Boston <u>immediately</u>. Expect letters and harrumphing! Dear Brother B. even threatens to come get Mr. Knight in Paris, though that isn't likely; you know what a stick Bucky is.*

Write back right away, dear, and tell me you'll play for us in New York.

ȣȣȣ

EVERY NIGHT among her prayers, Perdita asks God to somehow find a way to let Uncle Gilbert stay with Alexander, with them all, forever.

Anything else would be cruel. Now that he's staying with them, it's obvious that the only possible happy ending is this one. She hears them greet each other every breakfast-time, "good morning, Gilbert," "good morning, Alexander"; they sound so pleased. Uncle Gilbert talks about books he's found in the spare rooms, Alexander about patients at Jouvet. They're men so they don't talk about sitting round the same table at last, being a family at last, but that's what they mean.

Brother B. threatens to come get Mr. Knight in Paris—

What can she do, write Uncle Bucky in Boston and ask him to be merciful? She composes letters in her head but doesn't send them; letters will only remind him.

Uncle Gilbert gets letters from Boston, which he burns in the kitchen stove. Alexander gets letters too, which he doesn't share. But whatever is in those letters, it's not enough to make Uncle Gilbert go back to Boston. Uncle Gilbert is actually standing up for himself. He's *resisting.*

"I have never been to Paris," he murmurs. "I see no reason why I might not stay a bit. If I am not intruding—?"

"Never," says Alexander.

In long golden September, Uncle Gilbert takes Toby to the park. September turns into October; mists dance on the Seine, and Uncle

Gilbert takes Toby to see the *bouquinistes* and buys him picture books. Perdita plays the piano for them and works on her Carnegie Hall piece. All Saints' and cold November turn into December, and Uncle Gilbert stays with them, miraculously, though the letters from Boston come thick and fast. Uncle Gilbert ventures on speaking French and reads to Toby.

They hardly dare to shop for Christmas gifts for each other. But they do.

On Christmas Eve they go to midnight Mass at Notre-Dame. They stand elbow to elbow with thousands of other worshippers, listening to a wonderful tenor from the Paris Opéra sing "Minuit Chrétiens." Her dear husband says something that melts her heart. *This is happiness, isn't it,* he says.

And nobody has told Toby that happiness won't last. With Uncle Gilbert has come Elphinstone. Toby drops food and giggles as "Eff" snaps it up. Toby toddles after Elphinstone. Toby falls asleep on Elphinstone's dog-bed, curled up next to Elphinstone.

One day when she comes to breakfast, she finds her grand intellectual husband sitting on the floor talking to Elphinstone. "Yes, you vulture, you may have some egg. We treat dogs well here, don't we, Eff?"

Her husband, petting his uncle's dog. Family. Family. This is happiness.

Uncle Gilbert can't go back to Boston; he can't.

She is afraid because she's said yes to Aunt Louisa and the Carnegie Hall performance, as if she must stay in Paris on watch or Uncle Gilbert will be snatched away. But Alexander and Uncle Gilbert encourage her to go.

"There is a new ship going into service just about that time," Uncle Gilbert says. "Double-hulled and particularly safe. Unsinkable, they say!"

Uncle Gilbert thinks all ships are likely to sink. He has had such tragedy in his life, he's always looking out for the next disaster.

"I shall be fine, Uncle Gilbert. I can take any ship."

"Indulge me, my dear, and take this one."

So they all go down to the White Star Line office on the place de l'Opéra and Uncle Gilbert gives her a present of a first-class stateroom on the lovely new liner, on the liner's maiden voyage at that, very posh, she is quite impressed with herself; and she begins to feel that everything will be all right, that when she leaves Uncle Gilbert will still be in France to see her off aboard *Titanic*, and when she gets back he'll be there to meet her.

And then Uncle Bucky arrives.

╾╾╾

UNCLE GILBERT has wanted to hear her play in a real concert, before an audience who will admire her Conservatoire training. The French hate American pianists, but for him she phones and writes and trudges round until she finds a church in a suburb and a violinist who'll play with her. She programs crowd-pleasers and asks her friends to come. Uncle Gilbert (Uncle Gilbert, who's afraid of strangers and doesn't speak French well!) goes to every bookseller he knows, asking them to post programs. Uncle Gilbert is developing into quite a courageous person. But Perdita's friend Milly is in Egypt, her friend Elise has to work, Alexander's cousin Dotty wouldn't go to the suburbs on a bet; and on the afternoon itself, it's cold, sleet-down-the-collar weather that makes people huddle at home with hot chocolate and a cat.

The church is dead-of-winter freezing. The violinist and she huddle in the vestry until the last moment, in their coats with their hands in buckets of hot water. And then she strips down to her concert dress, and the violinist leads her on "stage," and she can feel there's no audience at all.

She plays. That's what you do. She plays for herself, for Uncle Gilbert, for Alexander, flinging notes of music like wave-spray against the great granite indifference of Paris. If things had worked out better than they have, she would have spent more time in America. She plays that it doesn't matter as long as her family is together. Perhaps Paris will appreciate her someday. And that's fine, until for an encore she does a solo, "Maple Leaf Rag," rich and elegant as cream, the way Mr. Joplin played it himself and Blind Willie Williams taught her to play it in New York, and she remembers what it was like to play piano in America; she remembers when she had a plan and a future and a life as a musician, and she almost bursts into tears.

As she takes her bows, she counts by ear. Eight, no, seven pairs of clapping hands. And that must include Alexander and Uncle Gilbert.

Uncle Gilbert hurries up to wrap her coat around her. "I was *concerned* for you all through the concert, my dear. You looked so cold!"

She wouldn't have been cold with an audience. "It's all right, Uncle Gilbert, I'm fine."

Alexander embraces her with one arm; the other's round Toby, who's yawning and grizzling. "Poor baby, you're missing your nap!" She puts her hands round his dear little hands. "Poor cold fingers!"

"You were marvelous, love," Alexander says.

For seven people. Music is nothing if no one hears it. "Let's go home," she says.

"Do you want to eat somewhere first?"

"No, poor Toby, let's just go home. But can we go in one cab, this once? It'll be warmer with us all together."

She doesn't mean warmth; she wants Alexander and Uncle Gilbert to cheer her up and tell her she'll make it in Paris.

"No, love. Two cabs." The Rule, Alexander's Rule: Toby's parents don't go in a cab together; not a cab or a train or a boat. For safety, Alexander says. What if there were an accident, Alexander says. Toby cannot lose both parents, he says, and doesn't add *the way Richard did.* Richard's parents drowned together in a stupid accident with a rowboat when he was four years old.

So she and Toby go in one cab, and Alexander and Uncle Gilbert in another, and two poor cab horses are rousted out of their blankets instead of one. Toby falls asleep inside her coat, clutching Puppy Lumpkin and nuzzling against her breast as though he were still her little nursing baby and not her big strong toddler; and she shivers all alone, freezing and sad.

She cannot, cannot, cannot do this. She presses one hand against her face and whispers into her fingers so not even Toby can hear. *I want to tour. I want audiences.* And that means America. Stay in France and she'll never play for a full house again, never solo with an orchestra.

"Toby, do you remember when we went on tour last year? You're too young. Mama misses being a musician. What good is Carnegie Hall if it doesn't lead to something? You and Papa could stay in Paris. And if Uncle Gilbert could stay too, you'd all be so happy—"

She wants America. And she wants a whole family to come back to. A family that includes Uncle Gilbert. She is tired, tired of living day to day. She's tired of having the family secret rule their lives.

She asked Alexander once why he didn't just tell the truth. *The truth,* Alexander said. *The truth is I don't want to be Richard.*

The truth. She is an American pianist in France, where they dismiss American pianists out of hand.

The truth.

The truth.

What is the truth they all can live with?

What truth makes them a family?

When she and Toby got back to Jouvet, Uncle Bucky's there.

"GILBERT CANNOT DO what he's been doing," Uncle Bucky says.

He and she go walking in the Luxemburg gardens, cold and deserted in the February rain. Sleet drums on their umbrellas and soaks her boots, but Uncle Bucky doesn't want to be overheard, so there they are. Uncle Bucky leads her, awkwardly, pushing her instead of letting her take his arm.

"This is the twentieth century, after all!" Uncle Bucky says. "The Knight Companies are outdated, old-fashioned. The new money is in big manufacture and oil. It is not simply that Gilbert has invested in," Uncle Bucky paused as if deciding what to call Alexander, "in *your husband's* company. Harry wants bigger things, now he and my daughter have expectations."

Is Harry's wife pregnant at last? "Congratulations, Uncle Bucky! I'm very glad for them. But you mean Harry wants to take control of the Knight Companies? He has had control for years."

"Harry does all the work but Gilbert owns the Knight Companies and can do what he pleases. All right while Gilbert did nothing. But now he's made this *investment* with your husband. If this sort of thing is going to happen, Harry threatens he'll go off and work for someone else. And who will take over the Knight Companies if Harry leaves? Gilbert must come home."

She hesitates. "If Uncle Gilbert promised never to do anything financial again, could he stay with us?"

The rain drums fingers on their umbrellas.

"Niece," Uncle Bucky says finally, "you are naïve. You trust your husband but Harry does not. Harry thinks Gilbert will do whatever your husband asks. You see I am talking to you like an adult. Harry—is not entirely reasonable about your husband's influence, but he's not wrong."

She folds her hands around her umbrella handle, praying and trying to be imperceptible about it. She appeals to his heart. "Uncle Bucky, you should see them. They care so for each other—"

"Don't you see, that simply proves my point."

"I shall speak to you like an adult too, Uncle Bucky. You know I want Harry and Uncle Gilbert to be family, no one more than me, and Harry must inherit; but—"

"You simply, simply prove my point," Uncle Bucky repeats. "We are talking about business; you don't understand." He takes her elbow so hard he pinches the nerves, as if he wants to guide not just her footsteps but her entire life. "Harry treats this very seriously, as do I, and he feels that he must remove Gilbert from you and your husband's influence by any means necessary. He is willing to say that your husband has exerted *undue influence* over Gilbert."

"'Undue influence,' what's that?"

"That is a crime, niece."

"Harry wouldn't dare say things about Alexander—"

Uncle Bucky hesitates. "Harry would be willing to say things about you."

"About *me*?"

"He might use something he knows about you. If he had to."

"What does he know about *me*?"

Uncle Bucky hesitated. "He said you told him the whole story about my sister Louisa. You know what story."

Her heart sinks. "I did tell him. He was going on about how he was glad I came from a respectable family, and he was going on so about respectability, I couldn't help it; I told him Aunt Louisa had divorced. He was so shocked at it, he didn't talk to me for days. But—"

"Do you know Louisa's former husband lives in Paris?"

"Yes, though I've never met him. But what could he have to do with me?"

"If you are tempted to interfere between Gilbert and Harry, go see John Rolfe Church. Explain who you are. Ask him to tell you the whole story of Louisa and himself. I do not know, or care to know, exactly what happened. But surely it was unpleasant or Louisa would not have divorced him.

"Harry will do *anything necessary*. He will spread any scandal about your husband or Gilbert that he can find, as long as it gets Gilbert back to Boston, and he will not hesitate to involve you. He will not hold back. I urge you, niece, use your influence to send Gilbert home to Boston where he should be, and it will be better for all of us."

❧❧❧

"PELHAM SAID Harry would bloody threaten you with some family secret of yours?"

She doesn't want to have secrets. "With something about John Rolfe Church. My Aunt Louisa's former husband. The secret is that John Rolfe Church is my grandfather. I think he is."

"John Rolfe Church?" Alexander says in an odd tone.

"I'm sorry I never told you."

"Family secrets," he says. "I know why you didn't." He sounds sad. She feels guilty. They already have his family secret. One is more than plenty.

"Do you know John Rolfe Church?" she asks.

"Unfortunately, yes. Tell me the story."

They're sitting in the family room, on the sofa, by the fireplace. She gets up and closes the door. She lowers her voice, though there's no real shame in the story.

"I believe he is my grandfather and my Aunt Louisa is actually my grandmother. Aunt Louisa left Mr. Church very abruptly and then, Mamma and I believe, she found out she was expecting. Uncle Bucky believes Harry could find out some horrible reason behind *why* Aunt Louisa left him, something that could reflect on me."

Alexander pats the sofa next him. She sits down.

"Details," he says.

"I don't know much but here it is." She leans against him. "It was back in Civil War times, when Aunt Louisa was young. She was a fervent Abolitionist and she wanted to do something. She talked her parents into letting her go to New York and teach black people to read. In 1863 she was eighteen and living at the Colored Orphans' Asylum on Fifth Avenue, teaching the children.

"Do you know about the Draft Riots? In 1863 Mr. Lincoln started drafting men for the Union army. In New York men revolted against it. They burned the lottery barrels, then the draft offices, and then—

"Alexander, it was murder. They lynched *people*. Lynched black people and set them afire alive."

"*Burned alive* in *New York?*" says Alexander. "My G-d."

"They burned the Orphans' Asylum. *Burned a building with children in it.* Aunt Louisa says they had almost no warning. One moment there was just smoke in the air and the next, Fifth Avenue was full of men with torches. She and the other teachers got the children out a back door and they all ran toward the police station, blocks and blocks away. The mob came after them. The children couldn't keep up and of course the teachers couldn't leave them. Aunt Louisa was sure they'd be killed.

"And then, in the middle of the smoke and fire, a young man appeared on a big horse and held back the mob with a pistol, all by himself, while the teachers and the children got away.

"That was Mr. Church. John Rolfe Church.

"The next day Aunt Louisa called on him to thank him. They talked for hours. They shared each other's dreams and ideals. He was a Southern man but working for the North, for emancipation. She wrote Uncle Bucky she had found her destined soul mate and they were going to start a school together for freedpeople."

"John Rolfe Church said this?" Alexander says.

"Who is he? Why would Uncle Bucky warn me against him?"

"Finish the story. She married him?"

"They ran away and got married at City Hall. She sent a telegram to Uncle Bucky; she said she was so happy. But the very next morning she left him. And she never has told us why."

ॐॐॐ

THAT'S THE WHOLE STORY, the mystery of Aunt Louisa's marriage. Why would a woman leave a man she loved? Perdita hopes she and Alexander never know.

"Surely she's told you more than that?"

"Nothing at all. Uncle Bucky went down to New York to rescue her. She refused to be rescued. She went West, supposedly to recover, and didn't come back until the next year.

"And just about that time, her oldest married sister—Grandma—had what she said was a surprise baby. Who was Mamma. We don't know for *certain* certain even now. But when I was a student in New York, Mamma came to visit, and she and Aunt Louisa and I all went to dinner and tried cocktails and got very sentimental, and Aunt Louisa said to Mamma *consider me your mother, if I had a daughter she would be just your age.* Mamma says she knew right then."

"And your Aunt Louisa's told no one why she divorced Church?"

"Mamma's asked her, and Aunt Louisa only said that her marriage was between her and Mr. Church but there was nothing wrong. She simply had to do what she did."

"Had to do it," he repeats.

"It doesn't sound like her at all, does it! Uncle Bucky doesn't know either, he says, but of course he thinks it's something dreadful. Do you know this Mr. Church?"

"I know a Church—a John Rolfe Church—living in Paris. But I wonder if it's the same man. You say he rescued black orphans? The man I know would have watched them burn. He knocked Barry Bullard down once at Longchamps, simply for the color of his skin."

She shivers. There is a detail of Aunt Louisa's story she hasn't told Alexander. One orphan didn't escape the asylum. She burned alive in the fire. Simply for the color of her skin.

"If this man is prejudiced," she says, "he can't be the same man who married Aunt Louisa. Though it's certainly not a common name."

"Do you know anything else about your aunt's man? Where was he born?"

"Northern Virginia. He lived on a horse farm. Fair something. Fair Home. He was at Bull Run and went north with the Union afterward because he believed passionately in emancipation. Shall we call on him?"

"You won't," Alexander says, "I will."

Reisden

JOHN ROLFE CHURCH is the duc de Varenne's horse trainer. The next morning Reisden visits the Varennes on the excuse of checking on Patrice, the son, who's a Jouvet patient.

Patrice de Varenne has his own floor of the family townhouse, with discreet bars on the windows; even the most elaborate of madhouses isn't enough for a duke's heir. Reisden leaves the contents of his pockets—penknife, propeller pencil, anything Patrice can use to harm himself—in a famille rose bowl by the door, and is let in.

Patrice is making rope, sitting on the floor, fingers busy. "You're getting good at that," Reisden says, sitting on his heels beside him in the denuded room. Even the mantelpiece and the mirror above it are gone.

"Never enough rope," Patrice says. "They take it away from me. I have to start over every day."

Reisden nods. Patrice's fingers are scarred, scabbed, callused. About four inches of strong rope dangle from his fingers.

"Does it help?"

Patrice unconsciously tugs at the length of rope, trying to make it longer.

"I want a long rope," Patrice says. "I could lower it to him. He could belay. I know he's dead. But—I want that rope."

The winter before last, Patrice was climbing in the Jura with an Irish friend, David Molony. On a cliff face, Molony slipped and was dangling in midair. Patrice was being pulled off the cliff by Molony's weight. "Cut the rope!" Molony shouted to him. "One of us should survive."

Eventually Patrice did it.

"You won't bring me a rope?"

"Only my attention," Reisden says.

"You think I'll hang myself?"

"Your father's worried."

"He's wrong. All I want is the rope," Patrice says. "I want the rope I didn't cut."

The gun that didn't go off. The runaway who didn't run. Who wouldn't want that?

Richard, apparently.

Patrice doesn't know about Richard, of course.

It's part of the choice Reisden's made that he'll never be able to tell him.

ᚙᚙᚙ

"WHAT DO I KNOW about John Rolfe Church?" Bibi de Varenne says. "John Rolfe Church is a liar."

Patrice's father doesn't even ask about his son any more. Instead he gets drunk in the middle of the day, and angry. He's angry now. "My trainer? The one who *calls* himself Church? He's been lying to me all these years. I was at the Jockey Club yesterday. Man there says he's met another man, just come to Paris: John Rolfe Church. In Paris with his *mother*. Well-known American trainer. The real Church. Isn't my Church." Bibi raises his bristled jowly chin.

"There's a *second* Church?"

This is not the information he's expected.

"There's an *only* Church. Coming to lunch today. *And* my Church. Whoever he is. Bring 'em together. Lunch." Bibi makes an explosive gesture with his hands. "Dog fight. Bang. You want to watch?"

No. "Yes."

"Good man."

They're in Bibi's trophy room. Stuffed heads snarl from every wall.

"That one, he's new." Bibi points at a huge wild boar. "Shot him at Varenne. Three hundred forty-two pounds dressed weight. Nearly got me. Never so glad to be alive, afterward. The air was sweet." He jerks his head in the direction of Patrice's rooms. "*He* says he can't stand to be alive. I've been in wars. You're alive or you're dead. Alive is better." Bibi's head swivels toward the doorway. "Look. Here he comes. Monsieur Who-is-he."

Church is standing at the doorway.

The man looks terrible; under his outdoorsman's tan, his face is gray. He's leaning against the door as if he doesn't have the strength to stand.

"M'sieu' le Duc, have you heard about this impostor?" Church has lived in Paris for twenty years, but he still has the slurred Southern American accent, or maybe he's as drunk as Bibi. He's trying to sound careless. It comes off as bluff.

"Monsieur," Bibi says coldly. "Monsieur What's-Your-Name?"

"Sir, my name is Church."

"Don't lie to me. I trusted you with my horses."

"Whoever told you I'm not John Rolfe Church, he lies. They all lie, lie, lie—" Half repeating the word, half stuttering, Church pushes heavily away from the door and advances across the carpet. "I am— I am not—" His lips roll round some word, trying to give it speech. "*You* lie, Sir, if you think I am!" Church stands in front of Bibi and, incredibly, draws back his hand as if he means to challenge the duke to a duel.

Bibi steps back. "I don't fight *servants*."

Church stands still, struck seemingly with the word, his hand held up as if he were swearing to something. "*Servant.*" He presses his hand to his chest and his eyes roll up theatrically as if he were about to give a speech. "I'm not a *servant*—" He laughs, or coughs. It's not until he stumbles and falls to his knees that they realize something's wrong.

Reisden rolls him over onto his back and tries to loosen his tie and collar. Church feebly pushes his hand away and takes a great awkward breath. "Bury me at Fair Home," he says. "They cannot deny a dead man."

He chokes and sighs and then he's dead.

❧❧❧

WHEN A DUKE'S TRAINER DIES in a duke's trophy room, and it isn't murder, phone calls are made. By the time Reisden gives his statement to the *procureur*, the investigation has been discreetly kicked upstairs to the Department of Let's Forget This Ever Happened. But Reisden knows people.

He calls Inspector Langelais. "Church?"

"You were there. I should have known. Anything weird, it's you. Come talk to me. You'll want to see the body. And we're bringing in the other Church to be interviewed."

"Do I want to see the body? But yes, Church."

He stops at *Le Matin* to beg a copy of Church's obituary. John Rolfe Church, trainer to the duc de Varenne for the past twenty years. Born on Fair Home Plantation, near Warrenton, Virginia, where the famous racer Whirlwind was trained. (Whirlwind? No idea.) Church went to Brazil in 1861 to make his fortune. (Leave America at the beginning of the Civil War? Odd for a Southerner.) He stayed in Rio training horses until 1890, when he brought his skills to Paris and began working for Bibi.

If Church was in Brazil from 1861, he wasn't in New York in 1863 marrying Perdita's Aunt Louisa.

Langelais meets Reisden in the courtyard of the Hotel-Dieu and leads him toward the *souterrain*.

"We're not enduring the whole autopsy, are we?"

"We'll do one for the newspapers, just to confirm. But it was a heart attack. His doctor says it was coming. That's not what you need to see."

The autopsy room is chilled the old-fashioned way, by Seine water. It isn't enough; the smell is appalling. Reisden offers Langelais camphorated Vaseline out of a jar. The windows that barely light the room are runneled with yellowish film. Only one of the zinc slabs is occupied. A sheet is thrown over the body.

Langelais draws a corner of the sheet back between two unhappy fingers.

"Have you ever seen anything like this?"

The dead John Rolfe Church is lying on his stomach. His back is covered with scar tissue, mounds and crevasses of gnarled slick skin, layered over and over each other, a map of agony from the shoulders to the buttocks. Against the violet of the livor mortis, the convulsed scars stand out grey.

"He was *whipped*," Reisden says.

"That's a Russian knout, that is."

"Or a bullwhip or a cat of nine tails." His voice sounds remote in his ears. Richard was whipped.

"Are you all right?"

"Furious." A good enough approximation. "He committed a crime somewhere, but *this*— He was in Brazil. Do they punish with the whip in Brazil?"

"Only on blacks. But in Russia," Langelais speculates.

"Where he's never been, as far as anyone knows."

"Two Churches," Langelais says and frowns. His job is to make all this go away.

"We need to talk with the other one."

∜∜∜

THE SECOND JOHN ROLFE CHURCH is already taking up most of Langelais's office. He's about seventy, big and white-haired and vigorous, with an open ruddy face and a magnificent curled white beard. Through the beard, like a lightning-bolt, runs a riffled scar. White suit, wide white hat: no one but an American wears white before Easter. Suit from a good provincial tailor, old-fashioned, carefully kept; a gentleman farmer's sturdy boots, polished and resoled. Gold wedding ring on the left hand. A well-loved tie pin, so old the gold is worn down, its shape a running horse smoothed to sheer motion. The skin around his eyes is creased with the complicated upturned lines of a man who smiles frequently.

This is the one, Reisden thinks; here's the man who enchanted Aunt Louisa; here's the man who talked with her about ideals. Here's Perdita's grandfather. The only mystery is why Aunt Louisa left him.

Langelais sits behind the desk and Reisden leans against the windowsill.

"He doesn't speak French," Langelais says. "Can you translate?"

"This is the most distressin' thing," the man breaks in in a mellifluous Southern accent. "My name is Dr. John Rolfe Church, and my wife read in the newspapers that I am dead. Miss Fan's French is not perfected, but she did understand that this Church was born at Fair Home, Virginia. And Sir, there has been no John Rolfe Church ever born at Fair Home but I. I do believe this man has died under false pretenses."

"Ask him if he has identification," Langelais says.

Reisden does, apologizing.

The old man draws himself up. "I have been John Rolfe Church of Fair Home for seventy-two years. I am not accustomed to proving who I am. But if you need to inquire further, you might speak to Mr. J.P. Morgan; I have sold him colts. And Mr. Federico Tesio; Mamma and Miss Fan and I have been in Italy studying his methods."

The owner of the White Star Line and the owner of the Dormello Stud. Solid gold names. Reisden nods slightly.

"And you have just arrived in Paris?" Langelais says.

"Yesterday. This man who was using my name, Sir? He asserted he came from Fair Home?"

Reisden nods. "Are you missing anyone at Fair Home, about fifty years back?"

The good humor and the color drain together out of the old man's face.

They take him down into the *souterrain*. Langelais phones ahead and they're given the relatively clean small viewing room. Langelais pulls the sheet down, showing the ruined back, the dead face.

"Do you know him? Do you know how this happened?"

The old man stares at the face. He moistens his lips, and his tongue finds the white furrow where the scar has notched his upper lip.

"I am sorry to say that is Bright Isaac."

❧❧❧

"HE WAS A *SLAVE*?" Reisden says.

They lead Dr. Church back out into the courtyard. He leans heavily on his cane, but waves off their offers of help.

"I don't suppose there's such a thing as a good Southern whiskey in this town?"

This is the center of Paris; there's a café-bar on every corner. Reisden and Langelais get coffee; the old man takes his with a shot of *marc*, sit with his back against the wall, scanning the room. Reisden knows the signs; this man has something to tell but doesn't want to be overheard.

"We were sure he was dead," Church says. "Fifty years ago. He never came back to Fair Home."

He sits vacant-eyed for a moment, collecting his thoughts.

"Bright Isaac.—I have no love for enslavement, Sir," he says finally. "My country suffered greatly for it. But at Fair Home we were always family together, without any great distinction. Many of our people with us now were born at Fair Home and continue with us, you know they could leave these days, but they choose to remain. We have always given opportunities to our people. Our principal trainer, our Mr. Otis, was born in servitude at Fair Home. I tell you this to say who we are."

Reisden notes *our Mr. Otis*, the patronage, the naiveté in *they choose to remain;* but this is a man who would have rescued black orphans.

"Bright Isaac was my body-servant, Sir. He was so high-yalla he could have passed for white, and he was restless, Sir, restless from his birth. He kept himself slim, he ate like a plantation lady, so my hand-down jackets and trousers would fit him and he could dress like a gentleman on a Sunday. When I learned to ride, Zack watched and practiced on a farm-horse and nothing would stop him but he would learn to ride like a gentleman too. He fanned me while my tutor gave me Latin lessons, and Zack learned Latin. Of course he knew horses. There was no preventin' the learning of that boy."

"He meant to escape?" Reisden said.

"Always, Sir, always."

The old man drains his coffee and brandy at a gulp. Reisden gestures for more.

"When the War came, I returned from military school with my friend Lafayette deMay, whose plantation ran next ours. Of course it was a matter of honor for Fate and me to volunteer. Honor and glory were costly in those days. I had to have my uniforms from the best tailor, and of course I needed to have horses and pay my share of the mustering. Fair Home was not prosperous as it is now. Papa was just dead, Whirlwind had not begun to make money for us, and Mamma had always taken against Zack." The old man looks down and considers. "I suppose I should tell you it was no coincidence Zack had the look of family. I blame Mamma for not lookin' the other way as a lady should, and Zack for actin' high. Now that Papa was in his grave, Mamma decided to sell Zack."

Langelais opens his mouth and closes it again.

"And Zack knew," says the old man, painfully, directly. "I mean he must have known. The dealer came to Fair Home, Zack knew what that man's business was—"

No one says anything. A fly lights on the café table. They might have brought the fly with them from the Hôtel-Dieu, where a man's body lies covered with scars.

"Goin' to another plantation would have been nothing to Zack. He had talents. He would have been able to buy himself free, even if we had won the War—

"But you know, he was one of *us*. He wanted to work with *our* horses, with Whirlwind. And he would not be a slave.

"Our uniforms were still being tailored when the Yankees marched on the rail-head at Manassas. It was but ten miles from us. Fate and I rode out in our ordinary jackets and trousers, gloryin' we was to be in the first battle and whip the Yankees and set the seal upon our independence, as our ancestors had at Lexington and Concord. Of course Zack went with us, all the boys did, to hold our horses and load our guns. The driver said the boy would run, this was his chance, but Isaac was family, and we *trusted* him. He should have been trustable.

"I can still hear the fifing and the drumming as we marched away."

The old man says nothing for a full minute. He touches his marred lip under the beard.

"Fate and I were both wounded. We fell in the grass. There was wild onions all through the field, I can still smell them, onions and gunsmoke and blood. Fate's boy Paul went for help and Zack was left to watch us. The next I knew, Zack was gone with my coat and hat and Whirlwind, and the Yankees had come back. They took me," Dr. Church's voice wavers, "they hailed me into prison and I never saw Fair Home again until after the war, but they killed Fate, bayoneted him on the field for their sport. He was a gallant man. He might not have died and I might not have suffered if Zack had stayed with us."

No sound but the old man breathing hard with the pain of memory.

"Do you mind my asking where you were in prison?"

"Various places, sir," Church says, surprised. "They had us workin' on roads. I was in a chain gang."

"Not in New York?"

"I was never that far north."

Not in New York during the draft riots. So he says. But the other Church, Bright Isaac, was supposed to have been in Brazil. Even farther away.

"You must have hated him even before he betrayed you," Langelais says in fragile English. "He was trying to become you, n'est-ce pas?"

Church only stares up at him blankly. "Are you accusing me of having to do with his death, Sir? I thought he was dead fifty years ago."

"You say that he was well treated," Reisden says.

"Always."

"But the whipping?"

The old man shakes his head. "We never did that, Sir. Never."

❧❧❧

REISDEN TAKES DR. CHURCH to his modest hotel in a taxi and meets "Mamma," who set this tragedy off. Adelaide Church, Miss Lady, is a solid sphere of a woman in a sprigged gown, with a high girlish voice and the curls of an 1850s belle; but she does not rise from her sofa, the shoes on her flirtatiously tiny feet are unscuffed, and there's a wheelchair in the corner, an old-fashioned one home-made from an American chair. He wonders how long she's been unable to walk. Was that the war too?

"Do you want to see him?" Church asks his mother.

"That boy who deserted us?" She dabs at her eyes with a tiny lace handkerchief. "I am just so disappointed and disgusted with that boy. I don't care to see his face.—Miss Fan, bring me my smelling salts."

Miss Frances, Church's wife, brings salts and a pretty Italian fan for Miss Lady and bourbon for the gentlemen. Miss Frances is dressed in plain grey with a lace collar, like an upper servant. Her face is set and quiet. She exchanges one sad look with her husband.

"He was *whipped*," she says. "I can hardly bear it."

"It don't bear thinkin' of," says Church gently. "How could it have happened?"

"I am sure he was whipped by a fellow gambler," Miss Lady says venomously. "He was a crazy boy. Takin' Whirlwind from us! He'p me up, I shall go rest and pray and give thanks we have survived him."

Reisden takes his leave as Dr. Church and his wife help the old woman into her wheelchair. Its back is carved with a horse's head, a long-nosed horse like African carving, and surrounding the horse, like a garland, are Confederate flags.

He walks back toward Jouvet down the Boulevard St.-German, thinking, his hands in his pockets.

If it can be proven beyond doubt that the second John Rolfe Church married Louisa, good.

But proving it is the problem.

He thinks of the Confederate flags. Does Dr. Church's family know, even now, how he spent the war? Reisden doubts it.

He knows about changing one's history.

What would Reisden have done in Church's place?

The game is power. The game is played for respect, love, happiness; for a self. John Rolfe Church, rescuer of black children, husband of the abolitionist Louisa Church, went back to his Virginia roots and fitted himself with the history he should have had. Reisden found another past and another name, and he's a better man than he'd have been as Richard.

What will Dr. Church do now?

Not confess to the marriage if it means facing his past. Reisden knows that.

He swears and goes home.

Perdita

WHEN HE TELLS HER, she cries in his arms and he holds her; but then she can think only one thing. "Toby and I *cannot* be black."

"It was the second Church who married your aunt."

"But how do you know? I could be black."

What she means is she and Toby must be white to be American.

To be black in America? She has friends who are black. Her teacher, Blind Willie Williams, was a piano prodigy when he was a boy; he played classical. But when he grew up and was free, all people wanted from him was "coon music." Now he plays ragtime for dinner and tips. When she got to know him, he agreed to teach her piano tricks, but what he wanted wasn't money; he wanted to know everything she learned at the Institute, because a black man can't even enter the Institute doors. No one will ever pay him to play classical. But he wants it, for himself.

Perdita's friend Garnet, Willie's granddaughter, is white enough to pass and has a genius for fashion. But Garnet can't try on clothes, can't even *touch* them, because a black woman can't try on clothes in any store in New York. Mostly Garnet cleans houses. But while she cleans, she dreams of hats and gowns and high-heeled shoes.

Blind Willie and Garnet are what Perdita knows about being black.

When she was pregnant with Toby, she had nightmares that he would be born with eyes no better than hers. She knows about prejudice; oh, yes, she does. She can see colors and shapes just fine, she's really no more than very short-sighted, but nobody cares about that; no, they decide she can't see at all, and if she can't see, she obviously can't hear. People ask Alexander questions about her *when she's right there to answer*.

Being called black would be like being called blind. People think *can't*. Think *stupid*. People have tried to make her that person for most of her life.

"And that is what Harry might learn," Perdita thinks out loud. "That a man named John Rolfe Church, who might be my grandfather, was passing as white. Would Harry use that? He wouldn't. He couldn't. It would be so cruel. How could Uncle Bucky think he'd use it?"

In America, even the rumor of black blood-- That is all most people would choose to know about her ever again.

"Toby and I *shall* not be black. Tell me about this other John Rolfe Church. Dr. Church. You think he's the one who married Aunt Louisa."

"I do."

"Then we only need to explain the situation to Dr. Church and ask him to say so."

"He won't do that," Alexander says.

"Why not?"

"His family thinks he spent the war as a prisoner, not working for the North."

They're in the family room, with the door closed. She gets up and locks it. This is that kind of family secret. As bad as Alexander's.

"Ask your aunt what happened," Alexander says. "The Churches are going to America via New York. Have her meet the boat and look at him. Ask her to confirm that the John Rolfe Church she married was the real one."

"Will that convince anyone? People lie for black people all the time." She's lied for Garnet; *this is Garnet, my white friend.* "It'd be better if Dr. Church backed up her story as well."

"Church has told another story for fifty years, love, and he's not going to change it for you."

"But perhaps he might write something at least, not something that might get to his family, but privately. It would be stronger than Aunt Louisa alone doing it. I have an idea," she says. "Perhaps I might talk with him myself and persuade him. When are the Churches going back to America? I'll change my ticket; whatever boat they go on, I'll go too. I'll talk to him myself. I'll be blind and helpless," if everyone's going to think of her that way, she'll use it, don't think she won't. "I'll ask him about Aunt Louisa and tell him why I'm asking. I'll telegraph Aunt Louisa to meet me on the dock and I'll introduce them. I want him to tell me 'I am your grandfather' and I want her to tell me 'I married that man.' And I want them both to write it down. Toby and I will *not* be driven out of America. We *cannot.*"

Driven out of America? That is the very least of it. It isn't just her secret, it's her mother's, her brothers and sisters. Phil is engaged to be married. If Harry knows this secret, and is willing to use it—

How could he?

But if he thinks of it, she is utterly at his mercy. She will have to do anything he says. Anything.

She will be caged by family secrets, forever.

She hears Alexander sigh. But "There's a chance it'd work," he says. "The Churches are going on the same boat as you. *Titanic.*"

"Perfect." She takes a deep breath and asks for what she wants. "Alexander? I want you to come with me."

"No, love. No matter how important this is, we don't go on the same boat."

She's good at hearing what people say, but not at meaningful looks, shifting eyes. There's an art to that. Alexander has it.

"You and I can go together this once, Alexander."

"*No.*"

The Rule, the blasted Rule. Toby's parents take two cabs because Richard's parents died together. "Alexander, this is Toby's and my future. This is more important than the Rule. I might be able to get Dr. Church to talk, but you and I could do it better together."

"I am not putting both of us on one ship," Alexander says.

"You can *see.* Come with me. Be my eyes." She hates that she has to spell out her need for him.

"No," he says. "*No.*"

"Richard," she doesn't want to use the name but it's Richard she's talking to. "We will not drown. Your parents did but we won't. Toby and I need you. I want you to be my ally with the Churches. Will you?"

∾∾∾

IT IS THE WORST QUARREL they've ever had. They say nothing to Uncle Gilbert, of course, because he would be distressed, but almost nothing to each other. It's Lent and there are no parties where they can pretend at least to be happy.

It isn't just about taking the same ship. Their quarrel is about family, Paris, marriage, secrets; everything, everything.

Three times she tries to tell Uncle Gilbert the story of John Rolfe Church. *Uncle Gilbert, Toby and I are suspected of— It is not true, but*—And then she can't go on.

What would Uncle Gilbert think of her? Would he treat her differently?

It would break her heart if he did.

She packs. She polishes her piece for the concert at Carnegie Hall. She doesn't know what to do.

Uncle Bucky has gone home after talking with her. Has Uncle Bucky heard the story of John Rolfe Church while he was in Paris? Is the story already traveling to Boston via some gossip on some liner? Is it already too late for Toby and herself?

It can't be. Alexander and she must— *She* must do something.

Alexander says nothing and spends evenings downstairs in the garage in the passage behind the building, tearing apart the engine of one of the cars.

What does she know about being black? Nothing. She's no more Negro than she is—she wants to say, than she's a French baroness; so much less than she is a musician. Anything is a lie that means she can't be with other musicians in America. She *is* white, Toby *is* white. It gives her privileges Garnet and Blind Willie should have too, but it is really who she is. She doesn't know how to be anything else.

Alexander must understand. They must get Dr. Church to talk.

❧❧❧

ON THURSDAY the servants have their half-day and Alexander and Uncle Gilbert are out. She and Toby eat an early dinner all alone, an omelette and a salad. Toby throws salad all over the floor, calls "Eff! Eff!" and drops bits of omelette for Elphinstone, who's out too. "Toby, no!" She crawls over the rug feeling for food, getting salad dressing on her skirt and putting her hand unexpectedly on a slimy bit of egg. Ugh; she sits up and hits her head on the bottom of the dining-room table. "*Ouch*," she whispers, trying not to cry.

"Mamma?" Toby asks, distressed.

"Mamma's all right, lovey." Mamma's sitting under the table with a big goose-bump coming up on her skull.

She gives Toby a bath, tucks him in his crib with Puppy Lumpkin, and starts a story about a heroic dog named Puppy who holds a signal-lantern in his jaws and saves an entire train from wrecking. She runs her fingers over her dear boy's face, comforting him, comforting herself with him, feeling his sweet little nose and lips, a baby version of Uncle Gilbert's and Alexander's. She rubs at a little worried wrinkle between his eyebrows. "Toby lamb, what's wrong?"

He began to sniffle. "*Not* America."

She curls into a ball of guilt.

"I must go. Toby, you and Papa will have a lovely time together and I'll send you postcards every day."

And I'm saving your entire life, but you're too young to know. Oh, blast.

"Now you go to sleep, and Mamma will play you some nice music while you do."

"Want Eff."

"Elphinstone is with Uncle Gilbert, lovey. Here's Puppy. Puppy will be sad without you."

She leaves him curled up with Puppy Lumpkin and escapes into the music room to play for him. (For him? For herself.) What? Not Brahms tonight. Tschiakowsky's "Lullaby."

The Wind's mother asks her

What have you done, my daughter?

She transcribed it back in New York, at the Institute, because it struck right to her heart, then and now.

I have done nothing, my mother. I guard a little baby, I rock his cradle softly...

Can she protect Toby? By herself? Without Alexander?

I have done nothing.

The girl she was at the Institute: how that girl played this song, wanting not to be left on the shelf, wanting love, marriage, children. She was full of the excitement of really studying music, all the wonderful world she'd earned because she'd decided not to marry Harry. But every night she thought to herself, will I ever get another chance at love? Blind girls don't marry. Harry had been her first boyfriend and she was afraid he'd be her last.

But then Alexander came to New York all the way from Paris to see her. He'd come on business, he said, but he spent so much time with her—

He was romantic; he was tall and handsome and utterly wonderful. He'd always been wonderful and she'd tried not to feel it while she was engaged to Harry. He treated her like a friend, but he took her seriously, he listened to her, he talked to her about his own new life, about deciding unexpectedly to buy Jouvet. He shared his own world of science, specialists, French officials, patients, madmen. It was a wider world even than New York.

Paris. Of course she thought Paris was glamorous.

They had both found their true places, the worlds they belonged in. Their lives were developing on such similar lines, she never considered they were on different continents.

One day he took her to a lake on Long Island and taught her to swim. (It makes her sad now to think this was part of his caring for her, to protect her from drowning.) That night, back in her single bed at Mrs. Gordon's, she felt his hands on her body as if he were in bed with her, and she faced her feelings for him.

She chose not to understand what she intended. Of course people who made love got married beforehand, if they were virtuous. She was a virtuous person. Of course she and Alexander would be married. Except that Alexander would want a *wife*, not a music student, and she wasn't looking for a husband, certainly not in Europe.

She'd lied to herself about what she wanted, but she'd come to Paris and had found it in his arms.

Now she loves Toby more than she could have believed. She knows what love is.

She loves Alexander more as Toby's father than ever she loved him before.

But *I have done nothing.* She's backed into life without ever having made choices.

And now this worst choice is being made for her. *Stay out of America because you may be black. Give up Uncle Gilbert because Harry may say you're black.*

She *will* not. She *cannot* accept it. She has to persuade Dr. John Church to tell the truth, who's kept a secret for fifty years.

But how likely is that? She might as well get Alexander to say he's Richard.

❧❧❧

AFTER THREE DAYS Alexander comes to see her, smelling of engine oil, and takes her hands in his long calloused fingers.

"I try to keep us safe," he says. "I try to be a good father to Toby. I don't want him to lose us both. Is that wrong?"

She wants to say *I know you care for us.* She wants to give him comfort. But she sits with her hands clasped tight in her lap, not reaching out to him, she is not so strong she can give him that, and she feels how much she can hurt him, but she can't give in.

"There are things we can do," he says, "other than playing Holmes and Watson ourselves. I have the name of a man in New York who will look into the American Church's background."

"But there's only this one chance to talk to *Aunt Louisa's husband.*"

"Yes," he says, "I know," and stops.

She waits.

There is no one else to rely on. And it isn't just that there's no one else; it's that, for both of them, it should be Alexander.

"I will go with you for one night," he says. "Not to America, Perdita. One night. *Titanic* makes a stop at Queenstown. I'll go from Cherbourg to Queenstown with you. That's all I can give you. I know people at White Star; they'll do us a private tour of the ship; we'll invite this Dr. John Church along, away from his family, and try to get him to talk to us."

It isn't enough. "Thank you," she says all the same, but he draws a little away from her.

"No, don't," he says. "I'm doing this because you ask me, not because I believe he'll talk."

"I know it's hard."

"It's useless, love," he says.

It isn't useless. *One night on a boat together,* she tells him silently. *On a ship together and not drowning. We won't die; we will work together, we will be a family, it will be love—*

And we'll get Dr. Church to talk. We must.

"We'll learn something."

But she's already learning something, and it's not that she can rely on him.

Reisden

GILBERT HAS A COPY of the special issue of *The Shipbuilder* on *Olympic* and *Titanic*, and reads the safety measures out loud. "*Titanic* is practically unsinkable, so the magazine says," Gilbert murmurs, horrified. "But that does not mean *entirely* unsinkable. You should not go together! You will be not simply on a lake, but *at sea!*"

Reisden can't reassure him. Reisden is sure *Titanic* is going down, sure in the same way he was sure he'd murdered someone, long before he knew he had.

Every morning before he starts work he unlocks the center drawer of his desk, where he keeps his gun and other private things, and reads a note he's written to himself. It started as an index card, the fall he came to Paris after he learned what Richard had done: the short list of resolutions he thought a repentant murderer should make. *I will hurt no one again.* Occasionally over the past years he's added something, and last year, after Gilbert came to Paris, he wrote the list over and put his family at the top.

I will trust Gilbert and Perdita.

I will be worthy to be Toby's father.

He updates his will. Richard's father wanted Gilbert to be Richard's guardian, but left no will. So Reisden has a will, and Perdita has one, which he's had drafted for her and she's signed with the air of someone indulging a heathen superstition. If they drown together, Toby will have sane, protective guardians.

But that's not enough. Toby must have living parents.

I will be worthy to be Toby's father. He reads, he locks the drawer again, he persists in a state of funk.

Toby is staying in Paris. At least Toby will survive.

Reisden sends a note to the Churches, presuming on acquaintance. His blind wife will be traveling on their ship; could he possibly ask the Churches to look after her? He himself will be on board for one night and would like to invite them to dinner.

Gilbert insists on coming down with them on the boat train, to get his last sight of them on earth. Can you believe it: he and Reisden consider seriously the chance of the boat train crashing, simply because all three of them are on it.

"A train full of millionaires," Reisden says, "wrecked on its way to the maiden voyage of the world's largest ship. Too symmetrical to happen, Gilbert."

"It would be unlikely," Gilbert admits. "They must be taking great precautions? But one cannot tell. I could take the train the day before, we would not be all on the same train," *et cetera.*

"We are being morbid over this. Nothing will go wrong."

"It will not," Gilbert says heroically.

Neither of them believes it.

&ce;&ce;&ce;

THE TRANSATLANTIC TRAIN would be magnificent if one were in the mood. The French head of the White Star line is aboard to look after the millionaire passengers. As a millionaire if not yet a passenger, Gilbert gets attention. The crystal wall-vases of their compartment sport little red and white silk pennons and *muguet,* lilies of the valley, the red and white of the White Star Line. Courtesy of White Star, stewards offer them cocktails and *petites bouteilles* of champagne.

"Champagne at breakfast!" Perdita says with determined cheerfulness. "Isn't this fun, Uncle Gilbert, isn't it, Alexander?"

Reisden doesn't reply. He has spent all night writing a postmortem letter to Toby, just in case. He's left out all the things he won't be able to say to his son for years, if ever. Just *I love you very much.*

The weather is ironically beautiful. At every station, villagers wave handkerchiefs and mothers hold up their children to see *Titanic's* boat train pass. Through the windows they can hear the cheering. *Catch your last sight of us victims.* Oh my G-d.

"Of course—though the ship will be *quite* safe—it *must* be—one should not count on being *too* safe," Gilbert says. "Perdita, if *anything* should happen, the slightest untoward thing, you must *immediately* put on your life-belt and go to the lifeboats. You cannot possibly be too careful."

Perdita makes a little hissing sound. "I shall be fine, Uncle Gilbert."

"Postcards?" A young woman is knocking at the door of their compartment. "Would you like some postcards of *Titanic*?"

Anything to change the subject.

"Take as many as you like, they're free." The young woman holds out a fan of postcards. "Write all your friends and mail these as soon as you reach New York! Compliments of New York Photo and the White Star Line."

"Why, how can this be?" Gilbert asks, taking one and turning it over. "The ship has not reached New York yet, but here *Titanic* is in New York."

There's *Titanic* steaming up the Hudson, between Battery Park and the New Jersey shore. Tugs hoot and a fireboat shoots white jets of water into the air, greeting her. In the foreground a pale cliff of windows, one of the new tall buildings, dwarfs the Battery Park Reisden remembers.

STEAMER TITANIC, he reads at the bottom of the postcard. WHITEHALL BUILDING N.Y. THE TWO LARGEST IN THE WORLD, and the date, April 17, next week.

It's a good magic trick, though the trees are in summer leaf in Battery Park. "It's *Olympic*, isn't it?" *Titanic*'s near-twin, in service since last summer.

"No, it's *Titanic*," the postcard girl grins.

"Alexander," Perdita says, "Uncle Gilbert, put a postcard in your pocket and think of me next Wednesday." She takes two postcards, holds them to her lips, and gives Gilbert one and one to him. "There; April 17, noon; the voyage is over; *Titanic* and I are safe."

He feels angry at her for patronizing him and angry at himself for needing talismans, and sad for both of them, and still he takes the postcard. He'll put it on the mantelpiece in his office and brood over it like an abandoned child until Wednesday, and snarl at everyone until she telegraphs she's safe in New York, and then he'll snarl some more because he doesn't want her there and he's worried for her, good *G-d.*

Perhaps by next Wednesday, she'll have got something from Dr. Church or from her Aunt Louisa in New York, and it will all have been worthwhile.

Gilbert tucks his own postcard into his billfold.

"Will you be on *Titanic?*" Perdita ask the postcard girl.

"I wouldn't miss it! I was in Egypt two months, taking stereo cards for Keystone. The sand got in everything! I'm ready for home. I'll have the first photos of the trip from on board. Find me on the ship, I'm Greta Nisensohn, I'll take your picture on *Titanic!*"

᚛᚛᚛

BUT WHERE IS *TITANIC?*

When the boat train reaches Cherbourg, *Titanic* isn't there. *Titanic* has had an accident in Southampton Harbor.

"Has the voyage been put off?" Reisden asks shamelessly. For a day? A week? Forever? Forever would do.

No. The ship's just late.

Cherbourg has a small station, suited for the smaller liners of an earlier day; though most passengers boarded in England this morning, almost three hundred passengers for *Titanic* are waiting here in France. Everyone who's already dealt with luggage is out in the spring sun. Gilbert leads Perdita away to confirm that her luggage has not been irretrievably lost on the train or smashed or infested. ("*Every* ship has rats, and they carry *diseases!*") Reisden stays on the pier, sitting on his overnight suitcase with its red-diamond White Star sticker, and watches the children.

Titanic coddles its millionaires but White Star makes its money from emigrants, families who've sold everything to go to America. Boys and girls, whole families of children swathed in layers for traveling, run up and down the long pier, their arms outstretched and flapping like bird-wings. The toddlers cling to their mothers' skirts, looking up timidly at Reisden.

Don't drown, he thinks. Don't lose your parents and be alone.

The third-class men stand marveling at the first-class luggage piled in an Alp by the ferry-boats. One boy is counting a set of matched luggage from Maison Vuitton, fourteen trunks, he gestures to a friend, fourteen! If he's like most emigrants, his ticket has been marked for "the first available ship," and he is only now finding out that the first available ship is the largest and richest and newest ship in the world. He'll be on its maiden voyage, sharing it with millionaires. Something to tell his American grandchildren.

The women are herding the children: women in wasp-waisted dresses and short jackets in the styles of twenty years ago, bright festival shawls round their head or waist. Every one going to America like his wife. They'll end up on the Lower East Side, sewing shirts in inside rooms, peddling elderly vegetables from a cart, hoping to be ladies' maids, which is as much beyond them as traveling first class. But they aspire to the same free world as Perdita: to the American world where women have careers and ride by themselves in railroad cars and play piano all over the United States.

"You do not suppose *Titanic* has been *damaged,* Alexander?" Gilbert says, coming up beside him with Perdita's luggage tickets. "The White Star Line would certainly not send it out if it were not in *perfect* condition, and it must have been damaged by hitting another boat—?"

"Oh, *Titanic* didn't hit anything, sir," a passing steward says. "Near as anything, but a miss."

"Not the start we expected, eh, though, is it, old boy?" an Englishman says. "Lost her chance at the Blue Riband. I wager Ismay had his eye on beating *Olympic* at least."

"No, surely not," Gilbert protests, "not *going at excessive speed*, not in April; why, this is just when the ice breaks up and is most dangerous."

This is true, and of course Gilbert knows it.

"You must speak to the captain," Gilbert tells Reisden, "to tell him to go *quite slowly*, and tell the stewardess that Perdita's sight is *less than perfect* and the stewardess must look out for her. And you *both* must practice putting on your life-belts as soon as you are on the boat."

"Gilbert, I shall be back Friday morning." If we're not dead.

"And you must both stay away from the rail. There are *large waves*, and they come *unexpectedly*."

The crowd is full of reporters trying to get quotes from millionaires. One of them spots Gilbert.

"I am seeing off my young friend the distinguished pianist Perdita Halley, who is playing at Carnegie Hall."

"Carnegie Hall! *Merveilleux!*" Carnegie Hall impresses even the French.

"She is the wife of the Baron Alexander von Reisden. Dr. Reisden is the head of Jouvet Medical Analyses and a business partner of mine. I am very pleased with my investment."

"Thank you," Reisden says when the reporter moves away.

"You will be careful?" Gilbert says.

"You know I will."

"I think of Tom and Sophie." Reisden's parents. Richard's parents. Gilbert looks up at the clear sky, the sun low over the water. "It was a bright day like today. And I never knew till evening they were drowned."

Don't. "I'll telegraph you from Queenstown. And I shall be home Friday morning; we'll have lunch and I shall tell you all the wonders of *Titanic*."

"I shall not be truly happy until Perdita is safe in New York."

"Nor I."

He sees her where Gilbert has left her, by the *Gare maritime*, slim in a light traveling suit and a big hat pink with the sunset light, holding her guide cane more conspicuously than she usually does. From this distance he can imagine rather than see her eyelids batting in helplessness; she hates so very much to be helpless. Miss Lady is leaning forward in her wheelchair and talking steadily while Perdita listens and nods. John Rolfe Church is looking for the ship, Santa resplendent in a wide-brimmed hat, and at a distance from the group, the wife holds the old woman's lap robe and scarf like a burden of grief.

He watches Perdita as a drowning man watches the shore. *You'll drown. You'll leave me. I'll never see you again.* Richard's parents drowned; and somewhere in the baroque recesses where he remembers everything but will never admit it, there's a child sick with fear, knowing how truly abandoned he'll be, screaming *Don't go on the boat, the boat is going to sink,* screaming to Perdita *Help me, pay attention to me, don't leave me, never leave me.* And she is going to America; she's following John Rolfe Church, but what she wants is America.

America, where Gilbert must go someday. America, which is taking his family.

And he is going with her. One night on *Titanic.* Not enough to help her. But flirting with disaster—

Flirting, oh G-d, head over heels infatuated with it. Is this the man he wants to be? Is this Toby's father?

"I've left a letter," he says to Gilbert. "Center desk drawer. Perdita's and my wills are in the same drawer. I don't think anything will happen; but if it does, you and Roy Daugherty will be Toby's guardians, with the Bullards and Dotty as backup." Is it enough? Nothing is enough. "I don't expect anything to happen," he repeats, and thinks that if Gilbert's left alone to open the middle drawer and read the letter, he'll see the list too. *I will* trust *Gilbert and Perdita.*

"I intend to survive to see Toby grown," he says.

Gilbert pats his arm awkwardly.

"Still," Gilbert says, "today I shall not go even so far as the tender. I shall stay here on shore."

"Good. I shall bring Toby toys from the ship for both of us. Tell him when Papa comes home he'll be the most indulged child in Paris."

"Oh, look—oh, Alexander, look."

He looks up and sees *Titanic.*

She comes out of the sunset, out of a sky luminous as tropical water. By now it is almost dusk and she has dressed her lines with lights, as if she is conscious who is watching her, who will sail on her, Ismay and Astor and Straus and all those emigrants to the beginning of the world. As they watch, more lights flare on; she comes on blazing. She rules the pier and the lighthouse, the harbor, the very sea. Everyone points and cheers.

Titanic is taking his wife to America and drowning them both on the way, but "Oh my L—d, isn't she magnificent."

"Truly she is."

Horns blare. Parents gather their children, leading them down the pier toward the tender-boats. The luggage mountain is melting away like hourglass sand. By the lighted windows of the *gare,* Perdita is waving to them.

"You remember my husband," Perdita introduces him to the Churches.

"I am honored, Sir, that you are entrustin' your charming wife to us—"

He remembers very little of their trip out to *Titanic.* Gilbert waves from the pier. Reisden points out the Astors to Miss Lady Church. A woman in deep mourning, with a thick black veil, stands in a corner all the way. He wonders what coffin she is accompanying. The rivet-studded side of *Titanic* looms enormously above them; they smell steel, coal smoke, new paint. The tender glides toward it through reflected portholes like drowned moons.

And then they are on *Titanic.*

❧❧❧

CHARLES "LIGHTS" LIGHTOLLER is now Second Officer of *Titanic,* and dreams of someday being her captain. Up until hours ago he has been First Officer, but in a last-minute reshuffle, Captain Smith has decided to give the position to Henry Wilde, who will be *Titanic's* next captain. The previous Chief Officer, William Murdoch, has been dropped down to First Officer and Lightoller to Second.

The original Second Officer, David Blair, was in charge of the crow's nest, where the lookouts watch for ice. When he left, he accidentally locked the crow's-nest binoculars in his cabin and took the key. This is now Lightoller's problem, with no fix unless someone breaks down the door. The lookouts will complain about the missing binoculars and Lightoller will make a note to get it all sorted in New York.

Lightoller's a methodical man. He'd make a good captain.

Lightoller is in charge of launching the lifeboats, should it ever be necessary. Here he's in good shape; he's done a drill during the sea trials.

But he doesn't know one crucial thing.

The lifeboats can be launched with a full load of passengers, but Lightoller thinks the davits can't bear so much weight.

He will send the first boats away only half full.

❧❧❧

JOSEPH BRUCE ISMAY, chairman of the White Star Line, is preparing for a triumph. J. Bruce Ismay—that tells you something about him, he uses his middle name—Ismay made his reputation with luxury ships, including the recently launched *Olympic.* Now he's perfecting the design with *Titanic.*

Ismay wants a grand, broad, uncluttered boat deck, a promenade. The designs have specified 48 lifeboats, enough for every person on the ship. But Ismay thinks it will look better to reduce the lifeboats to the legal minimum number, 16 regular-sized and four collapsibles.

Titanic will sail with 2300 passengers and crew on board, and lifeboats for only half of them.

Even if all the lifeboats are full.

Ismay will board a lifeboat, and survive.

❧❧❧

THE GOOD NEWS is that no one dies on *Titanic*, everything's fine, everyone's safe. *Titanic* steams from Cherbourg to Queenstown sedately as a teakettle. Reisden gets back to Paris, not in time for Friday lunch, best of Irish efficiency, but at least in time to join his uncle for dinner.

"It's a splendid ship," Reisden tells Gilbert.

"And Perdita is quite, quite sure of where the lifeboats are?"

"And the lifejackets."

On board, he's confirmed with the Churches dinner at the Ritz, which earns him her silent thanks; but then he wastes it by acting out every fear he has. They find her cabin, which is a single with one dauntingly small bed. The cabin is dim for her; he'll ask her stewardess for a stronger lightbulb. He retrieves her lifejacket from the top of the wardrobe and hangs it inside where she can't miss it. She squares her shoulders as if she were hearing a wrong note in music. He says "And now we are going to walk the path between here and the lifeboats."

"Don't we have to dress for dinner?"

"Not the first night, not even for the Ritz. Lifeboats. You know Gilbert will ask me." As if it were only Gilbert he's doing this for.

Perdita's stateroom is on A deck, near the Grand Staircase. "Out your cabin door, left and down the hall, right and forward to the stairs, up the stairs twelve steps. Right on the landing, up another flight. Now we're on the boat deck. Turn two o'clock, through a vestibule with a revolving door. Turn one o'clock, here are the lifeboats." He takes her hand, puts it flat against the side of one enormous boat; she has to reach up to feel the damp canvas cover.

"Out my cabin door," she repeats dutifully, all the way to "the lifeboats. And now, Alexander, I hope we are *done.* Let's find the Churches and talk to Dr. John."

"Not yet, love. If anything goes wrong," he persists, "you are to put your warmest clothes on and your lifejacket, and bring your muff and thick gloves to warm your hands, and a warm hat, and you're to come up here right away. Don't use the elevator. If the electricity fails, the elevator will stop."

"I'm glad you trust me to do the right thing and don't give me endless directions as if I were an idiot."

He doesn't take her up on that. One of the stewards is passing; he asks a few questions about which *The Shipbuilder* has been coy. How many boats? What's the capacity of each boat? Can they be launched fully loaded, or will the passengers have to climb down into the boats? Dunno, sir. Dunno.

"Alexander, is it time for dinner? I think we need dinner. I am feeling cross."

"I am not being unreasonable."

"Let's just eat and talk to Dr. John."

They do dress for dinner, since it's the Ritz—a ballet in the small cabin, both of them brooding, he losing a collar-stud underneath the bed, she holding herself very straight and stiff while he fastens her necklace. Gilbert has sent a sailing basket with flowers. The scent of American lilac fills the room. The basket also holds an electric torch, extra batteries, a whistle, chocolate bars, all the necessities for shipwreck. Reisden ties his evening tie in the scrap of mirror over the wash-basin; gets the knot wrong, which he never does.

❧❧❧

THE RITZ, THE BEYOND-FIRST-CLASS à la carte restaurant, is at the stern near the propellers. It's a strange combination, the muffled mechanical thrash and churn, the pink-shaded lights and brocaded walls and the string trio playing restaurant music. "The musicians have to buy all their own uniforms," Perdita says in an undertone, "and even pay for having the White Star Line buttons sewn on, and they can't complain or they'll be blackballed."

Of course she knows them. They're musicians.

"Here are the Churches," he says.

"Why," Miss Lady burbles, "isn't this the most wonderful restaurant you have ever been to in your life? I wonder what am I going to have? It all looks so good. I declare, I wish I could have one of everything."

Reisden reads the menu for Perdita, who has no sight in dim light like this.

"Lobster?" Perdita asks. American food. "How are they fixing it?"

"Broiled, with— Chili sauce?"

"Oh, that's *wrong*."

"Filet mignon," he reads, "*doucette*, dandelion greens, asparagus. American ice cream for dessert. Something like that? Madame Church, for you? Lobster? One of everything?"

"I will never have lobster, no," the old lady shakes her head vehemently, "that is Yankee food. I have no truck with Yankee things."

"You know, Miss Lady, I am from Boston," Perdita says.

"Miss Perdita, you're too young to know."

The Churches choose the second-cheapest dishes on the menu with the politeness of persons to whom money meant a great deal not long ago. Miss Lady's fan is new from Italy; she flirts it with the pleasure of a woman who has not had many lace fans with ivory sticks. The wife, Miss Frances, wears a new shell cameo, well-cut but not expensive. Their dinner clothes are out of date. No money for luxuries until this Italian trip, where fans and cameos are cheap. The Churches have been in Italy to learn the Tesio method of breeding horses and to buy two Italian foals, which have already gone to Virginia with their invaluable chief trainer, "Uncle" Otis.

"How did you become a horse trainer?" Reisden asks Church.

"Why, our Uncle Otis is our trainer, not John," Miss Lady says. "Dr. John is principally a dentist. Dr. John is known all the way from Baltimore to Philadelphia. I swear he has done every set of dentures in three states but mine. I remember when a person could make a livin' breedin' horses, but now we just *pour* Dr. John's money into Fair Home and the dratted New York bankers buy all the land around us. And Miss Fan's son is a lawyer. There are no more gentlemen of leisure, Sir, not in the South."

The Churches have never been in Europe before. None of them has ever been to New York. So Church says.

"I must show you New York when we arrive," Perdita says. "I'll introduce you to a few people. You must meet my aunt."

The hors d'oeuvres arrive, brie *bouchées* with slivered raw spring radishes, ruffled and scalloped as if they came from the Ritz on the Place Vendôme; not bad for the restaurant's first night. They must have practiced on the officers. Bruce Ismay himself comes in. Miss Lady coos with delight. The string trio works competently at popular music. *Come, Josephine, in my flying machine...*

"Excuse me," a woman stops at their table. "I know you," she says to Reisden. "Don't I know you, yes I do—!"

Round face, brown hair, a sample standard American girl, Noo Yawk accent. Her face is familiar. Where—? Magazines, advertisements, collars— Before he recognizes her, she assumes he has.

"Yes, that's me, Dorothy Gibson, the Harrison Fisher Girl!" She strikes a model's pose, index finger on her chin. "And now I'm in the movies," she says. "Aren't you in the movies too?"

This is the very least opportune moment for that to come up. "Just an amateur."

"Of course, *Citizen Mabet,* you were wonderful, amazing, I could have *eaten* your cheekbones, now you're here on *Titanic!*"

Go away, woman.

"Did you know Billy Harbeck's on board too? He's filming *Titanic* for the newsreels, Guggenheim's on board and of course he and Billy hate each other after Billy's Alaska film and Billy wanted to make Guggenheim and Morgan fight and film it but Morgan's not on board so Billy doesn't have much to do, he could film us, we could do a one-reeler, let's call it *Her Shipboard Romance,* I'll write it, I'm an amazing writer, my Jules says so, I'll write it tonight and ask Billy tomorrow, I really want to work with you, what's your name?"

"I'm afraid I'm leaving at Queenstown."

Dorothy Gibson gives him a camera-ready pout. "Come on, stay on board. We'll do the exteriors right here on the boat and the rest in Fort Lee, I've got a photographer to take location stills, she's from Keystone, a real professional, Nuss...Nissbaum... Never mind, it's perfect, you're not under contract to anyone, are you? Puh*leeze*, Jules and me, we can make you famous," her voice drops to a slinky purr, "those cheekbones belong in New York."

Her voice carries. The string trio breaks into *Oh You Beautiful Doll.* Perdita puts down her water glass and hides her face behind her napkin.

"You too, all of you! Be in my movie," Dorothy Gibson says. "We'll all be in the movies together. We'll be famous!"

✍✍✍

AFTER SHE'S GONE, Reisden makes his move. "We're touring the ship while my wife has my eyes to see it with. Would you care to join us? I'm afraid there will be stairs."

This eliminates Miss Lady. She sulks and orders Miss Fan to stay with her, but Dr. John promises to take the tour and tell them about it.

Of course this is what Reisden and Perdita want, John Rolfe Church away from his family.

"I must get my scarf and gloves," Perdita says. Reisden says it's crowded under the Grand Staircase clock, already the place to meet on *Titanic.* "Shall we meet you outside, love?" He and Church get their coats from the cloakroom and go out to the prom deck. In the chill night air they are as alone as they can be on a ship.

"I have a second motive in inviting you," Reisden says, "other than your kindness to my wife. Sometimes we at Jouvet are asked discreetly to find a thing out, and someone has asked us about the other John Rolfe Church."

"You mean Zack," Dr. John corrects.

"Yes, Bright Isaac. After he left Fair Home, he apparently went to New York, where he seems to have married a white woman. They had a child."

"A child?" Dr. Church asks sharply.

Not *a marriage* but *a child.* The child is news to him. The marriage not?

"A daughter, who now has children of her own. Obviously the family haven't any intention of contacting anyone, but they've heard about Bright Isaac and it concerns them that their grandfather might have been black. They want to know whether it might possibly have been not Isaac but you who married her. Here's Perdita. We'll talk later."

He and Perdita have timed it right. In interrogation, there are three principles. First, ask for only what you need to know. Offer the victim as much security as the situation warrants; be on their side. Finally, give them time to think.

Dr. John will now have time to think.

Dr. John has no children. Or thought he didn't, until now.

What motivates a man?

His children. His family.

Will a child get Dr. John to talk?

"And here's our guide. We'll continue later."

ॐॐॐ

THE NEXT HALF HOUR is pure British farce. They have been promised a tour of all *Titanic*'s splendors, the many-storied staircases, the elevators, the almost-outdoors Verandah Café with its real ivy and silk ivy; but their steward clearly was on another ship until this morning and he isn't quite yet here. He's twenty or so, with a twenty-hair ginger mustache; he has a treble voice and bright shiny buttons and he can't believe his luck in being on the world's greatest ship. "I'n't she fine, though?" But he couldn't find the Grand Staircase if he were standing on it. He leads them into culs-de-sac trying to locate the first-class dining room, which is, after all, the largest moving space on earth and shouldn't be that hard to find. He gets them on the wrong staircase. Finally they give up and go back to the Ritz. Reisden buys the group a bottle of Veuve Clicquot and invites the boy to join them on the prom deck, the next step in unlocking Dr. John's tongue.

They stand in the enclosed promenade looking out over the bow. In the light from the portholes Reisden watches Dr. John's face while champagne dissolves the steward's inhibitions. "Look 'ere," says the boy, showing them the patent windows that protect the first-class passengers from being splashed. "Named after Mr. Ismay. Ismay windows. You can open 'em." He lets one of the heavy windows down, desperate to show off something he knows. "'Ave you ever seen anything like?"

"Only the best for your passengers?"

"Right, sir!"

"Is it true Jack Johnson tried to take passage on this ship?"

"Oh, sir, there's a story behind that, there is. Went right up to the top birds, they say, up to Mr. Ismay 'isself, before they stopped 'im."

Jack Johnson is the great American boxer, who would be the heavyweight champion of the world if he weren't black. Last year he beat the champion, a white man. One would have thought the world had ended. The Boxing Commission refused to certify him.

So Johnson declared he'd return to America as a celebrity should, aboard *Titanic.*

"'e wouldn't 'ave been right for 'ere. Never mind 'e's a black-fella, travels with his wife *and* 'er sister, they do say they *all fancy each other*," the steward lowers his voice and casts a glance at Perdita, who's leaning obliviously out the Ismay windows, breathing the fresh sea wind. "*And* Johnson beats up people when 'e drinks, and there's plenty of places to drink on *Titanic*. Right clever of the directors to 'andle it the way they did."

"Why," Dr. John says, "what did Mr. Ismay do to stop him?"

"Got rid of all the blackies, Sir. Every one."

The directors of the White Star Line have not simply refused to sell a ticket to Johnson, who's known to stand on his rights and sue. No, they've issued a declaration.

"Not a one of them goes aboard us, Sir. Not a maid or valet, not a chauffeur, not a cook or stoker. The White Star Line is *white*."

"Is that so?" says Dr. John. He raises his chin a little. Under his mustache his scarred lips tighten.

Perdita turns to listen; she unconsciously makes the same small gesture, the same lifted chin and compressed mouth.

"Why, Sir, I would make a notable fuss if our Mr. Otis could not travel with us," Dr. John says. "We know how to value our people where I come from."

"To people being valued," Perdita says, raising her champagne flute. "Good for you, Dr. John."

She might as well have declared herself. She can't lie, doesn't know how. She might say the right words but her face, her gestures— Reisden clears his throat meaningfully.

"Oh," she says, "I am getting cold." She asks the steward to help find her cabin, leaving Reisden alone with Dr. John again.

"Your wife is very independent," Dr. John comments.

"Yes, very.—As I said about the daughter's family, you'll never hear from them, and I am bound to silence because of what I do. The family simply want to know whether they are your descendants rather than Isaac's. You know what trouble they would save themselves."

Dr. John looks up at him, and for a moment Reisden thinks he'll get a real answer.

But "Why should they care, Sir, what others think of them?" Dr. John explodes. "In Virginia we have a most liberal law, there is no 'one-drop' law for us, seven-eighths will make us white. And do you know why, do you know what my name means? Rolfe? My family boasts descent from John Rolfe, one of the first colonizers of Virginia, and his wife Pocahontas. What does Mr. Ismay think of red men, I wonder? I point out nothing, I do not sport a tomahawk nor adorn my hair with feathers. But it is so."

"Are you in favor of what Bright Isaac did, then? Passing himself for white?"

"His sin was not in wantin' to be a free man. It was wantin' to be me. I am in favor of leaving well enough alone, and that is what you may say to them. Let them value themselves and know themselves, and they will be known for who they are."

Leaving well enough alone should be the right choice.

"Louisa Church is still alive," Reisden says quietly. "She lives in New York City. She never remarried."

"Sir, the lady is nothing to me."

"And the children? There are grandchildren now. I've met one of them, the most marvelous little boy. He lives in Paris. He loves dogs and stories." Oh, Toby. "The family will not misuse whatever information you can give them. But it will make a great difference to them."

Dr. John shakes his head. "I am sorry. I cannot help you."

Dr. John would rather keep silent than help a child.

Reisden scribbles his private telegraphic address on his card. "If you should change your mind, telegraph me at this address. One word would reassure them. Simply say *Yes.*"

"Sir, I regret you will hear nothing from me."

ॐॐॐ

"I didn't expect him to talk," Reisden tells Perdita.

They meet back in the stateroom and sit together on the narrow bed. She sighs and leans against him. He smoothes his hand down the soft curve of her hip. His heart aches. If he had more time to work on Dr. John alone— It's Reisden's choice there's no more time.

"What shall I do?" she asks.

"You'll introduce him to Louisa in New York. You'll talk with both of them. Separately or together. It will work out."

"Do you think so?"

He hopes so.

He could go to New York with her. Theoretically he could.

He won't.

In the dark, in the scent of American lilacs from the traveling basket, he reaches out for her; she clings to him. They pull desperately at clothes, unbutton, unhook. The stiff sheets slide and crumple under them. They pull each other close, *oh please,* she says; *please what?* he says, trying to make her laugh, but "I don't know!" she says; there is no safe place here tonight, sex has no more power than love to keep her safe. He buries his face between her breasts. In what ought to be pleasure, he groans silently, inwardly, and she cries. "I don't know what to *do,*" she says.

The satin comforter is wound round them like rope round prisoners.

"You'll take him on a tour of New York," he says. Here she is, skin to his hand, here. They have so little time. "Get him alone and talk to him."

The sweat is chilling on them; the porthole is open, a void of stars in the dark.

Something jabs at their ribs. "Do you have a book in bed?" she asks, laughing shakily.

"It's the bed-rail." According to Gilbert's *Shipbuilder,* many of the beds on *Titanic* are a generous four feet wide. This is not one of those beds.

They rearrange themselves against each other. "Is that better?"

"Actually, not much, let me put my arm around you— Oh blast. No, stay in bed." He untangles himself, closes the porthole, turns on the electric heater. The bed isn't meant for two people; the genteel English sleep alone unless they think of England. Inexplicable. He finds his overcoat, which has been a blanket before in a pinch.

"You take the bed, I'll sleep on the couch." There is a couch, a tiny upholstered plank.

"Alexander, no."

No. He wants to sleep with her.

But they won't sleep together comfortably in this bed, he won't sleep at all on this ship, and in that farce of a tour, she hasn't had the advantage of his eyes. At least he can do one thing.

"Shall we see *Titanic*?"

࿐࿐࿐

TO HER IT FEELS like the very safest of ships in the storm her life has become. A handrail to grab, the solid thrumming and heartbeat of the engines. The number on her door is a smooth enamel plaque. She feels for subtle raised numbers, but finds none. The trouble with blind people is there aren't enough of them; if more people had trouble seeing, there'd be raised numbers you could feel. She takes out her little traveling perfume-atomizer and sprays a discreet scent at nose height on the door. There.

To him it looks like a cemetery. He watches her drifting down the corridor in her pale coat, a ghost in the night-lights. Boots and shoes line the corridor like epitaphs.

If she drowns he will not have even her body to bury—

Wearisome, Richard. Go away. Leave us alone tonight.

She smells the dye in the new carpets, the fresh paint, the brass-polish. She files away landmarks: fire extinguisher, smell of citrus soap marking the bathroom. A fresher air, a breeze against her cheek. A big space. She stretches out her arms, touching emptiness.

"The lounge and the Grand Staircase," he says.

He's borrowed *The Shipbuilder* from Gilbert and brought it with him; they should have had it this evening for the tour. He opens one of the folding maps and shines his flashlight on it. "Elevators behind the stairs. They come up only this far, to A deck. Up the stairs one flight to the boats," he reminds her.

"I remember."

She feels her way down the staircase, exploring. A bronze Cupid holds a glass torch at the bottom of the stairs. She touches chubby brass feet, kneels to run her hands over spiky iron flowers.

The floor-tiles are almost sticky, rubberized, with little grooves and treads like the bottoms of shoes.

"So as not to slip," he says. "So you'll be safe."

Safe, she thinks. "What's on this deck?"

"The lounge, the smoking room—"

"The smoking room? Where women can't go? I want to see that." She wants to do everything she can, in case she can never travel on *Titanic* again. The White Star Line is white. She shivers and puts the thought aside.

He leads her down another long corridor and through a lounge. Scattered lamps paint color on the carpet. A man in shirtsleeves is shelving books; with almost a year to prepare, they're still furnishing *Titanic*. Through another lounge past the aft staircase: "And this should be the smoking room." He pushes experimentally at a heavy door. Officially the public rooms close at eleven, but first class ignores the rules; in one lit corner men are bent over a card game.

"Oh look, oh look, *look*," she says, because the light is slanting just right and she can see a magic, a marvel; the window frames are glowing, the mantelpiece, the panels on the walls, as if the room were made of moonlight. "What is it?"

"You can see it? Mother of pearl."

"It's beautiful." She runs her fingers over the inlay.

Italian work, curlicues and flowers, goblin faces, lit to rainbows by electric sconces. There is always something exaggerated and unreal about the big liners, Reisden thinks; the smoking room wants to be in some fantasy Renaissance castle. All he notices are the bay windows. Bay windows on a ship, where high waves will crash through.

"I don't suppose Dr. John is here, though," she says.

"No."

"Then let's see the dining room. I'll want to know where it is."

For when you're gone, she doesn't say.

For when I'm gone and can't help you, he thinks.

The largest floating space on earth, *Titanic's* famous first-class dining room, is an echoing blackness; his flashlight doesn't reach to the end of it. He plays the light over a white coffered ceiling, white cubes of tables, cones of folded napkins, green leather chairs.

She claps her hands gently and then half-sings, "Halloooo." She knows it's here; she's written to the White Star Line and has the locations of all the pianos. *Halloooo,* the room echoes back, a soft-padded resonance, a harplike vibration of strings. She claps again, listens, and moves into the darkness, hands stretched out. "Here it is—" She raises the fallboard and plays a few scales to test its action and tuning. She's explained to White Star that she'll be playing at Carnegie Hall and has got permission to practice in the early morning, if she does it quietly. This is the early morning. She plays the first few bars from her Carnegie Hall piece and then closes the fallboard.

"Go ahead, love." He sits at the table next the piano.

"Are you sure?"

He watches her. All those times she was practicing and he passed by oblivious, taken up with his own work; he wants to watch her now, remember her, all of her, the percussive curve of her hands, her fierce soft happiness.

She closes the fallboard and comes to sit by him. He puts his hands on hers. She thinks of their uncertain marriage, their future and Toby's, sailing through these unknown waters, untested as

Titanic; and all the sailing of it will be in her hands, once she is alone with the Churches.

"Tell me all you know about *Titanic,*" she says.

You are going away on it, he thinks. "What do you mean, love?"

"So I can make conversation with Dr. John. *Titanic* has engines. Men like engines."

He laughs and turns on the table light to show her the deck plans. "Can you see?"

Blank pages to her; she shakes her head.

"All right. *Titanic*'s half hotel and half machine. Passengers see the hotel. But at the far end of this dining room is a wall, and beyond it, my love, are wonderful things. Electrical systems, telephone exchange, elevator machinery, kitchens. Post-office, with its own stamps and postmarks. The engines—" Under their clasped hands, the surface of the table thrums; the leaded windows, the silverware, every filament in every electric light. "*Titanic*'s engines are the largest ever built, five decks high."

"Do you want to see them?"

"Don't I. Shall I try to get us down to the engine room?"

"Alexander, let me. Watch me be more pathetic than Miss Gibson."

They make their way through the darkness, through the starch-and-heat smell of freshly ironed linen, and find the kitchen door. Reisden knocks and shows his letter from the White Star management, but it's Perdita who talks them in. "We have just had a private tour of the ship," she explains with pathetic-kitten innocence to the cook who's trying to make them go away. "My husband knows one of the White Star managers and we have seen all the pretty things, but we want to see where the work gets done!"

"Oh, but ma'am—"

"It's that I'm halfway blind, so when I tell my friends I've been on *Titanic,* I won't have seen all the things they have. But if I've seen the *important* things, where everything is cooked, *interesting* things like that—!"

She means it to be heartbreaking, but the worst is it's true.

In any case it works. An undercook shows off the largest stove in the world, nearly a hundred feet long with nineteen ovens; takes them into the enormous bakery room and the dessert preparation area. "We make ice cream right here!" He gives them a taste of it. Skillets clink overhead. The famous potato-mashing machine is taller than they are. The cook leads them down a metal stairway to one cavernous cold-store after another: dark swaying racks of beef and mutton, boxes of bacon and ice-packed fish.

In the engineers' mess, the cook introduces them to a man with a soft Irish accent, sopping up fried eggs with a slab of fried bread. "Of course ye've seen nothing yet, half the folk on this ship couldn't find their rump with a compass, excuse me, Ma'am. I'm on Mr. Andrews' team, the Guarantee Group, we're checking her out, testin' her all this voyage, fixin' what needs to be fixed, glorified man-Jacks, that's us. Changing lightbulbs this morning, I was. Six thousand lightbulbs on this ship." Reisden asks questions; the man draws in the margins of *The Shipbuilder:* main and auxiliary generating sets, metal-filament and carbon-filament lamps, electrical requirements of the elevators. All the innovations that make *Titanic* comfortable, dimming circuits in the cabins, illuminated signs, master clock to change the time all over the ship at once.

"And it's safe, isn't it?" Perdita asks pointedly.

Double-bottomed floors, watertight bulkheads to above the waterline— "She could hit another ship bang-on and make port on her own steam. *Olympic* did."

"And the engines?" Reisden asks.

"Would ye fancy seeing 'em? I'll warn ye, though, they'll get ye smutched."

He leads them down narrow stairs, down corridors muttering with engine-thunder, around obstacles that he names with an affectionate hand-slap against steel plates, and knocks on a white door. It opens onto oven-heat, an avalanche of scraping and clanging, a thrumming floor. Around them and above them and below them roar the engines.

Titanic is all engine. Above their heads, below their feet, the air dances with coal-grit and burning oil. Great pistons chop around them. Through the gridded floor, heat shudders upward.

Reisden puts his arm around Perdita for his own comfort as much as hers. On the decks far below them, the coal-trimmers run about like mice.

"A ton of coal to go a mile!" the engineer shouts. "All shoveled by good Belfast boys and them lubbers from Southampton."

Those five-story-tall behemoths are run by coal, and the coal is flung into the steam-boilers shovelful by shovelful like any ordinary house-furnace; but there are rows of furnaces. The trimmers' and firemen's heads are rocks in a flow of lava. The men have their own quarters in the bow of the ship, their own passages through it; from Southampton to New York, the Black Gang won't see the light of day.

"Are they actual black men?" Perdita shouts.

"No, ma'am, but the smutch gets ground so into 'em." He pours them mugs of hot sweet gritty tea from a spatterware pot sizzling on a boiler. "Now ye can say ye've seen *Titanic*. Not even Mr. Ismay's had boiler tea."

They take their sturdy round mugs with them out on deck; the wind cuts cold after the engines' heat. He draws her into the shelter of a deck-bay, where folding chairs are piled with steamer blankets. "Oh my shameless woman," he says. "More pathetic than Miss Gibson indeed." She laughs with pleasure. They cuddle in one deck chair together, in a nest of pirated wool blankets, arms around each other.

Morning comes too soon.

HE LEAVES HER TO THE DUBIOUS PLEASURES of the salt-water bath and has himself shaved at the barber's, which is also the *Titanic*

souvenir-shop. He gets the ship's newspaper and a copy of the passenger list; Perdita is on it but so is he, as if they were going together all the way to New York. He buys Gilbert a souvenir pamphlet about *Titanic*, Aline and Mme Herschner pincushions in the shape of life preservers, Toby a tin toy *Titanic* that is too old for him, but he must have it anyway because it is chubby and charming and not in the least like the real ship. Dotty's son Tiggy has one as well, and postcards because Tiggy has begun to collect them. He gets Perdita a *Titanic* ship's-wheel brooch for her coat, the traditional way of boasting one has been on one of the great liners; and gets her also, from him, something that surely should have been banished to the third-class barber shop for its Victorian sentimentality, a little brass bird flying through a little milk-glass lifesaver marked *RMS Titanic. Across the seas on thought's bright wings / My bird of love this message brings.* It has a dangling heart; of course it does. *Be careful, be safe; may we be like birds of one flock; oh my love, my heart depends on you.* He gives it to her at breakfast.

"Truly, Alexander, wasn't it a glorious adventure?" she says, pinning it on her coat, oblivious to irony. "We know what's behind the kitchen door. We've seen the engines."

Encouragingly, they have survived the night; they are almost to Ireland; perhaps they will not drown. If he survives as far as Queenstown, she'll make it to New York.

And perhaps she'll learn something from John Rolfe Church.

"We have seen the engines," he agrees. Glorious can wait till Wednesday morning when *Titanic* steams past the Statue of Liberty, Louisa Church meets them, and she identifies white Dr. John Church as her ex-husband.

Outside, on the third-class deck below them, a group of Swedish boys are playing soccer with a bundle of rags. "Mista, give us a quarter to buy a real ball!" Reisden, a soccer fan, tosses down a dollar.

"What's your name?" Perdita calls.

"Per! But in New York I change my name, I am Peter!" The boy runs off with the coin in his fist, kicking the rag ball down the deck.

"Alexander, I will miss you so much," she says.

"Let me hear how things go."

"I'll write you every day."

"Telegraph me if it works out. When it works out," he corrects himself.

He watches from the tender as *Titanic* sails away from Queenstown harbor, into the moist April light. Seagulls scream. Up on A deck, Perdita is wearing her red jacket so he can see her; she waves, and he waves back though she can't see him.

No one has died on *Titanic.* Everything's fine. Toby's father and Toby's mother have gone on a boat together, and Toby still has both of them.

Mr. Otis W. Church, trainer, Fair Home, Virginia

OTIS CHURCH WAS BORN IN 1856, just old enough to hero-worship his half-brother Isaac. His mother was Miss Lady's body-servant and Zack was Master John's body-servant, so, in spite of his field-dark skin, Otis was destined for a plum job too. When Master John had a son, Otis would be that son's body-servant. Otis would fall heir to fancy clothes and book-learning the way Zack had. When the son went to the races, Otis would go with him.

And what meant more to him than any of that, someday Otis might have his own horse.

His place was swept away with his world. Otis grew up in a long drab Afterward. Paint peeled. White people ate from tin dishes and wore mourning.

But there were still horses.

Otis became a jockey and a trainer.

It's early in the morning outside the Fair Home barn. The Italian foals from Mr. Tesio have settled down as if they were born here, not bothered at all by their long journey from Italy to France to Virginia. Otis leans against the paddock fence watching them. They're taking things good. Eating well, curious, no signs of colic from the new grass. That pretty little bay has already picked herself one of the barn cats for a pet.

He rubs her nose and feeds her a treat. "What we going to call you, pretty girl?" Plenty of time to pick out a racing name, but Otis likes things determined and settled. Ever since Whirlwind, Fair Home horses have been named after winds. It's luck. Mr. Tesio suggested l'Ostro, Wind from the South, but Otis didn't even halfway favor that.

He'll ask Miss Arbella for a name. Miss Arbella will think of something fine.

He walks up the path toward the summer kitchen. Breakfast is waiting on the table, grits in a pan, covered with a clean kitchen towel to keep them warm. With Miss Lady gone, Mamma is practically a lady of leisure; Miss Arbella has come down from the big house and they've taken their coffee outside to sit on the porch. Otis scrapes his grits onto a plate, takes a spoon, and looks up for a moment at the engraving of Whirlwind over the kitchen table, Whirlwind galloping down the straight at White Sulphur Springs, first big race after the war. The jockey in the picture is drawn to be white but it was Otis rode that day, rode and won.

He goes out to join Mamma and Miss Arbella. Miss Arbella is sitting on the step below Mamma, getting her orders for the day.

"Miss Arbella, you're going to let Vivvy dust Miss Lady's office before you go in there," Mamma says. "And I want to see you doing your pretty sewing and playing your piano before you start studying the breed-books."

"Yes, Mammy Jane," Miss Arbella says resignedly.

"And I don't mean it's all right as long as I don't see you. How are you going to get yourself a fine husband if you don't sew and play like a lady?" Mamma looks up and sees him. "Otis Church, do I see you using a spoon on your breakfast as if you don't know how to use a fork?"

"Don't you get on me, Mamma," Otis says comfortably. "Miss Arbella, what we going to call that Italian bay? Need to give her a name."

"Wish we could call her *Titanic.* Titanic Wind, maybe?"

"Titanic Wind sounds rude, honey," Otis says.

"Air de Paris, like that perfume my good boy Otis brought me," Mamma suggests. Otis brought her a tiny bottle of it from Paris and she's not even dared to open it, just smelled round the edges.

"Unc' Otis, can you bring out our postcards? Maybe I can think of something from them."

Otis gets up stiffly and goes inside, unpins from the kitchen wall the postcard of the Eiffel Tower Mamma got from him and the one of Longchamp from Miss Lady, very first postcards Mamma's ever got of her own. Miss Arbella has a postcard of a gargoyle from Otis and one of Versailles from Miss Lady, and one of the ship they're coming home on. Postcards are a new thing for Miss Arbella too, but the girl has pinned them up in the kitchen to make it bright for Mamma and Otis and the maids. Miss Arbella has a good heart.

Miss Arbella spreads the cards out on the steps like she's telling fortunes. Her father comes down the walk past the kitchen.

"Hello, Mr. Jeff! Fine day, sah!" Otis says.

"Hello, Uncle Otis, Mammy Jane. Too hot in that kitchen for you?"

"Yassuh! Too hot for us! Cook going to sweat herself to butter in there! And I just been lookin' at those fine foals for you, Mr. Jeff! We been asking Miss Arbella to pick names! She pick you lucky names, Sah!"

Mr. Jeff laughs and goes on.

"He don't want you folks sitting outside," Arbella says. "He don't know how hot that kitchen is."

"He doesn't want," Mamma corrects. "He doesn't know. Miss Arbella, he just wants to keep order. Your father should not condone servants being idle."

"He's right there," Otis says. "What we going to call that pretty foal, then?"

Miss Arbella wraps her arms around her knees and rocks back and forth on the step, looking at the postcards. Mamma rolls her eyes. "Miss Bella, you do look like the village idiot. How are you going to get a husband like that?" But Miss Arbella holds up her hand.

"That foal need something about her being brave, going on a long voyage to a new home." Miss Arbella taps the bright-colored card of *Titanic*. "What do they call a good wind for a ship? Got to be a name for that."

"Favoring wind."

"Favoring Wind," Miss Arbella says, trying it out.

Otis can feel that name settling right round that pretty little bay's neck like a victory wreath. "That's a good luck name," Otis says.

This is what I worked for, he thinks, watching Mr. Jeff's clever daughter. Little white girl, frizzy yellow hair, blue eyes, only but twelve years old. She own this place someday, but I have the horses under her like I do under Miss Lady.

This place is mine; this is mine.

Nobody talks about the cost of Fair Home's surviving. Maybe Miss Lady and Mr. Jeff don't know; maybe they just like to pretend they don't. Otis can look at it straight, though, all the way from when his brother told him Fair Home was his to look after.

If the South had won the war, he'd have been a better man.

More to life than being good, though.

He'd rather have Fair Home.

Perdita

WHAT DOES A WOMAN DO when she wants to find out something about a man?

She talks to his wife and his mother.

But Miss Lady would rather talk about herself.

"I was always meant to marry Mr. Charles Church," Miss Lady says. "I was married in white silk with apple blossoms in my hair. Mr. Church was thirty-nine and I was fifteen, and I must say, the wedding night was nowhere near pleasant."

"Miss Lady!" says Miss Fan, shocked.

"I knew what I was doing, Fan, I married Mr. Church for his horses. You may have heard of our horses, Miss Perdita? Our Whirlwind?"

Miss Lady's voice flutters lovingly round *Whirlwind.* They are on the promenade deck, Perdita in a deck chair, Miss Lady in her wheeled chair with Miss Fan holding a parasol over her. The sunlight is glorious, springlike and fresh and clear, the kind you never get except on water. The ship's dog walker runs past them behind a whuffling fan of dogs. It would be perfect, if only Miss Lady and Miss Fan would talk about Dr. John.

"I was not sure of Signor Tesio until he said that gray horses never win races. I would never own a gray horse. Didn't I always say that, Miss Fan?"

"Yes, Miss Lady, you always did."

"I knew it years before Signor Tesio. I say a man is a fool who bets, but a worse fool who bets on a gray horse. We do no betting at Fair Home." Miss Lady's flowery old-lady perfume smells hot with indignation. "I knew a boy bet *all his land* against our Whirlwind and lost!"

Miss Fan sighs.

Miss Lady has hundreds of anecdotes about her girlhood as a belle and heiress in the 1840s; to hear her, there was no other girl in the South. Perdita listens for clues to Dr. John, but gets none.

"Frank wanted to shoot himself for me, he said he would die rather than live without me." Miss Lady was the only child of her family's generation; Fair Home was hers. So she was the queen of balls and hunts, of love letters tucked into bouquets of camellias, serenades under her window, all from men who wanted to marry her plantation. "Eddie was the most handsomest man I ever saw and he told me the sun rose in my eyes. But I knew he would not be equal to running Fair Home." Duels at dawn; readings from *Ivanhoe*; champagne and broken hearts at midnight. "That Aubrey, he couldn't even *ride*." Miss Lady never mentions who washed the champagne glasses, mucked out the stables and put the tired horses away. "Oh, darlin', my father managed our people on the plantation and Uncle Davis and Aunt Lila dealt with the house the way my Jane does now. They were treasures upon earth."

Miss Lady is talking about slaves. Perdita dares to ask. "What was it like, Miss Lady, being the mistress of slaves?"

"Slaves and servants, darlin', it's all the same. You are not put on earth for their convenience. Know what you want and take nothing less," Miss Lady says. "Find the people who will run your house right and support them in their endeavors, as long as they support you. But if they do not, cast them off."

Cast-them-off, this privileged old heiress says, one stony little word at a time. Perdita has no trouble believing she sold Bright Isaac.

"What was Dr. John like when he was a boy?" she asks, trying to get back to him. "Was he such a good person as he is now?"

"He was triflin'," his mother says. "The War was the redemption of him."

"Trifling?"

"Why, darlin', think of his taking Whirlwind to Manassas!" Miss Lady snaps her fan venomously. "Of course the Yankees got both of them. I am sure there are fast horses up North that should belong to us."

"Was Dr. John trifling in other ways too?"

"Oh, he is changed now. Did I ever tell you what Varina Davis said about me?"

This is hopeless; Miss Lady's only subject besides horses is herself.

❧❧❧❧

MISS FAN, AT LEAST, should talk about her husband more readily, but Miss Fan is always in attendance on Miss Lady; Miss Lady sulks when she's left alone. So Perdita, who swims perfectly well thanks to Alexander's making sure she can, is forced to beg Miss Lady that Miss Fan may join helpless blind Perdita in the ship's swimming-pool during the women's swimming hour, to save her from a watery grave; it would be *such* a favor.

She hates doing helpless blind. But it works.

"Imagine, me in a swimmin' costume!" Miss Fan says, laughing nervously. Miss Fan, in a rented bathing suit, holds onto the side rail of *Titanic's* swimming pool and kicks her feet uncertainly. "I feel unclothed! And do you know, we are actually *under the sea* in this swimmin' pool?"

Perdita and she bob up and down in the quivering water and talk.

Miss Fan is Miss Lady's cousin; their grandfathers were brothers. Like Miss Lady, Miss Fan had land, and Miss Lady wanted to arrange a marriage between Miss Fan and Dr. John to bring Landrum Farms and Fair Home together. But when John Rolfe Church came home from military college, he brought his friend Lafayette deMay.

"I had no eyes but for Fate," Miss Fan says. "We were married in the parlor of Fair Home the evening before the men rode off to Manassas. When my Fate left in the morning I was so proud of him, I thought I would see him come back triumphant. But we had only the one night. Thank the good Lord. At least I have Jeff."

Jefferson deMay is her son, the only child from either of her marriages.

"What was Dr. John like when he was young?"

Miss Fan's voice sounds even more melancholy in the echoing and splashing. "Do you know, I hardly remember. My Fate eclipsed him entirely. My Fate was so perfectly tall and blond and handsome, with eyes as deep and sad as—"

And off she goes into five minutes of the wrong man.

"Had your Fate and Dr. John known each other long?" Perdita persists.

"Too long! John had a bad influence over him. My Fate told me later that when he saw me first, he was overcome with despair that he was not worthy of me."

"Why, what had he done?" At last here is some information.

"John had encouraged him to gamble against Whirlwind. He had lost his land!"

Land, land, land, the pool echoes. Perdita remembers Miss Lady: *I know a boy who bet all his land and lost.*

"Dr. John let him bet against Whirlwind?"

"Miss Lady said I could not marry him because he was landless." Miss Fan takes a deep breath. "But Fate was goin' to the war. I *defied* her!"

Good for you. "But how could Dr. John have allowed his friend to bet against Whirlwind?" That is horrible, and seems so unlike him.

Miss Fan considers and says finally, "I suppose he was carried away."

"But wasn't Whirlwind a famous racer? Didn't your Fate know that?"

"Whirlwind was a young horse, not tried yet. John must have been thinkin' to race Whirlwind before word got out, and make money to live like a general."

To take a friend's inheritance? "I cannot imagine Dr. John would do such a thing."

"In the end, I got Fate's land back. John and I agreed to have no children, so Fate's son would have Fair Home."

Oh goodness. That is entirely awful.

"John changed completely," says Miss Fan solemnly. "He was in prison for years and suffered beyond measure. He said he was in agony for what he had done and he was obliged to me for accepting him."

Miss Fan turns her conversation quickly away from Dr. John. Perdita tries to keep her astonishment from showing, and find out more about this new side of Dr. John. But throughout their swim and the steamy Turkish bath afterward, Miss Fan only wants to talk about her dear lost Fate deMay.

🙣🙣🙣

PERDITA SITS CROSS-LEGGED on her bed on Saturday night—it is sadly wide and comfortable with only herself in it—and considers Dr. John.

Good Dr. John isn't so good after all.

He let his best friend lose his land, because Dr. John knew Whirlwind could run fast and Fate didn't.

And then Fate died, and according to Miss Fan Dr. John was wounded and put in prison, and he became saintly. "Changed completely."

Except that Dr. John wasn't wounded and in prison. If Dr. John is Aunt Louisa's Mr. Church, he was in New York, buying horses for the Union Army and marrying Aunt Louisa.

Taking advantage of your best friend's ignorance! Abandoning your crippled mother and your best friend's pregnant wife, in wartime!

Aunt Louisa would have been appalled.

But would she have divorced him over it?

And the idealistic man she'd described? *Her* John Rolfe Church?

They would both have wanted him to make amends.

He made amends, she supposes. But— Marrying Miss Fan so his conscience would feel better? And agreeing not to have children? It's unnaturally saintly, and poor Miss Fan!

Alexander's right, he won't confess it publicly now; there'd be high hosanna to pay.

But will he confess it privately to Perdita?

She considers how she and Dr. John can talk alone.

Miss Dorothy Gibson, who wanted to devour Alexander's cheekbones, has a cameraman but no leading man. So for the last two days Miss Gibson has been having herself filmed in first-class places on *Titanic,* flirting with an invisible admirer. Miss Gibson has had tea alone at a two-person table in the Verandah Café, Miss Gibson has strolled on the promenade deck, Miss Gibson has shaded her eyes and looked soulfully over the sea, and the ticking of Mr. Harbeck's film camera has followed her like perfume. Miss Gibson is being awful and getting in everyone's way and everyone wishes they were her.

Perdita's cabin is furnished with a telephone, a wonderful indulgence on a ship. She pats the wall until she finds it and clicks the *accrocheur* to get the operator's attention.

"Miss Gibson, please."

Getting Dorothy Gibson to talk about her movie is as easy as getting Niagara to roar. Miss Gibson complains that the hero of *Her Shipboard Romance* will have to be added to the movie at the studio in New Jersey. "I wish we had your husband on board. But we'll be able to say it was filmed on *Titanic,* the posters won't say how much of it was and the audiences won't care. So is your husband coming to New York?"

"No, but do you come across to Paris frequently? My husband has worked with André du Monde, the director, and André always needs leading ladies."

She promises Miss Gibson an introduction to André, and recklessly throws in Alexander for a weekend's work on a picture in Europe; "Alexander would be delighted." Not in the least, but Alexander owes her. "And I have a great favor to ask you. Are you doing more scenes? Oh, good! Might I be an extra? It would be a grand surprise for Alexander to see moving pictures of me on

Titanic, and I have a scheme. If you could ask Dr. John Church as well, and have the two of us sitting together somewhere in the background, away from his mother and wife?"

There is nothing like making a movie for sitting around talking. It's as good as an ocean voyage.

After Miss Gibson, Perdita ropes in Greta Nisensohn, the postcard girl, and makes plans with her too.

❧❧❧

THE NEXT DAY, WHICH IS SUNDAY, Miss Nisensohn approaches Perdita and the Churches on the promenade deck after church services. She has her camera with her, she says, because she is taking photos of *Titanic* for Miss Gibson's film.

"Miss Nisensohn, would you take my picture with my friends?"

Click squeak click, Miss Nisensohn snaps off one Kodak after another, getting good clear pictures of Dr. John's face, just as Perdita asked her to do. If Aunt Louisa doesn't meet Dr. John right away, Perdita will show her the pictures and ask *Is this your husband?*

"Stand there," Miss Nisensohn positions them, "smile, say cheese! Now some close-ups of all of you, *close-ups,* listen to me, I'm talking movie lingo. I'll send this to your hometown paper. 'A Prominent Southern Family on *Titanic,*' how's about that?"

"A lady never appears in the *papers,*" Miss Lady protests, gratified. "But on the *social* pages, I suppose—"

"Wouldn't it be fun if we could be in Miss Gibson's movie!" Perdita gushes innocently. "When are you filming next, Miss Nisensohn?"

"Today! We're in the Verandah Café right after lunch. And the movie needs extras. Dr. Church, would you? Miss Gibson's short on men."

"On a Sunday?" Miss Lady shrieks.

"Oh, but you know the picture-people must work when they have light," Perdita says, "and we have been to services already. Won't you help, Dr. John?"

Miss Gibson admires Miss Lady's purple velvet coat and snares her into playing a rich lady. Miss Fan is given the role of the lady's companion. That takes care of them. Perdita and Dr. John are relegated to figures in the background of the long complicated scene. They sip tea (real smoky Assam tea served by a real waiter, because this is *Titanic*) and are left to make conversation all by themselves.

How do you ask someone to give up his secret?

Unfortunately it looks as if Dr. John doesn't intend to. "If you are speakin' with me on behalf of your husband, Miss Perdita," Dr. John says immediately, "I told him what I know. Which is nothing."

"I know the family too. Whatever you know, you may trust them to say nothing. I would be glad to take a word to them. One word would satisfy them. That's all they need."

"Miss Perdita, we'll say no more about it."

That's what he thinks. "Would you like tea?"

"Let me help you pour."

"Oh, I do perfectly well." She lays one hand against the outside of his cup to measure the heat-height. "There, see?"

This is April 14, the anniversary of President Lincoln's being shot, and the obvious topic suggests itself. Dr. John is not the typical Southerner; it turns out Lincoln is one of his heroes. "Don't tell Mamma. He is 'that no-count Kaintuck Yankee' to her. 'With malice toward none. With charity for all.' If he had lived, we would be a better country."

"I'm surprised you think well of him."

"I would not speak of it at home."

I bet you wouldn't, no more than you'd speak of being a Union sympathizer and running away to New York. But that was what you did, didn't you? Please?

"What was it like to go to the war?" she asks. "Believing as you did."

"I believed in nothing but myself then; I was mad for glory. I wanted handsome uniforms and a plumed hat."

She doesn't say anything for a bit. Was *mad for glory* the same thing as letting your friend lose his land so you could have more? "Did you change your mind about glory?" she starts to say, but he speaks across her.

"What's it like to have so little sight?" Dr. John asks. "If I may ask."

Well, she must set the tone of being frank.

"For me it's normal. I do see lights and shadows, I can even read, some, and see pictures with a magnifying glass, but most of what I suppose other people do by sight, I have to figure out my own way." The same way, she supposes, as a Southerner who favors the North might have to make life up for himself. She considers how to get the conversation back.

"What's hard, Dr. Church, is when people treat you like an idiot. In Paris, when they mean 'You understand?' everyone says 'You see?' And then they say '*Mais, Madame, vous ne voyez pas!*' and laugh and ignore me. I hate to be treated as less than other people." There, that is the tone. "Do you know how hard it is to be thought something you aren't?"

"No one thinks I am a dentist," Dr. John says.

That is not what she wants him to say.

"I am assumed to be a planter and a horse trainer," he says, "but it is Miss Lady and Mr. Otis who run the plantation. I truly like filling people's teeth. It does them good and they pay me. Mostly. What's it like to be a baroness, Miss Perdita?"

Did Sherlock Holmes solve crimes by answering questions about himself? "My husband would rather run his company and I'd rather play the piano. But what do we do? We go to parties. It's all for business. I pity Cinderella; once she married Prince Charming, the poor woman probably never had a second to herself. What's it like to be in prison?" Your turn now, Dr. John.

"We thought of food."

That sounds right. She pushes the sandwich plate at him. "Have a sandwich."

He laughs. "Mamma is dying to ask you about European society."

"She would have a fine time with it. No, really, what was prison like?"

"You truly don't care for society, Miss Perdita? Meetin' dukes and princes? You will never convince Mamma society is triflin'."

He is avoiding and they are fencing, but she intends to win.

"Society is a bother, like a dress you can never sit down in because if you do, it has to be ironed. When we go to some nobleman's house, I have to change clothes three or four times a day. Something to have breakfast in! Something else to go walking in! A tea-dress for tea and a semi-formal for dinner! Alexander's cousin Dotty has herself sewn into her dresses, can you imagine. Alexander just wears a black suit unless he's in evening clothes. He gets away with it because everyone lets him be eccentric. I wish I could become eccentric. Really, what is prison like?"

"So you would give up society?"

"What's it like to get out of prison?" she asks.

"Like life after death," he says on an out-breath. He is giving up something after all, he's telling the truth, she can feel it, like the breeze by the Grand Staircase, a bigger place, a fresher air.

"What did you do when you were freed?" she asks.

"I walked the streets. I took a bath. I selected new clothes. The smallest things—! To be free of restraint! To be my own man!"

She clasps her hands with pleasure under the table. He has just betrayed himself. He had money for *selecting* clothes. Where did he get it?

In New York, oh, please; he was in New York. Working for the Union. Marrying Aunt Louisa. Please.

"When you were free, did you go straight home?" she asks.

"First I found Whirlwind."

"You saw no one else? You went nowhere else?"

"I knew where he was, outside Baltimore. And Miss Lady would have griddled me if I hadn't brought him back. Whirlwind *was* Fair Home. He was all we had."

Miss Lady's and Miss Fan's money would have melted away during the war. "How did you get him back?"

"Stole him," says Dr. John.

"You stole a *racehorse?*"

"Stole him back. Not so hard when you are acquainted with the horse. One apple and he was mine."

"Like Eve."

Dr. John laughs. "And was I the snake?"

No, he is not a snake; he is not lying at his center. He has been imprisoned, somewhere, and got free, somehow; and freedom was like life after death. And after all that, he found the courage to go home and make that hard bargain with Miss Fan, so the son of the man he'd wronged would have land.

Does he have his freedom? Can he share his story with Perdita, when he can't with Miss Fan or Miss Lady, or with anyone, now, still?

Please say you believed in the Union and married Aunt Louisa. Just say it. Now.

"I tell you what it's like to be in a war," Dr. John says suddenly. "I rode Whirlwind all the way back to Fair Home. Taking it slow on back roads. We were under martial law and a Southern man with a prize horse would have been a dead man.

"I saw the ruins of railroads and farmsteads, burned houses, bones in the fields, skulls. You cannot imagine. Our people were gone or not willing to work, wanting land but not knowing how to farm more than a little patch of ground. The whole country was fallen away like the face of a dead man. I came to Fair Home. The barns were burned. The fields were shoulder-tall in weeds and the quarters deserted. Even the smithy was burned. The wreck was so large. I wanted to take Whirlwind and ride away.

"But I didn't know whether Mamma was alive or dead.

"So I had to go to the door and knock. And after that, I had responsibilities.

"I feel sometimes I have never left prison.

"But when I was free, Miss Perdita? That freedom was the saddest time of my life."

It is like herself, the morning she realized she was pregnant. Alexander and she talked about abortion. She would have been free to keep studying, keep on with her career, but neither of them could hurt a child; that was inconceivable.

So she married Alexander, and they have Toby, their dear perfect boy. And *I have responsibilities.* Responsibilities she chose.

She can't fault herself for choosing them.

But now she is trapped.

Not trapped. Just married. Just not free.

But *life after death* to be rid of trying to be French, trying to make music in the wrong country. And *life after death* to make a marriage into something stable, a family.

What does freedom mean? Which responsibilities do you choose?

This is not what she needs to think of now.

But she can't help thinking of Dr. John. He is in prison still; a loved prison that constrains him.

He is like her.

She must find out what happened. They must talk, and keep talking.

❧❧❧

THAT NIGHT she starts practice just after the lights dim, to get extra time, to think how she will get Dr. John to talk with her again.

The Churches have gone to bed early. Other people are tucking themselves in too, keeping warm under the bedcovers; the weather has turned freezing. She's wearing her Irish lace opera coat for warmth and has to turn up the sleeves to play. In one corner of the lounge people are still drinking and playing bridge, complaining and laughing. ("I mean, *Titanic*'s magnificent, still, hasn't one seen it all before? One even knows the dogs.") But the lounge is big, they don't bother Perdita and she doesn't bother them.

She does her warm-ups and plays her Carnegie Hall piece through; the fingering is all worked out, the legato is soft as kitten fur. She doesn't have anything to do until she meets her violinist. She begins to improvise around a ragtime piece she learned last year from Blind Willie. In honor of him, she plays a hymn with a walking bass, suitable for Sunday at sea: *Jesus savior of my soul, Let me to Thy bosom fly, While the waters round me roll...* One of the bright young things applauds. She bows in their direction.

Jesus, savior of my soul, let us talk to each other. Let us support each other. Let us be family.

🙐🙐🙐

TESTIMONY OF EMILY RYERSON:
"Sunday morning Mr. Ismay showed to a woman passenger a wireless message with an ice warning. She asked if the *Titanic* would not go slower and Mr. Ismay replied laughing, "No, FASTER!..."

Testimony of Frank Prentice, assistant storekeeper on *Titanic*:
"It was almost like murder, wasn't it?"

🙐🙐🙐

AND NOW IT STARTS. It's late at night, April 14, 1912. *Titanic* is steaming through the North Atlantic, the largest moving thing on earth or sea, the newest ship, the most beautiful, the safest. *We will go faster,* Bruce Ismay said. *Titanic* is racing through Iceberg Alley at night.

Her long Marconi antenna rises from the bow, past her funnels all the way to the stern. The telegraph has been down for most of the previous day and the *Titanic* wireless operators, Harold Bride and Jack Phillips, are still catching up. "Greetings from *Titanic*," the ship blasts. "Arrive New York Wednesday morning. Meet me in New York."

In the first-class lounge, the bridge players are complaining.

Sixty-five seconds.

In their cabin, Isidor and Ida Straus are looking at pictures of their grandchildren. In her cabin, Dorothy Gibson is reading about herself in *Photoplay*.

Bruce Ismay is asleep.

Forty seconds.

In third class teenagers are awake, flirting. Polish and Swedish and Irish, Italian and Turkish and Lebanese. In three days they will be American. All they know, they will be changed.

Twenty seconds.

Samuel Heming, lamp trimmer, is turning a key. A cook on D Deck is mixing the rolls for tomorrow's breakfast.

There is no tomorrow.

Ten seconds.

Nine. Eight.

It's too early to have to survive, not yet, not yet—

❧❧❧

ABOUT QUARTER TO TWELVE there is a series of little stuttering bangs under Perdita's feet. Once on the Fourth of July, when she was in a boat with Harry, some fireworks fell into the river by mistake and exploded underwater: that sort of sound, thumps on the hull.

"What was that?" one of the drinkers calls.

"Iceberg!" someone shouts from the deck outside. "We nearly hit it!"

With a sound like that, Perdita wonders about *nearly*. She follows the others out into the cold, shivering in her coat, to find out what happened.

"An iceberg! It went right by us! I think we scraped it!"

"Three stories tall! It was blue in the lights, bright blue!"

"Don't slip, Miss, there's ice on the deck!"

"Steward?" a man calls. "Get me some ice!" Someone laughs.

"Is everything all right?" she asks a steward.

"What I think, Miss, is the ice 'ooked one of our propellers. Feel 'er running rough? That'll be bad news. Be limping all the way to New York. May 'ave to be towed. Ismay will be 'oppin'."

Her Carnegie Hall practice starts April 22. "How long extra might it take?"

"Couple of days."

"That's all right then." She kneels down and gropes for a piece of ice. It smells like ancient cold, rotted plants, and fish. In her warm hand it begins to melt. An iceberg; they hit an *iceberg*. She goes back inside, into the warm, begs a spare bottle from one of the stewards, an ink-bottle with a chipped stopper, and feeds into it slivers of iceberg for Alexander to put under his microscope. The steward seals it with candle-wax and she tucks it into the opera coat's hidden pocket. *Look, Alexander, this is what you're afraid of: it's just water.*

Then she goes back to practicing.

The engines sound tired, laboring. The steady thrum slows, picks up again, then stops. Rats, the steward is right; something's wrong with the engine. A propeller.

All the more time to find out things from the Churches. Tomorrow morning she'll invite them to the dog show and tell them about the iceberg, and then somehow, some way, she will get Dr. John alone again and they'll talk about freedom and family.

Tomorrow.

Meanwhile she practices.

Garnet Williams/Miss Nanette Williams

NEW YORK, MONDAY MORNING, APRIL 15, the beginning of another week and another quarrel with Frog Jaw Johnson.

"I could protect you," Frog Jaw says, like he's in control of the world.

"From what?" Garnet says. "From what are you protecting me, Mr. Johnson?"

"Someday the white folks'll catch you."

"Well, they won't."

"I can look after your grandpa," Frog Jaw says. "Glad to do that."

"No need."

"Don't you get me courting my grandbaby for you, Frog Jaw," Blind Willie says. "Can't do it your own self, it ain't gonna happen."

They're talking by the subway kiosk at 103rd and Broadway. All their conversations take place by the subway. Every day Frog Jaw just happens to be coming up Broadway as she walks by and happens to stop to talk to her, regular as a sermon or a dripping faucet. Giving Garnet grief about her journey down to 34th St. and her daily life of crime.

This week, this last week she'll be herself, Garnet can hardly bear Frog Jaw giving her more troubles than she has. She wants to shout at him. What do you mean, trying to bring me down? Sure, you could look after Grandpa, but what's that leave me owing you? Take all my cares away and I'd be beholden to you forever.

"Mr. Johnson, I know you are the best man in all New York. You own a pawnshop and a funeral parlor and a jewelry store and a bar and a detective agency. You get yourself a church and you'll be everything to everybody."

"But not to you, Miss Williams?"

"I don't think so, Mr. Johnson."

In any other part of New York they'd draw stares and jeers. A no-neck wide-mouthed man, tall and athletic but dark as a privy at midnight. A pretty ivory-skinned brunette girl, very pretty if she does say so. An old chicory stick of a blind man in a fancy seersucker suit and a Panama hat.

And a dog. Fat lurching splay-eared Sturgis, in a saddle and bellyband like a horse, and a perambulator handle fastened to the saddle so Blind Willie can keep hold of him.

"I'm going to my *job*," she says. "Where no one's *catching* me. Good day, Mr. Johnson. See you tonight, Grandpa."

"Tonight I'm playin' at John Brown's, get my supper there. No need to fuss, darlin'."

"OK. Love you, Grandpa. Don't drink too much. You take care of him, Sturgie."

She turns and clatters down the stairs, pays her five cents, pushes through the turnstile, gets on the local, takes her seat on the cane bench and catches her breath.

At 79th St. Garnet Williams gets off the local, crosses to the IRT downtown express line—and Nanette Williams gets on.

It's so easy.

Nanette Williams.

Miss Nanette Williams.

Downtown white.

Now that people can live long subway rides from where they work, a New York girl with good skin and good hair can get a job downtown and her boss no wiser. *My family lives way up the Bronx,* Nanette says, *takes me forever to get here but it's such a good job!*

Passing is crime, is it? Don't you tell me what it is.

Her mistake was hiring Fred Troutman, one of Frog Jaw's detectives, to pass as her brother at the Macy's Christmas party. Fred is white as blank paper and just as stupid, he told Frog Jaw what she was doing downtown, and now Frog Jaw is making her business his own.

But it's *her* business.

She can take care of Blind Willie. She *can.*

She ducks into the Macy's employees' entrance on 35th St, punches her timecard, and takes the elevator up to the sixth floor, joking with the white elevator boy. Monday is show day and New York society has signed up to view the latest fashions. The dressing room is full of models. "Miss Williams, here's your list. Miss Van Rensselaer wants to see the peach linen suit and the beaded formal; only six minutes to change between them, can you do it?"

"Mrs. Pritchard, I can do anything you want."

Every outfit is numbered. Nanette shimmies into the peach suit and the coordinated accessories from the matching numbered box. Good-as-jeweled earrings, brilliant scarf, beaded gloves, leather slippers. Models stand in a row, posing and turning in front of Monsieur Édouard of Windsor Frères. "Good, Miss Williams." "Thank you, Monsieur Édouard." Models stand in a line, waiting their turn to go through the velvet curtains into the showroom. "Now sell, sell, sell!" Monsieur Édouard grins just for Nanette. Nanette smiles back.

And now it's her turn. From one side of the curtain to the other, she becomes still another person: Nanette Astor, society girl. The richest girl in New York. She's going to Paris; she's going to marry a European aristocrat; she'll be happy forever; and she'll wear this posh peach linen suit as she waves to her envious friends from the deck of *Titanic.*

In the audience, chubby Miss Van Rensselaer gapes like a fish. Nanette smiles at her, sharing a secret. *Buy this and you'll be like me.* Miss Van Rensselaer would look like Death's ugly niece in peach, but Monsieur Eddie will talk her into rose or blue.

"What did you do to Miss Van Rensselaer?" Eddie asks her at the end of the morning show.

"I thought of *Titanic* and made her think of it."

"Girls? Think of *Titanic.* Think glamorous! Think biggest and newest and best! Think like Miss Williams!"

"And look like me too." Nanette crosses her eyes and sticks out her tongue. All her girlfriends laugh. All her fashion-model girlfriends, who'd never talk to her if she weren't white.

They eat their tiny lunches in kimonos and underwear, nibbling at cheese and white grapes, nothing that'll spill or stain or spoil a line. They talk about the Strauses, the Big Boss and Aunt Ida, who are coming home on the real *Titanic.* The Strauses are everyone's favorite people. It'll be good to have them back.

Nanette wanders over to where Monsieur Eddie is eating his lunch. Monsieur Édouard; Eddie Cohen, half of the brothers Eddie and Bernie, with a factory on Sixth Avenue. Barely taller than Garnet, patent-leather hair; Eddie says he brings his lunch because he's on a diet but everyone knows he's kosher.

"Monsieur Édouard?" Garnet says. "I know a woman coming to New York on *Titanic.* She's going to play at Carnegie Hall. She's a musician *and* a French baroness *and* her husband's company treats all the mad rich people in Europe."

"Who dresses her?"

"Nobody here, yet!"

"Well!" Monsieur Eddie says. "Talk to me later."

It's a long exciting afternoon. Women are buying their high-season wardrobes: they need tennis whites just as if they played tennis, they want that perfect little frock, that summer suit, that drape, that lace, that frill. Miss This is going to Europe on the third voyage of *Titanic,* Miss That is jealous because she's only going on some ugly German soot-belcher. Mrs. Van Hoohah's daughter is already engaged and is buying her trousseau in Paris, but of course she needs outfits to shop *in...* This year's drape skirts make them all look like they have bear hips. Rich white New Yorkers, and they all belong to her.

Then it's over and the girls get back into their ordinary clothes and walking shoes.

"Come see me a moment, Miss Williams." Eddie takes her into a corner of the room. He spreads out silk tube scarves, his latest style, with long silk tassels on the ends. Raspberry, burgundy, colors to eat with a silver spoon: "This color is you, Miss Williams." It is. "Wear it, show it off. You really sold them today. Every time you wear my clothes, my accountant smiles. And your friend, what colors does she wear?"

"She's just about my complexion and she likes modern colors. Coral, dark violet, aqua."

"She'll like our summer palette. Give her this," he picks another scarf, perfect for Perdita, "and ask her to think of the House of Windsor."

You bet, Eddie.

"You thought about what I said?" Eddie adds in a low voice.

"I need to finish hiring somebody to take care of my grandfather. He's blind. As soon as that's done, you bet I'll take the job."

"I can get somebody to help you find somebody."

And have Eddie find out Willie's black? "Thanks, but I'm OK."

"Come see me Tuesday at the atelier. I'll show you some of the designs we're working on. I'll introduce you to my brother."

The Windsor atelier. His *brother*.

"Thanks," she stammers. "Just—I'm the happiest girl in New York."

Eddie grins. "You deserve."

All the girls are waiting for the employees' elevator. She twirls the tassel on her new scarf. "Aren't you the one, then!" says Annie O'Meara, who's Olga on the show floor. "What was he asking you about?"

"Oh, just bribing me for a friend's name. Did you see what he was doing with that striped linen suit!"

"Mother Mary, twenty-one gores in the skirt!"

"Gores are old," another model sulks.

"Not the way he does them. And he matched the stripes perfectly," Garnet says. "Just impossible with that pattern, and he did it. I want to cry about those stripes."

And she's working for him.

She's done it. She's on her way.

Up in Harlem, every woman sews; half the women in Harlem sew beautifully. Some of them have been to dressmaking college. But the way to succeed isn't to sew, it's to own a business. To set up fashion walks and show off the clothes. To make people want the glamor, the name, the story. If Madam Walker can do it with hair, Garnet can with dresses.

She only has to close her eyes to see her shop. Her name on the shop front. *Nanette*, in script. Like *Fortuny* or *Lucile*.

And sometimes she thinks her shop should be downtown.

Where she's white.

The employees' elevator takes a long time to come, and when it does, Billy, the elevator operator, is crying, sniveling onto his uniform sleeve. He's only twelve years old; of course he doesn't have a handkerchief. She runs back into the dressing room to grab a snip of cloth and wipes his nose for him. "Oh, honey, what's the matter?"

Billy breaks out into a wail.

"Ain't you heard? They're saying *Titanic* has gone down and the Big Boss is dead!"

🙠🙠🙠

IT WILL BE THE FIRST GREAT NEWS COUP of the wireless era. The White Star office on City Hall Plaza is still posting reassuring messages: VIRGINIAN IS STANDING BY TITANIC. NO DANGER OF LOSS OF LIFE.

But on the second floor of Wanamaker's, which has a Marconi station, the manager, David Sarnoff, and two assistants are intercepting actual messages from *Frankfurt, Virginian*, and *Olympic.*

Carr Van Anda, managing editor of the *New York Times,* believes what Sarnoff and his staff hear. Van Anda dares to print the unthinkable.

**Biggest Liner Plunges
to the Bottom
at 2:20 A. M.**

RESCUERS THERE TOO LATE

Except to Pick Up the Few Hundreds Who Took to the
Lifeboats.

WOMEN AND CHILDREN FIRST

Cunarder Carpathia Rushing to
New York with the
Survivors.

SEA SEARCH FOR OTHERS

The California Stands By on
Chance of Picking Up Other
Boats or Rafts.

OLYMPIC SENDS THE NEWS

The families begin to gather outside the White Star Line offices in New York, London, Paris, waiting to see who's survived.

Perdita

IF YOU DON'T SEE WELL, you learn balance. When your world begins to tilt, no matter how subtly, you feel it.

At the piano, Perdita feels herself reaching a little too far to the right, almost hitting wrong keys. And the engines have stopped entirely.

That iceberg can't have done anything to *Titanic* beyond perhaps breaking the propeller. Alexander and Uncle Gilbert would never forgive her for being in a wreck.

And then the dim lights all brighten at once. The bridge players shout and laugh. To Perdita's eyes, after the darkness, everything looks pale and startling. She blinks and listens.

"This could be a little serious, you know," a man says.

"There's always one worrywart in the party, and ain't he a bore."

"Want your ickle life jacket, old boy?"

"Steward?"

"Women and children first, you know. Helen, maybe you should—"

"Not me, spending the night in an open boat while you lazy lot drink up the whiskey. Steward? Is anything wrong?"

"No, ma'am, nothing to worry about."

There, Perdita tells her absent husband silently. You and Uncle Gilbert would worry. You would insist I get on everything I own and go up to the boat deck—

"Practically unsinkable," she mutters aloud and puts her hands firmly back in position.

But *she* promised.

She didn't promise to make their worries her worry, or their lives her life.

No. She sort of did promise that.

At least she promised, if anything even seemed wrong, to get dressed warmly and go to the lifeboats.

All right, all right, all right.

Suddenly the room fills with a shrieking like locomotive whistles. Perdita claps her hands over her ears. "Nothing to worry about," the steward shouts over the noise. "Venting steam from the engines."

The noise fills the entire room; she can't play anyway. She closes the fallboard, not quite slamming it, hoping this is all over very,

very soon, and makes her way through the unnaturally bright shrieking corridors to her cabin.

She is supposed to get her warmest clothes on and her lifejacket, and bring her muff and thick gloves to warm her hands, and a warm hat. She doesn't have a warm hat (she's going to New York in April, after all), and no muff and only thin leather gloves, but she puts on wool stockings and boots over her silk stockings and her spring coat over her opera coat, and wraps a scarf round her ears; the sirens and whistles are earsplitting even from inside and a deck down.

She turns on the heater and thinks of something heavier she can wear.

And then *Titanic* jerks; she feels the deck slip a little downward under her feet, all at once.

It's not a big thing, only a tiny tilting. But it reminds her of a set of bailing buckets Alexander showed her once, after the Great Flood in Paris. The first bucket filled and tipped, and the water spilled over and started filling the next one, and it went on in a series of jerks—

The watertight compartments reach above the waterline, so it's not that. The ship itself is safe.

But there must be a leak, and *Titanic* is shifting because of the water inside her.

Titanic's generators and transformers and all the electrical stuff are below the waterline. Perdita has no idea how big *Titanic*'s transformers are, but they must be huge.

In the Great Flood, when the water at St.-Michel reached the Métro transformers, they exploded.

And water is inside *Titanic*, going goodness knows where.

A man calls out in the corridor. "What's that noise?" He sounds a little panicked.

With all her watertight compartments, *Titanic* is safe enough. But the transformers could blow up. They'll have to be shut off.

There'll be no heat or light. Darkness is no problem, not for Perdita, but without electricity the heaters won't work and all those rooms of electrically refrigerated food will begin to spoil. Soon, in this lovely floating hotel, everyone will be freezing and starving. No one will be able to find their way anywhere and the crew will be just as lost.

She feels in Uncle Gilbert's basket and tucks the chocolate bars in her coat pocket; she breaks off a sprig of lilac and smells it to cheer herself up; she makes sure she has the Braille watch Alexander gave her and at the last minute grabs the pillow from her bed. She can wind it round her hands to keep them warm, or around her ears to keep out the noise.

She opens the door on a startled steward.

"Miss, we're 'avin' everyone up on deck."

"There's a leak, isn't there, because of the iceberg?"

"Yes, Miss, and a bad 'un. Water in the mail room and the squash-court. You'll want your lifejacket, just in case."

The steward helps her put on her lifejacket. (How could she have forgot that?) The stiff cork and canvas make her waddle like the Michelin Man. Other people are in the corridor now, bumping up against each other. What an idiot she is, bringing the pillow—

Water in the squash-court. She has no idea where the mailroom is, probably low down in the ship with the other interesting things, but Miss Fan and she saw the squash-court when they went for their swim.

The squash-court is on F deck.

Above the electrical equipment.

Titanic won't have electricity for long at all.

Oh my goodness, she realizes. Miss Lady.

The Churches are down on D deck, and Miss Lady in her wheelchair needs the elevators to get upstairs.

Miss Lady will be stuck in the cold and dark—

"Miss, where're you going?"

She's already plunging down the corridor toward the staircase. The stairs feel wrong, off balance.

On D deck she stops a moment. The Churches' cabins are somewhere at the bow of the ship; she doesn't know where. She goes down the whole corridor, banging on all the doors.

"Wake up! Get up!"

❧❧❧

BRUCE ISMAY, wakened by the collision, also believes the ship has thrown a propeller. He asks a steward, who doesn't know, then puts on trousers and an overcoat over his pajamas and goes up to the bridge. This takes him about ten minutes. Ismay, Captain Smith, and the senior officers meet with *Titanic*'s designer, Thomas Andrews, who has been belowdecks.

"Is the ship damaged?" Ismay asks Andrews.

In the first ten minutes after the collision, Andrews says, water has risen fourteen feet within the bow of *Titanic,* more than a deck's worth. Of the sixteen watertight compartments that make *Titanic* practically unsinkable, five are taking on water.

The ship can float with four compartments breached.

But not five.

The water is shooting through the gashes in the hull. The hull is beginning to warp and deform. Rivets are popping and the breaches are widening.

The weight of water is dragging *Titanic* down, and her bow has begun to slide into the sea.

❧❧❧

PERDITA FINDS THE CHURCHES' STATEROOMS at last and stands clutching the silly pillow, trying to persuade the Churches to get up. Dr. John and Miss Fan stand at their doors, frowsty and confused, but Miss Lady refuses to leave her bed. "Did anyone say the ship was sinking?" she says indistinctly, then gets her teeth in. "I am not going anywhere unless the ship is actually sinking under me. I was having such a nice dream; I was dancing."

"You can sleep up in my cabin, Miss Lady, but the elevators are going to stop working and you can't stay down here."

There is no steward in the corridor. Perdita runs upstairs again, five breathless panting flights to the boat deck, trying to find someone official who will come persuade Miss Lady. People are shouting and milling around.

"Miss, you get in a lifeboat. Someone will go to D deck and get your friends."

"Who will?" she says. "Everyone is busy here."

The sailors are actually loading the lifeboats. Crewmen are swinging the boats out over the side, and if Perdita were fulfilling her promise to Alexander she would be standing obediently in line to get in one. But there is no line; everyone is just standing around waiting to see what will happen. *Women and children first,* one of the officers is shouting in a proper British, curiously monotone voice, *come on now, lidies.* But no one wants to get in the boats. Pack yourself into a little lifeboat and get lowered seventy feet into the icy ocean? In the dark?

"I must go back to get my friends," Perdita tells the steward. "One of them doesn't want to come up. Will you talk to her?" She has to act all trembly and helpless and blind before the steward pays any attention. "She's in a *wheelchair,*" Perdita explains, "she might be *stuck* down on D deck."

The elevators rattle past; at least they're still working.

"You got to hurry, Miss." As she leads the steward down to D deck, Perdita hears wheezing from the elevator shafts, like someone with asthma trying to breathe.

"Mamma, you must come," Dr. John is saying. "Look, Miss Fan and I are dressed."

"But my hair isn't done. Miss Fan, do my hair!"

"Miss Lady, there's no time," Miss Fan says.

"Everyone's in their nightclothes," Perdita says, "it doesn't matter."

"What would you know!" Miss Lady snaps.

What a nasty woman. "Everyone interesting is up there," Perdita counters. "Colonel and Mrs. Astor and Mr. Guggenheim and his mistress are all together in the salon, and Mr. Ismay. It is such a chance to see them." She has no idea if this is true.

"Miss Fan, I need my purple velvet coat and my fan with the ivory sticks and I need my lace scarf for my hair!"

It takes what seems like half an hour to get Miss Lady into her wheelchair. The steward dances round them uselessly and then leaves them. Dr. John goes ahead to call the elevator while Perdita and Miss Fan push Miss Lady's wheelchair along the corridor. It feels as though they're pushing it uphill and it keeps veering off course.

The elevator doesn't come. "This is terrible service," Miss Lady says.

"Go on up to the lifeboats," Dr. John says to Miss Fan and Perdita. "Take the stairs."

"Dr. John—" Miss Fan says.

"I do promise, Miss Fan, Mamma and I will see you upstairs."

"But the elevators may stop at any time."

"Go. I'll carry her up; you see about the lifeboats."

The stairs tilt forward; as they climb, their feet slip and jam against the risers.

Upstairs, at least the steam-whistles have stopped. In the lounge, people are waiting for something to happen, talking noisily, ordering drinks from the stewards. It feels like a party where everyone wants to go home.

And then, right in front of her, something cold and awful happens. A man kneels down by a toddler-shape and begins talking in the rhythm that adults use to frightened children. "You and Mamma will go in the lifeboats, dear, just to be prudent. Look, other children are going to the boats."

His voice is shaking.

"Papa!" a little trembling voice says, so like Toby. "Papa! Pick me up!"

"I'll find out if they're loading from this deck." Perdita gropes her way across the tilted lounge to the outside door, suddenly careful not to think too much. She knows a frightened parent when she hears one. It's *cold.* Deep bone-chilling soul-freezing cold. She listens up and down the deck; there's no one waiting for a lifeboat here. But from the deck above her she hears a bumping and rasping along the side of the ship, women calling, men cursing "Lower her, lower her!" A woman cries out *No, don't leave me!* A man says *Darling, you must go.* The lifeboat scrapes and screeches against the ship.

"Cut the ropes! Cut 'em now!"

Perdita turns back into the lounge, cold inside. "We should go to the boats as soon as Dr. John gets here."

Because *Titanic* is— Because people think *Titanic* is— The men in the lounge are joking with each other, but the way that patients joke with each other in the Jouvet waiting room when they know they're there for the same thing, and it's serious. Their voices are loud and trembling and the room is thick with whisky fumes. She hopes the little boy got in a boat.

Dr. John and his story must get in a boat.

"She'll make us stay on this ship," Miss Fan says suddenly, her voice cracking. "She'll think we have to set an example."

"We aren't setting any examples. I promised my husband."

"She'll make John stay. You don't know her."

They hear Miss Lady's voice as the elevator screeches upward. "At least we sent the foals on ahead—I have never seen such incompetence!"

The elevator carpet smells like wet wool and salt water. It hisses under Perdita's boot-soles as she helps Miss Lady out. For a few moments the wheelchair is wedged inside the elevator because the door won't open all the way; Perdita leans her whole weight against the door and it scissors ajar. The elevator-boy says "That's it, I'm gone!" and pushes past them.

"How'm I goin' to get up those stairs?"

The wheezing in the elevator shaft is a breeze now, cold, smelling of seawater and pushing upward past them.

"I'll carry you, Mamma," Dr. John says.

"Without my chair? What am I goin' to do without my chair?"

"Somebody help us?" Perdita shouts.

A couple of men come forward, but one man swears at them. "My son's too old to go in the boats, girl, isn't that bitch too old?"

"Old?" Miss Lady says, moaning as Dr. John lifts her out of her chair. "Old? You watch your language!" Perdita and Miss Fan drag her wheelchair up the stairs. It veers right and catches against the banister and the sharp iron flowers. Something on Perdita's coat rips. She thinks *I shall have to have that mended.*

From the bar behind them, she hears a strange sound, a pretty sound really, glasses clinking against each other like little chill bells. Then a glass smashes.

Out in the cold on the boat deck, Dr. John sits Miss Lady in her chair again and they steal a blanket from a deck chair to tuck around her. Hundreds of people are talking and crying out for each other, jostling and shoving toward the boats, everyone clumsy in the stiff lifejackets, slipping because the deck is tilting and wet. "Women and children, only women and children!"

Half of Perdita thinks, *I'm a woman, I can get on a lifeboat.* But the other half knows *Not without Dr. John*—

There are so many people.

The salon orchestra is playing with mechanical cheerfulness. If you're a musician in an emergency, you play something happy. *Oh, you beautiful doll*—

"Women and children into the boats—"

"There just one boat left and it's full!" Miss Lady says.

"There must be more on the other side of the ship," Perdita says.

"Miss Perdita, honey, get in that boat! They'll make room for you."

"I'm not going without you. We all have to find a place."

Manhandling Miss Lady's wheelchair up the slope of the deck is like pushing a boulder up a mountain. A flare arches and bangs above them, smearing light. When they get round the corner and turn back down toward the bow, the wheelchair nearly runs away with them; they have to lean back and hold on.

"The lifeboats are gone here too," Miss Fan says, half-panicked.

"No, there's one left," Dr. John says. "And Mamma, Miss Fan, Miss Perdita, you are going on it."

"You too," Perdita says.

"No, Miss Perdita."

"You too."

There are crowds here too, pushing and shoving. "Only women and children!" an officer is shouting. "Men stand back!"

"Dr. John?" Miss Fan quavers.

Someone takes Perdita's arm and starts pulling her away from the Churches. "Here's the blind girl as plays the piano, make room for her! Miss, get in the boat—"

She twists away. "Dr. John," she fights her way back toward him. People rush to take her place.

"I am stayin' behind," Miss Lady says. "It seems I am an old woman. Miss Fan, when you talk to them about me at Fair Home, tell them that I gave my seat—"

"John?" Miss Fan repeats, very loud.

"Dr. John is stayin' with me, darlin', like a gentleman should. Now you listen to me, Fan—"

"Dr. John," Perdita says, "Miss Fan, I am so sorry, but please, I must talk with Dr. John for a moment."

She pulls him a few feet away from the others, into one of the bays of the promenade, and speaks quickly. "My husband told you there was a person who wanted to know about Louisa Church. I'm the person. It's me. Please, please tell me what you know! Please, just tell me you did marry my Aunt Louisa! Say yes."

There is a shot from the direction of the boats, and a scream.

"It has been a pleasure traveling with you, Miss Perdita," Dr. John says. "But I must speak with Miss Fan and you must save yourself."

"Miss, you got to come now!"

Dr. John pushes her forward. "Take my coat, Miss Perdita." He throws it round her shoulders and pushes his gloves into her hands. "Give these to Otis and ask him to remember me. I hope you remember me yourself."

"I am giving up my life for the young people," Miss Lady is announcing behind them. "And Dr. John is dying like a Southern gentleman— Miss Fan, hold my wheelchair, it's runnin' away!"

Perdita is suddenly grabbed round the waist and swung out into air with nothing under her feet, she bicycles trying to find a foothold, she is falling. She lands with a jar, bites her tongue, tastes blood in her mouth; her boots splash into water. The boat jerks downward. It isn't far enough; they hit the water too soon. The lights of *Titanic* hang over them. Someone guides her hands onto something large and heavy, a log, an oar. "Row, row fast as you can! We got to get away! Pull! Pull!"

All the women are pulling frantically at the oars, they tug and push against each other. She struggles into Dr. John's big stiff gloves; they dig at her fingers. She wishes for a note folded inside them, one word to her, *yes*. She has to go back to him. It is so cold; the icy air sucks the breath out of their bodies, even though they are packed together tightly in the boat. "Pull!" Above them, *Titanic* dazzles, her lights touching the water; the water glows green; there are lights below the surface. Dr. John is still up on deck and has told her nothing. Above their heads a violin leads a slow sweet heartbreaking melody. She can hear people on the ship, even individual voices. A man says "Bless you!" and a woman is crying.

Perdita can hear a man calling out as if he is preaching, *and there was no more sea.* She listens for Dr. John's voice saying *yes.*

And then *Titanic* flickers and dims to red-orange. Metal screeches. A heavy wave tosses the lifeboat; the women cry out. They are still so close to the ship.

The musicians stop playing, raggedly, in surprised off-key wavers.

She hears voices, hundreds of voices, calling out, and people begin to scream.

"Pull!"

And the sun of *Titanic* goes out and the whole world is dark.

"Row! Row! She's going!"

It is dark but Perdita can hear. Metal moans. People are shouting. "Mamma!" men call out. "God! Help me!" The telegraph wire breaks, pings, whines through the air. The ship shrieks, heavy things roll and tumble and thump and smash, windows shatter every pane at once, and all around her are thuds like hammers hitting water.

A groan like an enormous beast makes the sea tremble.

"Gorrum, look at 'er stern, it's going up— *Row! Row! Bugger you, ladies, row!*"

The lifeboat is pulled backward toward the ship as if by a tide. People are screaming, the living and the dying screaming together—men and women and—

She hears every cry right by the boat. She is listening for Dr. John still, as if he might call over the water, one word, one.

"Pull for your life! Row! Row!"

And she realizes what she is hearing.

"Mum! Mommy! Help!"

There are children in the water.

Perdita pulls Dr. John's gloves off her hands, and her own gloves, and puts her hands against the oar to try to stop the boat from rowing away, but there are too many people rowing, she only bumps up against them. She thrusts her hands over the side and gropes into the water as if one child might be close enough to pull into the boat. She feels in the water for one drowning hand, Dr. John, her past, her future, anyone, one hand to grasp hers and be saved. The freezing sea tugs her toward *Titanic*. The oar smashes against her shoulder. Her skin goes numb in seconds. It feels as if her hands are being crushed.

She has to pull her hands back out, moaning.

And it is too late.

ॐॐॐ

NEW YORK, APRIL 15, MIDDAY. Broadway is jammed with people, reading the latest news pasted on the windows of the *Times* building, the scrawled list of the saved.

So far no one is anything but saved.

No one can be dead on *Titanic*.

But the survivors can tell you. Seven hundred people hear fifteen hundred people die. Some jump from the ship and are killed instantly, smashing into the water as if they were hitting pavement. Some are sucked down. But over a thousand people float alive in the water. Husbands, brothers, sisters, children— For five minutes, ten minutes, twenty, they are held up by their cruel lifejackets, unable to drown. They freeze by inches. They scream in pain, they cry for help, they pray.

The survivors know their voices.

And the survivors have to listen.

The survivors huddle in the boats. They jam their fingers in their ears to keep out the screams. In one boat, the men tell the women that the screams are cheers because everyone has found a place, everyone is safe. In another, they sing "Pull for the Shore" to drown the cries.

"Go back!" some women shout. But only one boat goes back.

Slowly, one by one, the voices from the water die away.

Plugged ears cannot keep out silence.

The survivors strain to hear familiar voices. They yearn to hear anything.

"I should have stayed with him," a woman moans softly.

Bruce Ismay, who took a place in the lifeboats, who knew so many of those voices, sits in the stern of a boat, hunched over.

And it is dark. And it is silent, except for the oars slapping the water, the people rowing to keep warm, rowing to have some sound in their ears, a splash, an oarlock groaning, anything but silence. A splash, a murmur, the sound of human life. Even a scream. To hear a scream again. Anything but silence and the voices only they can hear, voices whispering to them, last cries, *Help me. Help me. Don't leave me.*

How many people die on *Titanic?* How many voices cry out and then go silent in that hour, in that sea?

Long years later, Renée Harris, who lost her husband that night, will be introduced to a completely clueless woman as "Mrs. Harris, who was on *Titanic.*" The clueless woman will ask, "And did you survive?"

Renée Harris will think for much longer than the question warrants.

"No."

Reisden

WITH PERDITA AWAY, the family descends into slovenly bachelorhood. Toby is allowed to go to bed without a bath, with his tin *Titanic* creasing his cheek and Elphinstone snoring meatily beside him. Reisden fills Perdita's absence by reading in bed until sunrise. The bed looks like a desk that's been slept in. He and Toby have leftover chicken for breakfast.

The weekend is for family. Since he's been away Thursday, he spends his Saturday half-day taking his nephew to the movies. Tiggy loves his *Titanic* model, though they agree that an even better one would be watertight and have a real engine and puff smoke through its funnels and steam showily across the rond' pond in the Luxembourg. The toymakers must have such a thing, and Reisden promises him one. Tiggy will be the envy of his friends.

At the movies, the newsreel shows *Titanic* departing from Cherbourg. The millionaire Gilbert Knight is among the passengers photographed on the boat train. Tiggy thinks he sees Aunt Perdita and Uncle Sacha among the passengers and waves at the screen. He gazes at the flickering ship in rapture. "I will go on that ship someday." Eight years old. Tiggy is the age Richard was when Richard—went away. Nothing unspeakable has happened to Tiggy. Reisden watches him and is content.

When he bring Tiggy back, he sits by the fire for a half hour with his cousin Dotty. "Cousin" in quotes, he was nothing more than a ward of the family, but he and Dotty were brought up together and share a family cynicism. She pours him brandy and accuses him of missing Perdita.

"I should have gone with her."

"Oh, darling." Dotty's front room is pure eighteenth century, glimmering gold and flickering with candles; she breathes beautifully at the nearest candle and blows it out. "She doesn't want you in her precious America. She'll leave you for America like that."

"Not if I can help it, darling. A question for you," he says, cutting her off. "What do you know about John Rolfe Church?"

"The trainer? Nothing. No one knew him. A brute. A Negro. Such a story. Darling, tell me all about *Titanic*. You were on it?"

Sunday, Gilbert is in the illustrated papers too, talking with the reporters at Cherbourg; of course they report he sailed on *Titanic*. The other big news is on the science pages. Next Wednesday, Parisians will see a total eclipse of the sun, the first in Paris since

1724, the only one this century. The Sunday papers are full of scientific articles and diagrams.

"We must all see it," Reisden tells Gilbert over the breakfast table.

"No, you must go inside and *close your eyes completely* till it is over," Gilbert says earnestly. "And you must tell Tiggy and Madame Dotty not to look either. People will go blind."

"No, we will see it." We have so little time left. We must cultivate it. Reisden makes a note to get slips of smoked glass and a pinhole camera. He wants them all to see the round shadows leaves make in an eclipse. When the next total eclipse appears in Paris, Toby will be ninety years old.

Sunday afternoon they all go by Métro to visit their friend Roy Daugherty at Courbevoie. Reisden spends his afternoon digging out English ivy from the garden. It's a perfect quiet afternoon, chill, foggy, but the little plants are brave and green and ready to burst out, and Elphinstone galumphs up and down the hill. Daugherty does an oil sketch of Eff sniffing at the ground, all curious nose and wagging tail. Gilbert is delighted. At nightfall Madame Suzanne serves beef stew to everyone, including the dog.

❧❧❧

THAT NIGHT Reisden works in the downstairs office catching up on his mail, oh L—d why do they *write* him, and then goes up to his own office to plan the testimony of a Danish forensic accountant, an expert witness in a murder case. The murderer says he killed his business partner in a fit of madness, but he's been cooking the books and he's not going to get away with it. When that's done, Reisden builds up the fire in the fireplace and goes over financials until he falls asleep.

When he wakes up, cold and stiff, it's four in the morning and Elphinstone is staring up at him mournfully, whining.

"You don't have to," Reisden says. "Do you?"

I do. Really. Right now.

Reisden stares at him. Eff stares back.

You know how it is. I'm only a little dog. The stew was wonderful and I had so much of it.

"Gilbert will take you out in an hour. No? All right, but we're just going out to the courtyard, not all the way up to the Seine. Agreed? *D'accord?*"

No use making the dog lie. Eff will lift his leg happily against any wall of Jouvet but won't do serious business unless he's more than a block away.

It's half-rainy in the predawn dark, soft intimate Paris rain; the streetlights are haloed with mist and a horse clomps past, head down, his hide steaming, pulling a delivery wagon toward les Halles. Reisden lets Elphinstone tug him up toward the Seine. Eff tracks and sniffs and backtracks and marks his territory; Eff does his transaction by the Gare d'Orsay; Eff barks through the balustrade at the river. Reisden lifts Eff up onto the parapet and holds him safe as they both stand watching the Seine. Eff whuffs with pleasure while Reisden scratches his chin: warm dog breath against his hand.

"I don't want Gilbert to go. Never. Never," Reisden says to the dog, who won't tell.

It's an ordinary Monday morning, April 15.

After breakfast he goes off to coach his Danish forensic accountant. Dahlberg is an amateur astronomer, has been fascinated with Tycho Brahe's experiments at Elsinore since he was a child. He sends Reisden back with slips of smoked glass and a pinhole camera for the eclipse. Reisden determines Gilbert shall watch it.

It's a conversation he'll never have.

When he drives the car into the courtyard of Jouvet, Gilbert is waiting for him with Perdita's telegram.

ߪߪߪ

"WHAT DOES SHE MEAN SHE IS *SAFE*?" Gilbert keeps saying.

Reisden reads the telegram, SAFE CARPATHIA, over and over, SAFE CARPATHIA, the words don't make sense. "Why must she tell us she is *safe?*" Gilbert asks. "If she says she is safe, she certainly is not."

Reisden wants to snap at him. He pours Gilbert a brandy and gets him to sit down. "She is safe," he says with a calm he doesn't feel. "She's told us so; let's not worry. What is Carpathia? Is it code?"

Jouvet has its own Marconi station; he calls their operator and decoder in. "It's a ship, Monsieur le Docteur," their operator Maffei guesses.

"If she is telling us she's safe on *Carpathia,* when she should be quietly on board *Titanic*— Maffei, keep your ears open for *Titanic* news. Anything you hear, I want to know immediately. The rest of you lot, back to work. You'll hear whatever we do."

"Something has happened to *Titanic,*" Gilbert says shakily. "There has been a terrible accident."

"Nothing can be wrong if she's safe."

He's repeating the word too much, *safe,* over and over, it's losing its meaning, *safe,* just sounds, hissing and ripping and F's like knives.

ॐॐॐ

IF THIS WERE THE TWENTY-FIRST CENTURY, there would be Internet video of the water rising up the stairs, the rush to the lifeboats, the ship's bow inexorably pulled down. But in 1912 Reisden phones round for news. Barry Bullard, who restores furniture for the Guggenheims, has heard wild rumors that Ben Guggenheim is dead.

"Stay here with Toby," he tells Gilbert. "I'm going to the White Star offices. I want news."

His concentration is gone; he cannot decide whether to drive or take a taxi, even what overcoat to wear, though his choice is black or black. He wants to take the telegram with him, SAFE CARPATHIA, but leaves it for Gilbert's reassurance.

His eyes fall on the postcard Perdita gave him at on the train, *Titanic* in New York.

⋗⋗⋗

ON THE PLACE DE L'OPÉRA, crowds have gathered outside the White Star Line office. Reisden moves through the crowd, asking grandmothers and uncles and wives what they've heard.

"My daughter-in-law sent a telegram. She and my grandchildren are on *Carpathia*. But she doesn't say anything about my son."

"I haven't heard anything from my brother," a grey-haired man says.

"Our firm was sending ten crates of ostrich feathers." A fat little man waves a blue telegram. "Our New York office thinks something's happened. They're very expensive, ostrich feathers."

"Attention!" A White Star Line official appears at the door with a chalkboard. "We have news of *Titanic* from our New York office. There's no need for alarm. She has hit an iceberg and sustained some damage, but everyone is safe on board. The *Virginian* is towing her toward Halifax and her passengers will be transported from Halifax by train. Any family members waiting for them in New York will be taken by train to meet them in Halifax." He sets the chalkboard on an easel and starts writing the news on it.

"Oh, thank Heavens," the grandmother breathes. People cheer, people clap. A few families leave.

Everyone's safe on board? Reisden crosses the street to American Express and learns that *Carpathia* is a Cunarder, currently taking American tourists from New York to Naples.

Carpathia is a single-stacker. Which means it's small.

It makes sense to move passengers from a damaged ship. But why a small ship going the wrong direction?

He telephones home from the Café de la Paix and reaches Gilbert. "Are her friends calling? Tell them she's safe."

Safe.

Jouvet has its traditions, older than the Red Cross: In a disaster, Jouvet takes care of victims and their families. It gets them clients but they'd do it anyway. Reisden hires a private dining room in the Café de la Paix and starts the kitchen making sandwiches, goes across the street and invites the waiting men and women to come inside. By now it's dark and April-frigid. It must be icy on the sea.

Inside the café, friends and family members whisper over untouched food. *I saw them off in Paris, I didn't go down to Cherbourg. They said 'Mother, don't you want to see Titanic?' I said I could see her anytime.*

I had a bad feeling when the ship was late.

"I know other firms with cargo on *Titanic*," the ostrich-feather man offers. "I could call round."

"Do it."

Some of the families in the café begin to get telegrams, brought by servants or family members. They're all from *Carpathia*, all very short, all from women reporting themselves and their children safe.

"Why nothing from *Titanic*?" the grandmother worries.

"They can't telegraph if they've lost power, Mother."

But no one has heard from men.

Someone realizes that Reisden's wife was on *Titanic*. "She's safe—?" the grandmother asks him timidly.

"Yes, *grâce à Dieu*, we've heard from her."

"You're going to America to see her?" The old lady goes on, assuming the answer is yes. "If— If— Would you call on my son's wife too? My son and his wife? And the children? Make sure they're all right?"

"Of course they're all right," her middle-aged daughter breaks in impatiently, "Walter knows how to take care of himself. Mother, don't be morbid!"

Everyone begins to protest that their people must be safe: their Florence, their Erik, their Lillian. They raise their voices as if arguing. *If the worst happens, he can swim. He swims every day, even in winter.— My brother. We've never been separated.* Their Ned, their Lucy. Their eyes are distracted, as if they're listening for something. The men stand by the window, looking across the street to the White Star Line offices, waiting for the next message on the chalkboard, looking for the messenger boy or the family servant bringing the telegram. They need news.

At Queenstown, Perdita wore her red jacket so he could see her and waved to him from the prom deck. He can see her now, standing straight at the railing, holding her hat and gesturing gravely, blindly, having faith that she was waving to him. He waved back though she couldn't see him. That's where all the families are now, everyone in this room, even Reisden who has had news; waving, having faith that someone they can't see is waving back.

"We'll send someone to New York," he says to the grandmother. "Someone reliable and good to check on your family. To make sure they're all right."

And he knows it can't be him, and he knows he has to go.

ࡆࡆࡆ

REISDEN LEAVES THE CAFÉ, with the sandwiches drying and curling on their plates, the exhausted air, the families waiting and waiting, and walks; walks without mind or purpose; and his walk takes him in the direction of his cousin Dotty's house.

"May I see Tiggy?"

"He's in bed, darling. It's late."

"Tell him his aunt Perdita's all right."

Does he imagine that Dotty looks annoyed? "Darling, you look terrible," she says. "Have you eaten anything?"

He considers, can't remember.

She takes him down into the kitchen, finds asparagus, bread, chicken; piles a Limoges plate high; takes him upstairs again and sits him down at her cherrywood dining table. She lights the half-guttered candles in their silver sticks and puts a fork in his hand. It's her family silver, eighteenth century, forks the size of pitchforks. He and Dotty ate off these plates with these farm implements when they were young in Vienna; now she has them. For years Dotty was all he had for family. What he remembers of a childhood, he shares with her.

She drops down in the dining-room chair next to his.

"What has happened with *Titanic,* Sacha?"

"Supposedly it's safe. I'm going to New York."

"Truly, darling, why?"

"Perdita's husband would go to New York to be with her. I am her husband. Therefore."

She shakes her head impatiently. "Don't worry. There's been some sort of an accident, but that's all. *Titanic* is fine. It's in the papers. You don't need to do anything."

He puts his head down on his hands.

"Sacha," she says. She puts her hands on his shoulders. "Eat, or I shall start feeding you like a child."

He turns the fork over in his hand, he puts it down. *I should have gone with her.* I should have stood up for Gilbert in the first place. I should have—

"Who'll take Tiggy to the movies while you're gone?"

"I must go. I will come back," he says. "Dotty? The families have been getting telegrams, from women and children only, and all from one little Med tourist boat. Why are they all on *Carpathia,* going the wrong direction? Why move anyone? Transferring from ship to ship in midocean—" Ropes, a basket swaying from ship to ship; a broken rope, tumbling bodies, drowning. Drowning—

"You worry too much."

"I think things went bad and there wasn't time."

≈≈≈

SAFE CARPATHIA. The Churches, Perdita, *Titanic;* they run through Reisden's mind like rats trapped in a flood, sharp-toothed and scratching and nowhere to go. He can't sleep; sits awake staring at the fire; almost asks Gilbert to come sit with him, but doesn't.

Around dawn he dozes, and wakes to nightmare.

Toby's nursemaid Aline is standing in the hall, holding *Le Matin*, tears running down her face. He reads the paper over her shoulder, then takes it from her. The front-page headline says *Titanic Is Sinking.* At the bottom of the page is a slag-line in bold: Latest Dispatches, page 3.

Page 3 is all bulletins, set in type as they arrived: hopeful, cautious, contradicting each other, until the final news.

Titanic is lost. She is not sinking; she is gone. Not even *Carpathia* reached her in time. The boats went off half full at first. No one believed the ship was in danger. The survivors spent the night on the open sea. Astor is dead. Ben Guggenheim is dead.

Reuters reports that half the survivors have gone mad from hearing the screams of the dying.

The postcard of *Titanic* entering New York harbor is on the sitting room mantelpiece. Perdita kissed it and gave it to him.

The telegram is not a mistake. She is not drowned.

But safe?

Gilbert, in pyjamas and bathrobe, is standing in the corridor. Reisden holds out the newspaper to him.

Gilbert looks at him wordlessly.

"Come in the sitting room, it's cold here."

He pokes up the half-dead fire. "Gilbert, I'm going to America. As quickly as I can; tomorrow; Wednesday. I want you to stay with Toby until I'm back. He needs someone from the family here."

His uncle shakes his head. "I shall go. I am the one who should go, I am the one they want back in Boston.—Dear Heavens, I told her to go on *Titanic* because it was *safe!*"

"It's not your fault. I have to go and I don't want Toby left alone." The rule of the sea, women and children first. Dr. Church is probably dead. "She needs my help with something in New York, and it's just become more complicated." He shakes his head. "That's not why I'm going. I want to see her. I won't believe she's all right until I see her."

The two of them look at each other, understanding completely.

❧❧❧

REISDEN CALLS DOTTY and asks her to pack for him. He calls the Jouvet staff together and divides his work among them. As soon as he gets to New York, he'll link his private telegraphic address to someplace he can pick up telegrams; meanwhile they'll telegraph him on the ship. Mme Herschner books him on a fast German liner. No trouble getting tickets; no one wants to travel. Barry and Elise Bullard show up with food and offer to take Toby for however long is needed.

Back upstairs, Aline is packing clothes for Perdita. She'll have lost everything. Cook is in the kitchen sobbing and baking a cake for him to take to her.

He's not scheduled to leave until tomorrow morning, and there's one conversation he hasn't had with Gilbert.

Gilbert is sitting in his workroom, staring at a pile of what look like very ordinary books. They don't look like French books; American, he'd guess. Gilbert is holding one of them, a shabby red-covered one, staring at it.

"Gilbert, I need to tell you why I'm going to America. Better if it were Perdita telling you, but she's not here. Did you ever hear anything unusual about Perdita's Aunt Louisa?"

Reisden sits down on the spare chair, moving the books onto the floor. He tells the story, watching Gilbert all the while. Elphinstone, napping on the floor at Gilbert's feet, wakes up, blinking at the tension in his voice. What if Gilbert is prejudiced? Gilbert is American. "Two men calling themselves John Rolfe Church," he finishes. "One is the real man; the other was his slave, who was passing for white. We don't know which one Perdita's aunt married."

"Perdita? Our Perdita?"

"We do believe it was the white man. Perdita was on *Titanic* to hear the story from him. Now he's probably dead, which leaves us to find out what happened. I'm going to help find out."

"But she could not be— Perdita is not—" Gilbert pauses and gathers himself. "It would make not the slightest difference, of course, in anyone's opinion of her— Certainly not in mine. *Certainly* not. No one who *knows* her. Never," he says, and repeats firmly "Never at all. She is the same Perdita."

Thank you. "But it will make a great deal of difference in America."

"Might the story get to America?" Gilbert says.

Twenty years ago it took a steamer a month to cross the Atlantic; gossip died mid-ocean. Now the world's too small, and Bucky Pelham has been in Paris. "Yes."

"But that would be dangerous for her," Gilbert says. "Even if it's not true. I knew a man in the War, a stretcher-bearer like myself. He was Italian, I believe, but the rumor went round that he was a colored man. He...disappeared. He simply *disappeared*."

"She won't disappear," Reisden says roughly. "But she'll have to leave America if we can't solve this."

"I will speak for her, but no one believes me about anything." Gilbert considers. "Harry."

Harry?

"If Harry were to speak for her... He is not well-disposed toward her, toward any of us, I realize, but he is a man of business and judgment. If he were to say there was nothing in the story—"

"Why would he?"

"I have something to give him, which he wants very much."

Don't give yourself. He is not supposed to say that.

"It is not only my going back he wants, dear boy." Gilbert looks across at him almost with apprehension. "I hoped I would never have to tell you this at all. You can give this to him yourself, to get his help with Perdita's story. This is what he wants, as much as me."

The shabby red book is still in Gilbert's fingers.

Gilbert hands it to him.

"Harry wants a book?" He can barely concentrate on it.

"After you left Boston," Gilbert says, "I got together Richard's books and put them together on a shelf in my office. Do you remember this one?"

Richard's books?

Reisden reaches out and takes the book. It's a textbook of elementary German, suitable for a student of thirteen or so. The cover is worn and ink-stained. It takes him a moment; then he recognizes it. He turns to the page he remembers: a child's picture of a puppy, and in Richard's unformed eight-year-old handwriting, *This is Washington a Dog. I love him.*

Richard's dog.

Reisden shoves the book back and wipes his fingers against his jacket.

Gilbert pages through it, still not looking up. "That is not the page." Gilbert finds a page and holds the book out, open. "I am sorry," he says. "I am so very sorry."

The page is blackened as if it were burnt. Someone—Richard—spilled ink, then smeared it trying to clean it up. William would have beaten Richard for it. *Do you think I am made of money, that you ruin your books?* The panicked blots and smears tell the story. Richard was alone when the ink spilled, hoped he might not be caught, tried to wipe the paper clean. Perhaps he got away with it. Reisden hopes so.

But in his haste and fear Richard got ink on his hands.

On the margin of the facing page, where a child would have held the book down as he scrubbed frantically, there are three quite clear child-sized fingerprints and the mark of part of a left palm.

Fingerprints.

He drops it as if it's burning. He stands up, steps away from Gilbert and the book.

"No."

"It makes quite a difference, do you see. Mr. Daugherty says there is no way to falsify such a thing."

"Those aren't mine." Of course they are, Reisden shouts internally at himself.

There has never been a way to prove he's Richard. There can't be. Richard is dead.

"Mr. Daugherty had them tested against yours."

"He—you—had my fingerprints tested? You stole something of mine, with my fingerprints, and had them tested?"

"It was one of Mr. Daugherty's own glasses," Gilbert says. "He did not steal anything. I am sorry to bring it up—"

"It doesn't matter what it was or what you did!"

"I didn't know then that it was important," Gilbert says.

And Reisden himself had gone through all the books, looking for proof he wasn't Richard, and missed this.

"When I realized, I put the book in the bank. I had Mr. Phillips send it to me in Paris after Mr. Daugherty thought I should have it."

"Harry knows about this?"

"Harry saw these fingerprints, yes."

"And?"

"But he believes it's a forgery, Alexander," Gilbert says shakily. "He believes it's your forgery."

Oh, fuck me.

"Is that's what he thinks I'm doing? He thinks I'm going to wait until you *die* and then 'find' the book and match fingerprints?"

"If I had proof of who you are, I would use it, wouldn't I?" Gilbert says bleakly. "That's what Harry believes we both want."

Gilbert has had the proof and hasn't used it.

No.

"Dear boy, I am so sorry."

"When did you know?" Reisden asks. "Five years ago? When? How long?"

Gilbert simply looks up at him, helpless.

"I'm not Richard," Reisden says.

He turns and walks out and leaves Gilbert behind.

❧❧❧

TOBY'S UP FROM HIS NAP. Reisden calls the Bullards and asks if Toby can come visit. He takes a cab, with Toby, with diapers and Puppy Lumpkin and more toys and blankets and all the toddler circus parade. Toby, who loves taxis, keeps up a babble of commentary as he looks out the window. Horse! Dog! *Red* taxi! He produces an entire beautiful sentence: "Papa, sky always up?" "You're going to stay with Emmy and Julien, and Aunt Elise and Uncle Barry." "Mamma?" says Toby, his face lighting up. "No, lovey, Mamma's in America. Papa's going to get her." Toby breaks into howls. "No America!" "Agreed, sweetness. When I come back I'll bring Mamma."

"Soon, Papa?"

"As soon as ever I can, my dear."

Toby thinks, and then he holds out Puppy. "Mamma have," he says.

They could both cry.

He stays talking to Barry and Elise. Barry says the Guggenheims are still hoping Ben Guggenheim's alive, in spite of reports, but someone saw him and his valet in evening clothes "prepared to go down like gentlemen."

Back at Jouvet, he is alone. Gilbert's gone somewhere. The lights are out, the stove is cold. Aline and Cook have gone to Notre Dame to pray for the dead of *Titanic.* Even Elphinstone is gone.

He stands in the deserted building, lost without his family.

He goes into his room to stare at the luggage Dotty has packed. Two trunks, mostly clothes for Perdita. She'll have lost everything she took with her.

Downstairs in his office, he takes the postcard of *Titanic* from the mantel, but leaves the telegram for Gilbert. On his desk, Dr. Jouvet's desk, is a pile of letters and memos, twice its usual size because he's answered none of them today.

If he became Richard, it would take care of Harry. Gilbert wouldn't have to go back to Boston.

No. Gilbert would go back to Boston. Because Reisden would be in Boston too. Being Richard.

Gilbert knew that too and didn't use the book.

Being Richard would be like standing at the top of a cliff and jumping.

He's not Richard.

He spends the night answering his mail and trying not to think.

In early morning, at the train station, the newspaper headlines are black with *Titanic.* Even the once-in-a-century eclipse barely makes the news.

Fifteen hundred dead.

As the train howls toward Cherbourg the sun is going dark.

Part 2: *The Silence After*

Perdita

SHE ROWS, through the dark, through a strange unmoving sea, toward nowhere. She pulls the giant oar with cracked and frozen hands until she can't feel anything, and then she wedges her hands under her arms until she can feel them again, and then she rows, to keep from freezing to death.

For a long time she can hear one last voice, a man calling *Help, help,* dazed, not as if he expects help but like a phonograph record forgotten, playing the last groove over and over, *help.* And then he stops.

There's silence.

Oars splash, someone blows a whistle in the distance, someone in another boat calls *Is anyone alive?*

"We're alive," says one of the sailors. "Got to be 'appy about that."

"Hush," says one of the women. "My husband's drowned."

"I should have stayed with John," a woman says hoarsely. It's Miss Fan. For the first time Perdita realizes that Miss Fan is in the boat too, Miss Fan is alive.

Dr. John is dead.

There were children in the water.

They're dead.

The waves begin to rise. They slap the boat like a hand across a face. The boat is overweighted, the water almost to the gunwales;

everyone's tossed against each other and freezing waves slosh over their feet.

"Maybe no one's looking for us."

A man dies in their boat. Perdita hears him whispering *I'm so cold,* and then he stops.

Rowing is all that is keeping them from freezing. A minute after Perdita hands over her oar to warm her hands, she's shuddering.

The blackness of the sky fades to washed-out gray. Time is still going on. How strange.

"Lights," a woman says hoarsely. "I see lights."

They count, one-two-three, and shout *Help,* as loud as they can in their cracked frozen voices. A searchlight shines warm through the dark on them.

A man calls to them through a megaphone. "Ladies, you're safe."

Safe.

The dawn breaks full of rainbows. White things float in the water, sheep, clouds, buildings, white hills: ice.

The steersman maneuvers the boat toward a dark solid haze.

A heavy piece of rope slaps Perdita on the cheek. She can't grip it. Someone helps her into the wide frightening mesh of a sling, and she is pulled up, bumping and revolving, her hands frozen and cramped and holding nothing.

And then she is standing on a deck again, feeling the thrum of an engine again. Someone bends her hands around a cup of bouillon. Someone leads her inside, to a lounge, puts a warm blanket around her. She maneuvers it around her hands. She had a pillow. It's gone.

Sometime later a man asks what her name is and whom she wants to telegraph. She gives him Alexander's telegraphic address but doesn't know what to say. "Safe Carpathia," he suggests. All right.

Every muscle and bone in her body aches. Her jaw is sore and stiff because her teeth are chattering. Her hands hurt worst of all; as they get warmer, they feel as if they're about to burst. She stands up, stiff and swaying; the lounge is so crowded she can't make her way through it. She should have her guide cane. Her cane is— for a moment she thinks it is still on *Titanic*.

It is still on *Titanic*.

When she tries to move her fingers, she realizes something is crusted all over both hands.

"Miss, can I help you?" a steward asks.

She holds up her hands with the curved stiff fingers.

"Right, we'll take you down to the doctor right away."

He takes her arm to help her down the stairs toward the doctor's surgery. For a moment she feels Alexander's hand on her elbow, escorting her down the Grand Staircase. The ship turns dizzily around her.

The corridor outside the surgery is filled with moans and sobs, half-familiar voices she has heard at lunch or dinner. A stewardess takes her into a cabin and brings her a basin of warm water. "Put your hands in here, Miss. Is that too hot?"

The water feels boiling. She makes a guttural sound she thought would be a scream.

"There, I'm putting in some cooler water. We'll have those gloves off in a few minutes and then we'll see."

She's left alone. She thinks of Dr. John's stiff gloves rubbing her fingers. Strained tendons, she thinks. Muscle spasm. Not frostbite. Please. She can't stop shaking. The water goes dark in the basin. Blood. Her hands are her tools.

In the corridor a woman sobs and shrieks hysterically. Perdita presses her hands against each other in the water, trying to get them to move.

"Let's take off your gloves now." The nurse bustles back in.

Perdita bites her lips while the gloves come off. They peel scabs of blood away with them.

"We'll wash that off." Perdita holds out her hands. The pain is worse; it frightens her that she can't tell exactly where it is.

"We rowed all night." Her voice is rough, shaky-strange.

"You've got blisters all up and down your fingers. We're going to soak your hands for a while, warm water and hydrogen peroxide, then we'll put some bandages on."

The woman in the corridor has subsided into muttering and sobs.

"You're the pianist, aren't you? I don't see frostbite. You should be fine in a couple of weeks."

She begins to cry convulsively, when she wipes her face her fingers hurt like fire; but it doesn't mean anything. Her hands are not frostbitten. She is not dead. Alexander and Toby are not dead.

Only Dr. John is dead, who could have told her what she is.

And children— the children in the water—

The nurse bandages her hands. "Do you want something for your nerves?"

"No, I— I'm fine."

She feels her way up the stairs.

The morning has turned thick and gray. People are still being brought aboard from the lifeboats. All along the rail, women are standing waiting for news of their husbands. "He's on another boat," one woman says. "Those voices in the water? It's only foreigners who scream like that. Not our men." "Have you seen my son?"

She hears Miss Fan calling to each boat. "John? John?"

She stands by numbly as each boat is emptied and hauled up. People are crying, vomiting, swearing, shouting. "Alfred?" a woman calls. "Walter?" People stagger up on deck, stammering with cold.

"I'm looking for my son," a woman says. "My little boy!"

Children—

Some people throw their bulky white lifejackets in a pile on the deck. Some refuse to take theirs off. Perdita keeps hers. She wants the warmth, she tells herself.

In the bottom of the boats, pale shadows are lying curled up, not moving, some of them wavering back and forth, half-floating in icy water. Sailors slide down the ropes and load the bodies into nets.

Everything is moving as quickly as possible; it's beginning to rain and the sea is choppy. Men shout *get us up quick, we're sinking.* Living and dead bump up the side of *Carpathia.*

"Have you seen my husband?" Miss Fan asks everyone. "He is wearin' a white suit. He has a white beard."

"None of them are gone," a woman says. "They are with Jesus."

"Shut your mouth, I want him *here,*" Miss Fan says.

"Don't talk nonsense," another woman says, "they are simply on another boat. There must be other lifeboats somewhere. And look at all this ice. Some of them will have climbed onto the ice. They are safe."

Sailors are bringing up the last of the bodies now. And then—

"*John!*" Miss Fan shrieks and runs forward.

A dripping whiteness, all bedraggled and crumpled, his beard a white shroud across his face—

"Come with us, missus, or stand aside, we got to get this one warmed up. He's still alive."

Dr. John is alive.

❧❧❧

DR. JOHN IS ALIVE.

Dr. John is alive.

He was swept overboard and washed up against the side of a collapsible lifeboat. He froze in the water until someone died on the boat, and then he was pulled aboard to take the dead man's place. Miss Fan weeps with joy and terror on Perdita's shoulder in the corridor outside the makeshift hospital.

He's unconscious but he's alive. There's still a chance for him to survive, to say *yes* he was Aunt Louisa's husband. She and Miss Fan get to sit with him for a moment. His breath is wheezing like the elevators, faint like the last man crying *Help me.* But he's alive.

All over the boat, the passengers of *Carpathia* give all their extra clothes, their coats and shoes and hats to the survivors of *Titanic.* In the dining room, the lounge, the library, crowded up against each other, women sit with women. A woman passenger on *Carpathia* asks Perdita how she is. Does she need anything?

"No, I'm fine."

In the Carpathia's lounge, other women are telling their stories. *I saw the iceberg aft and I knew what had happened. I heard a sound as if we had run over a thousand marbles. Titanic was so silent going under, only a bubbling, like a big pot of water boiling. The musicians played until the end. They played "Nearer My God to Thee." They played "Autumn."*

The dining room is turned into a women's dormitory with mattresses on the floor. Someone leads her to one and tells her to rest. She tries to pray for Dr. John, but she can't get out sentences, only *Help, help.*

Her Braille watch that Alexander gave her has stopped ticking. She holds her wrist clumsily to her ear, shakes it, asks someone to wind it; but it won't tick any more.

She lies with the watch against her ear, listening to silence.

She drifts into something half thought, half a dream. She is on *Titanic.* She is standing on the promenade deck with her hand in Dr. John's. Out on the ocean, Miss Fan and Miss Lady are safe in lifeboats.

Now you can tell me everything, Perdita says to Dr. John. *Now you are free.*

And he does. He tells her about life after death, love and freedom. He tells her who he is and he says he married Aunt Louisa. He tells her to be safe and says not to lie, never to lie again; and he tells her something more.

When she wakes, she doesn't remember that last thing he told her, only the feeling of it. In the face of death, he told her something so important that she felt she would remember it forever; now she only remembers how much it explained, and she longs for it, it's the only thing that holds her together, to hear what he said.

❧❧❧

PERDITA BRINGS MISS FAN soup and biscuits and an apple. She stands by the door listening to Dr. John's painful wet breaths.

The nurse bandages Perdita's hands again and says Dr. John's being kept under a steam-tent. It's all they can do for him until New York. There's a therapy, a serum. They don't have it on *Carpathia* but St Vincent's will have it.

"Will he get better?"

"He's an old man."

"I have to talk with him."

"If he gets better, wait until then."

"He must get better."

"If the therapy doesn't work, there may be a moment," the nurse says. "Sometimes they're quite clear at the end."

Perdita goes back and stands by his door, and simply waits.

A child is crying in the corridor.

Children cry in her ears. *Help.*

❧❧❧

THEY SAIL ALL DAY through icebergs and grey rain. There is a service for those who have died in the boats. All the survivors come up on deck. Perdita hears the dull pounding of bodies hitting water, the same hammer-thuds she heard as the ship was going down. *People were falling from the ship.* The lifeboats hang above them like wooden rainclouds.

"Where's Ismay?" the women say. "He should be here with us."

"Ismay—"

"He took a place in the last boat," the women whisper to each other.

There aren't enough children on deck. Most of the survivors are women, and most of them are first and second class. She finds out where the third-class passengers are and climbs down painfully to their deck. She calls for Per, or Peter, who was going to get a soccer ball, but no one answers.

"That brute Ismay—"

Ismay survived. He took a place in the last boat.

"Captain Smith died like a hero. But Ismay—" the women say.

She took a place in the last boat too. She was in the same boat as Ismay.

And there were children in the water—

That night it begins to storm fiercely. The sea tosses *Carpathia* side to side. The woman on the mattress next to Perdita's begins retching. Her baby squalls, and she holds her baby to her breast but then retches again, over the baby and onto the skirt of Perdita's salt-crusted dress. Perdita takes the poor bad-smelling baby, holds her in clumsy bandaged fists, shushing and rocking her, *there, little one, what's her name? Gladys.*

One of the women has lost a child. She keeps insisting her son is on another boat. Or on the iceberg. But safe.

Per is on the iceberg. Please.

Let every child be safe.

Please let Dr. John live.

Save us all.

But the children keep crying.

AT BREAKFAST all the women ask for extra napkins, sit on them, smuggle them away, and pass them to the mothers of babies for diapers. Every child is precious. Two children have no parents at all. *Carpathia's* passengers give them silk blouses for baby coats, jewels for playthings. The ship's store is emptied. Perdita shares out Uncle Gilbert's chocolate among the children in third class, hoping Per will come up and hold out his hand.

He wasn't grown yet. He should be alive.

There is a piano aboard *Carpathia*. She holds her hands above it but she can't play.

Some of the women sing hymns, sing them interminably, over and over in a drone.

Nearer my God to Thee.

❧❧❧

IN THE MIDDLE OF THE NIGHT, she is lying wrapped in her coat and Dr. John's coat, trying to ignore her bursting, aching hands, when she feels something like a rock or a bed-rail under her hip.

Do you have a book in the bed, Alexander? She smells lilacs and the ghost of her stateroom rises around her like walls. For a moment she is in Alexander's arms, safe on *Titanic*.

Paw-handed, she works the thing out of her pocket. It's an ink bottle with its chipped stopper still sealed with candle-wax and the wilted remains of a lilac-sprig clinging to it. She smells an undertone of sea, rotted leaves, cold. A steward went hunting for a bottle for her and brought this back and dripped candle wax over the stopper.

She smells the iceberg's dark decaying breath.

She shudders. She gets up, silent in her wool-stockinged feet, wriggles into both coats and her lifejacket, and makes her way to the deck. *Look, Alexander, an iceberg is just water;* that's what she said. She feels her way to the rail where the bodies slipped into the sea. She holds the bottle over the railing between her bandaged hands, thinking of the iceberg going to join *Titanic*. But the iceberg won't leave her fingers. She pushes the bottle back in her pocket.

She was so sure of herself.

Dr. John pushed her into the boat.

She took a place in the boat.

Children—

If she had stayed on deck with Dr. John—if she had taken a child with her—if she had reached a child in the water—if she had done something different, better—

Why is she alive?

She wants to be in Alexander's arms, safe and innocent, in the cabin, before all this, instead of all this. She wants to have one word from Dr. John, one word that will tell her who she is and that everything is all right.

If she had stayed, he would have talked to her. In those last minutes, he and she would have told each other the truth.

She wants those last minutes on the boat, when she would have been sure who she was. She wants to be on the tilting deck with Dr. John, listening to the last boats rowing and splashing away, full of children who didn't drown. And then she would turn to him and say *Tell me who I am, tell me what freedom is.*

She wants to be on *Titanic.*

And so *Carpathia,* and the survivors, and the iceberg come together to New York.

ॐॐॐ

CARPATHIA STEAMS UP THE HUDSON RIVER on Thursday night in the midst of a thunderstorm. The quarantine officer comes aboard, giving out landing cards without examining anyone. Thunder tumbles across the harbor like falling barrels. Lightning cracks the sky. At first the passengers don't realize what else is happening. But as they go past the lighted haze of the Statue of Liberty's torch, they begin to realize the other terrible thing that's happened:

They are news.

They are heroic, pitiful, heart-wrenching. They are survivors. "There are *thousands* of people on the piers," Miss Gibson says. "They want to hear all about us." Perdita is at the rail with Miss Nisensohn and Miss Gibson and Miss Gibson's mother, and men with microphones and even spot-lights are down below in boats, shouting at them. "Fifty dollars for your story!" a man is repeating in different languages, French and German and maybe Yiddish. "Fifty dollars cash! A hundred! Two hundred! Give us your story!"

"I'm getting three hundred," Miss Nisensohn says flatly. She has got a camera somehow and film from the onboard store and has been taking Kodaks of survivors. "Best money I ever made, I guess."

"You should have saved your pictures of *Titanic,*" Miss Gibson says. "What a lot of money they would have made.—I'm getting more than that," she continues smugly. "You'll see when we land."

Thunder growls headlines above them.

"Jules is not even divorced yet," Miss Gibson's mother protests.

"Mamma, mind your business. What are you getting, Baroness?"

"I don't know," Perdita says tiredly.

Carpathia turns in the river; her engine slows. "We're going into the White Star dock," Miss Nisensohn says wonderingly. The tugs nudge them forward. The dock is a dark eternal tunnel, built for the biggest ship in the world. Black walls loom around them; the ship slows, it stops; and then, once more, Perdita hears the splashing knock of a body hitting water.

"They're leaving the lifeboats," Miss Nisensohn says and she begins to cry.

One by one, hollow splashes; clods falling on coffins; people falling from a sinking ship; it lasts forever. Perdita sits down on a coil of rope and muffles her ears with her bandaged hands.

Titanic has arrived in New York.

The tugs warp *Carpathia* back into the Hudson.

Now at last the voyage is over, but something else, something horrible, is only beginning. "You can see flashlights and candles all up and down the shore," Miss Gibson says. "Look at all these people waiting for *us!*" They can hear ten thousand voices shouting on the shore.

Carpathia slows and bumps against the dock. The sickest and most wounded passengers are offloaded first, a line of stretchers going down the gangway into a roar of voices and a storm of clapping. Miss Fan goes past among the first, murmuring softly to her husband. "Help is here, John. We're in New York." The most important passengers leave, wives of dead millionaires, Mrs. Astor, Mrs. Widener. The crowd roars. It sounds like screaming.

Bruce Ismay is taken off alone, through boos and catcalls, surrounded by guards. Then the crowd begins clapping again.

We all took a place in the boats, Perdita thinks. But they applaud us.

"Such an *audience!* You stay with me," Miss Gibson instructs, "and clap when I say." At the foot of the gangplank the ground stops shifting; they are on land; but the voices rise even higher, calling for husbands, friends— They are suddenly jostled by crowding, shouting people who have not been on any boat at all. "Katie!" "Bobby, boy? Hey, Bob?" "Ellen? Delia?" People are calling names and hoping someone answers.

"Who's going to meet you?" Miss Nisensohn shouts to Perdita.

"My aunt."

Thunder, and harsh light cuts across the line. "OK, here we go. *Jules!*" Miss Gibson calls, loud enough to be heard over the crowd.

"Oh, my darling!" a man calls back.

"It was dreadful! Terrible! I nearly drowned!"

"I almost lost you!" the man shouts. "And I never knew until now how much I cared! Will you marry me?"

"Oh, Jules! I never want to leave you again!"

The crowd laughs and applauds just like at the movies.

"I'll make you a star, my darling! We'll make a movie about *Titanic!*"

Oooh, the crowd breathes.

"She is such a con," Miss Nisensohn mutters, "*nearly drowned, she was in the first boat,*" and then calls out "Gus! Nathan! Here I am!"

Miss Nisensohn is swept away into the arms of two tall brothers.

Perdita is left alone in the middle of people who are being reunited with their families. She is pushed back and forth in the waves of the crowd —

"Hey, Perdita!"

Someone takes her arm.

"It's Nanette," a familiar voice says. "Your friend *Nanette.*"

"Garnet?" she gasps. "Is that you?"

"Sssh! Come round the corner, Willie's waiting—"

"Oh!" she says, and is swept into her friend's arms.

ॐॐॐ

THEY FIND THE TELEPHONE KIOSKS on the pier and Perdita calls Aunt Louisa's apartment. Betty answers; the dogs are barking in the background. "I can't find Aunt Louisa, Betty. Tell her I'm fine for tonight, friends met me, I'll talk with her tomorrow."

When she faces Aunt Louisa, she will have to talk with her about Dr. John.

Garnet and Blind Willie and Perdita take the IRT, racketing uptown toward a part of town she doesn't know, toward her new apartment on Riverside Drive. Uncle Gilbert has offended Harry by buying the building, though it makes money. "*Miss* Nanette Williams," Garnet tells her over the racket. "I'm a mannequin. A fashion model. I'll tell you all about it later. I have lots of news. Are you hungry? I've brought chicken and biscuits. And nightclothes and underwear for you, and something to wear while I take you shopping."

"Oh, Garnet, Mr. Williams." She's near to crying. "I can't even find my way from the subway."

"Who you calling Mr. Williams, like we never met?"

"Ssh, Perdita, I'm telling you, call me Nanette. You don't know, it's taking a chance, both of us coming to meet you together. What happened is—"

"Lemme introduce you to my dog. You can call him *Mr.* Sturgis."

Sturgis is new. She can smell him, big wet sloppy dog smell; it reminds her of Elphinstone, of Toby, of Paris. She kneels and embraces the dog with her bandaged hands. Sturgis laps her cheek and she bursts into tears again.

"Don't cry," Garnet says briskly. "You're just hungry."

They get off at 96th St. and walk crosstown through the rainy New York spring night, Perdita holding Garnet's arm, counting steps and memorizing turns: uphill from the shops and lights of Broadway to West End Avenue, downhill towards the Hudson, bear right and uphill again on Riverside Drive. The building Uncle

Gilbert has bought faces the river. A cold breeze brings sea-smell from the Hudson. Perdita can hear a train huffing north. She smells coal smoke. *Ismay windows,* the steward said, and the window clattered down and she could smell the coal-smoke of *Titanic.* "Be careful," Garnet says, "the land goes down like a cliff across the street." *Titanic* went down. The building has a heavy door. Grates and figured iron. Her numb hands feel a Cupid with naked bronze feet.

"Wait a second," Garnet—Nanette—says. "Don't go in yet. Let's really be clear on this. Grandpa and I aren't related, not here. Just two people both named Williams."

Perdita takes a breath and pushes *Titanic* away. "Why, Garnet?"

"Nanette."

"I can go round the back door," Blind Willie says. "Or maybe I better go off now, you girls all talkin' about clothes and all, make an old man nervous. This some fancy building, too, I smell fancy comin' off it. All right I come back tomorrow, girl? Or you come downtown to see me?"

"You go now, Grandpa," Garnet says as if that was what she wanted all along.

"Mr. Williams, come in, and please always use the front door." Is she living in a place that might not welcome Blind Willie?

"Tomorrow afternoon, girl, when you got you'self settled, you come see me at the Tiger."

There's a doorman on duty. He calls her Baroness, tells her Aunt Louisa has left a message for her, and asks her what the building staff can do for her. He opens her door for her. The apartment smells like floor wax and fresh flowers, and for a moment she feels as though it is tilting and about to sink. *Help,* a faint voice cries all alone. Maybe it's her voice.

"Isn't this the fancy place, though!" Garnet says in admiration.

Newly painted rooms, unfamiliar rooms, luxurious anonymous brocade; her apartment is a floating hotel. "Do you mind if I take a bath before we talk?" She has to wash; she hasn't had a bath in four days. Not since *Titanic's* swimming-bath where she talked with Miss Fan. Garnet leads her down a dark hall. Hot-cotton smell of new towels. Vinolia soap. The citrus-flowery smell, the fresh paint, the new tile. It's just paint, just soap, just flowers; Uncle Gilbert has had someone lay this on for her to make her feel welcome. She must feel welcome. It is not *Titanic*; it is kindness. She must think that. She mustn't think that if it was Isaac who married Aunt Louisa, she's not welcome here.

Garnet unhooks her dress and corset and draws her bath. "Want me to wash your hair, Moddom?"

She smiles as best she can. "You might help untangle it later." She must ask for help. She must be strong enough to talk to people and find out everything. She must think and plot and get Aunt Louisa to talk, and Dr. John must speak.

"I'll heat the chicken, OK?"

Resistance of water against her body, her arms, her hands. Cold inside the heat of the water. In the tub, her long hair drags her down. She holds her bandaged hands above the water and almost slips underneath the surface; she feels as if she's fainting. She gets out quickly, half-clean, and stands in the middle of the tiled floor, feeling it vibrate under her bare feet.

Her bedroom is next the bathroom. Cased in stiff new nightclothes, buttons and ribbons undone, she finds her way by smell to the kitchen. "I'm making a list," Garnet says. "You need salt. Can you believe, no salt?"

"Are you working tomorrow? Would you help me shop for clothes?"

"Am I working? Perdita girl, I have a designer who wants to dress you. We're going to Macy's tomorrow and tog you out hat to Louis heels in House of Windsor. I know the suit for you. Black and white stripes."

Black and white stripes. Half mourning. She wants black, all black.

"And we'll make White Star pay for it. Eddie'll give you a good price; he'll get a story out of it. Dressing a survivor."

"Garnet, don't talk about stories and survivors."

"Was it terrible?"

In her chest she feels the screaming. She waits until it dies to one last voice, *help help.*

"The Strauses," Garnet says hesitantly. "The Big Boss and Aunt Ida. Did you see them on *Carpathia*?"

"I'm sorry, Garnet. They're gone. She stayed with him."

"Oh, of course she did," Garnet says, her voice furious with tears. She lays the spatula down and there's no sound in the kitchen for a moment but the chicken sizzling and Garnet sniffing back sobs.

"The Strauses had deckchairs near us," Perdita manages. For a moment she's back on the boat deck, with the cold wind rushing past her, hearing the tap of a thimble against a darning egg. "She darned his socks." She sinks down at the kitchen table and leans her forehead on her wrists.

"Let's have something to eat," Garnet says.

Perdita nods wordlessly, clumsily takes a piece of chicken, sits with it greasy in her bandaged fingers, begins sobbing like a child.

"Let me cut that. You're just worn out. Everything's going to be better in the morning. We'll go shopping."

❧❧❧

SHE FINDS THE PIANO. It's in a room by itself off the entranceway, facing the front of the building; a good place to practice except when the trains rattle by. The room has curtains round the walls to pad the echoes. She touches one key with a painful thumb. The piano is a Steinway by its tone, big and muscular, a little out of tune.

Once she told the truth by playing the piano. Now the truth is on the deck of *Titanic,* which she can never reach again.

She goes to bed.

In dreams she can see perfectly well. She is in the smoking room with its glowing decorations on the dark walls, and the smoking room is full of people. Mrs. Straus is there, a gentle white-haired lady in a blue dress, wearing a shawl, and so is Dr. John. Her chest aches with fear for them. "Mrs. Straus," she says, "please get in the boats, you can survive," but Mrs. Straus says, "I will not go into a lifeboat until everyone can go. Will you stay with me?" Miss Fan says "I am staying with Dr. John." Perdita goes from child to child, a little girl with round bouncy curls, a bigger boy with ball-shaped cheeks; a girl in a pink coat, a boy with a stiff brush of yellow hair, child after child. "Please go, please be saved, don't you realize you'll be drowned?" But they say the same thing to her, "None of us will go until we all can go. I want to stay with my Mamma, my brother, with Papa, with my family." And she is afraid, much more afraid than she had time to be then, because she knows that she won't stay, she will be the one to step into the lifeboat, she will leave and survive, like Bruce Ismay, a thoughtless coward. And they will stand on the deck of *Titanic,* the children, old Mr. Straus and his wife, her grandfather who still had things to say to her, holding hands, families together; and they will tell the truth to each other, and she will not be there.

Dr. John crouches down next to Miss Lady in her wheelchair and talks with her. She cannot hear a word he says.

One child is hiding behind one of the fat green leather chairs. She recognizes his voice. She runs to him and scoops him into her arms.

It is her own dear Toby, crying, scared.

"Oh, Toby, why are you here?"

"Be with you, Mamma."

She picks him up and stands in front of Dr. John. "This is my son, my baby, and for his sake you must tell!"

They must all get on the lifeboats, every one. They must talk; they must tell; they must survive.

But as she speaks, the room tilts and the lights go out.

❧❧❧

GARNET IS MAKING TEA in the kitchen. Perdita comes in barefoot, groping for the doorway, shivering in the blanket she's wrapped around her.

"Did you stay here all night? Oh, Garnet. What time is it?"

"It's only midnight. You were crying in your sleep. I almost woke you."

"I dreamed my little boy was on *Titanic.*"

Garnet sucks in her breath. "Come on, sit down, have some tea or coffee or something."

Perdita sits at the kitchen table with the blanket around her shoulders and a mug of tea between her hands. *Not even Mr. Ismay's had boiler tea.* Dr. John and she drank tea, the one real conversation she had with him.

Life after death, to be free.

"Garnet?" she says. "Do you know how many people died? They didn't want to tell us."

Garnet hesitates. "Fifteen hundred."

"How many of the children?"

"About half of them."

Oh no. No.

"I heard them," Perdita says. From the lifeboat. Where I was safe and a coward.

Garnet pats her arm. Perdita snatches it away.

"I've been reading what it was like," Garnet says. "Anybody was lucky to survive."

"You don't know what it was like." She fumbles her tea mug down, thumps it on the table, a feeble sound.

"Don't get angry at me. You survived," Garnet says, almost accusingly. "And that's great. So don't you get all morbid."

"There was a man on *Titanic,*" Perdita says. "I was trying to find out something from him. He didn't want to tell me. He pushed me away rather than tell. And I was frightened, Garnet, everyone was going to die, and people were saying *get on the boat, get on the boat, it's the last boat,* and his mother said *I'm dying for you, you have a child,* and I was frightened and stupid and feeble and I let it happen. Now all I want is to have stayed on the ship and made him tell me. He would have told me."

"What's worth dying for?" Garnet says.

"Talk about something else," Perdita says.

"Talk to me."

"No. I can't. Tell me about your job." She concentrates and tries to think what Garnet told her.

"If that's the way you want it." Garnet takes a deep breath. "I model at Macy's."

Macy's? "But—"

"Yes, that's a white store. No, they don't know I'm black."

"Garnet, isn't that dangerous?"

"All I wanted to do was to *try on clothes,*" Garnet says. "Was that wrong? You and I used to go shopping together and I would say *that dress works on you, that skirt works* but I never got to try anything on, I was so sick of it. One day after you left I went to Macy's by myself and I went inside, I said to myself, for one day in my life I want to try on clothes, I don't care if they rip them off my back, I don't care if they lynch me.

"And nobody stopped me."

Garnet's voice goes throaty and soft; this is truth.

"Inside Macy's there was a parade of girls in beautiful dresses, showing clothes on a stage. I had never seen a dress parade before. Perdita, it was like lightning struck me and cracked me like a rock. I said, 'I want to do that.' And the woman in charge said, 'I think you could.'

"I never meant to pass. I meant to go downtown and play Nanette for them, and then come back uptown and be me. Except," Garnet swallows. "I always was Nanette. Just nobody knew. I've been talking with Monsieur Édouard of the House of Windsor? His real name is Eddie Cohen, so he's passing too, right? He likes how I sell his dresses. He and his brother are starting their own dress parade in the fall and they want me to be their lead model. I can't give it up, I can't, it's my chance," Garnet says. "But he doesn't know who I am. He thinks I'm white. And I'm going to be white for him. Do you think I'm wrong?"

That's how they met first, she and Garnet: clothes. Perdita was living on her own for the first time. She'd never shopped for clothes without someone with her. She needed a recital dress. *Only if I can choose all your clothes,* Garnet said.

"This is who you really are, isn't it," Perdita says.

"I'm Nanette," Garnet says.

Perdita wishes she knew who she was herself.

"Nanette," Perdita says. "Then I'll help."

And if I do I can't lie to you, Perdita thinks.

She can't be loyal to Garnet without telling her. She can't give help without asking for it.

It's so easy to keep silent—

Quickly, before she can think, she speaks.

"Garnet, this is what I was trying to find out from Dr. John."

❧❧❧

"*You?*" GARNET SAYS.

"Me and Toby. My mother. All my brothers and sisters too. But they don't know."

They sit at the kitchen table and eat chicken and talk.

"You're afraid your Aunt Louisa married the other one, Black Zack, and she screamed and ran when she found out?"

"I don't mean that it's blameworthy to be black, Garnet."

"I know what you mean, girl, better than you do. Anybody else know your story? Anybody white, I mean?"

There is something in the way she says it, as if Perdita and she are now in a conspiracy. Garnet is talking differently to her.

"Do you remember Harry? The man I was engaged to and broke it off?"

"Him? Coming down to New York to tell you he was getting married to your cousin, like the sun was coming out of his ass, and thinking you were going to be all broken up and weeping because you'd missed out on him? *He* knows?"

"He knows Aunt Louisa married a Mr. Church. And he's likely to learn that a man named Church was actually a black man; it was all over Paris. But he wouldn't tell—"

"You think? Maybe not if he's married to your cousin. What are you going to do?"

"Sit with Dr. John and ask him when he's better. Get the story out of Aunt Louisa." There's so much to do. She's so tired.

"She'll tell you she married the white man," Garnet says.

"She'll tell me the truth," Perdita says uncertainly.

"You know she won't. Nobody ever tells," Garnet says. "People you never even met will lie for you. They'll make up stories for you. Because if you are passing, girl, it gets dangerous. People don't like not knowing what people are."

"But I want—"

She wants to know what she would have learned on the deck of *Titanic.* "I want the truth of it."

"Then you should talk to Frog Jaw," Garnet says.

"Frog Jaw?"

"Mr. Louis Johnson to you. He's a detective. If this Church might even the slightest be a black man? Use a black detective. Because nobody's going to tell a white man anything."

Perdita wants to know, but have the answer be the right one. She is really white; she has been white all her life. She wants to know her truth is true. She wants to believe it as she would believe Dr. John on the deck of *Titanic.*

What is her truth?

She took a place in the lifeboats. There were children in the water. *Titanic* is wrecked. Nothing will be true the same way again.

"I want to talk with your Mr. Johnson, then."

"You really want to?"

"Yes."

"Right after I take you shopping. You can't live in an apartment like this and have no clothes. Now get some sleep."

❧❧❧

No one keeps track of the survivors. The first- and second-class passengers exchange business cards or pieces of paper, promising to keep in touch. No one wants to. This voyage isn't going to encourage reunions.

They scatter. The Philadelphia first-class survivors go back to their city by private train provided by dead George Widener's railroad. The crew spends the night on a White Star ship or at the Jane Hotel, ready to return to England and their families. The third-class survivors are given hotel vouchers, issued tickets to their destinations. Tomorrow they'll get clothes from charitable New Yorkers.

Rich or poor, now they are on their own, in hotel rooms, in apartments, in St. Vincent's hospital, facing the night. Some of them pray, some of them drink, some try to sleep.

Perdita hears little screams, *help, Mommy, help!* Dr. John's voice rumbles in her ears but she can't understand what he's saying. Her hands are painful and numb. She wraps a pillow around her head, and thinks of the pillow she wrapped around her ears to muffle the sirens of *Titanic,* and shivers. She wonders if, even now, Dr. John is dying in St Vincent's without her there.

She gets up early to face what she can and to help Toby and herself: to be a white woman, the mother of a white little boy.

❧❧❧

Dorothy Gibson is making her plans. Cuddling next to her Jules in a midtown hotel, she jumps up every two minutes to jot something else down on an increasing list of things she must do—hairdresser, clothes, publicist, photographer. Jules is reading the late papers, checking the news about them. All the *Shipboard Romance* footage is at the bottom of the ocean, but Jules has already bought film of the *Carpathia,* the survivors, even dead Captain Smith smiling from the deck on *Olympic.* Out in Fort Lee, working through the night, the editors at Éclair Studios are patching it together.

"We'll get a ship from Staten Island," Jules says. "From the ship-breaker yards. Moor it right by the Palisades. Put a big canvas sign on it with our title, *Titanic* or something." He turns to the front page. "'Saved from the Titanic, 775 souls. Lost from the Titanic, 1565.' What a story. And, Mutsie, we'll have the first movie."

"Say that again, Julie." She cranes over his shoulder. "*Saved from the Titanic.*"

"What?"

"*Saved from the Titanic.* That's our new title."

"Starring you, Mutsie."

"Directed by you, Julie."

"I'm thinking, though," he says, "there's a problem. It's got to be a love story, right? But what do we do about the hero? He can't survive."

"Never mind, honey," Dorothy Gibson says, who rowed away in the first boat and survived. "We'll figure it out. Let's not worry about it at all."

Part 3: Survivors' Music

[DURING THE FIRST DAY OF TESTIMONY about the sinking], Ismay left the room and paced the corridors of the Waldorf-Astoria smoking cigarettes. He was joined by journalists who badgered him as to whether he had left a ship filled with women and children....

"What sort of man do you think I am? Do you believe I'm the sort who would have left the ship as long as there were any women and children aboard her? I think it was the last boat that was lowered I went into. I did then what any other passenger would do... I did nothing I should not have done. My conscience is clear, and I have not been a lenient judge of my own acts. I took the chance when it came to me."

The women passengers in Collapsible C remember the loading of their boat differently. Margaret Devaney...recalled being "caught in a crowd and pushed into Collapsible C", and Waika Nakid...saw two men from Lebanon being shot at.... "Sailors armed with revolvers drove the men away from the boats shouting, 'women and children first!'"

—Frances Wilson, *How to Survive the Titanic*

Perdita

SHOPPING FOR CLOTHES is trivial, heartless, comforting, all at once. Perdita tries on clothes in the private showroom at Macy's and Garnet decides what she should buy. Suits in Greek silhouette and Directoire style, big hats, clocked stockings.

The disaster haunts Macy's. The store is only halfheartedly open, in mourning for the Strauses. Garnet's friends the mannequins hover round, giving style advice but really wanting to ask about the Big Boss and Aunt Ida. Every once in a while one of them goes off in a corner to cry.

"There's going to be a service for them at the Educational Alliance on Tuesday."

"We should all go," Garnet says. "Come with us, Perdita. You can tell the family you saw her on the ship. They'd like that."

"I want a dark suit," Perdita says hesitantly, speaking clothes and meaning mourning.

Memorial services. She wants to talk about the Strauses. She doesn't want to. She wants to know what Dr. John would have said to her. She wants him to say it. She wants to talk about the screaming afterward, the silence, the children; she wants to talk about the feeble, thoughtless people who survived. She doesn't.

She walks out of Macy's wearing a dark linen suit and a blouse Garnet has picked out, very dark but not black, not mourning. She can't mourn; she's lost no one; she has no right. "You look good," Garnet says. "Don't you feel better now?"

They take the Broadway car downtown toward St Vincent's. Garnet wants to show her something before they visit Dr. John.

Garnet points out a green-and-brown-striped cliff. "The *Evening Post* building." Garnet drops her voice to a whisper. "That's where the National Association for the Advancement of Colored People has its offices. They write about people in the South lynched for being black. Every day you wake up alive, girl? Celebrate."

Nearby is City Hall Plaza. Garnet takes her to look at the lists on the window of the White Star Line offices. Perdita stares at the long white panels of newsprint on one side of the door, the so much shorter list on the other, the short list of the saved.

"Look. There's your name." Garnet stretches up her hand and points to a blurred place on the white list.

She stands there, safe in New York, in her new fashionable hat and suit, in the spring sunshine and the spring breeze: alive. She goes up to the window with the long list and stands with her nose almost up against the glass. She doesn't know what to do with *alive* any more than she does with *black*.

"Let's go to St Vincent's," she says.

At St. Vincent's she only wants to hear about Dr. John, but they treat her like a patient. A nurse cuts blister skin off Perdita's screaming fingers and dabs mercurochrome on them. Perdita stamps her feet silently with pain. The nurse bandages her hands again, finger by finger this time.

"Dr. John Church was being given serum therapy. Do you know, is it working?"

"He was the one who was in the water so long? Poor man."

"Is he—?"

"He's not doing very well yet."

A crowd marks the part of the hospital given over to the survivors. Charitable ladies are donating flowers, clothing, Teddy bears for the children. The ladies bring their autograph books and their Kodaks; they have their pictures taken with survivors. The reporters flash big professional cameras. The ward smells like fireworks.

Miss Fan is sitting by Dr. John's bed in a private room, still in the nightdress and brown coat she wore on *Carpathia*. Dr. John is unconscious, breathing in slow rasps.

"I can't leave him; what if he should start talking?" Miss Fan swallows and goes on. "What if he should wake and want me?"

"I can watch for you," Perdita says.

"No, I need to stay here with him myself, every minute. Miss Perdita, I hate to ask, but if you would do something for me? My son and granddaughter and a few of our people are comin' up from Fair Home today. Would it be possible to send someone to meet them? They have no idea of the city or know a place where they might stay."

From Fair Home? "I will go myself. And all of you must stay with me."

"Oh, honey, it's not just my son and his daughter comin', it's Mammy Jane and Uncle Otis." She means *do you want black people staying with you.*

"All of you."

"Jeff, he wants to see Dr. John in case," Miss Fan doesn't say in case of what. "Arbella and Mammy Jane are goin' on up to Halifax when the funeral ship comes in. To bring Miss Lady back to us..." Miss Fan's voice trails off.

A ship is going out from Halifax to where *Titanic* sank, to gather bodies.

"I don't know how I will tell Mammy Jane about the other one dyin' in Paris," Miss Fan is saying. "I don't know what I'll say."

Of course "Mammy" Jane must have known Bright Isaac. "Was he special to her?"

"I'm sorry, you don't know. Zack was Mammy's son."

"ZACK'S *MOTHER*!" Garnet carols when they're out on the street again. "What a lot we can find out from *her*! And all the rest of them are staying with you too! We'll be detectives, better than Frog Jaw!"

Mr. Louis Johnson's neighborhood is only two stops beyond Perdita's, but it's another world. The two women come up out of the subway to a Broadway in chaos. On all the side streets it's moving day. Cart horses are snorting, wheels are grinding against curbs, movers are bumping trunks downstairs; an iron bedstead jangles and clangs. The Jewish families are racing to finish by sunset.

"Tomorrow our folks move in," Garnet says.

Our folks, Perdita thinks.

"This is *our place.* Not a crooks' den like downtown, not a slum. A real neighborhood. Black people renting to black people."

Mr. Louis Johnson's detective business is on the second floor of a jewelry store, which he also owns. Mr. Johnson himself is a tall athletic shadow behind a desk. Someone is typing in the corner. Perdita takes in everything curiously.

"My friend Perdita's looking for a good detective," Garnet explains. "But you'll have to do."

"I never mind Miss Williams," Mr. Johnson says comfortably to Perdita.

"And I never mind him," says Garnet.

"Ma'am, why don't you tell me all about it and neither of us will mind Miss Williams?"

He sends the typist out and Perdita explains. The two John Rolfe Churches. Bright Isaac. Miss Lady. Miss Fan. Fate deMay. Fair Home. Manassas. Prison, Brazil, or New York. Aunt Louisa. Dr. John now in St. Vincent's with pneumonia. She needs to talk with him.

"And Harry," Garnet prompts.

And Harry.

"Your Aunt Louisa," Mr. Johnson says, "your grandmother, you're intending to ask her what happened?"

"Yes."

"But she'll lie," Garnet says.

"Unless she did marry the white man," Mr. Johnson says. "You're looking for independent confirmation that she did? And you'd like to know when Dr. John is conscious."

"Perdita has all the Churches coming up to stay with her," Garnet says. "The whole Church family from Virginia. Including Isaac's mother. Isn't she clever?"

"Fair Home," Mr. Johnson says. "I've heard something about that name. Whirlwind?"

"Dr. John stole Whirlwind back for Fair Home. To make up for having taken him away."

She smells Assam tea, tastes sandwiches in the Verandah Café. The film camera clickets in the background. *Am I the serpent?* Dr. John says, and laughs. She shivers.

"You tell me everything you know about Dr. John," Mr. Johnson says.

Fate deMay, she says; the bet, Manassas. "He encouraged his friend to bet and the friend lost his land."

"Would your aunt have left him for that?"

"She'd have wanted him to make things right."

But Aunt Louisa said *nothing was wrong.*

"The Churches' employees are coming?" Mr. Johnson asks. "And one of them this Isaac's mother? First. We can have someone watching at the hospital to tell you when your Dr. Church wakes up. And, Ma'am, I would suggest you hire an employee. A good housekeeper, cook—"

"I do have to find someone. I can't monopolize you, Garnet."

"Dummox," Garnet says, "he wants to put a woman detective in your house."

"Are there woman detectives?"

"He'd like *me* to be a detective," Garnet says.

"You could do anything you please, Miss Williams—"

"I *do* do anything I please, Mr. Johnson."

Mrs. Clementine Daniels, cook and detective, arrives a few minutes later. She is a substantial middle-aged woman in a wide red hat and matching red boa, who has caught two bank embezzlers, a forger, and too many philanderers to mention. She has her own gun, makes lavender tea shortbread, and will not only cook but do light housekeeping.

"I cannot ask you to do cleaning, Mrs. Daniels—"

"Oh, Miss, no trouble dealing with one young lady and her friends. I make this and that, I sit and gossip with the other servants, Isaac's Mamma particularly, and I tell them stories about my employers, and they tell me stories about theirs. No trouble at all. Nobody holds anything back from a woman who's baking."

Mrs. Daniels is sent off to buy Garnet's list of groceries, though this seems hardly the way to begin using a detective.

Mr. Johnson will also have a friend in Washington check the records of Union prisoners. "Dr. John was captured at First Bull Run? I might have something for you by Tuesday or Wednesday. And if he was on the Army payroll buying horses here—You leave it to me."

"Of course you can do everything," says Garnet. "You know everyone, everywhere. He has everything but his own church, Perdita. Frog Jaw, how can I take you seriously if you aren't the Reverend Mr. Johnson?"

"Take me seriously, Garnet," Mr. Johnson says.

❧❧❧

"A WOMAN DETECTIVE," Perdita muses when they are walking back toward her apartment.

"And we can detect too. Aren't you clever to have the family," Garnet says. "Zack's mother!"

"Why don't you like Mr. Johnson, Garnet? He seems a nice man, and trustworthy." She trusts him, a man she's just met.

"I don't like him judging my business. He thinks I'll get in trouble, doing what I'm doing."

"Will you get in trouble?"

"Don't you worry," Garnet says.

Which means yes. "Oh, Garnet, be careful."

They stop to buy grapes from a greengrocer's stand on West End Avenue, and discreetly say nothing until they walk on.

"How did Mr. Johnson come to be a detective?"

"Frog Jaw's always looking for ways to make money. He started as a bicycle racer before the whites drove black racers out. He got medals, so he learned the difference between gold plated and gold, and he started up a jewelry store down on 53rd St. Sold wedding rings and ear-bobs to our folks, slept under the counter. And then some of those marriages didn't work out, and people would come to him asking what their husband or wife was up to, and Frog Jaw decided it'd pay to be Sherlock Holmes for black people. Now he's moved uptown, he part-owns a bar where all the betrayed husbands and wives drink and an undertaking parlor for when they shoot each other. He's a special constable too. Practically delivers the ice and the milk. Just a miracle, Frog Jaw is."

"He's very successful."

"Always successful and always black."

"Garnet!"

They wait to cross the street.

"The thing is," Garnet says in a low voice, "he wants me to pass too. But for him. Pretend to be a white woman, be an operative for him. How different is that from what I'm doing?"

"Not at all," Perdita says loyally. "Except that you're doing what you want."

Garnet takes her arm and they cross the street together.

❧❧❧❧

BACK AT THE APARTMENT there's a huge vase of flowers from everyone at Jouvet, roses and lilac—Uncle Gilbert must have asked specially for lilac—which leaves her feeling sad and cold and frightened. She sits down in a chair, exhausted. Lilacs will never smell good again. She gives the flowers to Garnet.

Mrs. Daniels has arrived with groceries; Perdita sends her out again to the New York Association for the Blind with another list—guide cane, extra cane tips, magnifying glass, and her Braille watch to leave at a watchmaker's in case it can be fixed. The apartment doesn't have enough sheets and towels now the Churches are here; Mrs. Daniels must get some too.

A detective buying sheets. Sherlock Holmes never had to buy sheets; they just appeared. Mrs. Hudson bought them.

"You have a basketful of cards and messages," Garnet says.

"Would you read them to me? Garnet, I'm making you wait on me hand and foot."

"I jes' purely loves to wait on you, Miz Perdita."

"Garnet!"

"Well, you've made my Monsieur Édouard very happy, and I owe you."

"I thought that was me owing you."

The very first item on the pile is an envelope with two copies of Aunt Louisa's marriage certificate and a letter from a New York detective agency, telling her that Alexander ordered these and the agency will be looking into John Rolfe Church's background. Which is what she's just asked Mr. Johnson to do. She must tell Mr. Johnson about these people so he can steer round them. She realizes, with a twinge of disquiet, that she doesn't want Alexander's detective agency to find out too much. She trusts Mr. Johnson to be more discreet.

There's a telegram from Alexander that she puts aside to puzzle out later. He will be worried for her and she can't face reassuring him.

Miss Alden from the NAWSA Fundraising Concert Committee has asked her to call. Perdita winces. Mrs. van Rensselaer from the New York Relief Committee for Titanic Survivors has left a card. Miss Dorothy Gibson, please call.

"I'll call Miss Alden."

Perdita painfully flexes her bandaged fingers while she waits for Miss Alden to come on the line; but Miss Alden is out at a meeting.

Will she be able to play at Carnegie Hall? She won't. It doesn't matter. It shouldn't matter.

Teachers and friends from the Institute have written congratulating her on her escape. Dr. Guttmacher has telephoned, her most beloved teacher at the Institute; he made solfège and transcription actually inspiring. She phones him back. "I'm fine. It was bad, let's not talk about it." She levers off her shoes and massages each tired foot against her other knee, standing on one leg like a crane while she holds the earpiece.

Next up— But the doorman whistles through the pneumatic tube; she has visitors.

"Harry Boulding and Buckingham Pelham."

ᔥᔥᔥ

IF SHE WERE ALEXANDER she would swear.

"Come in," she says. They're already in. They fill the hall with the smell of cigars. Harry has taken up Uncle Bucky's smoking habit.

"Put on your shoes," Harry says to her. "You look stupid."

"Good morning, Harry." She does slip on her shoes. She always did what he asked.

"Would you like some coffee?" she asks.

"We have heard a very unpleasant story from Paris," Uncle Bucky breaks in. "About Louisa."

They have heard the whole thing.

"Oh," she says innocently, "that strange man in Paris who was *pretending* to be John Rolfe Church?"

"The *black* man," Uncle Bucky says. "Your aunt Violet is very distressed that my sister might even be thought to have married a *black* man. It cannot be true, but of course we are all appalled. Such rumors might affect the family."

"Not my family," Harry says. "I married the right girl."

"The man in Paris was not the man who married Aunt Louisa, so there is nothing to worry about." There, she is lying.

"But how does one know there is nothing to worry about?" Uncle Bucky says. "When did this *black* man in Paris begin this vulgar charade? Niece, we have no proof at all that he was in Brazil and not in New York."

He knows far too much. "I'll get coffee," she says and flees to the kitchen.

Garnet and Mrs. Daniels have been listening at the kitchen door. "They're worried their family's getting smeared with black cooties!" Garnet whispers. "Couldn't happen to more deserving people."

"They want to believe the worst," she says and realizes she's called being black *the worst* to Garnet and Mrs. Daniels. "What they think is the worst. I am sorry." But she thinks so too, doesn't she. She is being a hypocrite to apologize.

"I made coffee and scones in case folks stopped by," Mrs. Daniels says.

"They want to use that story," Garnet says. "Can't keep their fingers off it, can they? And look at that Harry. 'Not *my* family.'"

"Don't you worry about anything," Mrs. Daniels tries to reassure her.

Perdita wheels the tea cart back down the hall.

"Your husband is coming to America?" Uncle Bucky says.

"No, he's not. You know he doesn't like America."

"Sure he's not coming," Harry says. "No, I don't want your coffee. You could never make coffee."

"This is someone else's coffee." A *black* woman's coffee. Harry is putting her down and she is justifying herself; why does she always do that?

"Your husband has left you all alone with this, niece," Uncle Bucky says disapprovingly. "He should be protecting you."

"There's nothing to be protected from," Perdita says.

"Nothing to be protected from!" Uncle Bucky says. "Niece, think of the family!"

"Uncle Bucky, you could have asked your *sister* yourself and saved anxiety. Aunt Louisa will confirm that she married a white man. You both have nothing to worry about."

"*I* don't have anything to worry about," Harry says. "It's not *my* wife's grandfather."

The speaking tube whistles. She jumps nervously up to answer it.

"Mrs. John Rolfe Church," the doorman says.

"Louisa?" says Uncle Bucky.

There is nothing to do but let Miss Fan in. "They have sent me away to rest," Miss Fan says faintly. "There's no change."

"You're Mrs. John Rolfe Church?" Harry says.

"Why, yes," Miss Fan says.

"Did you marry Perdita's grandfather too?"

❧❧❧

OH HEAVENS.

Perdita pushes Harry and Uncle Bucky out the door, sits Miss Fan down, pushes Mrs. Daniels' excellent coffee and a scone on her, and then she has to explain.

"My John was married?"

"I am afraid he was," Perdita says. "Married and then divorced."

"Oh my L—d."

"I am so sorry. It must be shocking to you."

"Is the lady still alive?"

How much should she tell Miss Fan? "Yes, she lives here in New York."

"Oh my L—d. You are John's grandchild?" Miss Fan says. "John had a child?"

She wishes she could keep this from her. "I told him who I was, on the ship, just at the last. I am sure he had no idea before then." She considers saying Dr. John has six other grandchildren, but Miss

Fan doesn't need to hear that. "It's very new to me. You know of course that I have no claim on him; I would never dream of such a thing."

Miss Fan stands up and goes to the window, looks out onto Riverside Drive.

"I wondered where he was during the War!" she says.

"You didn't think he was in prison?"

"Oh, no, we lied about that." Miss Fan sits down, exhausted. "His teeth weren't all wore down or fallen out from the sawdust-bread the Yankees gave our men. But—I never thought New York. He was helping the Yankees? The Yankees?"

"He was buying horses for the Union Army."

"Oh my L—d."

"I know he was thinking of you at Fair Home while he was in New York."

"That would have been good of him," Miss Fan says, shaking her head. "Oh, Heavenly Father," she says. "Working for the North. Miss Lady, Heaven have mercy, she'd have shot him where he stood."

"He brought her back Whirlwind," Perdita says. "He said he had to know his mamma was safe and bring Whirlwind back."

But poor Miss Fan he had not talked about at all.

Miss Fan takes hold of her arm with frail hot tired fingers. "Don't say anything to the family!"

The family! They are coming in two hours.

"Promise me!" Miss Fan says. "Best if we forget this entirely and never speak of it."

"Of course. This is between us alone." For now. "Lie down and rest, Miss Fan." Perdita leads Miss Fan down the hall to one of the guest rooms. Miss Fan lowers herself down on the bed just as she is, coat and hat and shoes. Perdita pushes the curtains closed to darken the room.

"Promise me, Miss Perdita!" Miss Fan whispers. "Don't talk to the family. Please don't talk about this at all."

ॐॐॐ

PERDITA GOES BACK TO THE LIVING ROOM. Garnet and Mrs. Daniels are there. She closes the glass doors and sinks down on the sofa, her bandaged hands over her mouth.

"He didn't tell her he'd been married?" Garnet whispers.

"You heard?"

"You can hear through the ventilator if you stand on a chair."

"He didn't tell her *anything*. He didn't tell her about going North."

I have never been out of prison since. Dr. John has said never a word to Miss Fan about his first marriage, how he spent the whole war. He's forged his own bars and manacles of lies. Alexander has at least had Uncle Gilbert and Perdita to be honest with. Dr. John has had no one.

I should have been on the deck of *Titanic* for him.

Wake up, Dr. John, she thinks. You have to talk with me, and with your wife. If you're going to die, you can't die lying.

❧❧❧

"DR. JOHN AIN'T DEAD, IS HE?" says Jefferson deMay. "Where's Mamma?"

Perdita goes to Penn Station to meet the Churches. There are four of them, Mr. Jefferson deMay, his daughter Arbella, the trainer Mr. Otis, and Isaac's mother. The servants are swathed in dusters and traveling scarves and all the Churches have wide bands of black on their sleeves for Miss Lady; Perdita is glad she's wearing near-mourning too. Both Mr. Jeff and Mr. Otis are short and lean. Southern children, Perdita thinks, starved by the War and hard times, the way every French person who was a child in the Paris Commune is short.

And Dr. John took away Whirlwind, who was their livelihood, and left them to starve out the War; and Miss Fan suspected it, but has only found out now; and the rest of them don't know at all. Oh, what a cage of lies this is. *Forget this entirely and never speak of it,*

Miss Fan said. Alexander's right; Dr. John would never have spoken.

"Uncle Otis, you go get our baggage," Mr. Jefferson says. "This is my daughter, Miss Arbella deMay," Mr. Jeff introduces, "and this is our Aunt Jane, our Mammy."

Bright Isaac's mother.

If Isaac was practically white, "Aunt Jane" must be very light-skinned, able to peer over the wall of race. Perdita squints but can't tell what color Aunt Jane is; everyone is dark at night. She's only a thin stooped figure in a broad straw hat, wearing the duster and a scarf or shawl around her neck.

"Ma'am," Perdita says to Aunt Jane, what is her last name? Church? "Please accept my sympathies on the loss of your son in Paris."

"I thank you, ma'am." Aunt Jane has a sweet cultivated voice. Her teeth whistle a bit; she has dentures. Perhaps Dr. John made them for her.

"How was your travel up here?"

"Why," Aunt Jane says, "it was up and down, up and down; thank you for asking, ma'am."

"It was dirty," says a new voice, young and high and raw. "Papa, you said we could all sit together up beyond Washington and it would be clean. But they put Uncle Otis and Mammy in the first car, away from us, and me and Otis couldn't sit together and talk about horses."

They have been traveling in segregated cars. The servants' dusters and scarves are to keep the train-smoke from their clothes.

"Hush now, Miss Arbella," Aunt Jane says. "Otis and I. And a young girl shouldn't talk about horses all the time. Miss Arbella, you say hello to the baroness."

"Hello, ma'am, Mis' Baroness," Arbella bobs, a movement in the dark.

"Miss Arbella will be glad to help you while you're here."

"Yes ma'am, Mis' Baroness," Arbella says resignedly.

CRIMES AND SURVIVORS ~ 175

"Would you rather leave your things at the apartment first or see Dr. John right away?"

"Master John, ma'am, if you don't mind," Aunt Jane breathes.

"Yes," Mr. Jeff says, "Papa first. Where is Otis? Where has that boy got to with the luggage?"

Boy.

They find Mr. Otis standing by their pile of luggage, waiting, and it's obvious why he hasn't come back. He can't carry the luggage alone but no porter has stopped for him. As they arrive, Perdita sees a uniformed shadow with a rattling empty cart pass by, hesitate for a moment, and go on.

Mr. Otis is a black man. With luggage. *Must have stolen it,* Perdita's inner Garnet comments. And not even other black men stop for him.

As soon as white Mr. Jeff stands by the luggage, a porter comes to help.

The porter takes them to the taxi-rank outside Penn Station, and at the taxi rank it happens again. Mr. Otis stands in the cab line while the rest of the family guards the luggage, and the next cab suddenly remembers it's off duty. And the next. And the next.

I am simply encouraging wrongdoing, Perdita thinks, but she steps forward to stand beside Mr. Otis and waves her guide cane. "Hello," she pleads to the next cabman, "would you do such a favor before you go off duty and oblige a poor blind woman?"

"Well, I'm sure I didn't see *you,* Miss," the cabman says.

"Oh, it's not for me," and she gestures Mr. Otis into the cab before the driver can say a word. She calls Mr. Jeff and Aunt Jane and puts them in too. "Thank you so much!" she calls up to the cabman, *thank you in spite of yourself, you nasty prejudiced man.*

Toby cannot be black. She cannot. Not in America.

൙൙൙

THAT EVENING, Mrs. Daniels entirely justifies herself as a detective.

Arbella deMay is very young, twelve or thirteen Perdita would guess, too young to watch at a sickbed, so she comes with Perdita and the luggage up to Riverside Drive. Arbella unpacks luggage as if she were the family servant. Clementine Daniels, who is doing the favor of staying late, helps her.

Then Mrs. Daniels comes in to see Perdita.

"Miss Perdita, would you like me to serve tea?" she asks out loud for the benefit of Arbella down the hall, and then delivers her report in a whisper: "(Jane Church has a picture of John Church and Isaac just before they went to the war!)"

"Why, thank you, Mrs. Daniels, I would appreciate that. (Just about the time he married Aunt Louisa? Golly!)"

"I'll do that right away. (Get her to show it to you.)"

She can do better than that. "Could you possibly bring tea in a few minutes? I just remembered something I must pick up on Broadway."

She goes off to test her knowledge of the neighborhood and buy a camera.

Garnet Williams/Miss Nanette Williams

"Good mornin', Miss, how are you this bright morning?"

Macy's is closed Saturday in mourning for the Strauses, so Garnet goes to Perdita's. A little girl answers the door.

"Who are *you*?" Garnet asks.

"I'm Arbella deMay," the girl says. "From Fair Home. I'm helping."

To tell what kind of a place Fair Home is, you only have to look at Arbella deMay. She's a little stick of a thing, round blue eyes, kinky yellow hair, black cotton mourning dress with a big white apron. If she's Jefferson deMay's daughter, she'll own Fair Home someday, but (Garnet sees water all down the front of her apron) she's been doing the washing-up and she's answering the door. Fair Home is a working farm, and the daughter of the house works with the rest.

Maybe she's a white Negro. Frizzy hair, yes; blue eyes, maybe. She certainly talks black.

Garnet sees other people through the door of the dining room. "Who are those?"

A sixtyish whippy man is standing by the kitchen door, shifting about, nervous as a toothpick being chewed. "That's Uncle Otis," the little girl says. "Our trainer. He's just a *brilliant* trainer. He's teachin' me. And that's my Papa." A chinless white Southerner, a few years younger. "And Grandma and Mammy." Two white women at the table talking. One of them is Miss Fan, still wearing her ruined clothes from *Titanic,* Garnet must do something about that. The other is very old and—

Not white. Garnet stares at her. This has to be Zack's mother. But that is the only, only way Garnet can tell. Jane Church's skin is less lined than a white woman's would be; her hair is thicker; but that's all. She's a handsome old *white* woman.

"Mis' Baroness Perdita, she's just coming," Arbella says.

"I'll wait right here."

Left alone, Garnet watches the Churches like Sherlock Holmes. They are talking about the dead woman, Miss Lady.

"—Miss Lady was a demandin' woman," the white man says, "but you know, no one cared more about Fair Home."

"My little Lady," Mammy Jane says. "We knew each other for eighty-five years." She speaks with a good educated accent, a soft murmured suggestion of a Southern voice—but *we knew each other!* What she means is, she was that Miss Lady's *slave. Slave,* that's the word you should use, you stupid woman who could have been a white lady. Garnet narrows her eyes.

"Judged her horses better than anyone," the whippy old man says.

"Told you so too, ever' day, Uncle Otis!" the chinless white man chuckles.

"Sure she did, Marse Jeff."

They are having their little own memorial service right here, Uncle Tom and Aunt Jemima and the white folks, hearts are breaking 'cause Old Miss dead. Old Miss probably ran you 'servants' down every day of those eighty-five years, and you jes' laugh 'cause dat de white folk way.

"Miss Lady was so strong," says Mammy Jane.

"How'm I ever going to be as strong?" Miss Fan says, quivering like coconut jelly.

Oh, honey, you'll figure it out.

"Miss Fan, we are all standing with you." Mammy Jane, the *white* woman, is talking to her mistress sweet as Old Auntie right off the molasses jar. Garnet listens, mortified. "We all take care of you. My Otis and Mr. Jeff, they take care of the horses, and Miss Arbella and I, we bring Miss Lady back to Fair Home, I help her same as I ever did."

"Do you think I shall be able to do my part?" Miss Fan quavers.

"Oh, darlin', of course. The Lord give you all you need. The Lord take care of you."

"I take care of you," Mr. Otis chimes in. "Take care of Fair Home."

"Mis' Williams?" Arbella appears again. "Mis' Perdita be right with you. I go back and finish up the dishes, you don't mind."

"Arbella," Garnet says, just in case this little country girl is actually a white Negro and needs her horizons widened. "Have you ever been to New York before?"

Arbella looks round for the person Garnet must be talking to.

"Yes, asking you, Arbella. Have you ever been to New York?"

"No'm."

"Wouldn't you like to see something of it?"

Arbella considers. "Dunno," she says. "Mammy says it's dangerous."

"No, Arbella, the answer is yes, you would. Have you been to Times Square?"

Arbella stares at Garnet with alarm, like a cow at a steam shovel.

"Perdita or I will take you. They've got electric signs in Times Square, all made of lights. Galloping horses and a girl walking in the rain. The raindrops splash and her skirt moves. You never saw anything like. And the news goes round the *Times* building. You can read it from the street and see all about *Titanic* and everything."

Moving signs? Arbella smiles carefully as if in the presence of a madwoman.

"Times Square is famous," Perdita says, coming up the hall. "Arbella, you can go with me in the subway."

"The *sub*way, Mis' Baroness?"

"A train underground. Much nicer than the taxi we took last night." Perdita sounds uncharacteristically grim.

"Oh, Mis' Baroness, underground *train?* I don't know."

"Nanette," Perdita says, "would you come with me for a moment? I need to consult with you about clothes."

Perdita still looks bruised and pale and in pain, but she's not the dripping gravestone she was yesterday. Shopping always helps.

"Mrs. Church," Perdita calls, "do you mind if Nanette and I look in the closet in your room? I'm trying to find some clothes of mine that were sent here—"

"Oh, Ma'am, why you even ask me? And don't you call me Mis' Church, I'm just old Auntie Jane."

"Those are the most old-fashioned people," Garnet says when Perdita closes the door, "and that is not a compliment. Is that little girl white or black?"

"Arbella? White!"

"Her hair could use straightening. I hope you aren't getting out your old clothes from music school."

"There aren't any clothes, that's an excuse." Perdita's carrying a bag. Out of it she pulls, to Garnet's astonishment, a camera. "Mrs. Church—Jane Church—Aunt Jane—has a picture of Dr. John and

Bright Isaac when they were young. Can you find it and take a photo of it? I went out last night and bought the camera and the clerk kept trying to remind me I was blind." Good kind little Perdita is angry. "Do you see the picture?"

There it is, on the nightstand by the Bible and the tin dish for Aunt Jane's teeth, in a black hard-rubber frame. Garnet pulls up the shades and tilts the glass so the light falls across it.

"This blonde one must be Fate deMay," Garnet thinks out loud, "and the really dark one must be" Fate's *slave,* what was his name? "But you should see John and Zack."

Four men in the picture. Two young white men sitting in front, laughing at the camera, smiling a little too wide and proud and nervous; they're going to the war. One of them has bright curly hair like little Arbella. The other's more tanned, brown-haired.

Two other men stand behind them. One, dark as a tar road, grins down at the white men. He's not going to fight, not him, he's going to hold the horses, he's safe.

The other's not laughing. Not smiling. He's at his war already.

And he's white too.

He was like me, Garnet thinks. Dark skin shows darker in photographs, but Bright Isaac is as white as his brother. Privileged John Rolfe Church rode out hunting and let himself go tan. Good-skin *slave* Zack probably wore a hat every time he could. Garnet wears hats.

"Stand at the door," Garnet tells Perdita, "keep them out."

"What do John and Zack look like?" Perdita asks. "Tell me they look completely different."

"Shush, let me take these photos." Garnet peers through the viewfinder. One white face laughing nervously; the other white face cold and proud and serious. "They don't look like twins or anything, but they were half-brothers—"

"Al and Phil don't look alike." Perdita has twin brothers.

"The thing is, though, Zack? He could pass in an instant." Garnet points and presses the button and winds the film to shoot another, as if taking more pictures will show her something more.

Three men smiling.

One man with nothing to call his but who he is. Needing himself too much to smile.

As she's putting the picture back on Aunt Jane's nightstand, she sees the other photo there. No need to ask: a woman in a wheelchair, fat white face scowling with privilege. Garnet snaps a picture of her too, just because Miss Lady wouldn't like it. You, Miss Lady? Black woman just took a picture of you.

"Let's go out for breakfast," Garnet says. "These people give me the awfuls."

❧❧❧

THEY WALK OVER TO BROADWAY, get tea and bagels at the counter of a delicatessen, and find a booth at the back.

"At least there's the picture to show Aunt Louisa. So she can say 'I married this one' and not Zack."

"She'll *say* that if you show her a picture of an elephant."

There's an awkward silence. "What do you think of the Churches?" Perdita asks.

Garnet looks round. Nobody can hear them; the deli is empty. On a Saturday morning there's only the Shabbos goy at the counter reading the *Racing Form*.

"Uncle Tom and Aunt Jemima. In their hearts they are still," Garnet swallows the word like a mouthful of dry bagel and then coughs it out, "slaves, slaves, slaves. Zack was *white!* She's *white!* Of course he'd run. Why didn't she?"

"She sounds devoted to Miss Lady."

"The Miss Lady you described to me?" Garnet says. "Going to sell her son? Girl, let me tell you what that sort of devotion is. That is pure fear. I don't know how people pretend it's anything but fear."

Garnet lowers her voice. "Sometimes I don't understand how our people pretend to like white people at all."

Across the table, her innocent friend looks stunned. Her innocent, maybe-white, hopes-she's-white blind baby friend.

"You're all right though," Garnet says.

"You'd say that," Perdita says.

"I'd be nicer to you if I didn't like you."

Perdita half-smiles, a little uncertainly.

"At Penn Station last night?" Perdita says, and tells a familiar story of porters and cabs. "It was terrible. I was humiliated." *She* was humiliated, Garnet thinks. "Garnet, I apologize to you. Of course you want to be treated like everybody else."

"Well, thank you, I do."

"It's not right at all. I understand about passing."

That's too kind of her, but Garnet won't tromp on Perdita about it now. "Don't want to change the world. Just want to work for the House of Windsor."

"When I'm out with them," Perdita says, "I mean with the, the servant Churches, what should I expect? More of that?"

Innocent Perdita doesn't even know that *servant's* code for *slave*. "That was nothing. And don't call them servants. Call them employees."

"They're not employees either, they're all one family together. Literally, Garnet."

"What a surprise, girl.— I'll take those pictures up to Frog Jaw. He can get them developed today and you can show them to your Aunt Louisa. You get her to say the right thing and shut everyone up."

"I hope it's the true thing," Perdita says.

Well, that might be a little much to ask.

Perdita

PERDITA SENDS GARNET off with the films. Back at home, she calls Aunt Louisa to invite her for lunch Sunday. Then she goes through her messages.

Miss Gibson has called again. She's making a movie, *Saved from the Titanic.* She wants Perdita in it because Perdita is a survivor. Perdita hisses and drops the message in the trash.

Miss Alden has called and wants to see her; that she has to do. She leaves a message with Mr. Johnson's office, giving Miss Alden's telephone number in case something happens with Dr. John.

She takes a horse-cab through Central Park to Miss Alden's apartment on the Upper East Side; the driver goes slowly so she can enjoy the trees and sunshine. All she can smell is lilac, and all she can think of is lilac in her cabin on *Titanic.*

She thinks of the song she heard over the water, one wavering violin, then the second violin, the viola and the cello joining in. They played popular songs to keep people from panicking, and then they played the truth: We are all going to die.

Get Wallace Hartley to play for you; he was a real musician.

"I AM SO SORRY," Miss Alden says, "you have traveled so far and suffered so much."

Charlotte Alden's apartment is full of sunlight and twittering birds. The birds suddenly sound louder, a roar. Miss Alden takes her arm and sits her down.

"You are taking me off the program because I *survived?*"

"It is *Titanic,*" Miss Alden says. "Haven't you heard what's being written about the women on *Titanic*? 'VOTES FOR WOMEN when things go easily—BOATS FOR WOMEN when men had to die.' It is always like that," Charlotte Alden says bitterly, "they pamper us and then blame us; they are heroes and we are children. *Women* are saying this! 'Useful men should have been saved in preference to women, who are no good except for shopping. The women should have stood back and given an example of heroism.' So the board voted not to ask you, as a survivor, to play in this concert. It would be too hard on you. You lived, dear, that's the important thing. You will have other chances. If there's anything I can do for you—"

"I blame myself for not staying on the ship," Perdita says.

"Oh, surely, dear, that's too much. They are thinking of Ben Guggenheim and Colonel Astor and Mr. Straus, that's all, and want to recognize them as heroes; they died for the women and children. We don't all need to be Mrs. Straus. You have a child."

"Miss Alden, I do blame myself. But *examples of heroism*— Who talks about what the mothers said to their children, those last few minutes before the ship sank? Who talks about that heroism?"

"Well, of course—"

"Miss Alden, who should have been heroic and insisted that *Titanic* have enough lifeboats? Who should have told Mr. Ismay to stop the ship and wait for morning? *Blame* people for surviving, Miss Alden? Everyone might have survived if people had been heroic enough. Had just been responsible. Aren't we suffragists asking to be responsible too? Isn't that what the vote means?"

"I know, of course I do, yes of course women's lives, the lower classes' lives, count for as much as Jack Astor's or the Widener men, and it was criminal to have so few lifeboats. But it's the wrong time to say so."

"When is the right time?"

"I understand you're disappointed."

"I didn't choose," Perdita says. "I was not heroic. I didn't do the right thing, I didn't stay, I didn't listen, I let myself go on a boat, I didn't even take a child with me on my lap, as if," though it is not her place to blame anyone else, "as if it weren't my place to think or be responsible or make choices. And I am alive now and they are dead and I did the wrong thing and I didn't even decide to do it, I was not even cowardly by choice."

"My dear, you must not blame yourself—"

She can't stop. She should just let Miss Alden throw her off the program, this is her perfect excuse not to play when her hands aren't in shape for it, but she can't stop. "I feel as though I have not really survived. The best part of me has not survived. I feel like Bruce Ismay. But that does not make it right for anyone to tell me what I should do and think and feel. It does not make me unfit for the vote, Miss Alden, or unfit to play music, or unfit to choose ever again, it makes me guilty but that is no excuse not to do something. I was wrong but I will not be silent. Isn't it up to us to learn to think for ourselves, to care for ourselves, to mourn for ourselves, to know we were wrong, but to say ourselves that the men cannot choose how we live and die? Or are we to be always considered all thoughtless and selfish or all good and sacrificing, fit to be governed only by someone else, our lives to be determined by someone else, and for us to go along so completely we don't even know it?"

Charlotte Alden says nothing for a long moment. "You don't have to talk to me as if I were some man!"

"Women died," Perdita says. "Children died. They were us, Miss Alden. I must say something. I must choose to say something. And the only way I have to speak is to play."

ᐰᐰᐰ

SHE HAS FAILED, utterly failed. She has lied about being fit to play music, lied about everything except it's the only thing she has and she has to do something. She walks back through the park; she is so shaken she doesn't even want to take a taxi.

Her hands are still bandaged. She hasn't played since *Titanic*.

But if she can't do music? She must do something. She doesn't know what.

Who is she to talk like that? What does she think she can say?

At home, the piano is waiting in the music room like a challenge.

She sits at the piano, not playing.

Tomorrow she will hear Aunt Louisa's story.

Garnet is right; Aunt Louisa will say that she married a white man. The only thing Perdita is doing is getting for herself and Toby a place on the lifeboat of whiteness.

And that is what she should do.

But.

Perdita will not make Toby go through the same things as the black Churches and Garnet and Blind Willie do.

But.

She will not make him lie, the way Alexander does.

But.

She leans her elbows on the closed fallboard and leans her head against her wrists.

But what? Is whiteness just a lifeboat that she and Toby will escape on?

Surely not if she really belongs on it?

A visitor is buzzed in, a Mrs. Oliver van Rensselaer from the Titanic Relief Society. Mrs. van Rensselaer asks how she is holding up. "Your husband was on *Titanic*?" she asks. "I am so sorry for your loss."

"He isn't dead."

"Oh," says Mrs. van Rensselaer. She sounds as if she disapproves of his surviving.

"He got off at Queenstown," Perdita says. She's making excuses for Alexander's survival to this woman she doesn't even know.

"Oh," says Mrs. van Rensselaer. Yes, she is, she's disappointed, this horrible stranger was looking for a dead hero and a mourning widow and hasn't got them.

"I was the one who got on the lifeboat and survived," Perdita says. "I left children on board, like Bruce Ismay."

There is a silence Perdita can't read, and then Mrs. van Rensselaer laughs nervously as if Perdita has made a vulgar joke. "Let me tell you why I've come. The Relief Society is raising funds for the families of the victims. We're having a benefit to provide the women and children with clothes and transportation and a start in life. Caruso is singing." A bit of Perdita hopes she's being asked to play; she swats that down. "As a fellow sufferer and a musical person—I see your piano—may we count on you to take some tickets, and to ask your friends to support us as well?"

Perdita duly writes a check for two tickets, holding the pen between thumb and fingers. This is the first time she's used her hands to write. It hurts.

"It's a very good thing for them," Mrs. van Rensselaer chatters on. "The women will actually have better clothes and better prospects than if they hadn't been shipwrecked. It gets them enormous sympathy—you can't imagine how much we have raised already! We have a perfect mountain of Teddy bears!"

"Tell me," Perdita says, blotting the check; this conversation is like picking a scab. "If I were a black woman, would you be asking me to take tickets?"

"No black woman would care to attend," Mrs. van Rensselaer says. "It's not their kind of music."

๛๛๛

WHAT CAN SHE DO, Perdita thinks when Mrs. van Rensselaer has left.

What can she do.

She must talk to Aunt Louisa.

But first she'll apologize to a friend.

On her way, she goes to St Vincent's to check in on Dr. John. Outside St. Vincent's the sea-chill blows through the streets. For a moment she feels the thrum of the deck of *Titanic;* then she shakes her head and goes in.

There are even more flowers in the halls than this morning, more stink of flash-powder in the air. The patients have been given their lunch; she smells steamed vegetables, beef and potatoes, hot linen napkins, and hears momentarily again engines thrashing behind the walls. "Are you one of the survivors?" a reporter asks her. She blind-canes past him, determinedly not hearing him, then thinks that she is probably contributing to prejudice about blind people being deaf. She is doing nothing right.

"He is the same," Dr. John's nurse says.

"I've come to sit with him for a bit."

"His family is here too. You look pale. Would you like something to eat? Some Coca-Cola? Tea?"

Coca-Cola. She hasn't had any since the last time she was in America. The nurse goes away to bring her some.

No way to talk with Dr. John. All the Churches are there but Arbella: Mr. Otis, Aunt Jane, Miss Fan, Mr. Jeff. Mr. Jeff rises to give her his seat. They sit as if they're at service, listening to Dr. John's rasping breath. Miss Fan clasps Perdita's hand. It doesn't hurt as much as it would have a few days ago, which is half-encouraging and half-sad. She drinks her soda silently. Nobody says anything. They don't miraculously leave her to talk with him. He doesn't miraculously wake and speak. There is no moment of truthfulness. They all sit there until she leaves.

She goes downstairs to have her hands looked at, and is given salve and medicated gloves to wear instead of bandages. Tentatively, painfully, she moves her fingers one by one. She might even have been able to play something, if she had still been on the NAWSA program.

Outside, she checks the time, feeling first for her blind watch; without it she's adrift. She has to ask a passerby. Three o'clock.

By now, Blind Willie will be at the Tiger.

෭෭෭

MINETTA STREET SMELLS LIKE A WC, urine and horse-dung; she twitches her skirt up to keep the hem clean. Minetta Street is the center of the Black-and-Tan clubs in New York, one of the few places in the city where a white woman and a black man can play at the same piano. Of course, almost nobody comes here except for sex, so she sweeps her new cane ostentatiously from side to side of the broken sidewalk, grateful for once to be blind and therefore unattractive.

Good luck. "Hey, pretty! I got something amazin' for you! Want to feel it?"

"You get out of my way, I'm Blind Willie Williams's granddaughter."

"Blind Willie? You ain't his grandbaby, I know that gal."

"I'm Susan. The other one." Mr. Williams actually has a granddaughter named Susan; he had a granddaughter, at least. Susan was white enough to pass and Susan disappeared long ago across the color line.

"You Garnet's sister?"

"Cousin. And don't you get Blind Willie after you. He has a gun. You don't want to cross a blind man with a gun."

What Harry and Uncle Bucky would think of her knowing Minetta Street this well. When she and Blind Willie first started teaching each other piano tricks, they had difficulty meeting anywhere. It was scandal even at John Brown's that a white woman should sit at the same piano bench with a black man. A white man explained to her once that black men got excited from sitting down on a bench that a white woman had sat on; it was the warmth of her derrière that excited them, dear Heavens. Willie and she play four-hands, too, which means reaching over and under each other's arms and bumping elbows and such. Scandalous.

But Susan Williams scandalized no one; she was just another black woman, meeting her grandfather for piano lessons at a Black-and-Tan because Susan was passing. People at the Tiger gave Susan the same kindness Garnet depends on now, the kindness of people who will never give her away.

It was a game then for Perdita to play at black. She was shamming and could go back to herself at the end of the afternoon.

She thinks about the Jouvet apartment in Paris and the elegant Riverside Drive apartment uptown, and hopes for the right truth.

She pushes open the door of the Tiger. Mary Margaret McGee, the bartender, calls out to her. "That you, Susan girl? Haven't seen you in dog's age."

"Yes, it's me, Mary Mags; is Blind Willie here?"

"Right over here, grandbaby, right here in this corner having me a beer this nice afternoon. Sit you down. Start out with, lemme see your hands, Garnet says your hands all done in." He runs his fingers over hers. "What you do to you? I got something for you." He passes her a round-cornered tin box. "Rub it in your fingers."

The familiar greasy, leathery smell takes her right back to the Institute. Bag Balm. It's been years since she thought of Bag Balm. They don't have it in France.

"Buy you a beer?"

Susan Williams drinks beer.

They sit in their corner and Blind Willie gossips about New York things, new restaurants, new musicians. "That Jim Europe set himself up a music agency, Clef Club. That boy always want to be in charge of things. Scotty Joplin finished his opera, got some folks to sing it but it ain't hit Broadway yet, don't think it ever will. You been to Joel Rinaldo's restaurant? Joel's started doin' tamales, man, real Mexican hot stuff, an' he got some good new players up there. Always looking for folks to play gigs. I got to get me a gig there. How's Paris doing for ya?"

"They hate Americans." Not as much as Americans hate black people.

"Ain't nobody love a musician."

Perdita massages her right hand with her left.

"Knew you were coming to New York," Willie says casually, "started workin' up that Schubert, thought we could play it. I got me some real troubles with the fingering."

"I can't play it now," she says soberly.

"Hands?"

"Hands and. Everything. Willie, I don't know what to do with my life."

"Tough thing to happen."

"I should have stayed on *Titanic*. There was someone I should have talked to, while the boat was going down. I did everything wrong."

"Course you feel bad. Course you do."

Somebody's got to die, he sings softly. *Somebody's got to mourn. Somebody's got to feel real bad. Somebody's got to die and somebody's got to feel real sad, Well, she's gone to the graveyard, best girl I ever had.*

"Only don't you go to no graveyard before your time. So," he says, "what you think of Garnet, getting herself a job like that and all?"

"What do you think?"

"She got to do her thing."

"Of course she does."

"She movin' downtown. Going to have her a nice place like she always wanted. House of Windsor, they going to want her to go out to the theater evenings, show off they clothes."

"But who'll take care of you? Don't say you don't need anybody."

"Oh, we got that all worked out now. Garnet hire Liddy Boswick to be lookin' after me."

"Lydia *Boswick*?" she says, shocked.

"Ain't nothing wrong with old Liddy."

"Willie, she takes *opium*."

"Hash, honey, just hash. Ever'body takes a little hash. Don't keep her from cookin' fine," Blind Willie says easily. "Besides, I got me Sturgis. You didn't meet Sturgis proper. Say hello, Sturgie."

A deep dozy woof echoes from underneath the table.

"Willie, Sturgis is a *dog*."

"He a finer dog than anything natural. He lead me like the kindly light. I'll loan him to ya someday, you gonna want you one just like him—No, I'm lying, you try him now, let's us take him round the block."

"You're changing the subject, Willie. You need someone better than Liddy Boswick."

"You let me and Garnet fix that," Blind Willie says.

"I will not. I don't want anything happening to you."

She wants to invite him to stay at the Riverside Avenue apartment if he needs a place to stay. To her shame, the words won't come out. What if he isn't welcome?

"Sturgie, take us blind folk round the block? You show off for us, you can have some beer."

Sturgis whoofs. Perdita leans down while Sturgis sniffs her outstretched hands and sneezes at the smell of Bag Balm. Sturgis is large and has beery dog breath and his fur sticks out in tufts.

He is the very Liddy Boswick of dogs.

They can't even walk round the block together, not even in Minetta Street; when the two of them go out the front door and Blind Willie shows her how to hold Sturgis's handle, the comments start. "You got you a fine little white thing, Willie?" "You let my grandbaby be," Willie says, but the two of them give up on the street and practice walking with Sturgis through the festering trash in the alley behind the Tiger. From the way Sturgis smells and lurches, you'd think he couldn't make it across the street without a stein and a stop to rest, but he's really wonderful, like a living cane. She takes painful hold of Sturgis's handle—"take a hold on just like a subway strap"—and Sturgis leads her, padding and weaving round the piles of muck, like real proper eyes.

"He c'n cross streets just like a man."

"How'd you train him?"

"Didn't. He a herd dog. Come from a cowboy friend of mine down by Caldwell, Texas. He got a trick for herdin' but he too lazy to run."

"I do want one like him."

Back in the Tiger, Sturgis gulps down a bowl of beer and plops under the table, gurgling intestinally. They show each other new piano tricks and talk about Schubert. Neither of them has sight enough to follow fingering by eye, so piano lessons for both of them involve holding each other's hands and feeling finger-shapes. The men at the next table make rude comments.

"Don't you go gettin' a mouth on y'all," Blind Willie says, "you respect this girl. Her hands all scrouched up from saving her own life an' nearly freezin', she still play better than y'all. Show 'em how you play that blues, girl."

"Yeah, shatcha mouth," Mary Margaret says. "You show 'em, girl. Give us something."

She can't play.

She can't play. She sits down at the piano with her hands in their medicated gloves; drowned children are sitting round the piano, and if she played she would play for them, but what can she play? The pretty trained hands she used to have, all her pretty music, they're no use, what she wants to do for them is jump up and cry out like a musician, *Save yourselves, don't panic, we'll play for you.* What will she say, what can she say, about drowning? There is no place in music for *Titanic,* for a boy who wanted to play soccer but died in the ice, for Miss Fan screaming for her husband, for Dr. John throwing her in the boat with their last words unsaid. *Save yourselves or you will die.*

"What you got, girl?"

"Come on, you give us some music, jazz girl."

"I can't."

She sits there at the piano bench with no music in her. *What you got, girl?* Nothing. A little talent and no heart. In the darkness, in the lifeboats, with the screams echoing in their heads, someone burned a straw hat for light. The light did not change the darkness; out of the darkness the voices still called *Help,* and there was no help. Music is a straw hat burning. She has nothing to give. There is no truth here. This nothing. This drowning.

"I can't, I can't." She gets up and feels her way back to the table.

"I play for you then," Blind Willie says.

He gets up and pats her shoulder, feels his way to the piano. He plays, "Jesus Lover of My Soul," *Don't!* she whispers. *I was playing that when we hit the iceberg!* but he keeps on, the bass line rumbling like ice and iron, *while the waters round me roll,* and she lays her head on the table, lays her head on her arms right there in the spilled beer and stickiness, and tries not to cry. Mary Mags comes out from behind the bar and sits next to her, hugs her and lets her cry against her comfortable shoulder; and then very softly, when Blind Willie is done, Mary Mags begins to sing in her old cracked voice *that* hymn, the only hymn anyone is singing in all New York this week, and the people in the bar begin to sing with her, the men in the booth who have been making fun of her and Willie, the old rummies at the bar:

Nearer my God to Thee
Nearer to Thee
E'en though it be a cross
That raiseth me...

It's all a lie, she thinks. Music is a lie; God Himself is a lie. Where was He when the children drowned?

What is music, what is God, who is Perdita?

"You get your hands, we play some good funeral music like we used to play for the folks in N'awlins. You ever heard N'awlins funeral music? I teach you some."

Going uptown in the subway, she stares at her plaster-white gloved hands. She doesn't recognize them. She has no idea what they should do.

ॐॐॐ

"YOU COME TO CHURCH WITH ME."

Sunday morning Garnet shows up blithely in a new spring hat.

"I don't want to go to church." Church will mean sermons and "Nearer, My God, to Thee."

"You come anyway; Clementine Daniels and I are having breakfast after. I bet we can find a church in Harlem that won't care white folks drowned."

Perdita calls Mr. Johnson's office, telling his clerk where they'll be. Dr. John hasn't got worse but hasn't woken. They walk uptown, holding their hats against the spring wind off the Hudson.

"Garnet," Perdita says as they walk, "*Liddy Boswick?*"

"She was available."

"Of course she's available. Garnet, she has *habits*—"

"That won't bother Grandpa any."

"I know it won't, he'll drink and puff right along with her. Garnet, she," Perdita is speechless. When she first came to New York, she had no idea what a social disease was. She'd thought it might be an overpolite word for a cold. "Garnet, that woman probably has— fleas."

"She got 'em from Sturgie, then."

"No. You've got to do better. I'll pay if it's money. I have money from touring." That is the only meaning she can find in music this morning; people have paid her money to play; she can save Blind Willie from being looked after by Liddy. "I don't mean to interfere but he's my teacher."

"You know Grandpa. He doesn't want anyone competent and respectable. It'd mean he needed someone."

"You mean the only competent person he wants is you."

"Yes!" Garnet bursts out. "And I'm not going to wait until he's— Well, I won't. Opportunities don't wait."

"But not Liddy. Please."

They walk on, Garnet's hand on Perdita's arm, until Garnet abruptly stops, as if they've reached a curb.

"Is it my fault?" she says. "People keep talking about being a good black woman, or a bad black woman, as if having a certain skin and hair gave them a right to tell me who I should be. It's like, 'Girl, sail right or you're going to be smash like *Titanic*, that white iceberg is going to roll right over you.' But it's them, they're pushing me toward the iceberg and the iceberg toward me," Garnet takes her hand away and claps her hands together angrily, "and if I don't smash the first time, they'll keep pushing until I wreck, and then they'll say 'Oh isn't that a tragedy, poor light-skinned woman trying to pass.' But it's all their tragedy, you know? They made it. They can keep it. I just want my life."

"Garnet, *Titanic* isn't a story," Perdita says. "Don't talk as if it is. Let me help with Willie."

"You leave my business to me."

"I'll put him up in the apartment."

"No, you won't. That'd be a scandal. You can't do that, not now."

They go to St. Peter's, the church that started all this migration toward Harlem by buying land and building a row of decent houses for its parishioners. But the preacher gives his sermon on "A String of Pearls," the famous $100,000 pearl necklace lost on *Titanic*. The string of pearls of great price is the path that leads us up to Jesus. "Say amen!" The congregation shouts "Amen!" And then the choir sings "Jesus, Lover of My Soul"—

Let me to Thy bosom fly
While the waters round me roll

The bridge players are clapping in the lounge. *Steward, get me some ice!* Perdita clenches her stiff hands and waits the music out.

∾∾∾

AFTER CHURCH they go out for coffee and beignets with Clementine Daniels. Today it's warm and they sit outside at sidewalk tables, French-style. Mrs. Daniels, talking in her educated voice instead of the one she uses with the Churches, reports that she has been learning about Fair Home, which according to Miss Arbella is Paradise on earth for "colored folks." Off duty, Clementine Daniels has a talent for sarcasm. "Dr. John treats everyone so *good*," Clementine Daniels imitates Arbella's enthusiastic bird-voice, "ain't *no*body *ever* want to leave.— The poor child! She has been learning about horse-breeding from Otis Church, the trainer, and from Miss Lady. But the child has never been to school."

"Ignorant as pitch," Garnet agrees. "Southerners. Oh, look who's coming," she says disgustedly. "Hello, Frog Jaw."

Mr. Johnson looks sleek and resplendent in a churchgoing suit even Perdita can tell is well-fitting. He pulls up a chair and joins them.

"Have you got Perdita's pictures? Have you got news?"

He lays the copies of the picture on the table.

"Thank you, Mr. Johnson. I'm giving Aunt Louisa lunch today and I'll show these to her."

"We haven't found the divorce decree yet. When exactly did they get married?"

"The Friday of the draft riots." Aunt Louisa and Dr. John married when the fires were still smoldering. Just days before, they had rescued children, leaving the Colored Orphan Asylum burning. *Oh, Mamma, help,* the little voices cry. All the engaged people among the survivors of *Titanic* are getting married right away, this week, and Aunt Louisa and John Rolfe Church married the week of the riots.

What could have driven them apart when they had survived that?

"His Army payments end a month later," Mr. Johnson says. "He took another job or left the city."

"And she moved out West. She must have divorced there," Perdita says. "She doesn't even approve of divorce. She wouldn't have done it in front of her family."

"Try to find out when and where."

MRS. DANIELS HELPS WITH LUNCH, providing eyes. ("Don't you mind, Miss Perdita, detectives work all hours.") Poor little Arbella is pressed into service laying the cloth in the dining room while Mrs. Daniels plates the lunch and Perdita waits nervously for Aunt

Louisa. While she waits, she gets her magnifying glass out and takes another look at the picture.

Understanding pictures isn't something she's good at, but this much she can see: Bright Isaac is just as white as his half-brother.

What must he have thought, what must he have felt! His brother would go to war and be a hero; he would hold the horses. His brother would own the land and the horses he loved. Zack would be owned, like a horse.

No wonder he took Whirlwind.

No wonder he took his brother's name.

Nothing else would have been fair.

Wasn't it a risk? But wasn't that who he'd always been in his heart, learning his brother's lessons, wearing his brother's clothes? Wasn't his whole life a risk?

She remembers Garnet saying *I was always Nanette. Just no one knew.*

Life after death. Freedom.

She sits at the piano, not playing, but stretching her fingers painfully.

Who would he want to marry?

He'd marry a white woman, like his brother would.

❧❧❧

"HELLO, DEAR! Are you keeping strong? I've brought Opal and Betty along, just to cheer you up."

Opal is Aunt Louisa's lawyer and Betty is her maid. Oh *no.* Aunt Louisa was supposed to come alone.

"We won't stay long," Opal Lee says, "but I've brought your insurance forms for White Star and Betty has brought you a cake."

"Oh Miss," Betty says, hugs her, and bursts into tears. "I made chocolate, Miss. Oh, the poor people!"

Aunt Louisa holds out her arms; Perdita falls into her familiar beloved embrace, wondering how she can make Opal and Betty go away.

Aunt Louisa is a winter wren, small and brisk and shabby at her jacket cuffs, but the shabbiness is merely that she has better things to do than clothes. Rich men have courted Aunt Louisa, even though they knew she was a divorced woman; she accepted none of them, but asked every one the name of his broker. Aunt Louisa owns stock in railroads, Western Union, Edison, AT&T, and now automobiles. For Perdita's Institute graduation, Aunt Louisa presented her with a modest string of pearls, a hundred shares of Ford stock, and an introduction to Aunt Louisa's own (female) broker and (female) lawyer, Opal.

Aunt Louisa gives half her income to women's suffrage, believes in Graham crackers and a vegetable diet, works tirelessly for many causes, and has four big white foofy poodles, the Girls, who eat meat and lie about all day having their hair brushed and their nails done. If dogs could vote, the Girls would certainly vote for the wrong party.

"Hur*rah* for you," Opal says in her deep voice, "I hear you shamed that spineless Charlotte Alden."

"The NAWSA women are complete idiots," says Aunt Louisa. "Sometimes I think all women are idiots except for us right here. You know, Opal, Perdita's making a huge success in Paris."

Perdita says nothing.

"We must make this right," Aunt Louisa says. "New York wants to hear you, dear."

"I can't play now."

"What are you putting on your hands?" Opal asks professionally. "My esthetician has a marvelous healing cream."

Aunt Louisa has brought St.-John's-wort tea and Graham crackers; they have tea and talk about Roosevelt and Taft and Wilson, all running for President. Which would they vote for if women could vote? Who is more sympathetic to women? Roosevelt is sympathetic to black people, Perdita does not say. Poor Taft is devastated to have lost his advisor Archie Butt on *Titanic;* he has given up campaigning entirely.

Betty eventually goes back downtown to Washington Square to walk the Girls and Opal leaves for her dancing class at Cooper Union. It is odd that a lawyer does esthetic dancing; but women lawyers are women and why not dance?

With the others gone, Mrs. Daniels serves perfect mushroom-and-cheese omelettes and salad. Perdita closes the glass doors, sits down, and tells Aunt Louisa all the story. The two John Rolfe Churches in Paris. *Bury me at Fair Home, they cannot deny a dead man.* The scars on his back. (She listens for reaction from Aunt Louisa, but hears none.) Dr. John, the second John Church, who identified the first as Bright Isaac, the slave.

Perdita holds out the photograph.

"Here they are, both of them. Aunt Louisa, what concerns me is that both of them look white, and both of them used the same name." She takes a deep breath. "You must tell me. Which one did you marry?"

At this moment Arbella comes in with coffee. Neither of them says anything until she's gone.

"Dear, you concern me," Aunt Louisa says when they're alone again. "I almost hear you expressing prejudice."

"It is prejudice. I hope it's not mine. But I don't want Toby to choose between being American and being human."

She is conscious she's instructing Aunt Louisa what to say. She can't do that. "Aunt Louisa, whatever you tell me about your marriage, I am prepared to hear it. No matter what it is. I shall say what I have to, but I would like the truth."

Aunt Louisa takes the picture and looks at it, but says nothing.

Oh, to have Alexander or Garnet here, anyone who can see; oh, to have someone look at Aunt Louisa while she recognizes the man who was her husband! Has Mrs. Daniels found some way to watch Aunt Louisa? No, she's in the kitchen; she can hear but she can't see. In complete silence, for what seems like years, Aunt Louisa looks at the picture. Which one? The right one, for everyone's sake—

"Of course I married the white one," Aunt Louisa says. "There is nothing to concern you at all."

"There would be no shame if it had been different," Perdita says. "Only if Toby felt in any way lessened— I couldn't choose that for him as his mother. You know."

"I do know, and it doesn't matter, dear, because I married the white man."

Of course she'd say that, Perdita's inner Garnet says. If Perdita believed Aunt Louisa, she'd say something relieved. She says nothing. Neither of them has remarked on what Aunt Louisa has just admitted, that Perdita is her granddaughter.

"I'm sorry to ask this," Perdita says, "but there have been rumors—Uncle Bucky's been speaking to me."

"My brother is an idiot," Aunt Louisa says.

"Would you write that down? I don't mean Uncle Bucky's an idiot. Which one you married."

"Right now, dear," Aunt Louisa says. "Do you have a pen?"

Perdita doesn't know whether she does or not; they find a pencil by the telephone. Aunt Louisa sits down at the dining-room table and scratches out a half-page of writing. "There. Look. I've written on the back of the picture: I married John Rolfe Church of Fair Home. I'm circling him on the front." Another scratch and flourish. "I'm putting it back in this envelope. And that will take care of my brother."

Perdita takes the envelope in both hands. "Thank you." But are they telling each other the truth, or is Aunt Louisa simply protecting Perdita and Perdita letting her do it, getting herself and Toby into the white lifeboat?

"Give Bucky a copy. Make him beg for it. He should never have married Violet, he hasn't had a thought of his own for thirty years. Did he say 'it will reflect badly on the family'?"

They sit for a moment, neither of them saying the next thing. The envelope feels as stiff and important as Uncle Bucky himself.

"Aunt Louisa, now this is done, between you and me, I want to ask you. Why did you leave your husband? And why did you give Mamma away?"

"Do you have another copy of that picture?" Aunt Louisa says. "I should like to have one. He looks so young."

"I'll have one made right away. But, Aunt Louisa, why?"

"John is here in New York?"

"He's in St Vincent's, but ill."

"I would like to sit with him, if I may. I mistreated him," Aunt Louisa says. "I did very badly by him."

"His family is here," she says, and hesitates, because she has to give this other news as well, and it will distract Aunt Louisa from answering. "I am sorry, Aunt Louisa. He has married again. His wife's with him."

"His wife?" Aunt Louisa says. "Oh no. No." She jumps up. "But that's impossible."

"I am sorry."

"No, dear, you don't understand, it is much worse than *sorry*. It's really impossible. The poor woman!" Aunt Louisa gets to her feet. "Dear, I must go. I must talk to Opal."

"What is wrong?"

"I have made a horrible mistake! I shall never forgive myself!" Aunt Louisa is almost crying. "John is still married to me! I never divorced him!"

ॐॐॐ

PERDITA WALKS A SHAKING AUNT LOUISA to the subway.

"I was foolish!" Aunt Louisa says. "I had religious scruples about divorce! I was thinking in a conventional manner! I wrote him at his Army office, I told him I *would* divorce him, but when it came to the act itself— I am completely to blame for this."

"Miss Fan and he aren't married?"

"The poor woman! We must help her. But heavens, what can be done? I must ask Opal right away."

"What got between you and him? *Why give away Mamma? Please tell me.*"

"He wasn't to blame at all. The shame my child would have felt, the child of a broken marriage— That was my only reason. No more than you would have your Toby suffer, would I have had a child of mine suffer. I was *never* ashamed."

"I understand."

"But now— I must do something immediately, whatever I can."

Perdita leaves her at the subway and walks back toward Riverside Drive, stunned, devastated.

She has the photograph with Dr. John's face circled. She has Aunt Louisa's letter on the back. Toby is safe. She is safe. Whatever the morality of the lifeboat of whiteness, she and Toby are on it.

But.

I understand, she's reassured Aunt Louisa because one cannot criticize people's reasons at such a moment; but give your baby away? To save the child *shame*?

She doesn't understand. And she is afraid she does.

Aunt Louisa says she married the right one and there was nothing wrong. She says it was all her fault.

But Aunt Louisa gave away Mamma.

Perdita walks up and down the gravel path of Riverside Park and tries to make up a story that would explain how Aunt Louisa could give away her child.

Perdita was sent from Arizona to Boston when she was only five, to be trained as a blind person, but she wasn't sent *away*, has never felt sent *away*, no one in her family would do that. She cannot explain it, it does not make sense. Aunt Louisa is a suffragist and has marched and talked in front of big unfriendly audiences and spent nights in jail. Wouldn't even a very young Aunt Louisa have faced down shame and kept her child?

I was never ashamed, Aunt Louisa said.

Perdita stares out over the blur of the Hudson. She herself talked to Aunt Louisa about Toby, about how being black might make her little boy feel ashamed of himself; how she wants to save him from that.

Aunt Louisa took my story, Perdita thinks, and she changed it around to be divorce instead of blackness, and she fed it back to me.

When Aunt Louisa talked about her reason for giving her child away, was she telling the truth?

What could Dr. John have done to make Aunt Louisa, who loved him, feel she had to divorce him?

But if she married Isaac unknowingly—

When would Aunt Louisa have found out her husband was a black man?

On her wedding night, when she touched his scars.

And the next morning she left him.

❧❧❧

SHE SHOULD WRITE TO ALEXANDER and tell him about this. There was a telegram from him that she should find and answer. But nothing is in a proper place in this apartment yet; letters and postcards are on every flat surface, overflowing the basket where Garnet put them, mixed with the scores in the music room, and she can't find it now.

She telephones Mr. Johnson and checks for news instead, then tells him the whole story, being discreet because she's on the phone.

"I was hesitating about calling you since it's Sunday," Mr. Johnson says, "but I have some information for you and someone you should meet. I recognized one of the faces in that picture you showed me, and I've just called on his widow."

"His widow?"

"Mrs. Paul deMay. She lives here in New York and would like to see you tomorrow morning. She has a story for you about Fair Home."

Perdita has to think of the picture for a couple of minutes before she realizes who Paul deMay is.

The grinning young black man standing by Bright Isaac. Fate deMay's slave.

"Of course I'll come and see her."

"And come see me first. I have another story about Dr. John, and not a good one."

❧❧❧

"MISS FAN'S NOT MARRIED?" Garnet whispers.

"Ssh! We can't talk about it here, Arbella's in her room."

Sunday night. A week ago, she was just finishing dinner with the Churches on *Titanic.* Garnet and Blind Willie (and Sturgis the Dog Alcoholic) come over to have dinner with her, Garnet through the front door, Willie through the back, which grieves her but Garnet insists on it. In the front room afterward, Perdita whispers to them what Aunt Louisa has said.

"But at least she said the right thing about you," Garnet says.

"She *said* it," Perdita says.

"Let me see."

Perdita brings out the picture with Aunt Louisa's note. "I'm going to get it photographed and get lots of copies and give one to Harry."

"You feel all right about everything now?"

"I want to believe her."

Garnet doesn't say anything.

After a while, Blind Willie clears his throat and asks what they played at church this morning. "'Jesus Lover of my Soul'? Bet they played it mincin' at that St Paul's. Down in N'awlins, coming back from the graveyard, we used to play those hymns smokin' to wake the dead. Where you got your piano?" Perdita opens the doors into the music room. "A whole room for just your piano? Girl." He sits down at the piano and begins to play. "You c'mon, sit down too. You just plunk me out some rhythm here, plenty of work for the both of us. Let's rouse us some souls."

He starts playing jazz, "c'mon, girl, you walk that bass for me," she sits down but hesitates; Willie reaches across her hands and slaps down chromatic howls and screams in the treble. "Come on, you just play what you can, just one finger if that's all you got. *Come on to the water*," he begins in his rough grinding voice, and Garnet sings too:

Come right on into that water, children,
Come on to the water
Gonna be baptized in the water...

"Shush!" Garnet says. "I think I hear someone coming."

It's Miss Fan and all the rest of them. Perdita jumps off the piano bench, leaving Mr. Williams there alone. She tries to look especially white. I am white, Perdita reminds herself. Aunt Louisa married Dr. John. She wrote on the picture saying so.

"Good evening, Miss Fan, Mr. Jeff; how is Dr. John?"

What will happen to Miss Fan if Dr. John doesn't survive and Miss Fan isn't his wife?

"They are doing a little procedure," Miss Fan's voice shakes. "They asked us to leave."

"I going back to watch him soon," Mr. Otis says.

"Have you eaten? You must eat. This is a pianist friend, Mr. William Williams, and of course my friend Nanette you know. What a coincidence, both of them named Williams."

"I been playing some good old holy hymns," Blind Willie says smoothly. "Would some gospel music soothe ya?" He starts playing again, as well-behaved as any honey-fed angel, "Lead Kindly Light." Perdita and Garnet retreat to the kitchen to hunt something to eat. Clementine Daniels, bless her, has left brown bread and four kinds of cheese and a meat pie, and lemonade and beer. They come back with the serving-trolley to hear all the Churches singing soft and low, "Abide with Me."

Mr. Jeff is going back to Virginia. "I hope to see Papa fully restored to health and with us at Fair Home," he says bravely to his mother, and accepts a sandwich and a bottle of beer as he goes off.

Miss Fan retires to rest, Mr. Williams goes off to a gig, and Garnet leaves too, pointedly in the other direction.

So Perdita's alone with Mr. Otis and Jane Church. "We'll go to our rooms, ma'am," Jane Church says.

"Oh, no, please stay." She hasn't had a chance to ask questions of Jane Church yet. She sits down in the chair next to hers and begins to talk with her about her son Isaac.

"He ran away from home, didn't he?" Perdita prompts.

"I never understood that," Jane Church says.

"He didn't intend to gain his freedom?"

"But if it meant leaving Fair Home," Isaac's mother says. "He loved Fair Home. When he didn't come back from the fight at Manassas, we all thought he was dead."

"Don't you go talking about Zack, Mamma," Mr. Otis says. "No one want to hear about Zack."

Oh, yes, they do.

"After Manassas, all us folk went up to the railhead to find him and Mars' John and bring them home. There was a stream near the road and a little stone bridge. That stream ran red. I thought, his blood. My heart broke in two." She clears her throat. "We are going to find Miss Lady, we are going to bring her home. After Manassas, she held everything together. For all that time, Master John in that prison, both my boys gone, poor Master Fate dead, Miss Fan a widow before she's barely a wife? Miss Lady held it together. No one knows how strong that woman was. Truly we are as dew in the morning. The first fine time she ever had, she drowned."

Perdita shivers.

"Would you like to see my picture of my boys? If you can see a picture. I am sorry for your affliction. I have my picture of them with me, I always look at them and say my prayer for my boys before I go to sleep. Miss Arbella, would you kindly bring me my boys' picture for this poor crippled old woman? Bring Miss Lady too."

Arbella brings the pictures and Jane Church hands it to Perdita. Perdita tips the lampshade to give herself more light and focuses her new magnifier on the picture. But what she looks at is Aunt Jane's hands holding the picture. Aunt Jane's hands are pink.

Every single time Bright Isaac looked at his brother, what must he have felt? What must Miss Lady have felt? The family history is sitting right by her, old Aunt Jane who was young Jane once. Miss Lady's husband had his will with Jane, unless Jane gave in to him; and Jane's son looked too much like Miss Lady's son.

She cannot ask Aunt Jane more in front of Mr. Otis. But she can ask about the rest of them. "That is Dr. John, and your son, and the other white man must be Miss Fan's first husband."

"My grandpa," Arbella says. "Lieutenant Lafayette deMay."

"Who is the fourth man? The dark man?"

"Paul? Why you want to know about Paul?" Mr. Otis asks.

Because I'm seeing his wife tomorrow.

"Oh, poor boy, he died long ago," Aunt Jane says.

"He was uppity," Mr. Otis says.

"Here, this is my lady when she was young," Aunt Jane says, handing her another photograph. "This is my Miss Lady."

And there she is, Miss Lady, scowling, as if she were saying *Fetch my purple velvet coat! Fetch my fan with the ivory sticks!*

"You knew her on the boat, ma'am?"

Perdita nods wordlessly.

"Could you tell me how she died, ma'am?" Aunt Jane asks. "Miss Fan said she died well."

Suddenly it all comes over her, the heavy unwieldy wheelchair veering into the side of the corridor, the smoke and whiskey in the saloon, the cold outside the revolving doors and Miss Lady saying *I am dying for Miss Perdita.*

"Oh, ma'am, you all right?"

"Yes," Perdita says. "She died heroically. She and Dr. John both chose to stay— She gave me her place."

"Hers was a life of sacrifice." Aunt Jane reaches out to pat her arm. "Nobody knows the trials Miss Lady endured. Nobody knows how good she was."

"There weren't enough spaces for everyone. I should have known."

"Here, ma'am, you take my hand. I tell you something about her."

Perdita reaches out a hand and takes Aunt Jane's. "I didn't even think about her," Perdita says helplessly. I thought she was putting on airs, dramatizing herself. But she was dying.

"She wasn't easy, Miss Lady. She did screech and carry on," Aunt Jane says, "worst woman in the world sometimes. Would you like a handkerchief, ma'am? I always kept a clean handkerchief for her," Aunt Jane says, and adds, choked, "never get to give her a handkerchief again."

"Thank you." Aunt Jane hands over a handkerchief, soft cotton; when Perdita holds it to her eyes she feels a careful mend.

"I tell you something about Miss Lady," Aunt Jane says. "Her being crippled and all, and the only child? Her father hated her for that. Hated her like poison. She was not a kind woman or a nice woman. She tongue-lashed me to tears sometimes. But she gave and she gave, and nobody knew, not even herself, how strong she was at giving. I mean to bring Miss Lady back from Halifax, Miss Arbella and I, if the Lord wills that her body comes back to us. Take her to Fair Home to be buried. It's the last thing I can do for her. I've got my place in the graveyard and when it's my time I'll be buried beside her."

"You liked her," Perdita says, careful not to make it a question.

"Sometimes you get such a big gift, honey, you got to accept it. Comes like affliction sometimes but it's a blessing. Those are the holy gifts. She was a gift to me. You take your gift and you carry it with you, you treasure it and you accept it. You got to take it when you get it, and never say no."

They sit in silence. Aunt Jane's *gift?* That useless, spoiled woman?

Who died a hero.

Adelaide Landrum Church. A heroine of *Titanic.*

"Ma'am?" Aunt Jane says. "Miss Nanette says you're a famous pianist?"

"Not at all."

"She says you are. Did you ever play for my Miss Lady?"

No. She never did.

"I would be glad to hear you play, ma'am."

"I will play for you before you go."

"That'd be a pleasure to me, ma'am."

"And I'll ask my husband in Paris to send a picture of your son to you, if he can get one."

ꝯꝯꝯ

SHE GOES TO BED, hugging her pillow, and thinks. Half of her just wants to like Aunt Jane. Half of her has to think like a detective.

Aunt Jane is a good and loving woman. But her story is as wrong as Aunt Louisa's, and for the same reason: what happened to their children.

Aunt Jane talks as though Miss Lady is the most admirable woman who ever lived. Aunt Jane and Arbella are going to Halifax, a long journey for an old lady, to identify Miss Lady's body and bring it home.

But Miss Lady was going to sell Aunt Jane's son.

If anybody were going to sell Toby, Perdita would hit them with an ax, and throw clods on their coffin and dance.

Aunt Louisa gave away her child.

Aunt Jane somehow forgave her son being sold.

A holy gift?

They both are lying.

Mr. Otis W. Church

"PAUL," OTIS SAYS. "Why's she asking about Paul?"

They are all of them in the servants' rooms in back. Mamma has the biggest room and they're sitting there. Arbella has come in to help Mamma with her buttons.

"Who is that Paul deMay?" Arbella asks. "Was he my grandpappy's boy?"

"He was a friend of Isaac's," Mamma says. "Came to see us at Fair Home."

"He was uppity," Otis says. "Got himself killed."

"He got *killed?*" Arbella says, eyes wide.

"Shot."

"It was way before you were born, Miss Bella," Mamma says. "Nothing to do with us."

"Then why is Miss Perdita going to see his wife?"

"She going to see his *wife?*" says Otis.

"She said. I going to ask her why."

"Say 'I *am* going to ask her,' Miss Arbella. But you are not. You leave other folks' business to other folks."

"He knew my grandpappy deMay," Arbella kicks her heels against the leg of the bedroom chair. "It's my business. Miss Perdita and Miss Nanette want to take me shopping. I go shopping with them and I ask her about Paul."

"You stay out of that," Otis says. "I telling you, Miss Arbella. You start asking questions about that Paul and I ain't going to let you go down to the barn any more."

Arbella stares at him, eyes wide and filling with tears. "You can't do that."

"Never see them colts any more," Otis says. "Never again."

"You take that back," Arbella says. "You ain't nothing but a servant. You can't keep me from coming to the barn."

"You shush," Mamma tells her.

"I'm sorry, Uncle Otis," Arbella says after a moment. "But you take it back or I don't tell you what else I know about Mis' Baroness Perdita."

"What else you know?" Otis asks.

"Don't," Mamma says to him.

"You taking it back?" Arbella asks Otis.

"I taking it back."

"You all shush!" Mamma says.

"An old lady come to lunch," Arbella says. "Mis' Daniels and me, we serving. I come in with coffee and I hear something, I listen through the kitchen ceiling pipe. That old lady was Mis' Perdita's grandmother. Her name Louisa Church. And Mis' Louisa Church say Grandma Fan ain't married to Dr. John at all. Mis' Louisa Church is."

Perdita

"I HAD A COUPLE OF MY MEN go to visit Fair Home over the weekend," Mr. Johnson says. "A fine place, just what the Churches say it is. Green fields, handsome horses, plaques on the barn from the prizewinners they've raised."

Perdita has gone to visit him before her appointment with Mrs. deMay. One of Mr. Johnson's operatives has brought coffee and doughnuts and they are having breakfast.

"But—I don't know how to say this," Mr. Johnson says. "Our people are inclined to exaggerate how well the white people treat us, especially when we're talking *to* the white people. When you said that Dr. John treated his people well, I was expecting the field hands had doctoring on a Sunday and turkey at Christmas, but that's not how Fair Home is. My operative Fred Troutman, he's white, stayed at the Warren Green Hotel in Warrenton and asked about Fair Home, and all Fred was hearing was, 'Well, they are good folks, breed good horses, but that John Church do let his folk turn uppity.' Meanwhile his valet, who's my operative Liss Lincoln, was talking with the servants and hearing that Fair Home is the best place for black folk short of Heaven on Judgment Day. Our people are given responsibility there."

"Dr. John said they treat people well."

"And that is...gratifying," Mr. Johnson says slowly. "But from what you told me of Miss Lady, I would not have expected her to allow our people to rise high."

"She treated Miss Fan like her bond slave. And yet the woman who *was* her bond slave seems genuinely to like her."

"And Jane Church's other son, her black son, is Fair Home's head trainer."

Perdita blinks inwardly for a moment. "Mr. Otis is her son too?"

She has barely thought of Mr. Otis, apart from the horrible incidents with the porters and the taxi-cabs.

"Yes, her younger son."

Mr. Otis is old enough to have been born into slavery, which means Miss Lady had something to say about who his father was. And he's dark, which he must have got from his father. Miss Lady decided Aunt Jane's other son would not be mistaken for white.

"I do not understand these people, Mr. Johnson; do you? Miss Lady's husband had his way with Jane, Jane was Miss Lady's slave, Isaac was Miss Lady's son's slave, Miss Lady made sure that Aunt Jane's younger son couldn't run away as white, Miss Lady was going to sell Isaac. You would think the black people would whip out revolvers and shoot the white people. But everyone stays at Fair Home and they seem to like each other. Aunt Jane said she doesn't know why Isaac didn't stay, and Isaac even wanted to go back when he was dying, *Bury me at Fair Home.* Can anyplace be that wonderful? Is this a Southern thing?"

"I don't know, ma'am, my family comes from Albany. But it doesn't seem natural to me."

"Then what is the real story?"

There's a silence while the two of them think. Mr. Johnson takes another doughnut.

"I would counsel you to leave Fair Home to itself," Mr. Johnson finally says.

"You mean, not care, since Aunt Louisa says Toby and I are white?"

"It is a great advantage, being white."

"That's different from not caring."

Mr. Johnson considers.

"I heard a story," Mr. Johnson says, "years and years ago, and I might be just now hearing the other end of it. I think the story's about your Churches. And if it is, I'd let other people deal with them."

"Is this the bad story you heard about Dr. John?"

"You're sure you want to know?"

She doesn't want *not* to know.

"What do you know about Bull Run?" he asks. "Manassas?"

Dr. John and Fate and Isaac and Paul were there; that's all.

"What John Church told you about it wasn't so," Mr. Johnson says.

She doesn't understand. "He wasn't at Manassas? But he was."

"Not at the end he wasn't, ma'am. Manassas," Mr. Johnson says. "The first big battle of the War. Manassas railroad junction was the railhead for all of northern Virginia. The Union thought they could get control of the railhead, stop the trains, and be done with the war in a week. A whole church-picnic of Union civilians came down from Washington to get sight of the war before it was over.

"But the Union lost. The Confederates whipped them and the Yanks fled back toward Washington, higgledy-piggledy any way they could.

"Your Dr. John said that Yankee soldiers came back over the field and hauled prisoners away? Didn't happen. Your Dr. John lied."

"Why would he?"

"You were asking what your Aunt Louisa might object to, besides her husband being black?"

Perdita leans forward.

"An acquaintance of mine in Washington has made quite a study of the Battle of Bull Run because he was there, holding his own master's horse. Among the men on the battlefield, he said, was a Mr. Robert C.J. Champion Strounge, who was a notorious dealer in slaves. Mr. Champ Strounge had himself a reputation. If you had a strong young buck you meant to sell out of the neighborhood, you called Mr. Champ. He'd take them and sell them where no one would ever find them, and if they objected, Mr. Champ was known to like the whip."

The scars on Isaac's back. Perdita's eyes widen.

"I think Isaac was sold," Mr. Johnson says. "But not by Miss Lady. As my acquaintance was stealing his own master's horse and following the Union, he saw a Confed selling Mr. Champ Strounge a light-skinned slave who was wounded and unconscious. The Confed was a young man with a handsome young horse, a bay."

"*Dr. John* sold Isaac?"

"I think your Dr. John sold Isaac to this slave dealer right there on the battlefield, for folding cash, and took the money and rode to join the Union. My acquaintance thought it was very piquant a man would sell his slave for money to fight slavery."

"Dr. John let his people think Isaac ran? Let Isaac's *mother* think it?"

"Would your Aunt Louisa have left him if she found out he'd sold his own brother?"

"Oh, Mr. Johnson. In an instant."

There was nothing wrong. Nothing wrong with the child.

Only with the father. And it was not that he was black.

But give away her child?

To save the child the father's shame?

"But if Isaac were sold, why didn't he come back after the War?" Perdita asks.

"Because he was in Brazil. Some of the Confeds went to Brazil at the end of the war, and whoever bought him might have taken him there. The Brazilians didn't abolish slavery when we did."

"You mean Isaac didn't get free in 1865?"

"Ma'am, Brazil didn't abolish slavery till 1888."

Twenty-three years later. A lifetime.

"Oh no."

And Dr. John?

He must have thought he'd killed his brother.

"Isaac never came back," Perdita says, "and Dr. John thought he was dead. So Dr. John took care of everybody he hadn't taken care of before. He made Fair Home a place where black people could get their due."

"That would be as good an ending as that story could get."

"But it was too late." Isaac was dead, or so Dr. John thought; his *Titanic* had sunk, his lifeboats were gone; and Dr. John was condemned to live. "He regretted it forever."

Oh, I must speak with him.

"I'm not so sure that's how the story went," says Mr. Johnson. "Regretting it forever? Because, years later, Isaac's best friend, Paul deMay, came to Fair Home to find out what had happened to Isaac. Mrs. deMay is going to tell you that part of the story. But I warn you, it's not going to be pleasant. Paul got killed."

❧❧❧

"WE THOUGHT Paul died because we were too successful for America," Mrs. deMay says. "Because I looked too white."

Paul deMay's wife owns a whole brownstone in Harlem. An Irish maid shows Perdita in. The living room is full of the scent and pink cloudiness of roses, not in season yet, and the chair Perdita is seated in is delicate, ancient, French; Alexander's cousin Dotty wouldn't scorn it. Mrs. deMay has been coaching an elocution student, a young man with a cotton-picker's voice, excruciatingly polite; Mrs. deMay patiently corrects him, and every once in a while the voice of an educated man comes startled out of him for a full sentence or so, like a fledgling cracking its shell. Mrs. deMay sends him off with vowel exercises and the Irish maid serves them tea.

May deMay is the most eminent actress Perdita has never heard of.

"I was born in England," Mrs. deMay says. "My family has been free for two hundred years. We were quite ordinary people there. My grandfather was a vicar before he fell into misfortune."

Mrs. deMay has a picture of her husband and brings it out for Perdita. Perdita gets out her magnifier and her glasses and makes a production of looking at it, not only to see but to show she is paying attention. Paul deMay is a smiling, distinguished, successful man, unrecognizable as the dark slave boy who stood in back of his master and grinned like a minstrel show.

The Happy Slave might have been the first of his roles.

Because that was what happened to Paul deMay. He became an actor.

"Paul was born on the Landrum plantation in northern Virginia. His best friend was Bright Isaac, on the next plantation, Fair Home. Paul and Isaac were both ambitious young men, each in his way. Paul believed that, after Manassas, Isaac took advantage of his light skin and went North."

"Did your husband see him do it?"

"No. Paul had gone to find help for Lieutenant deMay." Mrs. deMay doesn't use the word *master*. She walks up and down a bit, preparing herself for the story.

"Once Paul had his own life to live, he decided to emigrate from America and try his fortune in England. Paul had always had a good singing voice and could entertain, you know those things made one's life easier when one was in the position he rose from. When I met him, he was singing plantation songs in a minstrel show in Liverpool and I, oh my dear, I had a dog act. Little May and her Dog Professors. The impresario asked Paul and me to do a comic turn, Othello and his Desdemona. With the dogs.

"But oh my dear! The man could act! And I could act with him! That marvelous deep voice. 'She loved me for the dangers I had passed, and I loved her that she did pity them.'" For a moment, through Mrs. deMay, Perdita hears a deep Southern-tinged baritone, handsome and confident. "We were lightning. Lightning. The impresario had to let us keep on with it. That was how we started.

"You don't act, do you? You cannot imagine what it's like to adore your leading man. We were everyone to each other, Beatrice and Benedick, Antony and Cleopatra. *Othello* was our signature role, of course, but you should have seen his *Hamlet.* I would have finished my role by his death scene, I was Ophelia, and I would stand in the wings and cry into a towel so as not to ruin my makeup for the curtain calls— My dear, I was a candle to his sun, and I am not so bad myself.

"We were scandalous, of course, a black man with a what-color-is-she wife. 'Oh, I'm ivory,' I would say, 'do I look white?' In Britain we are not prejudiced as you are, but my mother and aunt were very unhappy that I had married a man of Paul's coloring."

"Ivory?"

"'Ivory' you know is code with us; poor Garnet is ivory."

That is where she's heard Mrs. deMay's voice before: in Garnet's. "Is Garnet one of your pupils?"

"Was, my dear, and I wish I could have taught her more than elocution. She would be happier black as coal. Fashion!" Mrs. deMay snaps her fingers. Perdita has no doubt Mrs. deMay dresses in perfect fashion. "Fashion doesn't last; people do. She could have Louis Johnson any day. The man could run New York and he adores her.— Where were we?"

"You were acting with your husband."

"For twenty years. We were a success everywhere in Europe. We went to Russia, we played before the Czar. Do you know there are black Russian nobles? We played Dumas, *for* Dumas. *La Dame aux camélias.* So right for a black man to play the lead in a black man's play. I wish Paul had done D'Artagnan; wouldn't one thrill to a black D'Artagnan?

"And then, in 1890, we were asked to tour America.

"Twenty-five years since the War. We heard things were better, but one still had to be very careful. We were playing in Washington under the patronage of the Bruces. Have you met Josephine Bruce? The most beautiful woman in America in her day. She could have passed in a heartbeat and chose a husband as dark as my Paul. When one has one's difficulties, thinking of Josephine makes everything possible.

"One night, Paul told me he had seen his old friend Isaac in the audience."

"But Isaac was in Paris, or in Brazil—"

"Shush, dear. Paul sent his valet Roscoe to look for Isaac, but the man was with two white women, whom he was calling his mother and his wife."

"Dr. John, then."

"Paul wanted to know more. He arranged to go to Virginia, only for the day, you know, because of the difficulty of accommodations overnight. He gave out publicly that he wanted to visit his birthplace. He went very simply, with only Roscoe, and arranged for one of our local people to pick him up at the station and take him out to Landrum Farms.

"A day or so before he went, he discovered that Landrum Farms was now part of Fair Home and that he was actually going to Isaac's old plantation.

"I should have gone with him. I was too proud. One may be stared at on stage, but I was not eager to be ogled by farmers. I thought Paul could tell me everything afterward. One is so thoughtless when one is happy. I should have been there."

Mrs. deMay pauses, moves around the room, takes a stem of roses from the pink cloud: every move considered, graceful. Perdita only imagines she hears Paul's wife breathing hard, as if she's being careful not to cry, as if she too is regretting the lifeboat she was saved in.

"What I know I heard from Roscoe. It was an awkward day. Dr. John Church said he had seen Paul act in Washington. The Churches were gracious. They showed him round. They offered him lunch. Everyone ate on the porch, so that Fate deMay's old servant would not be eating at their dining room table. It was the sort of politeness that gives us finger bowls to wash our hands in and smashes the bowls when we're gone. Roscoe said that all the time he felt Paul understood something that wasn't being said. But Roscoe had no chance to ask.

"After lunch, they toured the stables. Whirlwind's last son was still alive then, very old and long-toothed. Of course one had to see a foal of Whirlwind. Roscoe said a man from the stables spoke to Paul privately during the tour, as if he were answering a question or making an appointment to meet."

"Did he describe the man?"

"A little man. Twitchy. Jumpy. One of us," Mrs. deMay adds.

Mr. Otis.

"At the end of the tour, Paul told Roscoe and the carriage driver to go down the road and wait for him at the crossroads. He would walk back through the fields of Landrum Farms and rejoin them there.

"They went to the crossroads. And they waited. And waited. And they heard a shot.

"They left the horse and carriage and ran into the fields, looking for him. They found him and he had been shot dead."

Mrs. deMay breaks off abruptly and stands silent. Perdita can hear no tears. A woman who wept into a towel to keep her makeup dry knows not to cry in front of strangers.

"I am so sorry," Perdita says finally.

"Don't. *I* was sorry, because I thought we had been too successful." This time she breaks out. "Oh, stupid, stupid, stupid! Paul for going to meet whoever it was. They for thinking he'd tell. One doesn't tell. It's how one survives in America.

"Paul found out something," Mrs. deMay says. "Perhaps something about Manassas. Louis Johnson has hinted at that story."

"But Dr. John did not murder him!"

"If no one murdered him," Mrs. de May says savagely, "my Paul is alive."

There's nothing to say to that.

"Americans do not think we are capable of great loves. I think of those poor women on *Titanic*," Mrs. deMay says. "I only hope they had a marriage half as complete as mine. I do not have a bad life. I tour on the TOBA circuit, I have my students and my friends, and I will never want. But the love of my life is dead. I know you were on the ship. Did you meet the Strauses?"

"Mrs. Straus sat near my friends and me."

"Her devotion to him. Staying with him. If you should ever speak with the family, tell them, from a woman who lost her husband, just say *a woman,* don't say who, that what she did must have been so completely what she wanted. I would have gladly died on *Titanic* if I could have died with Paul.— How well do you know Garnet?"

"Pretty well, I think."

"I have known Louis Johnson since I invested in his first business. Louis and Garnet are meant for each other. The man adores her, and she likes him too, you can see from her flirting with him. But she's afraid to let go of her skin." Mrs. deMay takes a breath. "If you find the chance, tell her this from me. The color line is nothing. The color line is a jump rope. Hop one side, hop the other, like a little girl. But the love line? Tell her to get on the right side and stay there, because on the right side she will find the other half of her soul. Tell her from me, the White Negro, the Black Bernhardt, I who have taken nonsense about my color all my life: Tell her to volunteer. Be counted. Don't run, don't hide, stand up, claim your love, claim yourself: *do* what you are! The thing in my life I am most proud of is ignoring the difference in our coloring and finding my Paul. That is the only truly worthy thing I have done.

"But I shall tell you this. It wasn't Dr. John who killed Paul, not alone."

"It wasn't Dr. John at all!"

"It was the murderous system. No one looked into Paul's death; it was as if he deserved to die. We were too successful, too human! In England, anywhere but here, we would simply have been people and my Paul would have got justice. Here?" says Mrs. deMay. "It's why I stay in America. I mean to find the man who killed him.

"And then I will shoot him myself."

Mr. Otis W. Church

WHEN OTIS WAS A LITTLE BOY before the War, being trained up to be a body-servant like his mamma and his brother Zack, he was told to follow Zack around and learn what Zack knew.

Zack knew how to escape.

"On land?" Zack said. "Take a horse or lift up your feet and walk. When you get to a river? Swim. You know how to swim?"

"You gonna take me with you when you go?"

"I don't know if that'd work out, Oatie. Have to take you as my servant."

"I be your servant. I do whatever you need."

"You learn to swim, then."

Otis learned to swim. Four years old, he could swim.

He walks down to St. Vincent's alone, while Mamma and Miss Fan and Miss Arbella are still asleep. He knows better than to even try the subway in this New York. But halfway down Broadway, foot-sore, he sees a dilapidated horse-car clopping by and there's a black face on it, so he gets on too.

At St. Vincent's, Dr. John is under the breathing-tent again, muttering. The white nurse looks at him suspiciously.

"That my Mars' John," Otis says, "I just watching my Mars' John."

"Oh, I suppose that's all right then."

White woman thinks he's trying to steal cash off sick folks. "He ain't say nothing, Ma'am?"

"No."

When she's gone, Otis gets a bottle and spoon out of his pocket. Miss Lady's medicine for when she was feeling poorly. She had a case of bottles in the storeroom. Otis felt poorly too once and took a spoonful. Like having a tree fall on him. He staggered round all day.

"You just swallow this," Otis says, looping the breathing tent up. "Slip it down. You ain't gonna say nothing you shouldn't say."

Fifty years, near to, they've kept their family secrets. Almost came out once when Paul deMay came to Fair Home.

Now it's happening again.

That Baroness girl is talking to Paul's wife.

The Baroness girl and the old lady know more than is safe.

And I got to fix it again? You think it going to be on me this time again like it was before? You think I'm just your third hand, your two good hands can sit in your lap in their white gloves and your dark black third hand sneaks round behind your back doing bad things for you? That what I am?

That's what he is, all right. For Fair Home.

Miss Fan and Mammy arrive to sit watch. Otis's restlessness comes on him. "Going out walking," he says.

Up here in this New York, men and boys swim in the Hudson. He walks up by the river toward the girl's place, watching the groups of men and boys gathered on the piers. When he sees black men in the group, he stops.

"Watch your clo'es for a nickel," a little white boy offers.

"You don't want to go swimming round here, you a stranger," a tall man says. "Suck you right out into the harbor when the tide turns."

"Turning yet?"

"About half an hour."

"I got half an hour then."

He strips. The water's mucky, full of oil and silt. He's not swimming to get clean.

Time to think.

I never divorced him, the old lady said when she and the white girl were having lunch yesterday. *I'm still married to him.*

The girl's her grandchild, and asking questions.

He'd be crazy to try stopping them. He could do it in Virginia maybe. But here?

This is why you swim a tidal river. There's a moment as the tide turns. The river slows and holds its breath. For a moment nothing moves. It's like that moment in a horse race when you're in the middle of the pack of riders and you see the path through. You just follow the path to winning; you are that path, you take that path; you bring that path into your heart and it stays.

There is a tide in the affairs of men

That taken at the flood, leads on to fortune—

Before Otis shot Paul, he was up in Washington with the rest of the family. Sat up in the colored seating, watched the rest of them below, saw Paul act. Considered well what he was going to do. It was murder. He knew that.

But he was protecting Fair Home.

There is a tide. There is a river. There is a race.

Freedom is knowing what path you're on.

CRIMES AND SURVIVORS ❧ 225

Freedom is protecting your home and your horses.

The water bubbles and whirls around him and begins to tug, and he strikes grimly in toward shore, riding the tide like a horse. He staggers and skids into the shallows.

"Man!" the tall man exclaims. "I was gonna bet you'd drown."

"I don't drown."

Reisden

WHAT REISDEN REALIZES on his efficient German ship, going toward America, is how much has changed in the past few years. The first time he visited Perdita in New York, not quite courting her, the trip from Cherbourg to New York meant days of isolation. Now every morning and two or three times during the rest of the day, a steward arrives with a packet of telegrams. The steward jokes he'll spend more money with Marconi than on his passage.

In the dining room he's seated with a table of businessmen and one Episcopalian priest, all traveling alone. They talk about Ismay.

"I wouldn't be Ismay. What a rotter."

"Never Ismay."

"I'd've stayed on board."

They know he was on *Titanic.* "Reisden, what would you have done?"

"Got on a lifeboat if I could."

"Seriously? Like Ismay?"

"On a boat, on the iceberg, anything I could do to survive. I have a son who needs a father. I have a business that needs me."

"Yes," the priest says. "'To him who is with the living, there is hope, for a live dog is better than a dead lion'—"

"Rot," the Englishman interrupts. "You don't think Ismay's better than Captain Smith or Thomas Andrews, do you? Andrews went down with his ship. That's the man I admire. Not Ismay."

"I don't say Ismay is admirable," the priest says somberly.

&ptext;&ptext;&ptext;

ON SUNDAY there are no telegrams. Reisden walks round the deck, which is shorter than *Titanic's,* with no protection from the wind.

The weather is cloudy, grey, frigid; they are in Iceberg Alley. The ship slows. Men drift out on deck, staring at the sea like lookouts. "This is where it happened."

From where he's sitting in first class, he can look down at the third-class passengers on the well deck. All the Swabian farmer emigrants, all the Poles and the Russians are standing at the rails, scanning the sea for ice. Among them are children, solemnly staring over the side, one clump of children with a white-wimpled nun herding them; some orphan train or Dr. Barnardo's group going to Canada for a new life. The nun says something to the older ones and takes the littlest one inside. Reisden's eyes narrow; he doesn't like children being left alone near a railing.

"Oh, G-d, look."

Up by the first-class railing, a man shouts and points into the mist. The sun is a tarnished farthing; the light is spectral; they all look for an iceberg; but on the colorless waves, they see not a white mountain but a field of white-and-black dots, as though a flock of birds are nesting on the water.

They're not birds.

Reisden gets up, horrified, and stands by the rail too.

"Go round," one of the men at the railing says in his throat. "Don't steam *over* them."

It's too late. The corpses of *Titanic's* wreck are spread all across the ship's path. A steward moves down the first-class deck. "No need to see this, sir. Help the ladies inside." Men traveling with their wives lead the women away. The women look back, appalled, fascinated. Below them, a female corpse's head bobs sickeningly near the ship's keel. She bumps against the side and is tossed high, arms flailing.

Even from the height of the first-class promenade, the corpses are almost identifiable. Men in evening clothes, men in pajamas. Women in fur coats and nightgowns. A man with a horrifying propeller-gash across his face and his arm trailing half-severed. A woman with a sea-soaked embroidered shawl over her head, holding (*no*) a child.

An old woman in a purple coat, her long gray hair spread out across the sea.

Miss Lady.

He stares, his eyes wide.

The nun guarding the orphans hasn't come back. The children are still standing by the rail, watching this.

There are five of them and the oldest can't be more than eight.

From the well deck the children have a closer view than he does.

The railing separating first and third class is padlocked, but it's no real barrier; Reisden goes down the stairs to intervene.

"Mister, are those dead people from off *Titanic*?" The oldest boy's a Londoner: a frowst of old jacket, a tattered scally cap, smudged all-knowing eyes.

"Are we going to see 'em close?" a fat boy asks.

Not if I can help it. "Let's go inside," Reisden suggests to them. "Do you like hot chocolate—what's your name?"

"And cookies?" the little girl asks timidly.

"Scavvins," says the oldest boy.

"I likes chocolate," the fat boy ventures. "Mick, I am."

"I ain't goin' inside," Scavvins says. "I wants to see 'em."

"Maisie," the little girl wavers. "That's my name. Mister, what happens to people when they die?"

How do you explain cadaveric decomp to children? It's like a lollipop in the jaws of death, darling, they just melt away...

"They rot, you nerk, Maisie," Scavvins says.

"It's like they're standin' under water," Mick says. "Dancin', with their 'eads 'angin' down."

"Their lifejackets are holding them up," Reisden says.

"They gonna get eaten by the fish."

"I ain't never eating fish," Maisie says.

"There's a ship coming for them," Reisden says. "They'll be taken home to their families."

"Fat lot of good that does 'em. Eaten by fish 'ere, worms there, wot's the change?"

"You ever going to eat worms, Maisie?" Mick says.

"Do they go to Heaven?" Maisie quavers.

"My ma's going to Hell," Scavvins says. "My da said so."

"Our ship will telegraph where they are and they'll be brought home," Reisden says firmly. He kneels down among the children. "And their families will be very sad and wish they were still alive."

Maisie nods.

"But sometimes the families will be relieved, and that's sad too," Reisden says, glancing at Scavvins. "Meanwhile you don't need to see them. Shall we go in?"

"I ain't sad about anything!" Scavvins says. "And I wants to see 'em!" He turns toward the rail. Reisden looks helplessly after him. Maisie comes and leans on Reisden's knee.

"I saw a little baby in the water," she confides in a whisper. "Wrapped in a blanket, floating all alone."

The boys drift toward the railing, pointing out bodies. They watch for bodies of children. Maisie puts her thumb in her mouth and hides her face against Reisden's shoulder. He can't save them. After awhile he picks Maisie up, shielding her eyes with his hand from whatever she might see, and goes to the railing too, standing with them.

❧❧❧

SURVIVAL is as dangerous as a bagful of knives.

The fatherless baby Perdita held on *Carpathia* is nursed at St. Vincent's, with her mother and her two-year-old brother. The Relief Fund gives them a suitcase of lovely new clothes. Grief and a suitcase are their only possessions.

Baby Gladys knows, love and marriage end in death. Gladys Millvina Dean never marries; she lives almost a hundred years, the last survivor of *Titanic,* supporting herself by selling postcards. On them she writes in a tiny shaky hand, "When this you see, remember me, the baby saved from the sea."

Her nursing home fees overwhelm her. She tries to raise cash by selling the Relief Fund suitcase, which she has kept all these years. James Cameron buys it and gives it back to her.

When she dies her ashes are scattered in Southampton Harbor, a smudge on the sea drifting toward America.

Lillian Asplund is five and a half years old, returning to Worcester, Massachusetts, with her mother, father, and four brothers. Her father drowns with three of her brothers, including her twin brother Carl. Her mother's nerves are shattered. From then on, Lillian is the parent of the family.

Lillian never marries.

At ninety-four, she speaks for the first and only time about that night. She was passed through a window into a boat already being lowered. She remembers looking up at her father, who was holding Carl. Her older brothers were standing on either side of him. Filip was thirteen. Clarence was nine.

She never speaks their names again.

Henry Adams, the American essayist, was scheduled to sail on the return voyage of *Titanic.* After the wreck, he dismissively compares *Titanic* to the American political situation; America is in worse shape than *Titanic,* "at the bottom of the deep sea, and the corpses are still howling on the surface." But he cannot stop hearing the corpses. Nine days after the wreck of *Titanic,* he suffers a stroke, hallucinates that his mother has gone down with the ship, and attempts suicide.

Col. Archibald Gracie, first-class passenger and historian, survives *Titanic* but dies six months later. He has never really left *Titanic;* he has spent those six months writing a history of the sinking. His last words are "We must get them into the boats, we must get them all into the boats."

Even the richest families are shaken apart. Isidor and Ida Straus were inseparable in life. His body is found; hers, never. Their sacrifice becomes the Straus family ghost. A hundred years later, speaking at a *Titanic* memorial service, their great-grandson will still measure his life against theirs, their courage against his. "What would I have done?" he is asking still.

"And did you survive?" the clueless women asked Mrs. Harris. "No," she said.
Rich and poor, child and adult, none of them has survived.

And Reisden knows all this.
What the survivors will learn from *Titanic* is the most lasting lesson they will ever learn.
When he finally goes back to his cabin, the walls tighten around him. He lights the lamp and finds in his steamer trunk the photo of Toby he packed, Toby grinning next to Elphinstone on the office rug by the fireplace. He thinks he's brought it for Perdita, but tonight it's for him.
He gets dressed and goes out on deck, takes possession of a deck chair and a stray steamer blanket. He thinks of Perdita warm next to him in the deck chair on *Titanic*. Tonight there's a moon. If there were icebergs, the lookouts could see them. All the same he's too restless to sit; he gets up and stands staring at the sea past the lifeboats. The white dots on the water are only moonlight.

Another man is outside, by the lifeboats, someone else who can't sleep. Reisden doesn't want company and stands to move away—

A man in a grey coat and a grey American Homburg hat.

Hallucination.

They never travel on the same ship. Gilbert knows that.

It can't be Gilbert.

But it is.

Perdita

"WHAT DID PAUL DEMAY KNOW?" Perdita asks Mr. Johnson over the phone. "And who shot him? Could it have been Mr. Otis who gave him the message? And here is Mr. Otis living in our apartment."

"Send him to live somewhere else," Mr. Johnson says.

She hesitates, unwilling to do it and not willing to say why. If Mr. Otis were a white man she could simply plead inconvenience, but since he's a black man it looks like prejudice. She says this to Mr. Johnson as best she can.

"I never find any trouble being prejudiced against murderers. You want Clemmie Daniels to have to shoot it out with him?"

This gives her pause. "I'll find some way to get him to leave."

❧❧❧

SHE'S STILL THINKING THIS OVER when she arrives back home and finds Aunt Louisa waiting for her. They go into the front room and close the glass doors for privacy.

"Opal and I have been considering what to do about John's marriage," Aunt Louisa says. "The best thing would be for me to divorce him so he can marry her, but that takes time and it's not possible while he's ill. We presume that now his mother is dead,

John owns Fair Home. If he," Aunt Louisa's brisk voice quavers for a moment, "if he does not get better, Opal says there is a danger that his will might talk about 'his wife' and 'his wife's heirs' rather than naming the woman to whom he believes he has been married all these years."

Perdita nods. "You mean he might accidentally leave Fair Home to you?"

"And his wife's heirs would be you," Aunt Louisa says. "You are my heir, dear. Don't think it's about your eyes, I am supporting your music. But we must make sure that Fair Home goes to her. Opal has put together a document for me saying that I renounce any interest in anything of John's, and specifically in Fair Home, in favor of the woman who should be his wife. Opal wanted me to ask if you'd sign a document as well."

"Of course I will; did she give you one?"

They find a pen in the kitchen—*nothing* here has a place yet (where is Alexander's telegram?). Perdita signs three copies on the kitchen table, one for Opal to file, one for herself, one for Miss Fan.

"Opal says this is no better than a legal good-luck charm, but it'll have to do for now. Now, dear, we'll have fun. Freshen up and come with me; we're going to have lunch with Oswald Garrison Villard and advance your career in New York."

"Oswald Garrison Villard?"

Oswald Garrison Villard is one of the most influential men in New York. He owns the *Evening Post.* He supports the New York Symphony. He's the grandson of William Lloyd Garrison, who was an Abolitionist saint. His politics are as impeccable as his suits. Just knowing Oswald Garrison Villard is a coup for a musician.

But not a musician whose fingers are covered in Bag Balm and medicated gloves. "I'm not ready for this, Aunt Louisa."

"Oswald and Julia are great friends of mine. They've heard how you've been treated by NAWSA and they are indignant."

"Of course they've heard, Aunt Louisa, you told them. But *I cannot play.*"

"Today you're simply going to their house for lunch. And if we don't leave now, dear, we'll be late."

ᔊᔊᔊ

THE VILLARDS live in an elegant building in the 50s. Perdita sits dumb, impressing no one, while Aunt Louisa catches up with them.

"Do you believe, Julia, because she's a survivor, those idiotic women mean to keep her from playing! Everyone at NAWSA should be shot," Aunt Louisa says.

"What an anarchist you are, Loulie," Mrs. Villard says comfortably.

"And you have been at the Conservatoire?" Mr. Villard asks Perdita.

Yes; and got thrown out, she does not say. She talks about the Conservatoire and the concerts she's given in Paris. She can give this interview in her sleep and she gives it now.

Interviews are not about the truth.

They have lunch. Perdita waits to have one of the Villards ask what it was like on *Titanic*. Neither of them does, for which she gives them much credit.

But then she's asked if she would like to play.

"She's just being shy," Aunt Louisa says determinedly.

"I am not."

"Do you have a piano?" Aunt Louisa says. "Perhaps we can just leave her with the piano a bit, Oswald, Julia."

"I really cannot," Perdita insists.

But they take her to the music room and sit her in front of the sinuous black mass of, she touches it experimentally, yes, a Steinway, and leave her alone to spin straw into gold.

Her chance. She is sitting in Oswald Garrison Villard's music room, at his own piano, and has been invited to impress him. The girl she was a week ago would have been breathless at the chance.

Around the Villards' Steinway all the victims gather. The Strauses, the children. *Save yourselves*, she tells them.

I had responsibilities, Dr. John says in her head, so strongly that she thinks for a moment he must have died just then and is coming to her as a ghost.

What responsibilities does she have? To whom?

By the piano, near enough to play four-hands, Perdita sees herself, Perdita. Seventeen years old, with her hair down, in a white dress; she has not even met Alexander yet.

That Perdita she understands, but she doesn't understand herself.

Am I the one who scraped together all her little triumphs in cold churches? And wanted to play something in Carnegie Hall because it was Carnegie Hall and that must make me important?

Who am I?

The musicians on deck played to help people survive. Wallace Hartley, all alone with his violin, played "Nearer My God to Thee." Mary Mags and the drunks in the Tiger sang "Nearer My God to Thee" too—

Music is—

She takes off her gloves, and scrubs her fingers with them until the salve won't make her fingertips slide on the keys. The thin sensitive skin flares in pain.

She stretches her fingers and lays them on the keys. (Whatever else, there is no sensation as good as putting your fingers on the keys of a really good piano.)

And she begins to play her confession. Every note hurts and her hands are stiff.

I have hired nurses for you
The wind, the sun, and the eagle—

The waves roll under her left hand, the mother's voice weeps in her right.

The Wind's mother asks her
What have you done, my daughter?
Have you chased the stars through night
And fought waves' icy might...

She transcribed it because it stuck in her heart, then and now.

I have done nothing...

The girl she was at the Institute: that Perdita: how that girl played this song, wanting not to be left on the shelf, wanting love, marriage, children; wanting to be like other people.

She has got what she wanted.

But other people don't play the piano.

And she does.

I guard a child.

A shiver of cold and darkness goes over her. She is back on the water and a child is calling "Mamma!" As she plays she plunges her hands into the water, and in the burning cold she plays the song for that child whom she did not guard.

It will be all right. No one will hurt you. The wind, the sun, and the eagle protect you. It will be all right, I tell you—but you and I know it won't. The water is freezing. The water is your only cradle. Your mamma cannot help you. She drowned. We forgot you in the lifeboats. The ice and the waves were stronger than anyone who loved you. Sleep, child, sleep; sleep in your lifejacket; sleep in your mother's arms. Sleep and freeze to death.

I am so sorry.

Child, forgive me.

I survived.

When she is done, there is a silence like the top of a mountain. She is alone.

The worst part is she knows she has played well.

She massages her hands, which hurt.

"Dear," Aunt Louisa says from outside, "it's no use pretending we weren't listening. May we come in?"

"Your aunt hasn't exaggerated," Mr. Villard says.

"I told you, Oswald. Such expressivity!"

I didn't mean it for you, she wants to say, and wonders if she did. She meant it for someone. Music is always for someone.

"We will get to know each other better, I hope. Dear heavens, what did you do to your hands?"

"We were rowing." The skin has split along one of her knuckles. She resists sucking it. "Aunt Louisa, Mr. Villard: I played well because they died and I took a place in a boat."

She can explain but they don't understand.

"Your hands must recover," Mr. Villard says. "We should not have asked you to play today. But *es ist der Geist, der sich den Körper baut.* The spirit builds itself a home. You have a gift."

A holy gift, Aunt Jane said. She shivers. How is she to live, what is she to do?

"Let us show you off a bit. Our friend Friedrich Guttmacher is putting together a small fundraiser. I don't know if you know him? Might I have him get in touch with you—?"

"I studied under Dr. Fritz at the Institute," she says automatically.

"Did you really? Such a genius! I wanted to study at the Institute," says Oswald Garrison Villard. "I envy you, being able to concentrate on nothing but music; having nothing to distract you. That is the way a life like yours should be."

❧❧❧

"THANK YOU for the introduction," she tells Aunt Louisa when they've left the Villards. Ordinarily they'd take the subway in sympathy with the masses, but today they take a cab. I am a musician, she thinks; and not because Oswald Garrison Villard said so. It's frightening. She's responsible. She doesn't know what being responsible means.

"Oh, dear, you did everything yourself. And I am so very glad you did; I am so proud of you. Do you know who the fundraiser is for? The NAACP."

The National Association for the Advancement of Colored People. "Should I do that, Aunt Louisa?"

"Of course you should, dear." There is a pause that might or might not be meaningful. "I belong to it myself. All proper-feeling people do; it is not for one race alone. I'll send you a membership application."

"I shall join. That reminds me that I have tickets for the *Titanic* memorial concert. Caruso is singing. Would you like to go? And I have a copy of Dr. John's picture for you." Perdita passes Aunt Louisa the picture of the four men, not specifying why the NAACP might remind her of Dr. John.

"Aunt Louisa. Why did you leave him?"

Could it have anything to do with why Mr. deMay was murdered? It is not only the family who needs to know now; it is Mrs. deMay, who thinks she will have to avenge her husband herself. What did Paul know? What did *Isaac* know? Is Mr. Otis involved? "It is important."

"Perdita," Aunt Louisa says, hesitating. "I have helped you do something I know will benefit you. I was honored to do it, but I would like you to help me in return. I want two things from you. First, don't ask about my marriage. There may come a time when I'll tell you, but don't ask."

I will keep asking, Perdita says, but silently.

"And second—" Aunt Louisa takes a breath. "I would like you to introduce me to John's wife. I must give her the letters of intention we signed. I owe her an apology and reassurance, one woman to another. And— I would like to see John." She says it quite simply, but for once Perdita doesn't need eyes to tell what someone's thinking. "I shall not stay long. She truly has nothing to concern herself from me."

Perdita takes Aunt Louisa's hand. Aunt Louisa grasps it. It hurts her fingers; Perdita makes not a sound. "John was a good man and I treated him terribly," Aunt Louisa says a little shakily. "I regret it."

"Please trust me and talk about it."

"It isn't the time, dear. But— Look, look there! I don't know if you can see it, but there is a sight!"

"Aunt Louisa, please don't change the subject."

"It's the film people," Aunt Louisa says. "They're towing a ship up the river. I suppose it's for one of those moving pictures they make at the Palisades. They have a big white sheet of an advertisement on the side. Last year they did something about Henry Hudson, they had an old Dutch ship anchored by the Palisades, it was quite evocative—"

"What does it say?" Perdita asks; she'll hear nothing more now. She puts her head out the cab window. They've taken one of the West Side avenues, 10th or 11th, catching the breezes from the Hudson and missing the midtown traffic. She can smell the sea-smell of the Hudson and see the ship, a shadow, a lean heavy blackness on the river.

Aunt Louisa looks out the window. "Oh dear."

She knows what it must be. "Is it *Titanic*?"

"I'm afraid so."

"It's Dorothy Gibson. She's got the idea of a romance aboard *Titanic* in her head and she can't get it out. I was in the first movie, on board. She's asked me to be in this one."

"You should do it," Aunt Louisa says. "Go face it, dear. One must face things. It's the only way."

But then why do you not face whatever happened between you and Dr. John?

She has an idea. "Will you go with me, Aunt Louisa? We can go and be in the movies together." And we can talk, she thinks, you and I. Movies are as good as a voyage for talking.

"Not before— Is it possible you can speak to John's wife today?" Aunt Louisa says. "Let's not put it off. Tonight."

❧❧❧

BEFORE SHE GOES TO ST. VINCENT'S, Perdita buys a box of rainbow-colored cookies from an Italian bakery. Inside, Miss Fan and Mr. Otis are watching over Dr. John. With them are three or four people Perdita doesn't know; Miss Fan says they're friends and colleagues from dentists' offices Dr. John has helped in Baltimore. At least one of them is black.

See, he's the man Aunt Louisa married, the one who helps black people.

To Perdita's ear, Dr. John seems worse. His breath is ragged and liquefied, he seems to be struggling less. When she holds his hand it's cold, freezing, as if he's slowly slipping underwater.

I know you're the right person. I do. Don't die without talking to me.

Perdita takes Miss Fan out into the corridor, gives her the cookies, as if cookies will help, and whispers Aunt Louisa's request.

"Meet *me*—!"

"And, I am sorry, Miss Fan, she wishes to see Dr. John."

"But someone is always here, Uncle Otis, Mammy Jane —"

"It's very difficult, I know." But do it, do it please, so that Aunt Louisa can see the man she still loves; do it soon, before it's too late.

And let him wake and talk with me.

"I know she'd like to see John, but— No. I'll arrange it. This evening. Have her come late. After midnight if she can. I'll send them away."

"Thank you, Miss Fan."

"Have her come alone. You and I will talk later, Miss Perdita. I promise we will."

We'd better, Perdita thinks.

"Miss Fan? If—" How do you say *if he's about to die?* "If it looks as though Dr. John's situation is changing at all, please, I would like to be there."

❧❧❧

ARBELLA is helping to watch Dr. John. It's too much to ask of a girl twelve years old. A couple of Perdita's friends from the Institute have asked her to tea at a new automated restaurant in Times Square and she asks Arbella to come along.

"You'll do me a favor. Without someone to help I'll probably work the machines wrong and end up getting pie with gravy. And we'll see the lights in Times Square."

"There's really moving signs?" Arbella says. "And food that comes out of walls?"

"Yes, truly."

It's a chance to question Arbella. They take the subway up toward Times Square and have to shout over the rattling. "Tell me about Mr. Otis."

"He is the smartest man. He been training me about horses since I was five, and Miss Lady taught me horse-breeding. Papa, he say Miss Lady and Mr. Otis and me, he take our advice which horse to buy. Every time."

Does he have a gun? Did he shoot Mr. deMay? "What is he like?"

"Oh, just Uncle Otis."

"Will you become a trainer yourself?"

Arbella laughs. "Got to get me some rich husband pretend to do it, get him to marry me and I do it behind him. He got to be rich, though," Arbella says earnestly. "We always trying to make money at Fair Home."

"Arbella," there is no really polite way to say this, "aren't you usually at school? I mean did you get leave from school to come to New York?"

"I don't go to school, Mis' Baroness."

"I never went to school either," Perdita says, but she's dismayed. Her parents sent her to Boston so she could go to the Perkins School. Uncle Bucky and Aunt Violet thought it would make her act too blind and they kept her home, but at least she was tutored. "Do you have tutors?"

"Just Miss Lady and Uncle Otis. Mammy tries to get me to talk good." Arbella giggles. "I got to go off to be finished sometime, Mammy say. But Miss Lady say, a girl with a horse farm got all the finishing she need. I just got to find me a rich man who likes horses."

❧❧❧

ANOTHER THING SHERLOCK HOLMES DOESN'T DO is go out for tea with his girlfriends. In the new restaurant where she meets them, there are no waiters; you put nickels into a slot and food comes out just as if it were being manufactured right there. Uncle Gilbert would wonder *how long that food has been in there* and *who put it in* and *did they wash their hands?* Perdita chooses not to.

But as soon as Arbella opens her mouth, one of Perdita's friends draws Perdita aside.

"That girl— From the way she talks, I do think *she is black.*"

"She is only from the country. And she's my companion, she is helping me." Too late she feels ashamed for saying that Arbella is white.

"I'll help you choose and put your nickels in for you, but honestly, Perdita, that sort of person isn't allowed in a restaurant in New York."

Perdita insists that Arbella sit down at their table. The other girls ignore her. Arbella goes over to the wall to try to work the food-machines. She can't figure them out and comes back to ask if one of the other ladies will help her. There's a silence round the table. Perdita gets up to help, but isn't any good at all.

"I don't want anything, I guess," Arbella says, "I ain't in the mood. Guess I'll go outside and watch the lights and you talk with your friends."

"I'm sorry, this isn't nice for you. I'll finish up and get away."

"No'm, I'll just go back. You showed me that subway; I can get back to the apartment."

"No, wait; I'll come with you."

Awkward, awkward, awful. Perdita goes back inside and spends a few minutes with her friends. Her friends are working as typewriter girls and doing music at night; they're teaching private students or accompanying films in movie theaters; one woman has got a job as a member of a women's orchestra, but that won't last, nobody buys tickets to see women play music. Still they think they're something holy because they're musicians. And they ignore an ambitious and successful girl who will train horses someday, because they think she's black.

Perdita leaves, and at least she and Arbella see Times Square. She buys Arbella a hot dog and a Coca-Cola from one of the street vendors, and has one with her so Arbella won't eat alone, though this is the third time today Perdita has had lunch. It's dusk among the high buildings and the lights show beautifully. Arbella and she look up at the whirls, spirals, fireworks of color, the dancing theater signs, the electric clock with fountains of light pouring out of lions' mouths. There are new ones since she was here last year: a kitten moving its tail and playing with string, a high-wire girl crossing the street on a rope of lights. The movie theaters all have electric signs now, sparking and winking together. Dancing figures shimmy; Johnnie Walker struts and twirls his umbrella. News wavers in lights across the *Times* building that gives the square its name. Perdita thinks she sees a T, for *Titanic*.

One of the signs is a horse-race, which Arbella criticizes. "What do horses really look like?" Perdita asks.

"Smooth as fire, ma'am. Not blinking and twinkling."

"My husband wishes I could see them running."

"He go to the races?"

"No, maybe twice a year, to be sociable only."

"Mis' Baroness? Is it true, my grandpappy's boy Paul's family lives here in New York?"

"Arbella, how do you know that?"

"Mis' Daniels, she said something."

Perdita bets Mrs. Daniels did not. Arbella has been spying from the kitchen. "His widow lives somewhere up in Harlem. Why do you ask?"

"Just I never knew my grandpappy. She might know something about him. You know where she live?"

"I can't say," Perdita says. "Why would you want to see her?"

"To ask if he was as good with horses as me," Arbella says. Perdita is ashamed for mistrusting her.

They go down into the subway. Arbella hands her nickel in carefully to get her ticket, a person getting back in control after a trying day.

"How did Miss Lady learn to be a horse-breeder?" Perdita asks.

"It come from bein' in that chair all those years. She have all that time to read. That's what I'd like to do," Arbella sighs, "just sit all day and think about horses, stead of having to help round the house. Except I wouldn't want to be crippled up like she was. Mammy Jane been looking after her ever since they was two little girls."

"Miss Lady was crippled all her life?" It makes such a difference in how people think of you: *Was there a time when you weren't blind? Were you ever normal?*

In Perdita's memory, Miss Lady is boasting about the men who flirted with her, the duels and champagne breakfasts, the dress with embroidered violets. Balls and hunts, she says. But hunting and dancing? Did she say anything about the first fox she hunted or the time she opened the ball?

She never did.

Crippled and an heiress.

"How terrible for her."

"Well, she have Fair Home."

"And Dr. John. She has her son."

"Yes'm," Arbella says. "But mostly she have the horses."

❧❧❧

ARBELLA GOES UPTOWN but Perdita walks crosstown to Aunt Louisa's.

Aunt Louisa is waiting. The Girls bark and churn and beg for treats around Perdita's knees.

"Take them out, Betty," Aunt Louisa says.

"Already took them out, Miss Louisa."

"Take them out again."

"Silly dogs!" Betty scolds them, meaning probably *silly Aunt Louisa.* "All right, come on."

When they're alone, Perdita gives Aunt Louisa the message. "May I come with you?"

"No, no, dear, I must face this by myself."

"Call me afterward."

"I'll call you or come to see you, I promise."

ಹಿಂಬಿಂ

WHAT ELSE CAN PERDITA DO to be useful? She telephones Harry and Bucky at the Waldorf-Astoria. "Come to dinner with me." She will become completely spherical, this is her fifth meal today, but she has the pictures with her and she wants to pass them on.

She takes them to the Cartoon Room at Joel Rinaldo's, off Broadway by the Met. When she was a student she dreamed of being cartooned at Joel Rinaldo's. If she were consulting their comfort, she'd get dressed up and take them to Delmonico's, where they could eat steak and potatoes.

If she truly consulted their comfort, they'd go with someone else.

"Here, Uncle Bucky. Here, Harry." She hands Harry and Uncle Bucky copies of the picture. "The man Aunt Louisa circled in the picture is the one she married. The *white* man," she says, lowering her voice.

Uncle Bucky looks it over. "Hmph," he says, which is as close to approval as Uncle Bucky gets.

Harry doesn't say anything. Oh, Harry, believe it.

"Try the tamales, Uncle Bucky, Harry, they're supposed to be good."

Uncle Bucky leafs through the menu warily.

"I don't eat dog meat," Harry says. "Why doesn't the city close places like this?"

Joel Rinaldo's is reasonably famous and as clean as most restaurants in New York, but Harry wouldn't like even a lobster palace with her at the table.

The room is stuffed with noise, conversations, music. Someone breaks into song, *Ay ay ay ay, canta y no llores*. Uncle Bucky decides he will try the chili con carne; "you promise it is made with *actual* beef?" He orders a Blue Moon to wash it down. Harry orders a Blue Moon. Perdita orders tamales and lemonade; she knows about Blue Moons, Joel Rinaldo's revenge on the bourgeoisie.

"This photograph, though," Uncle Bucky says, tapping it with his finger. "This man, standing, isn't this the man Louisa might have married? You wouldn't know, but one of the slaves looks almost white."

Uncle Bucky has never quite understood that she can see at all. "Uncle Bucky, he's not the man Aunt Louisa married. See which one she circled."

"But is she quite sure? Could she be mistaken? They look alike."

"Alexander says they don't look alike at all, and he met both of them."

"They look alike to me."

"'Alexander says,'" Harry says. "What about your *other* grandfather?"

She doesn't understand.

"You've been playing music with 'your grandfather' in some dive downtown. He's a black man! And you're calling yourself Susan Williams?"

She is sadly not surprised at all. "Have you been following me, Harry?"

"Well, obviously I didn't follow you *myself.*"

"That is my teacher, Mr. Williams. I'm sorry, I need to call myself Susan Williams in order to work with him—"

"Your teacher!" Harry laughs. "Is he the same man as in the picture?"

She stares; even she can tell that round-chinned Mr. deMay is not skinny Mr. Williams. "That is Mr. Paul deMay, an actor."

"'Mr.' deMay! 'Mr.' Williams! You're sneaking round to see a black man," Harry says.

Uncle Bucky clears his throat. "We wish no stories put about, Harry. Think of the family!"

"It's not my family," Harry says. "I married the *right* girl."

Their food lands on the table with a thump of heavy china. Downstairs, a pianist begins playing ragtime with a good tricky beat. She doesn't recognize the player. Uncle Bucky spoons into his chili and says in a strangled voice, "That's hot."

Harry says, "At least the drinks aren't bad.— You still think your husband isn't coming to America?" he says.

"He isn't, Harry."

Uncle Bucky begins to say something but chokes and takes a big gulp of his Blue Moon.

"You don't want him here with you?" Harry asks.

"He needs to be in Paris."

"You don't love him."

"I do."

"Like you 'loved' me?" Harry bursts out.

"I did love you, Harry," and I still do care for you very much, she decides not to say; no, she should say that and mean it. "I do care for you very much still, I wish you every good thing, but I was too young."

"Harry, niece, this is unseemly."

Harry leans forward. She smells Blue Moon on his breath. "You got married to a fraud because he knocked you up. If I'd known that was what you wanted, Perdita, I'd have done it myself. And I can tell you, I'm glad I didn't."

"*Harry!*" Uncle Bucky says.

"Your husband is a crook and he's trying to get my uncle's money."

"He's not!" She must not antagonize Harry or let him bait her, but this is her chance to speak for Alexander. "Alexander doesn't want your responsibilities, Harry. He has his own job."

"His 'job' is deceiving my uncle and stealing from me!"

"Did you ever hear about his red doorknobs?" she asks desperately.

"Red doorknobs?" Uncle Bucky says hoarsely, breathing chili fumes, trying to help her change the subject.

"This is how much Jouvet suits him." She addresses herself to Uncle Bucky. "You know Jouvet does a lot of testing. One day Alexander tested my eyes. He found I could see red best, so now we have red doorknobs."

"He didn't know you couldn't see, huh?" Harry says.

It had been a wintry rainy afternoon in March; she and Alexander had been married only about two months. She was morning-sick and had been thrown out of the Conservatoire for being married. Their apartment was full of the last Dr. Jouvet's dusty stuff, and the livable part ended abruptly in tarpaulins and hammering and the smell of wet mortar. Alexander was as bad at putting together a household as she; worse; much worse.

How do you see? Alexander had taken her downstairs to the Jouvet lab and made her sit in front of one machine and another, peer into lights and mirrors, have her head clamped in machines. *Do you see that? What do you see?*

He couldn't fix anything else that day, so he fixed that. It's how he loves. Protecting and fixing.

"He likes helping people." How will she convince them that Alexander will not harm them? "Jouvet's his way to care for people. He doesn't want anything but Jouvet. He certainly doesn't want to come to America."

"Which is why he's not coming," Harry says sarcastically. "You didn't marry him for doorknobs. You married him because you had to."

"Harry!" Uncle Bucky says.

"I *respected* you," Harry says. "A kid is so great, right? You wanted a kid that much."

I didn't know I did. Not then. But yes, oh, yes. "You must feel very happy now that Efnie is expecting."

"Happy. Yeah. Was it him who made the first move or you?"

"Harry!" Uncle Bucky says.

"He knocked you up because you wanted somebody to *luuuuv* you. He lies to Gilbert because he wants the *muuuney.* You thought the kid would help?"

"Don't you bring my Toby into this," she says, narrow-eyed. "And Alexander isn't Uncle Gilbert's heir. You are."

"I'm going to have a son too. And my kid's not going to get robbed. You don't know anything," Harry says. "And you know what?" He shakes the picture she's given him. "Your aunt, your grandmother, she says she married the white one? Look at them. You can't, can you?" He's making fun of her eyes, which is below anything he used to do. "The two of them? Alike as brothers. Used the same name. Which one she married?" He raises his voice so as almost to be heard above the noise. "She doesn't know who she married. I'll say that if Gilbert doesn't come home."

෨෨෨

AND AFTER THAT, Harry and Uncle Bucky insist on seeing her home. At her front door, Harry says "See you Wednesday" as if they've made some appointment.

"Why Wednesday?" she asks.

But Harry simply says "Bye" and goes to sit in the cab.

"Niece," Uncle Bucky says, "the photograph is all very well, and Harry is being—excessive—but you must not keep this Williams man among your acquaintance."

"I certainly *will*, though! What did Harry mean by Wednesday?"

"You do not understand the way the world thinks, niece. Harry will be a rich man. That makes his words valuable. If he chooses to speak as he did tonight, Heaven only knows—"

"But it is not true! Your own sister says it is not!"

"Do you think that makes a difference?" Uncle Bucky says bleakly. "People will believe *him.*"

Left alone, she telephones Aunt Louisa, but Aunt Louisa has already left for St Vincent's. "Betty, will you ask her to phone me as soon as she gets back?"

Clementine Daniels is still there. The two of them sit in the kitchen and Perdita fills her in on all the events of the day. Dr. John selling his own brother. Mrs. deMay's story about Paul at Fair Home. Mr. Otis. Harry. "I don't know whether to cry or kick Harry."

"I wonder if Otis Church has a gun," Mrs. Daniels says.

"Mr. Johnson says I should ask him to leave." It still feels prejudiced.

"I'm going to look in his room."

They bolt the door and Perdita stands guard in the front hall, ear pressed against the door in case someone comes. It takes only a minute for Mrs. Daniels to return.

"Right in his traveling bag," Mrs. Daniels says.

Mrs. Daniels hands the gun to Perdita. It feels heavy as death. She hands it back quickly.

"Oh lawksy me," Clementine Daniels says in her servant voice, "I just purely hate to see a gun in the house like this. Miss Perdita, can I lock this up in your jewelry safe, where no burglar can get in and use it against us?"

"That's a good idea, Mrs. Daniels. Mr. Otis can apply to us if he needs it."

They both break into nervous laughter at the thought of a possible murderer asking for his gun back.

"I'll stay the night if you want."

"Thank you, but my aunt's probably coming over later."

When she's alone, Perdita sits in the front room waiting for Aunt Louisa's call. Clementine Daniels has brought the *Matilda Ziegler,* New York's Braille magazine, and she reads it dutifully, first page to last. An article about how to maneuver on the subway.

Something stickily heartwarming about a blind person who has triumphantly learned how to use a typewriter. But nothing about murder or music or love.

What has happened to Alexander's telegram? She goes round the apartment gathering up pieces of paper and putting them on the dining-room table. She finds more good wishes she must answer and another message from Dorothy Gibson, but not the telegram. She wanders round the apartment trying to hear a clock ticking so she can open it up and find out what time it is, but she can't. She must get a proper clock.

Mrs. Daniels has brought her a book from the Braille lending library, *The Hound of the Baskervilles,* all thousand or so heavy pages of it. She takes it to her bedroom. Balances it on her knees and tries to read. Sits up with it. Lies down with it. "They were the footsteps of a gigantic hound." Sherlock, it's just a dog. She thinks of beer-drinking Sturgis and Liddy Boswick and Blind Willie. What with Liddy's opium drops and both of them smoking hash, Willie might as well stand in the middle of Broadway and set himself afire and have done with it.

Whatd would happen to Garnet then?

You must not keep this Williams man among your acquaintance, Uncle Bucky told her. You must get on the white lifeboat and leave Blind Willie; but no, not this time. She'll see Garnet tomorrow at the Strauses' memorial and she'll insist on helping out.

Someone gets in late. It's Mr. Otis; she hears his boots creak down the hall. She holds her breath and silently slides a chair under the doorknob. She listens, ear to the door, and thinks he pauses outside.

But he goes on past. A few minutes later she hears him go out again, back to St Vincent's to watch over Dr. John.

Miss Fan and Aunt Jane don't come back at all.

Aunt Louisa doesn't call.

She listens until the early birds start cheeping, then gets up and takes a bath and starts water for coffee, yawning—

And stands with the pot under the faucet, struck.

Alexander's telegram.

Alexander's telegram arrived the day Harry and Uncle Bucky were here.

And now it can't be found.

Just like her own letters to Uncle Gilbert in Boston.

Which "disappeared."

Letters Uncle Gilbert never got because Harry took them.

Last night Harry jeered at her when she said Alexander wasn't coming to New York.

"He stole it," she says out loud. "Harry stole Alexander's telegram. And Alexander *is* coming."

She doesn't want him here. She's finding out too much, and what she's finding out won't help Toby or herself. Alexander will tell her, "Lie for Toby's sake." Lying and leaving America worked for him. He will insist she take the lifeboat.

She needs more time before she has to face him.

➴➴➴

AT LAST THE PHONE RINGS. But it's not Aunt Louisa; it's Greta Nisensohn, the postcard girl from *Titanic.*

"I'm supposed to get you into La Gibson's film. Can you come have breakfast with me at least and let me tell you about it?"

"I'm waiting for a phone call—"

"Please. I got to talk to you. Please."

"Then you come here."

Mrs. Daniels has arrived and serves them coffee and rolls at Perdita's grand unfamiliar dining-room table.

"OK," Greta Nisensohn bursts out, "Her film. Will you do it? The thing is, La Gibson's driving me crazy. She's making things way too authentic on set, you know what I mean? She hired a whole ship up from the Staten Island breaker yards. This time she's not going to leave on the first boat. She'll leave like you did, at the last moment. G-d of Israel, she has a scene with her boyfriend on the deck, the whole *goodbye-my-darling* bit, *see you in New York*. He makes her leave. Of course the boyfriend survives. He swims to one of the boats with a child, saves the child— What's wrong?"

"Nothing." Chills run all the way to her fingertips. "Miss Gibson is saving a child. That's good."

"Do you know what I think? She wants to have do-overs. She wants to sink *Titanic* again and this time she'll be a heroine."

The only heroines aboard *Titanic* are dead. "Miss Nisensohn— Greta—why are *you* doing this?"

Greta Nisensohn doesn't answer for a long time. "Why she wants me, that I know, I was taking photographs all over the real ship, I know what it looked like. But— You have trouble being on a ship?"

"I don't know." She hasn't been anywhere closer to the water than Riverside Drive.

"When I go on the ferry to Jersey? I can't even look at the river, I go inside and hide in the ladies'. Last Sunday I'm coming through Madison Square Park, I turn around, there's the Flatiron Building, I think it's the bow of *Titanic*. I screamed. Out on the street I screamed. La Gibson's got a string trio playing on set, sometimes I just can't stand it.— Could you come Friday? Maybe Thursday too? I don't care about her. You come for me. Thursday and Friday they're doing the sinking. With the real boat," Miss Nisensohn says. "I got to have somebody I can talk to. Will you do it?"

"May I bring my Aunt Louisa?"

"Oh sure.— My brother Gus said this would be healthy for me," Miss Nisensohn says.

"Aunt Louisa says the same thing and I don't believe her."

"How are *you* doing?"

"I—" She really doesn't know. "I want to have stayed. I want to have talked with Dr. John at the end. I want to have done better."

"Yeah. I know. But who was I? I took pictures."

Neither of them says anything for a bit.

"You were with those people, on the ship," Miss Nisensohn asks. "Are they OK?"

"Miss Lady died, Miss Fan survived. Dr. John survived but he has pneumonia. He isn't doing well," she adds in a low voice in case Arbella can overhear.

Greta Nisensohn doesn't say anything for a bit. "Do you still want a picture of him?" she asks.

"It wouldn't be right to take pictures of him in the hospital."

"I mean— I don't need to take a picture," Greta Nisensohn says. "I have one. Some. I have all of them. I have the ones you asked me to take." She lowers her voice still farther. "I still have them."

"What do you mean?"

She doesn't say anything for even longer this time.

"I have the pictures I took on *Titanic*," she says. "I was all over *Titanic* taking pictures, that's why La Gibson wanted me. I was the only pro with a camera on board, I was so proud of myself, they were going to be huge news. When I went up on deck, I brought all the rolls of film I'd taken, and my camera and extra rolls of film. Because it was going to be a story, you know? *Titanic* hitting an iceberg, I was gonna be famous. I mean, it's who I am. I take pictures. I always have my camera with me.

"So I took more pictures. Up on deck."

Greta Nisensohn reaches into her bag. Black metal cylinders spill dark as blood onto the table.

"I didn't know *Titanic* would sink, did I? I sold the pictures I took on *Carpathia*. Three hundred dollars. You know how much I could get for *these*? *Titanic* before the wreck? Those people, that night? My folks aren't rich. *And I didn't know it was going to sink.* It was just going to be a huge story. Now, you know what? I sell them to somebody, they'll be all over the newspapers and I'll have to see them. People were about to die and I was taking pictures. I don't know who I am any more."

"Yes," Perdita says.

"Your friends' pictures, they're in there somewhere. Maybe I'll ask for them back one day. But right now I just can't have them. You get them developed, but not where somebody's going to make copies, OK?"

She pushes the cylinders into Perdita's hands. Perdita's fingers close over them. They feel huge and hard and heavy, like the shadows of lifeboats.

"And you come be with me when they film on the ship. Come Thursday if you can. I'm not trading. I'm asking. I'm not doing so well here."

"I'll come as soon as I can and I'll bring my aunt. I promise," Perdita says.

ॐॐॐ

SHE TELEPHONES MR. JOHNSON. No change in Dr. John. Mr. Johnson will get the photographs developed; she can drop them off or send them by messenger. Aunt Louisa still hasn't called, though it must be near ten.

Garnet calls from a drugstore. She is packing and wants to know if Perdita can come up to the apartment; she has clothes to give away.

Perdita telephones Aunt Louisa's, but no one answers. She will not call every five minutes. She will not drive herself crazy and use every nickel in New York calling.

She'll go to Garnet's. Mrs. Daniels will call Mr. Johnson if Aunt Louisa calls, and Mr. Johnson will send a messenger.

ॐॐॐ

"HOW COULD MRS. DEMAY say I should volunteer to be black!" Garnet says.

Garnet is discarding what seems like all her clothes. What suited Garnet won't do for Nanette.

"Try on this." Garnet tosses Perdita a hat.

"Mrs. deMay thinks you and Mr. Johnson would suit each other," Perdita says, pinning the hat on her head.

"So does Frog Jaw think so," Garnet says grimly.

Nothing for a bit but Garnet making disapproving noises about clothes.

"This jacket would look good on you," Garnet says finally. "Don't wear it anywhere important, though; it's last season."

The jacket is, she moves to the window to look at the color, deep coral, just a beautiful color; let Paris fashion think what it will. "I lost my red jacket. Now I'll wear this so Alexander can see me if he comes to New York." She hopes he's not coming; *please* let him not come yet.

"Here, I forgot, I was supposed to give this to you." Garnet hands over a scarf, a long silky thing in a splendid plum color. "A present from my new boss, Monsieur Édouard. Wear it with the jacket— oh, that's *right.*"

You wouldn't think the colors would go, but they do. No mistaking the pleasure in Garnet's voice.

"I know you have to take this Windsor Brothers job," Perdita says. "But Garnet—Liddy Boswick? If it's a matter of money at all, please, please let me help pay for someone better."

"Liddy will do OK. You stay out of that."

"Blind Willie's my teacher and I don't intend to lose him. If you're my friend, understand that. I would do the same for Dr. Fritz."

"No you wouldn't," Garnet says. "You'd trust his friends to look after him. Willie's got neighbors in this building, folks across the hall and upstairs and downstairs."

"Yes, but I'm one of his friends. What if all of his neighbors think *I'm interfering where I'm not wanted* and keep out? Garnet—"

"Folks don't keep out. We look after each other," Garnet says tightly.

"I can help."

"*We* help. You come tomorrow night. I'm having a party," Garnet says. "It's my farewell thing. You come. See Liddy, see who else will be looking after him. There'll be lots of people."

"I'll come."

"We can look after our own."

"I don't say you can't."

"I don't need you to help me."

There's a stiff silence.

"Frog Jaw told me how Paul deMay died," Garnet says. "You think Mr. Otis shot him?"

"I hope not, since he's staying at my apartment."

"I think it has to be Otis. Paul trusted the person he was going to meet. Who else would he have trusted at Fair Home? Not Dr. John. Not the white man."

"Paul deMay learned something," Perdita thinks aloud. "Or knew something. Was it that Dr. John sold his brother?"

"That was common enough!"

"Really?"

"Sure."

"But I can't imagine why either of them would have told Paul. Or why Mr. Otis would kill Paul."

Perdita feels her way toward Garnet's couch and sits down to think. Garnet sleeps on this couch every night; her grandpa has the bedroom. Bedroom, couch, piano; a gas ring to cook with; that's what Garnet and Blind Willie have in Harlem, and it's better than their apartment was in San Juan Hill.

Toby won't live like that.

What did Paul deMay learn?

He came down from Washington, to a place he hadn't been for almost forty years. Dr. John, Miss Lady, and Miss Fan gave him lunch. He went to the stables to see Whirlwind's son. Mr. Otis talked to him. And then he did what Mr. Otis must have asked. He went to the fields to meet someone and the someone killed him.

Mr. Otis? He'd been a little boy when Fate deMay and Paul had come to Fair Home. What could Otis have told Paul?

If it weren't Otis, who would Paul have trusted and gone to meet without a second thought?

She realizes, almost with a shudder, the only other answer.

"But he wasn't there," Perdita says aloud.

"Who wasn't?"

"Paul would have gone to meet Isaac. But Isaac wasn't there."

He could have been. By 1890 he would have been free.

Did Isaac come back to Fair Home?

Bury me at Fair Home. They cannot deny a dead man.

And then the whole story flips round, and she closes her eyes, but still she sees.

"You know what's strange?" she hears herself saying in a tight pale voice. "Paul deMay saw Dr. John at the theatre, with Miss Lady and Miss Fan. Dr. John should have been obviously Dr. John. But Paul said to his wife that he thought he saw Isaac."

Say it's not strange.

"That is strange," Garnet says.

Perdita presses her lips together but she must go on. "Then Paul went to Fair Home. He wouldn't have gone if he thought it was dangerous."

"What are you talking about?"

"He went to Fair Home," Perdita says, feeling as numb as if she were on the cold sea. "Because he thought he was safe. He thought whatever he found out wouldn't hurt him. The man he found it out from wouldn't hurt him. Because Isaac was his friend."

"What? Where does Isaac come in?"

She doesn't want to say this. But it's a responsibility; a gift; a truth, implacable as an iceberg.

Who would Paul trust? His best friend. She feels it closing in upon her, a bulk, a freezing cold—

She opens her eyes.

"Paul thought Dr. John was Isaac," Perdita says. "And, oh, Garnet. He went to Fair Home and he found out it was true."

⮞⮞⮞

"BUT THAT'S NOT POSSIBLE," Perdita says. "Garnet, tell me it isn't possible."

Garnet puts down the clothes she's sorting and sits down by her.

Because it can't be true. Because Aunt Louisa has told her she and Toby are white. Because Perdita and dear Toby can't be black. Because they want to be American.

But I never believed her.

"Because Miss Lady would never have called Isaac her son," she says. "That's why it can't be true. Not only because he was black. Because her husband was Isaac's father and she hated that."

Garnet lets out a big puff of breath.

"Or it's true and they're all in it together," Garnet says.

"No."

"It could be," says Garnet. "Your Miss Lady could have been in on it. The way you talk about her."

"She absolutely wouldn't have."

"Your Miss Lady?" Garnet says. "Think about her. The end of the War, nobody had any money, people didn't even have food. Her son was gone. And then one evening he comes back, riding down the road toward the plantation. He's bringing her Whirlwind, the horse she lost.

"Then he gets closer and it's the wrong man.

"You think she couldn't look at him and think it'd be so handy if it was her John who came back? You think she couldn't want that, couldn't, no, not her? Because the man who did come back wasn't white? Honey. Here's a crippled woman with no man in the house, and here's a man who sort of looks like her son and could pass for him and take care of her?"

"John and Isaac didn't look that alike, Garnet!"

"Before the War John was clean-shaven. After the War he had a big long beard and a scar on his face. Sure he didn't look like he used to. After four years of war, probably no one did. It didn't matter. She said he was John and she was his own mother and why would she lie?"

"She wouldn't do it, though."

"What would have happened to her if he'd gone away again? With his money? And with Aunt Jane?"

With Aunt Jane. Isaac's mother. Aunt Jane, who had taken care of Miss Lady all their lives.

Who wanted to stay at Fair Home.

No.

"It's impossible." Perdita hesitates. "Garnet," she lowers her voice; she is ashamed of saying this but it's what Miss Lady would have felt. "Garnet, Miss Lady wouldn't have stood for his *marrying Miss Fan*. Miss Lady wouldn't have married her own cousin to a black man."

"Just because your aunt screamed and ran when she realized she'd married a black man."

"I'm sorry, Garnet, but Miss Lady wouldn't have done it."

"Not until she'd lied good and solid to herself and decided he maybe was her white son after all and if she ever thought any different she jes' must be plumb mistaken," Garnet says. "You don't know how people can lie to themselves. She would have been desperate."

I saw the ruins of railroads and farmsteads, Dr. John says in Perdita's head; *burned houses, human bones in the fields, skulls.*

They had all been desperate. "But that desperate? And what about him?"

"I think Miss Lady offered him a chance to be white at Fair Home," Garnet says. "And wasn't that what he wanted his entire life?"

Dr. John had gone up to the door, past the ruins and skulls, with no intention of staying. To give back the horse, because Miss Lady wouldn't rest until she found Whirlwind.

But he hadn't come only to give back the horse.

Her skin chills.

He'd come because *I didn't know if Mamma was alive or dead.*

Dr. John said that.

His mother.

But if his mother were Miss Lady—

She feels as cold as if she were outside, on the deck, with the ship still shuddering from the iceberg and the deck covered in ice. Ancient rotted cold, a dark smell that spears her nose and lungs and heart and bones.

Rich or poor, Miss Lady owned Fair Home. She was important. If *Mamma* were Miss Lady, everyone in four counties would have known she was alive.

Dr. John wouldn't have had to go home to know that.

He wanted to work with our horses, Dr. John said about Isaac. With Whirlwind, and all the horses of Fair Home. Whirlwind, whom Dr. John had wanted enough to steal; who knew Dr. John so well that he followed him for an apple.

I wanted to work with our horses.

Dr. John went back to Fair Home to see what had happened to his mother.

Not Miss Lady.

Aunt Jane.

Who had not known why Isaac would leave Fair Home. Who thought freedom was not worth as much as Fair Home.

So he stayed.

I think I have never been out of prison since.

But I don't want this, Perdita thinks. I don't want my boy to drink from rusty water fountains and go to bad schools. I don't want my Toby in prison.

Garnet of all people should understand that.

"You want to be white," Garnet says.

Perdita says what Mrs. deMay did. "I want to be human."

"You know what white is?" Garnet says. "White is what's convenient for white people. There was some legislator in South Carolina, of all places, who said they shouldn't pass the one-drop rule because every family he knew had mixed blood. Georgia used to vote people white, I'm not kidding. If you had some acreage and folks could see you in the dark, you could have someone sponsor a bill and they'd just law you up white. Look at them changing the law now, that one-drop rule, changing what it means to be black, that's what one-drop means, it's convenient for white people that some people are white and some aren't and so they *pass a law*. Well, I say it was convenient for Miss Lady to have a live white son, so that's what she had."

"But then Miss Lady and Miss Fan must know all of this."

"And Mr. Otis too, I bet."

"But then what happened at Manassas?"

"Don't you know?"

Perdita shakes her head.

"Two men just after a battle?" Garnet says. "Smoke everywhere and everybody's filthy from gunpowder? One man's wounded and unconscious? And the slave driver's right there?"

"No."

"Who'd have been wounded? Isaac was back with the horses. Isaac whips the coat and boots off Massa and gets dressed in Massa's clothes, and he goes to the slave driver, *take him now*, Isaac says, *take this boy now, he's hurt but he'll get over it*, and who's selling who?"

"The slave dealer would have known who was who."

"He wouldn't. Slave dealers didn't hang round a neighborhood. That man hadn't probably seen either John or Isaac but a few times. Now someone in a coat and boots is offering a fine barefoot boy cheap. You think he's looking hard?"

Garnet's crisp clear downtown tones change a little, broaden a little; it's Willie's granddaughter speaking.

"It's happened before, a man selling his master. Grandpa heard this story in N'awlins before the War, and if it's not true it should be." There's a different cadence in Garnet's voice. "There was a young Massa, a whiskey-sippin' fool, drunk all night, asleep all day. His man Rastus was cool and clever and light. They were visiting N'awlins. One afternoon, Young Massa's asleep dreaming of bottles. Rastus strips him to pants and bare feet, gets dressed in Massa's best jacket and boots, goes down to the Exchange. 'I have me a bad slave, drunk all the time, I got to get rid of him. Give me five hundred dollar, he's yours.' Slave driver gives him the money. 'I want to warn you about that boy, he is difficult-minded, might say you got no right to him, but you just show him this paper.' And Rastus signs his master's name to the bill of sale and pockets the five hundred dollars and by the time things get straightened out, Rastus is a free man in Canada."

Garnet laughs for the first time since Perdita's arrived in New York. A real laugh.

"Can you picture that young drunk's face," Garnet says. "'You just show him this paper.' And it's signed with his own name. Grandpa says everybody who could, white and black, went down to see that white boy in the slave jail before his folks ransomed him."

Some part of Garnet will always be her grandfather's granddaughter, even if she crosses forever over the line. And no matter who Perdita's grandfather is, Perdita will never know in quite the same way how to laugh at that joke, or feel it's her joke she has a right to laugh at.

She can't be black, because she isn't. Dr. John can't be.

"You want the real white John Rolfe Church to somehow magically end up in New York. But how's that going to happen?" Garnet stands up. "No. Here's what happens. Miss Lady's son wakes up and says 'I'm white.' The slave dealer says 'Your master told me you were going to say that, but it don't wash, boy.' 'I'm John Rolfe Church of Fair Home.' 'And I'm Queen Victoria, Empress of India. You shut up, boy, or I whip you.' That slave dealer whipped him to make him black and then he sold him. Took Bright John to Alexandria probably, put him on a coastal boat to New Orleans or Galveston."

"But his family would have been looking for him."

"Not if they thought he was dead."

"But eventually he must have got free."

Eventually. From Brazil? In 1888?

"And he would have gone home."

They cannot deny a dead man.

He did go home.

It must have taken him such a long time. He was much farther away than anybody could have guessed. But finally he got home, expecting to get the prodigal's welcome. And when he did—

John Rolfe Church was already there. Head of the plantation, married to John Rolfe Church's best friend's widow—

And Miss Lady denied him.

Cast-him-off.

"Miss Lady would *not* have denied him," Perdita says, cold all through. "She couldn't. He was her son."

"She already had her son," Garnet says. "She had her *boy*," and the sudden bitterness in her voice is startling. "Her perfect *boy*. Her *boy* brought the horse back. Came with money. For her." Garnet's voice goes slow and low, like narrowed eyes. "Wouldn't that be dynamite for Paul to know? Sweet little old white lady denies her own son and calls her slave her son? Marries him to her own cousin? Nobody would invite *her* to a party again."

Could it have been white John Rolfe Church who went to Paris and hated all black people, even Barry Bullard?

But Miss Lady? When she went to Paris? Her own son was there dead and she didn't want to look at his face? "No," Perdita says. "He was her *son*. Her only child. You can make her out a monster, but she wasn't."

"I make her out whatever she had to be. Southerners! They made their own children slaves."

"But," Perdita takes a deep breath. "But who killed Paul, then?"

"When a man gets lynched, what does it matter who throws the rope over the tree? Paul went down to Fair Home and he saw John was Isaac. The Churches would have stood in line to shoot him."

"Do you read Sherlock Holmes?" Perdita asks desperately.

"Do you think a black woman doesn't read Sherlock Holmes? What does Sherlock Holmes have to do with it?"

"I'm asking *you* if *you* read Sherlock Holmes, Garnet. You know how complicated those stories are, gigantic hounds and stuffing a snake through the ventilator. But real people don't work that way. Why would somebody kill their stepdaughter with a snake? Isn't it just so Sherlock Holmes can look smart?"

"Of course. And?"

"Why would Miss Lady deny her own child? Why would Miss Lady take her slave for her son and reject her own son? She wouldn't. It's a snake through the ventilator."

"She did it because she could. It's not about skin color. It's those that can against those that can't. And if you don't see that," Garnet says, "you must be blind."

❧❧❧

IN THE SILENCE Perdita tries to say something about Uncle Gilbert and Alexander and about the force of family. About Uncle Gilbert, who looked for Richard eighteen years and could take no one else. But she can't talk about them even to Garnet.

It is not true. Miss Lady would have asked Isaac *What did you do with my son? Where is my son?* Perdita can almost hear her. Miss Lady would have taken no one but her beloved only son. Miss Lady wouldn't have put someone else in his place and denied him.

But why did Aunt Louisa give away her child?

"I don't believe it," she says.

It is so small a place, Garnet's and Blind Willie's apartment. There's only the tiny scrap of parlor, full of the sofa and Blind Willie's upright piano. There's a closet with a gas ring for a kitchen, and Blind Willie's bedroom off the kitchen. Garnet and Willie pay a lot for it. But now Garnet will be renting white.

Garnet is not wrong to want an easier life.

Neither is Perdita.

All she has to do is not think any more about this.

But to be white, what would she do?

Would she give away Toby?

Never.

Would she make her cousin marry a black man?

Miss Lady would never go that far.

What would she do?

Would she shoot a man?

People shoot people. Alexander did.

And she left children to die. Because her only thought was having Dr. John say she was white.

"I'm sorry," Garnet says. "Believe what you want." Garnet is moving around the apartment now, tidying up her knickknacks. "Do you want a picture of Willie? I can't take it.— Here."

Garnet thrusts the frame at her and she holds it to the light. A dark shadow in a white mist; she sees the stripes of one of Willie's gaudy vests.

Would she give up playing piano with Blind Willie, to be white?

What would she do? What is she capable of?

She is capable of anything.

Cowards are capable of anything.

"I'll keep this picture till you can have it back," she tells Garnet.

"You keep it for you, I won't have it back."

Garnet, you cannot deny him.

Neither can I.

"Here, I'm putting it in your purse," Garnet says. "You should have a little bag, not that big thing like a postman's sack, it's ugly."

Never any more to call your grandfather your grandfather.

Never to call your child your child.

Who could do it?

Could Miss Lady deny her son?

"I'm going to call Aunt Louisa again," she says.

Of course Garnet doesn't have a phone. Black people don't have phones; even if they can pay for them, the phone company doesn't think they can.

"I'll come with you to the drugstore," Garnet says.

From the drugstore phone booth they call Aunt Louisa. "Please please please," Perdita whispers into the phone.

But the phone rings and rings, and Aunt Louisa doesn't answer.

"I've got to shop for food," Garnet says. "Come with me," a sort of apology.

"No, I need to talk with Aunt Louisa. I'll see you at the Strauses' memorial service."

"All right," Garnet says, and hesitates. "Willie? He might not even be my grandfather. He was married to my grandmother, but that doesn't necessarily mean— Look at the color he is and the color I am."

"Garnet. He's your family."

Miss Lady would have wanted her son. She could not have denied him.

"Aunt Louisa will tell me the man in St Vincent's is John."

"Of course she will," Garnet says.

❧❧❧

BRUCE ISMAY, when forced to talk about *Titanic,* finds it increasingly difficult to say what happened. He is asked about the lifeboats. Did he know that the final design of *Titanic* specified only sixteen, instead of the 48 that would have saved everyone?

Certainly he knew. But, his biographer Frances Wilson writes, "Ismay denied having ever seen *any such design.* Nor did he *know that anybody connected with the White Star Line saw such a design.* Moments later he conceded that, *I saw the design I have no doubt; I saw the design with the rest of the ship,* after which he once again insisted that *I tell you I have never seen any such design....*"

For him, the only truth must be that he is not to blame. So it becomes not only harder and harder for him to tell the truth, but even to know the truth.

⁊⁊⁊

AT WEST WASHINGTON SQUARE, "Have you seen Aunt Louisa?" Perdita asks the doorman. "Have Aunt Louisa or Betty walked the Girls? Is she out?"

"Haven't seen either of them, Miss. Haven't seen the Girls all day."

The Girls on a walk are conspicuous, four huge white poodles galloping off to Washington Square dragging Aunt Louisa or Betty.

"I was expecting her to call me."

Perhaps Aunt Louisa is trying to protect her by refusing to say anything.

"May I leave a message for her?" Why hasn't she called?

She leaves a note. Over on Broadway, she gets herself a cup of coffee at a place with sidewalk tables, almost like Paris, and sits and thinks.

Miss Fan could not have even considered marrying a black man. The thought would not have come into her mind, a Southern lady marrying an ex-slave.

That is quite certain.

Is it? She sits with her coffee cup between her hands.

People are not Southern ladies and ex-slaves; they are themselves. They were not two melodrama-characters of their race and their time, they were Miss Fan and Dr. John, Miss Fan with a landless child and Dr. John who wanted to work with Whirlwind and the horses of Fair Home; two survivors of a war they lost.

Still—

Mr. Otis? She doesn't know him. He seems an ordinary man enough. She has hardly spoken to him. He tiptoes down the hall to keep from disturbing people.

Dr. John laughed with her over tea and talked about freedom.

Miss Fan let herself be under Miss Lady's thumb.

Aunt Louisa gave away a child.

Aunt Jane—

Miss Lady—

Miss Fan—

These are ordinary people.

Ordinary people do terrible things.

It's *wrong*, that's all. Dr. John is Dr. John.

"What time is it?" she asks the waiter.

It's five already. The Straus memorial service is at seven.

Aunt Louisa must be home by now.

❧❧❧

THE DOORMAN still can't reach Aunt Louisa's apartment. Perdita's note is still in the mailbox.

Discouraged, angry, Perdita takes her way toward West Fourth Street, ticking her cane dejectedly against the wall of Aunt Louisa's building, the way she'd kick a chair leg if she were sitting down. She thinks of standing outside, chaining herself to Aunt Louisa's railings like a suffragist, until Aunt Louisa comes out and they both face what they have to.

And then, just as she's carefully pausing at the corner for the traffic, she hears something. Aunt Louisa's apartment is on the corner, to get the breezes in the summer.

She hears dogs barking, frantic to get out.

It's The Girls.

They haven't been walked.

They sound as if they haven't been walked all day.

❧❧❧

STRAUS MOURNERS OUT IN VAST THRONG

Such a Crowd at East Side Hall That Memorial Services Are Postponed.

MAY HAVE TO GET GARDEN

The memorial services which were to be held last night in memory of Isidor Straus had to be abondoned because of the great crowd which assembled and which, because of its congestion, threatened for a time to create serious injury to many people.

It was planned to hold the services in the auditorium of the Educational Alliance, which was founded by Mr. Straus, and of which he was President. The Alliance Building is at East Broadway and Jefferson Street.

As early as 5 o'clock last evening about 10,000 residents of the east side had congregated about the auditorium's vicinity, blocking traffic. Capt. Liebers of the Madison Street Station called out his reserves to keep order. By 7 o'clock more than 25,000 people choked every avenue of access to the auditorium.

Those in charge of the services, fear-
ing serious consequences because of the
crowding of the narrow streets, appealed
to the police for additional help, and
Inspector Cahalane sent reserves from
several neighboring police stations. The
iron railing at the Jefferson Street side
of the auditorium was broken down and
a number of persons fell into the area-
way.

Perdita will hear about it later. The enormous crowd, so closely packed that people's feet can't touch the sidewalk. The crowd tilting, swaying, uncontrolled, shrieking with sorrow. East Broadway rolling beneath them like waves. Musicians hurriedly called out of the Alliance Building to play the mobs quiet, because when the people panic the musicians must calm them; but no use, the mourners weep and shout and press tighter, tighter, until a piece of Jefferson Street turns into a sinkhole, the crowd falls, women and children. Metal groans, people scream, people fall, crying *Help*, people are drowning in a sea of people. Garnet Williams and the other models from Macy's are caught at the edge of the crowd, horrified—

But Perdita isn't there, because she turns back and pushes open the door of Aunt Louisa's building. "The Girls are up there all alone," she tells the doorman breathlessly. "They are distressed, they haven't been walked, I can hear it. I am" her granddaughter "her great-niece, I will take responsibility, but please, please, open her door, I think something is wrong."

Even with the doorman, she has to play the blind card. *I am so distressed, so helpless.* The doorman sends finally for the janitor, and the janitor slops up the stairs jangling his keys and muttering "That Betty will take my ear off."

"Betty will give you a piece of pie and I will give you a dollar." The janitor tries one copy of the master key and then another.

The dogs boil out of the door as he opens it.

And the smell hits them.

The smell of blood.

ᴓᴓᴓ

IN NEW YORK, on the banks of the Hudson, another memorial is taking shape. Actors from every film being made at the Fort Lee studios, newspaper reporters, stringers from *Photoplay* and *Motion Picture News* gawk as a nameless wreck from Staten Island is painted fresh again: her black hull, her White Star black-and-caramel funnels, and the great white name on the side, *TITANIC*. Enterprising photographers work the crowd, offering to pose them with props: a railing, a quickly painted superstructure backdrop, a lifesaver marked *TITANIC*. A puff piece appears in the *New York Times:*

SAVED FROM THE TITANIC!

Last Moments of Luxury
Liner Recreated on Film

NEW YORK TO WITNESS

Miss Dorothy Gibson, the young actress who barely escaped the sinking *Titanic*, tells her own story in a new adventure film. This coming Friday morning, in full view of New York, the actress will re-create for Éclair Films her escape from the doomed liner.

"No expense has been spared," says photoplay director Jules Brulatour, fiancé of the New York beauty. An actual ship has been engaged to stand in for the doomed giant and is being equipped with Welin davits and lifeboats identical to those used on the fateful night.

Spectators are invited to watch from the banks of the Hudson by the 125th St. ferry as Miss Gibson and other survivors recreate the last moments of the disaster. Doctors and nurses will be standing by to assist those whose nerves give way...

Everyone wants to be on board this time.

This time nothing bad will happen.

No one will die.

Part 4: Titanic

Mr. Otis W. Church

OTIS FOLLOWS THE OLD LADY from St. Vincent's, prickly-skinned all over. Following a white woman. Even at home where they know him, it'd be dangerous. He moves from alley to alley.

The old lady stops at a church. He comes in behind her. Nuns are praying and singing by the altar. Nothing he can do here. He kneels two rows behind her. She whispers into her hands.

Outside, he comes up behind her. She turns and sees him.

She isn't afraid. Of course not; white woman, big city, street lights, everything bright like a store window, people passing by.

"I'm from Fair Home, ma'am. Got a message from him for you. Something he told me before he got sick."

"From John?" She looks eager to break your heart. "My home is just round the corner. We can talk there, and Betty will make us tea."

There's a Betty. Maybe he can do what he has to without rousing Betty.

He hasn't got his gun. He's got his hoof pick, a hand-wrought pick with one side sharpened.

"The building management dislikes some of my guests, I'm sorry to say." She has a key to the alley door. They go up the back stairs. He fingers his hoof-pick out of his pocket, meaning to do it on the stairs, but too late, she's opened the door.

"I'm afraid my dogs may bark at you. They are completely unreasonable. Shush, Girls! Betty," she calls, and goes inside into a dark hall, and turns just as he raises his arm.

She raises her hands to protect herself, but too late. He whips the sharpened edge across her neck. She clamps one hand around her throat, trying to stop the blood, and whispers "Oh, Betty, go back."

Otis turns and sees Betty.

ॐॐॐ

IT'S EARLY, NOT EVEN DAWN YET. On the streets it smells like country early morning.

In Heaven, if Otis gets there, it will always be early morning. He will always be in the barn at Fair Home. Four o'clock, dark and chill outside. In Heaven it'll be just him and the horses in the barn, him moving among them, warm with their warmth, rubbing noses, saying *good morning, boy, good morning, girl, here's day.*

He's just killed two white women.

What now?

Think.

Nobody knows the old lady had a connection to Fair Home except the girl and Miss Fan, Miss Arbella, and maybe Mamma. Mamma, Miss Bella, and Miss Fan never read the papers.

But the girl knows.

He goes back to the apartment. The girl's there. He stops by her door but sees a line of light underneath it. She's awake. She'll scream. The doorman's right outside and Miss Arbella's down the hall. He can't do it here, not in front of Miss Bella.

He changes his shirt, looks for blood on his jacket. He doesn't see any. In the closet in the hall is the coat John gave the girl to wear on *Titanic.* Better coat than Otis ever had. Warm, and he's shivering. He shrugs it on. Big on him.

He walks downtown by Riverside. His group of black men swimmers are splashing and shivering in the cold Hudson water. *Here's Otis,* they say, *Otis who don't drown. You swimming today?*

Zack told him, *swim and you can escape.* Otis thinks of swimming out past the shallows into the cold, into the thick muscled tide of the river, swimming like one of those people who drowned last week trying to escape the ship. What good did it do them, swimming?

"Not today."

The girl.

Can't make it look like another robbery.

But she's blind.

He can make it look like an accident.

Perdita

BETTY IS STILL ALIVE and is taken to St. Vincent's. In a nurse's office at the hospital, Perdita is interviewed by the police.

They want to know why someone would want to murder Aunt Louisa.

Mr. Otis was at St. Vincent's last night, she tells herself. Tell them I heard him coming back to the apartment late. Say I think he murdered Aunt Louisa.

Say why.

But she can't say why.

Over the raw empty stink of disinfectant, she smells Aunt Louisa's apartment: St-John's-wort tea and graham crackers and dog and over it all, the cutting copper edge of blood.

"When did you see your aunt last?" they ask her.

"At lunch Monday." It's as if she's telling them about her trip on *Titanic,* lifetimes ago.

She can't tell them.

She can't.

"Did Betty see who it was?" she asks.

"No, ma'am."

She has to tell.

The police leave her alone for awhile. She sits with Betty. "Oh G-d, Miss, what'll I do?" Betty sobs. Betty says she woke up in the middle of the night, hearing the Girls barking. "Miss Louisa told me she'd be out late so I was asleep. She never makes me wait up. But the Girls don't bark when she comes in so I thought it was a burglar. I took the baseball bat I keep under my bed, and I went out of my room. And I heard her in the hall calling out to me, it was dark but I heard her, all faint, I think she was saying 'Betty, go back.' She thought of me." Someone wrestled the baseball bat away from Betty and hit her on the head with it. Betty has a bad concussion and a broken collarbone and she may be blind in one eye forever.

"It's not so bad, Miss, is it?" Betty pleads, holding onto Perdita's hand. "Being blind?"

Someone dragged Betty, unconscious, all the way down the hall to her room and closed the door. Someone dragged Aunt Louisa's body to her room and closed her door too.

And then the same somebody fed and watered the dogs.

Like a person whose job it is to care for animals.

Mr. Otis.

ℛℛℛ

THE POLICE leave Perdita alone for a bit and she goes upstairs to see Dr. John. There's no change; he is asleep, his breath drags heavily in and out. Miss Fan and Aunt Jane are drowsing in chairs by his bed. Mr. Otis isn't there. Miss Fan comes out into the hall with Perdita and offers her a cookie. It's the cookie that convinces her: Miss Fan is innocent, she doesn't know.

"Miss Fan, did Aunt Louisa come last night?"

"She knelt by his bedside and held his hand and said she was sorry. Then she told me. She gave me a paper and told me I had nothing to worry about," Miss Fan said. "I suppose I should take against her but I can't. She is the nicest woman. You are lucky in your relatives, Miss Perdita." Miss Fan pats her hand.

"She said nothing at all?"

"Just she was sorry."

"Did she ask you anything?"

"No, Miss Perdita." Miss Fan sounds puzzled.

Miss Fan and Aunt Jane have been watching Dr. John all night. Neither of them have left Dr. John's side since Aunt Louisa came and went.

But Mr. Otis did.

🙰🙰🙰

THE POLICE ask Perdita more questions. Did Aunt Louisa have enemies? Was she worried about burglars? She went out late Monday night; does Perdita know where?

Aunt Louisa was here in St Vincent's.

She can't say so.

My grandmother married a black man. She gave her own child away, my mother, rather than tell her her father was black. She knew that Dr. John wasn't Dr. John. She was killed for that.

And I can't tell you.

The police ask the same questions again and again. They don't believe her story. Alexander says she can't lie.

"Whoever it was cut her throat with a hoof-pick," a nurse says. "For cleaning the dirt out of horse's hoofs. All the cabmen have them. They sharpen the off-edge and fight and cut each other with them and the cuts get infected."

A hoof-pick. Mr. Otis must have one.

Stupid blind girl. She's dead and you can't tell the police who did it?

The police ask, who did Aunt Louisa leave her money to?

"To charities and me. She told me" yesterday morning. Only yesterday.

"Did she have any enemies?"

"No."

Only me.

Betty has been sedated but can't sleep. A doctor is going to operate on her eye later today. "Do you remember how she sang?" Betty quavers. "She couldn't carry a tune in a bucket. I know she'll sing in Heaven. Do you remember how much she loved Caruso?"

"I was going to take her to the *Titanic* memorial to hear Caruso. I was going to take her to New Jersey to watch a movie being made."

I must tell.

"She used to make me so mad, Miss Perdita. She and that Miss Opal or Miss Alden would be planning a protest with papers spread out all over the dining-room table, and there I'd be with dinner burning. The wrongs of women, what about the wrongs of me?"

"Betty, did you hear the person who did this?"

"Who would do it? No one would *rob* her," Betty says, clutching Perdita's hand. "She never has any money in the house, she'll give it to any poor woman— Oh, L—d, what'll become of me? What'll happen to the Girls? Nobody will take four big dumb dogs and a blind woman."

"I'll make sure you're all right, Betty, you and the Girls too."

Betty cries like a child, still gripping Perdita's hand as hard as a woman can do who kneads bread every day. Her sobs slow; finally she is only snoring. Perdita gently twists her fingers free and sits massaging her hand.

She thinks, exhausted, I must talk to Aunt Louisa, I must get her advice on this tomorrow—

There is no tomorrow.

"Perdita?"

It's Opal Lee.

"Come outside and talk."

Tenth Street smells of late night and garbage and ashes. They find a café, deserted and chilly and too bright for their tired eyes, and seat themselves at a sticky zinc-covered table. The counterman rouses himself enough to give them hours-old bitter tea; they can hear him yawning as he slumps back, sloshing cups through the rinsing-sink for the morning. Two glasses clink against each other like cold bells.

"How are you holding up, dear?" Opal Lee asks.

Perdita hears Aunt Louisa: *Are you keeping strong?*

"How could this happen? To *her?*"

I shall never see her again, never have lunch with her, never play music for her at the Villards' or anywhere else; never be the person she teaches about investing or NAWSA or the NAACP; never be her beloved granddaughter, never hear her whole story. She asked me to introduce her to Miss Fan *and I did it.*

I have to tell the police about the Churches.

I must do something or I am guilty of her death.

"It wasn't robbery," Opal Lee says. "She had her mother's gold earrings on, as if she had dressed up for someone.—I *simply don't know why.*"

Perdita can't do this; she can't stay silent.

"Miss Lee, Opal, you are my lawyer. Is whatever I say to you in confidence? Aunt Louisa came to see someone here at St Vincent's last night."

She explains about John Rolfe Church, Aunt Louisa's marriage, Miss Fan, Dr. John; she almost tells her the rest, but not about Isaac. "Last night, Aunt Louisa brought the papers that you drew up for us and told Miss Fan not to worry."

"And someone followed her from there?"

"There's a man staying at my apartment, a Mr. Otis Church, one of the family servants. He was at St Vincent's last night and then he left. He," she phrases it carefully so as not to cast suspicion on Mr. Otis in case he's innocent. "He may have been involved in a killing before."

"My G-d. Who is this Otis Church? Does he have a stake in this?—Never mind, of course he does, the servants always have a stake. I know of a housemaid who killed her mistress for a fifty-dollar inheritance."

"I don't know for sure that he did it."

"This man is staying at your apartment? We are going there right now and you're going to pack some clothes and stay in my spare room where he can't find you."

"Aunt Louisa and I were going to Fort Lee together," Perdita says, and puts her head in her hands. "I kept phoning her and phoning her. But she was dead."

❧❧❧

AT RIVERSIDE DRIVE, Opal Lee is so nervous about Mr. Otis that she asks the doorman to go through the apartment beforehand. Nobody is there, though, not any of the Churches, not even Mrs. Daniels.

"Why didn't I bring my gun?" Opal Lee says. "I never think to bring it." She rummages in the kitchen drawers for a knife.

By feel, in her dark bedroom, Perdita goes through the few clothes in her closet. She should have asked Garnet to get her mourning. She has nothing dark but the suit she's worn for two days.

The doorman knocks at the door. "Ma'am, you have a caller. Mr. Buckingham Pelham."

"Don't stay to talk," Opal Lee says. "Let's get out of here. Never mind about clothes, we'll buy you something at Macy's—"

"I have to talk to him, he's Aunt Louisa's brother."

Uncle Bucky is knocking at the door. "Niece—"

"Or you could borrow clothes from Loulie," Opal says in a suddenly shocked voice. "I thought that just now. Loulie could lend you something." She bursts into tears.

"I don't know what this is about," Uncle Bucky says as she opens the door for him. "Why are you crying? Niece, I must tell you—"

"Are you not here about Aunt Louisa?"

"Louisa?"

She is the one who has to tell him his sister is dead.

"*Why?*" he says.

She'll have to tell someone why. She has to say. She leans against the wall. All she can think of is trivial things. Here she is again the way she was on *Carpathia*, in wrinkled clothes and stockings that need changing.

Aunt Louisa's dead.

"Loulie was still married to John Church," Opal Lee says to Bucky. "We think it was a matter of inheritance."

"Uncle Bucky, did Aunt Louisa talk to you about her marriage?"

"Never."

"Did you know she never divorced her husband?"

"What?"

"The husband's near death now," Opal Lee says, "he never knew, the supposed wife didn't know until *Loulie told her*. Perdita thinks a family servant killed Loulie to keep her from inheriting their farm. And Perdita is Loulie's heir. I am taking her off to be safe."

"No." Uncle Bucky clears his throat. "I am sorry, niece. I mean you must be safe, but—I did not know, there is a complication. I have just found out—I'm sorry—your husband is arriving in New York today. And I am afraid Harry has done something very inadvisable. Gilbert Knight has come too. And Harry has— There is no good word for it. Harry has virtually kidnapped Gilbert."

Reisden

"What were you thinking?" Reisden says bleakly.

Gilbert has spent the entire voyage in his cabin. The porthole's open, with a view of a lifeboat. Gilbert has laid his life jacket out on the sofa-bed and piled neatly on it a flashlight, cheese, and a box of crackers. Reisden moves these preparations for shipwreck aside and sits down.

"I didn't wish to worry you, Alexander."

"Worry me, my dear G-d."

The cabin is punctiliously neat but Gilbert looks as if he hasn't slept since he left shore. Reisden knows about that.

"You were supposed to be in Paris taking care of Toby."

"Mr. Daugherty is doing that," Gilbert says. "And this was the only ship going as fast as you— I am sorry, Ri— Alexander."

"You were supposed to be *safe*," Reisden says with an anger that surprises even him. "To stay in Paris with Toby, take Tiggy to the movies, and keep bloody well out of the way. Now here we are, never mind that we're on the same ship; it'll look as if we're conspiring.— The book. I hope you left it back in Paris."

Gilbert glances at his steamer trunk.

"May we throw it overboard?"

"Mr. Daugherty feels," Gilbert hunts for words. "He feels that if there is any question of your exerting undue influence on me— Not that Harry would actually assert such a thing."

"Harry knows who I am. And even he must understand why I'll never go back."

There is a silence. "It is not a subject I would bring up with Harry," Gilbert says. 'He— I— Certainly he does not act as if he knows."

It takes Reisden a moment to understand the implications of this. They don't talk about Richard. Gilbert said once, *I knew you were Richard because you didn't want to come back.* But Harry—

"I can't believe I don't know the answer to this. But does Harry know what Richard did?"

"It is not something I would speak of with him, Alexander."

"But does he?" Would he act this way if he did? "Does Bucky Pelham know?"

"I have never spoken of it."

"Do I have the privilege of explaining what happened? To them?"

"You did nothing anyone would blame you for."

"I *killed* someone." He stands up. "I have a patient. He was a mountaineer, he cut a rope and his friend fell a thousand feet and died. He makes rope now. I asked him what he meant by it. He said, I want the rope I didn't cut."

"You were *not* to blame."

"I want the rope I didn't cut. I want it not to have happened. But it did."

"It was *not your fault.*"

He leans against the wall. Cold; it's a ship in the North Atlantic. He puts his hands in his pockets; he's shaking a little and doesn't want it to show.

"It doesn't matter. The rope doesn't uncut. What I can do, I do; and what I can do is be someone else. I am never going back to being Richard. Why don't Harry and Pelham believe it? They think I'm a moral defective instead.— Dear Heavens, why didn't you stay in Paris."

"I am to blame. I went out for a smoke," Gilbert said.

"What?"

"I smoked then. Back when—then. I went out for a smoke and left you. And when I came back, you were gone."

"Forgiven," Reisden says, and then adds, "I probably waited until you left before I ran."

Then he listens to himself.

"I don't forgive myself," Gilbert says; but Reisden isn't paying attention.

I ran, he realizes; I ran, and left you to look for Richard for eighteen years. I don't blame myself for running. It was the best thing I ever did.

But I ran and I left you not knowing. You had eighteen years not knowing whether Richard was alive or dead.

What would I have done if it had been Toby who disappeared?

Gone mad and kept hunting for him.

Exactly what you did.

And if Toby were gone for eighteen years and came back?

I would walk across the floor of the Atlantic to be with him again.

Unless Toby didn't want it.

And that is what I've done to you. Said I didn't want it.

I lied. And oh G-d, I'm sorry.

You are the rope I should not have cut.

☙☙☙

"THIS IS WHAT YOU'LL DO," he tells Gilbert.

The arrival of a ship in New York Harbor follows well-known routine. A liner officially scheduled for Wednesday noon may get to the Ambrose light-ship as early as Tuesday night; the exact time is a matter of the captain's pride and the weather.

The liner anchors at the Ambrose until the quarantine officer and the harbor pilot arrive in the early morning. The harbor pilot stays on board to enjoy breakfast and guide the liner to her pier on the incoming tide.

But the quarantine officer is a different story. He has only to certify the health of the first- and second-class passengers. (Third-class are examined on Ellis Island.) Then he leaves. On a modern ship, quarantine inspection is usually empty ritual. It makes the quarantine officer, not bribable precisely, but bored and easy to persuade.

Occasionally he'll let passengers leave with him.

"The *Bremen* will dock at Hoboken," Reisden tells Gilbert. "Harry will be waiting for you there. But you'll have got off on the quarantine officer's boat and landed at Battery Park. You'll stay at a hotel you've not used before, under another name. When you're settled, telephone—" Not the apartment. "Telephone Louisa Church, Perdita's aunt, and leave a message." He has her number in his memorandum book; he writes it down for Gilbert. "As soon as possible, I want you back in Paris."

"Shall I stay at the Astor House, do you think, Alexander?"

The Astor House is the venerable upper-class hotel for the venerable upper class; exactly where Gilbert would go. "No, someplace in Times Square. You can watch the lights from your window. Have your meals ordered in, stay out of sight."

"What will you do, Alexander?"

"Meet Harry on the dock and find out what he intends. Try to persuade him he has nothing to fear from me."

And because I know what I've done to you?

Try to save you from going back to Boston.

❧❧❧

THE *BREMEN* REACHES THE AMBROSE LIGHT Tuesday just before midnight, a fast crossing. Reisden and Gilbert have had dinner in Gilbert's cabin. Gilbert has packed a suitcase for the hotel.

"Why come *on the same boat* with me?" Reisden asks

"I had to speak with you."

"But," he protests, trying to make a joke, "by being on this ship together, do you realize we could have drowned everyone on it?"

It would be a joke if he didn't more or less mean it.

Over the water they can see the great colossus of the harbor, Lady Liberty outlined against the lights of New York: her crown, her torch, her back to them.

"I suppose from here we could swim," Reisden says out loud, and looks at Gilbert. And sees on Gilbert's face something very like what must be on his.

"We must not pass on such fears to Toby," Gilbert says.

"He gave me his favorite toy to give to Perdita," Reisden says.

"He sent Puppy? Ah, the dear child."

Just a filthy little scrap of toy, but so beloved; and Toby gave it to him for Papa to take to Mamma for her comfort. He wouldn't take it back. Reisden wrapped Puppy in a shirt and plans to have the shirt laundered before he wears it; but Puppy smells not only of floor-dirt and spit-up and Elphinstone but of Toby, dear Toby, and Perdita will smell Toby and take heart. "Toby isn't afraid. Yet.— But I'm so afraid for him, Gilbert, afraid for Perdita. How they could be taken from me. What the world could do to them. I don't want them hurt."

It might as well be Gilbert speaking.

I don't want you hurt. I don't want you to leave us.

When I meet Harry on the dock, what happens then?

ᕔᕔᕔ

THE QUARANTINE OFFICER'S BOAT is expected around five AM; being the cautious men they are, they are on deck by four. Reisden listens to the rumble of New York traffic over the water, the neighs of horses and chutter of engines, the grumble of delivery trucks, the strident *shooga* of limousine horns pushing lesser traffic out of the way, ferrying the rich home from late parties. No Astors in those cars tonight, no Guggenheims, no Strauses. Times Square colors the haze with multicolored heat lightning. Down on the Battery the pale bulk of a new skyscraper is dotted with lights.

The Whitehall Building. In postcard sepia, a huge liner steams triumphant up the Hudson, surrounded by toy-sized tugs and fireboats spraying water to welcome her. *RMS TITANIC. WHITEHALL BUILDING N.Y. THE TWO LARGEST IN THE WORLD.* And the date, April 17, a week ago.

Reisden's steward brings last-minute telegrams. He folds them and stuffs them into his overcoat pocket, where he's already put Jouvet's code book and other telegrams he hasn't read yet.

"So many," Gilbert says.

Reisden shrugs. "I enjoy myself, Gilbert."

"Would you like to work on your telegrams before New York?"

They ask the steward to tell them when the quarantine officer arrives and set up shop in the corner of the lounge. On one side of a bridge table, Gilbert decodes telegrams, paging through the Jouvet codebook. On the other, Reisden answers them and recodes his answer. They pass the codebook back and forth. Reisden orders coffee; Gilbert tea, not too strong, and no milk. Gilbert doesn't trust milk that's spent a week at sea.

Reisden looks up once, when Gilbert has had the codebook for some time, and sees him staring at a telegram.

"Gilbert, what is it?"

Gilbert looks up, startled. "Oh. This is from Mr. Daugherty, for me."

He reads Gilbert's expression. "What news?" Bad news.

"It is Elphinstone," Gilbert says. He folds the telegram and puts it in his pocket. "He is quite all right now, but he ate a piece of chocolate and was greatly distressed. He is all right, Richard. You must not worry."

Reisden doesn't notice the slip for a moment, then "Don't call me Richard, Gilbert. Be careful."

Gilbert hasn't noticed it either. He stares past Reisden miserably.

"Don't look that way. It'll be all right."

"I am distressed over Elphinstone. Never to see him again-"

"You'll see him again soon. This is difficult, but soon over."

Will Gilbert ever see his dog again? Will he get back to Paris?

"I shall go and walk on the deck a bit, if you don't mind." Gilbert smiles at him. "Go on with your work, don't mind me."

Instead of working, Reisden thinks about Gilbert, and Harry, and the d—n dead boy Richard. An eight-year-old boy who did something inconceivable. His uncle, who didn't know and treated him like an innocent. And Harry, later, who has never been part of the family.

Harry wants revenge on Richard.

Gilbert wants Richard.

Richard is dead.

He shoves the problem aside and concentrates on finishing the telegrams. He'll need a clear head for Harry on the dock.

And what is he going to say to Harry?

Something bumps against the hull of the ship. *Iceberg,* Reisden thinks, and then *harbormaster's boat,* and looks out the thick-glassed window (out of which, of course, he can see the lifeboats; he and Gilbert chose this table). But it's only cargo being staged for unloading and Gilbert is out of view.

He should either avoid Harry or stage a scene to outdo whatever Harry does. And what would that be?

He hasn't seen newspapers since Paris, apart from the thin news summary their ship prints every day. For obvious reasons the paper has downplayed *Titanic*. But he knows how newsworthy it is.

If Perdita's all right, not hurt, not broken by *Titanic,* she'll be on the dock to meet him. He telegraphed her before he left.

She'll hate this, but they both know how to play to an audience.

He leaves a note on the table for Gilbert, *Back soon,* stuffs telegrams and codebook in his overcoat pocket, and goes to find the Marconi office. Since the *Titanic* disaster, ocean telegraphists are theoretically on duty twenty-four hours a day. If this were a British ship, they'd ignore the rule now they're at the Ambrose, but the *Bremen* is a German liner and a bristle-headed telegraph man is nodding at his station, trying to stay awake. Reisden sends a second telegram to Perdita at the apartment to make sure she'll meet him, makes it as sentimental as the pin he gave her on *Titanic*. He hopes the tone gives her her cue. *GILBERT AND I ARRIVE 12 NOON BREMEN stop SO WORRIED stop LONGING TO KNOW YOU ARE SAFE stop MEET US stop ALL MY LOVE R.* "Gilbert and I": no need to tell the world that Gilbert won't be on the dock.

On almost any ship there's at least one reporter or photographer. On *Titanic* Reisden would have used the postcard girl; he wonders if she survived. On the *Bremen* the reporter is a middle-aged Parisian who writes restaurant reviews for the *Times.* Reisden gave him a quote on Sunday about sighting the victims; now he writes a note for the steward to deliver. *I've come to New York to be with my wife, a survivor of Titanic, and to bring the survivors letters from their families. I'll see her for the first time on the docks. She's playing soon at Carnegie Hall. Something for you?* The reunion of lovers after *Titanic* is worth perhaps Page 4. He looks over the note and amends it to "a well-known Parisian pianist and survivor of *Titanic.*"

Harry's scene will depend on Gilbert. Gilbert won't be there, and he and Perdita will be staging a more attractive story.

He goes back to the lounge. His note is still on the table; no Gilbert.

A steward is passing through the lounge. "Have you seen the man who was with me?"

"He asked me to give you this, sir."

It's the telegram that Gilbert said was his, from Daugherty. But it's for Reisden, coded of course. He has to look up a word; the word is QUARANTINE.

H COMING BY QUARANTINE BOAT FOR GILBERT.

On the back Gilbert has written *Dear Alexander— I know what we have said. But this is mine to do. It is my job to talk with Harry.*

He runs outside to the deck, looks round wildly. But it's too late. The quarantine boat is already heading away from the *Bremen* toward New York. On the deck he sees two men.

Harry raises a fist triumphantly.

Beside him, thin and frail and terrified, stands Gilbert.

Perdita

"HARRY DIDN'T TELL ME what he was doing until he had done it," Uncle Bucky said.

"He *kidnapped* Uncle Gilbert?"

"It is not kidnapping, Niece, Gilbert came with him willingly—"

"You must come away, Perdita," Opal Lee said.

"No, I have to meet Alexander."

She doesn't know who she's more angry at, Harry or Alexander or possibly Uncle Gilbert. *Alexander trusts me to take care of myself,* she said to Harry, but he didn't. And Harry thinks she is his to manipulate—

292 ☙ SARAH SMITH

"I'll come with you," Uncle Bucky says.

"I will go alone."

"But Otis Church—"

"Doesn't know where I'm going. I'll take a cab. *Alone.*"

Why has Alexander come?

To save her, of course.

And she has nothing but bad news to give him.

If Mr. Otis killed Aunt Louisa, it is because Dr. John is Isaac. If he killed Paul deMay, it was because Paul recognized Isaac. And John Rolfe Church in Paris—

Was John Rolfe Church. Who hated black people, all people, because they betrayed him.

And she is black, and Toby is black, and they must be second-class Americans or exiles.

Toby *will* not be second class. Which means exile.

When the cab lets her off, she stands confused at the edge of the docks, hearing trucks and wagons rattling over stone blocks, handcarts rumbling and men shouting in a hundred languages. She doesn't know the docks at all; she has to ask at every corner and then feel her way down the street with her cane. She will meet Alexander disheveled and helpless and blind.

People jostle her and she cannot find her way. Sails whack in the wind, engines chuff, seagulls and steamers screech metallically; over the silty stink of the river she smells the sea. She is standing on the stone quai at Cherbourg, in a white suit and a wide hat, two weeks ago, a thousand years, with Miss Lady talking and talking and Miss Fan saying nothing, holding purses and handbags and shawls, and Dr. John calling Miss Lady "Mamma"; but everything is changed now.

"The Christopher Street ferry?" she asks passersby. "To Hoboken?"

Someone takes her arm and propels her through the maelstrom. "Hoboken, here you are, Miss."

She pays her nickel at the gate. She walks down the rope-and-plank bridge to the boat, holding hard to the rope handrail.

She steps onto the deck of the ferry—

And the engines start, and she is on the Cherbourg tender-boat going out to *Titanic,* the same long scything glitter of windows, the same dark paneling smelling of coffin-wax, the same wooden benches; the rolling rise and fall. The chattering passengers move inside, pushing her forward. Children are laughing.

Her heart clenches. She cannot catch her breath. Everyone here is going to drown. She gropes and pushes her way toward the door against the tide of the crowd; she runs out onto the deck, stumbles down the gangway just as it is being withdrawn, onto the lifeboat of safe land, the docks and the shore. She leans against a post as people move past her.

"Is there any other way to get to Hoboken?" she gasps to the ticket-taker.

She can take the city railroad, he says, through the Manhattan & Hudson tunnel. It is blocks away.

Shaking, she gropes her way uptown all the way up to 23rd St, through neighborhoods she doesn't know. As she waits for the train to Hoboken, she hears the bells of noon.

She is too late by the time she gets to Hoboken. She waits in the remnants of the crowds, not even sure she is at the right pier. Alexander has already gone.

It is—she doesn't even know what time, she still has no watch— before she gives up. Getting back to Manhattan by the under-river train is a miserable maze; she has to ask and ask, she is helpless. Every once in awhile she remembers that Aunt Louisa is dead, that she and Toby are lost, and simply leans against a wall, sinks onto a bench. She doesn't have the heart to leave the 23rd St. station to find a cab; she simply takes the subway.

All alone in the car, she cries on the way uptown. On the 96th St. station platform she has to stop to wipe her eyes and collect herself.

Now she will have to face Alexander.

She unfolds her guide cane, and just then, someone takes her by the arm. She turns, surprised.

"I'm sorry. I got to," Mr. Otis says, and pushes her off the platform onto the tracks.

Reisden

THE DOCKSIDE FILLS WITH THE FAMILIES of passengers, waving up at the ship.

But Perdita isn't there.

In the echoing dimness of the pier building, he finds his own and Gilbert's luggage and waits for the customs inspector to chalk it. He looks out for Perdita's red jacket. Nothing.

Harry isn't here either. Why should he be? He has Gilbert.

The inspector opens Gilbert's trunk. On top of Gilbert's punctiliously folded clothes, Reisden sees the red book. The inspector moves it aside.

It sickens him to think of the book. But it's too loaded with meaning to leave; he picks it up and stuffs it into his overloaded coat pockets with Puppy, the codebook, and the telegrams from Jouvet.

Outside, among the crowds, he looks for her, for the red jacket that she would wear to be conspicuous for him.

I want you to go to New York with me, she asked him. *I want you to be my ally in New York.*

He left her to go through the wreck alone.

No sign of her.

In the pier building, a blue-and-white sign marks a row of telephone booths. He calls the number for the apartment.

"This is the Baroness von Reisden's": unfamiliar voice with a Caribbean lilt.

"This is the Baron von Reisden. May I speak with her?"

"She's gone to meet you, sir."

He fights down panic. "When did she leave?"

"Two hours ago, sir."

He goes out onto the Hoboken docks, conspicuous, a tall man in a top hat; the photographers snap their flashes at him; if Harry has prepared some surprise for him, he's painted a target on his own back. No red-jacketed Perdita in the crowd. With a pinching at his heart, he thinks she had the jacket on *Titanic;* she wouldn't have worn it in the cold; it's lost. She bought it the first time he came to see her so he could find her in the crowd. He remembers her laughing up at him on the dock in New York. Bits of their past are being stripped away.

He looks for her until the crowd thins.

He finds a phone, trying to ignore the voices in his head.

"She's still not here, Monsieur."

"Has she telephoned? When she returns, will you tell her to wait at the apartment for me?"

Oh G-d, what's happened to Perdita?

He takes the railway under the Hudson and the West Side Line uptown, the fastest route. He looks at the advertisements, he goes to the front of the car and looks down the square steel-framed tunnels; anything to avoid thinking of being here; anything not to worry about her or Gilbert, not to think at all—

He takes out the red book and opens it, looks at the frightened smears of ink. Richard was terrified for years and then he picked up the gun. Eight years old.

Harry wants to revenge himself on Richard? Wants to be Richard?

In the afternoon the subway car going toward 96th St. is empty; the New Yorkers are downtown in their offices making money. The rattle of the subway car jars him. He's alone in the car with forty-eight hours of no sleep and nothing but dark thoughts.

Through the doors in the next car, a young woman is sitting alone in a dark suit. She's all alone, in such a crowded city, wearing mourning, perhaps for someone on *Titanic*. She is crying, her hands over her face, trying to be private—

And it's Perdita.

It's Perdita.

She's safe. She's alive. For a moment all he feels is the shattering relief of that.

He flattens himself against the glass door at the end of the car and looks through the glass at her.

She is facing him, but doesn't see him, of course; and she is not safe; she's crying. She gathers herself, gropes in her purse for a handkerchief. Her face is pale and tears are running down her cheeks. He almost opens the door and goes through to her; looks at the rails whipping by underneath. It is not that he couldn't step over, though he wouldn't have been so cautious before Toby. It is her face that he hesitates to trespass upon, her open grief.

He watches her.

Oh my G-d, love, what are you going through?

96th Street station; she gets off, he follows her from his own car, twenty feet or so from her. She still doesn't see him.

A short black man is standing on the platform, jittering on the balls of his feet; apparently not waiting for this train, perhaps for an uptown local.

The train clangs closed its doors and shrieks off into the dark. Reisden starts down the platform toward her, hesitates, unsure of his welcome.

She wipes her eyes and stands defiantly straight—he knows that straight back—takes out her folding cane, unfolds and opens it, fits the pieces together.

The short man comes up beside her to help, or because his train is coming; the rails have begun to thrum. He takes her arm, says something to her—

And he pushes her toward the rails.

She punches out at him, grabs his arm, fights back, hitting him with her half-unfolded cane. The cane spins away. She grabs round an iron pillar that holds up the station roof, screaming *No!*, kicking out so the man has to dance back. Reisden is running toward them. The little man dodges behind her, peels one of her arms from around the pillar and doubles it behind her, grabs her other wrist, and pitches her off the platform onto the rails.

Perdita gets to her knees, gropes not toward the safety of the platform but out toward the middle of the tracks, toward the express line. "Stop!" Reisden calls. There's an electrified rail and he doesn't know where it is. The man runs toward the stairs. "Perdita!" he shouts. "Stand still!" He jumps down onto the tracks and starts toward her.

Under his feet the ties shudder. Light from the tunnel touches her and him.

There's no time to get out of the way; he doesn't even know which track the train will take, whether it will stop. Between the uptown and the downtown tracks are open steel arches; he grabs her bodily and pulls her into one. "Hold on!" He braces himself and her.

The express screams by, ripping at them; they're standing in a tornado. Startled faces blur at them through windows. She struggles in his arms. "Don't move, I can't hold us!" The train slows and passengers boil out, staring at them; a conductor shakes his fist at them; the ticket taker clatters down the stairs, shouting.

He lets her go, stands in the arch, head down. His arms ache as if he's been lifting trucks off her.

"I didn't fall! I was pushed!" she says to him.

"I know, I saw."

"You were in the train with me?"

"Next car. Hello, love."

"Hello, Alexander." He hears a whole history of emotions in how she says his name; none of them are welcome.

The two of them are helped separately across the rails. Someone lifts Perdita up onto the platform.

The ticket taker looks at Perdita's guide cane, abandoned. "You fell onto the tracks?"

"I was pushed," Perdita says.

"Someone pushed her? Is that true?" the man asks Reisden.

"Yes." To his annoyance, he can answer only in gasps. "Short man. Five feet."

"He really pushed the lady, sor?"

Perdita opens her mouth, closes it again.

"Lucky you were here, sor. The lady should take better care of herself."

❧❧❧

"HE ASKED *YOU* if I was pushed!"

She turns, furious, pushes through the turnstile, begins climbing the stairs, away from him. He looks after her, abandoned, angry.

"Do not go off by yourself," he shouts up. "Wait for me."

"Come *on*, then, Alexander."

She storms ahead of him, under the underpass and upward to 96th Street. He gets a brief glimpse of the new neighborhood. High New York apartment buildings rearing overhead, older mansions small between them. On the other side of the street is a newly-planted park and a terrifying drop-off to the railroad tracks and the river.

She turns to him with angry tears on her cheeks.

"He asked *you!* And I know who it was!" she says. "It was Mr. Otis. He *spoke* to me."

"Mr. Otis?" he says. "The trainer?"

"*He tried to kill me.*" She turns to him. "I have to see Mr. Johnson."

"Who is Mr. Johnson? Wait. Talk to me."

"Come on." She hails a cab.

They ride up Broadway, silently. She is shaking. It's only twenty blocks or so, but a different world: shabby, quick-built buildings two or three stories high. Half the people on the street are black. Otis Church. A black man in a bowler hat. He might have discarded the hat now and be on the sidewalk next to them, unrecognizable.

"Mr. Johnson" is apparently a detective, but the address Perdita gives the cabman is a utilitarian cheap store called Johnson's. He hesitates a moment, wondering if she has the right place. "This is a jewelry store, love—"

"I know." She opens the door. "I need to see Mr. Johnson," she says to the clerk behind the counter.

Louis Johnson, jeweler or detective, comes downstairs from the second floor. He's tall, dark, fleshy-jawed, surprisingly young, with the friendly self-assurance of a local politician. He takes Perdita's hand—startling, in America, a black man holding a white woman's hand—and says something sympathetic. Johnson holds out his hand to Reisden with the wariness that Reisden remembers from early meetings with Barry Bullard.

How does Perdita know a black detective?

Johnson shows them upstairs into a smallish room with a desk, two chairs, and a bald Negro man typing in the corner. Johnson sends the typist out.

"Let me talk. Mr. Johnson, Mr. Otis just tried to push me off the platform at 96th St. It must be because I know what Paul deMay knew."

"Who is Paul deMay?" Reisden asks.

They both look at him. Perdita starts to say something, but turns to Johnson instead. "Where was Mr. Otis on Monday night? Do you know?"

"Left the hospital right after your Aunt Louisa did."

"He followed her from there. He came back to the apartment late, and then went away again. *I heard him.*"

"Changing his clothes, maybe," Johnson says grimly.

Perdita closes her eyes.

"We might have saved her if we'd had him followed!" she says.

"I could have saved her if I'd put a man on her," Johnson says bitterly.

"Saved her?" Reisden asks. "Will someone please tell me what is going on?"

🙠🙠🙠

LOUISA CHURCH IS DEAD.

Reisden can't even remember Perdita's aunt well; a little woman, a decisive nod, strong opinions. Dogs. Louisa Church was murdered by Otis the trainer.

Who apparently killed a man named Paul deMay years ago and tried to kill Perdita this afternoon.

"Mr. Johnson? Aunt Louisa didn't divorce John Church," Perdita says. "She told everyone she had, but she didn't. Aunt Louisa didn't know that her husband had married again until I told her; and Dr. John didn't know, I'm sure he didn't, that he wasn't divorced. So Miss Fan and he are married bigamously, that is, they aren't married at all."

She turns to him. "Alexander, Aunt Louisa visited the hospital on Monday night and told Miss Fan all of it. She told me she was going to reassure Miss Fan." She takes another hesitating breath. "I'm sorry, Alexander. I'm so sorry. I don't think Miss Fan knows that Dr. John is Isaac. But he is."

"He's not." That would make her and Toby black.

"We must tell the police about Mr. Otis," she says, "but, Mr. Johnson, how can we do it without letting out the whole story?"

"You can't go back to your apartment," Johnson says. "You've got to go somewhere else while I deal with Otis."

"Mr. Johnson, how can you deal with him? *The police didn't even ask me if I knew him.* Will anyone believe I recognized him?"

🙠🙠🙠

JOHNSON SENDS REISDEN AND PERDITA round the corner to wait in a hotel.

A commercial travelers' hotel in a Negro neighborhood; it's clean at least and, toward the end of the afternoon, the lobby is full of the sort of aspiring young men who read salesmen's handbooks and Bibles and sell insurance. There is a dining-room off the lobby. Four or five men are sitting together, dining early. They frown at the sight of a white man and a white woman without luggage, no doubt using the hotel for immoral purposes, until Perdita says innocently to the desk clerk "We are the people Mr. Johnson sent" and the frowns smooth away. The men go back to their dinners, respectable men in a respectable hotel.

Their room has a double bed, clean sheets; why should they not be clean? Reisden considers himself to be less prejudiced than that. It's not someplace he feels comfortable, though; this place belongs to black people and he doesn't know the rules. He takes off his overcoat and jacket and shoes, stretches out in his shirtsleeves and vest.

"Lie down with me. Start at the beginning and tell me everything."

There's a chair by the bedside; she sits down on it. "You don't know this and it won't be welcome. Aunt Louisa was killed because she knew the Churches' real secret. Dr. John is Isaac. It was Isaac who married Aunt Louisa."

No, he wants to object. He holds himself back. She tells him a confusing story: disguise on the battlefield, a convenient slave trader, a white man sold as a slave. Years later, she says, a man named Paul deMay was killed because he recognized the wrong man. While she talks he watches her hands. She is doing stretching exercises unconsciously, her long fingers moving painfully against her knees. Her hands are reddened and blister-scarred. He reaches over and puts his hand over hers. "What happened to your hands?"

She shakes her head. "We had to row away from *Titanic*. It's all right."

He waits, hoping she'll talk about it; hoping she'll fall into his arms. He wants just to hold her and give her what comfort he can. He wants not to have this to think about; to tell her about Gilbert; to say how much he's missed her; to know that she's all right, that Toby and she are all right. And she's insisting they are not. She moves her hand out from under his.

"I'm sorry," she says. "I'm so sorry. I was meant to find out something else."

"I don't think it's true."

"It is true," she says. "I'll lie."

You can't lie, he thinks.

"I just didn't want to lie to myself," she says in a whisper, as if she's apologizing. "I thought it would come out right, I guess. Well, it didn't."

"I think you're wrong. John is John."

"Oh, go ahead," she says. "Prove me wrong."

D—n the subway official for not believing her.

"You're quite right that Miss Lady wouldn't let her cousin marry a black man," he says. He thinks of Miss Lady's wheelchair with the crossed Southern flags. "And as for the men? You don't have this famous picture?"

She takes an envelope out of her bag. A photographic copy. Two men, one sitting, one standing. The sitting man's face is circled. The two resemble each other a bit, like brothers, if one looks only at their physical features. But—

"The switch between John and Isaac? No. Anyone could tell the difference between them."

"I know it's not what I was supposed to find!" Perdita says.

"*Chérie.*" He holds up the picture. "Bright Isaac, this man," the unsmiling face, "he's the one who died in Paris."

"How do you know?"

"Because I knew him. I met both of them. They look alike enough, eyes nose mouth certainly, but they were entirely different in personality. Everyone would have known the difference."

"I wish I could think so," Perdita says.

"Do think so. For Toby's sake. For yours."

There is a momentary silence between them.

"Is it better for Toby to lie all his life," she says, "than to live with the truth?"

Far better than to live with that one. "It's not the truth."

"Then what did Paul deMay know?" she bursts out. "What did he know that got him killed? What did John Rolfe Church know? And Aunt Louisa, what secret did she know, and what do I know that would make Mr. Otis try to kill me, if not that?" Perdita says. "Dr. John said he came home because he didn't know if his mother was alive. He would have known Miss Lady was alive."

This is too much; he feels angry with her, which is simply wrong. "Why did he come home?" he asks. "Because he had to see her. Why do you think I came here? I knew you were alive. I didn't know if you were suffering—" She turns round and faces him almost defensively. "He'd have heard she was alive, perhaps, but if he'd cared for her at all, he'd have needed to see her. I needed to see you," he confesses, giving her all his vulnerability at once, like a wilted bunch of flowers.

"You wanted to make sure I was safe," she says resignedly.

Dear G-d, woman, *Titanic* did sink. He sits up, takes her hands. "He'd have wanted to see her face and hear her voice, and say 'Are you safe?' and to be with her— I should have been with you."

"You'd have drowned!" she says angrily. "I'm sorry. I shouldn't have asked you to come on *Titanic.*"

"Are you angry at me because I came to New York?"

Silence.

"Of course you worry about me," she says finally, bitterly. "You want to take care of me."

"Darling. This Otis just tried to kill you." You need looking after. I need to look after you. Give me that—

"Mr. Johnson will find him."

"And then what?"

"And then I don't know!" she says passionately. "What can he do? You've no idea how black people are treated here. Paul deMay's murder was never investigated at all. I guess we could have the police arrest Mr. Otis for trying to kill me, but we'd have to say why he would want to. And the policeman didn't even ask me who had pushed me," she says. "It's going to be one more blind thing. One more *Negro* thing. Mr. Otis is going to get away with it."

He doesn't have anything to say. Is it better to lie? Do you doubt it, in a country like this?

"Mr. Otis cannot get away with murdering Aunt Louisa," she says.

"I will lie for you and identify him positively," Reisden says. "But will you believe, for your sake and Toby's, that Louisa's husband was the white man?"

She looks down at her hands.

"'They cannot deny a dead man,'" she says after a moment, raising her head. "He came back. The real white John did. He wanted to see his mother and his home. To know she was safe. It had been such a long time. But when he came to Fair Home, Miss Lady denied him. Because Isaac had come back to Virginia and taken John's place. Paul knew that. Aunt Louisa found it out and I know it too."

"Think of Toby," he says. "You have to be wrong."

&ce;&ce;&ce;

LOUIS JOHNSON MEETS THEM in their hotel room. The room is small with him in it.

"Don't worry about the police," Johnson says. "It won't be the police that take up Otis Church. It'll be me. All my operatives are out on the street looking for him."

"But what will you do with him?" Perdita says. "How can we explain why he murdered Aunt Louisa? I don't think he ever met her, and he's barely ever spoken to me." She waits, then "What will you tell the police, Mr. Johnson? Will you tell the police?"

Johnson doesn't say anything for a moment, then asks Reisden "You'll watch over Miss Perdita?"

He has to do something about Gilbert. But "Of course."

"Mr. Johnson, you do not intend to," Perdita looks for words, "give him to Mrs. deMay, do you?"

"No," Johnson says.

"Then what do you intend to do with him?"

"You go to Fort Lee. You were going to go there; go now," Johnson says. "I'll have my operative Fred Troutman come and watch you."

"What about Dr. John?"

"I phoned from my office; he's still the same. If anything changes, I'll come get you."

"I was going to New Jersey to help a friend," Perdita says to Reisden. "They're making a movie of *Titanic* and she doesn't want to be there alone. Mr. Johnson—"

"Dorothy Gibson," Reisden says, "the friend?"

"No, Miss Nisensohn, the photographer. Dorothy Gibson is making Miss Nisensohn help with the movie and she's hardly able to bear it."

Johnson clears his throat. "Ma'am, do you mind going to New Jersey by way of Garnet's? Her going-away, it's tonight."

ॐॐॐ

REISDEN PHONES THE WALDORF-ASTORIA from the telephone booth downstairs, trying to connect with Gilbert, Harry, or Bucky Pelham. More of the Negro commercial travellers are eating dinner by now and two or three respectable married couples have joined them. From the telephone booth, through the door to the restaurant, he watches an anonymous woman spooning soup with almost painful good manners, little finger out. She is wearing a careful hat with a single curled feather, too respectable, too tightly curled, the hatbrim small and conservative, as if any flourish would be punished by the world outside.

Perdita can't be black; she can't live like that.

Toby can't live like that. Not his boy.

Over the crackling telephone wire, the Waldorf-Astoria operator has a British accent, lower-class Liverpool pretending to London. Reisden hates this raw pretentious New York, it's not his city, he's homesick for Paris, he is sick at heart.

"Do you have a guest Gilbert Knight?"

No one under that name, the Liverpudlian replies. Which means Gilbert's not staying there, or isn't being allowed to have phone calls, or who knows what it means.

He has a fantasy of invading the Waldorf and rescuing Gilbert. Rescuing him, putting everything back together somehow, making things as they were; making them better; going home.

"Let's go," he says as if he knows where they're going.

ෙෙෙ

LOUIS JOHNSON HAS A CAR, a long black taxi-style landaulet. He replaces his suit jacket with a black uniform jacket, puts a billed cap on over his curls, and holds the car door for them, a perfect servant, a chauffeur. They drive north into Harlem.

With the approach of night, the neighborhood has become a city in Africa. Almost everyone on the streets is black: a woman in a fur stole, a mother herding children, couples shopping for vegetables, a child carrying a bucket. Johnson stops the car at a corner to buy roses from a black man selling flowers from a cart. Descending from the car, he's a chauffeur; hesitating between red and pink, he's a man buying roses. For this Garnet, who, judging by his expression, won't like any roses from him.

Faces look curiously in at the passengers of the car, and stop smiling. He and Perdita don't belong here.

The party is at a fifth-floor walk-up; Johnson leaves the car on the street without locking the wheels or removing the distributor cap, which says more than anything else about his position in this New York. The cramped hall smells of cooking, shared hall bathrooms, meager fires, lye soap, the smells of poor respectability. Shadows watch them from the cracks of doors. Perdita knows them, greets them by name. "Mrs. Allen, are you coming up to Garnet's?" Perdita has never introduced him to any of these people, not in any of the times he visited her in New York before she came to Paris.

"How are you, Susan girl!"

Susan?

A tiny apartment, hardly big enough for the three of them to stand in. Two people and a stout brindle dog are already in the room. A tall bony-faced black man, garishly splendid in violet-and-red striped waistcoat, red ascot, seersucker suit striped green and tan, silver rings on every spidery finger. Blind blue eyes under a hat too big for him; alert as a cat. Stretched out on the lump-sprung sofa, a gold-faced slab-toothed woman, reddish bushy hair, face all cheekbones, eyes sunk deep into black pits; the blind man's mistress, or someone's. The dog sighs down under the sofa like a dropped pillow.

And there's a piano, of course a piano, a cheap veneered black upright that Perdita should scorn to play.

On top of it, Reisden sees a bottle of whisky, a box lined with dusty velvet, and my G-d, a human skull.

"How your hands doing, girl?" The blind man stretches out his hands. Perdita puts her hands in his. She must be able to see his rings.

"Better, Mr. Williams."

"We going to play us some music for Garnet?"

The old man gropes his way past Reisden and Louis Johnson, leads Perdita over to the piano bench; he and Perdita sit down together. He strips off his rings one by one, dubious silver, a snake ring, a skull ring; he piles them in the velvet-lined box. Perdita takes off her gloves and adds her two small rings to the box, engagement ruby and wedding ring.

Reisden crosses his arms over his chest. He dislikes seeing her take off her wedding ring to play.

Johnson whispers to the blind man. "I am sorry for your loss," Williams says to Perdita.

She stops; her face crumples; she puts her reddened and scarred hands up to her face.

"Let's say us a little prayer with you," the old man says. He reaches out and takes both of her hands again. Louis Johnson bends his head and folds his hands. Reisden, dedicated agnostic, keeps his arms crossed. From over Louis Johnson's head he sees the yellow woman's insolent stare. She abruptly sticks out her tongue, a dark snake-flicker, purple, almost black, and folds her hands. The rest of her face is impassive.

"Lord protect my grandbaby Susan," the old man says. *Grandbaby* Susan? "And my grandbaby Garnet. Bad things been happening here. People dying, people troubled in mind, people crying out for help. Waters of sorrow rolling over them. Reach down Your healing hand, Lord, reach down and comfort Your people, Lord."

"Oh yeah," the sallow-faced woman says raspily. "Reach down, Lord!"

"Yes, Lord," Louis Johnson says surprisingly.

"We never talked," Perdita says. "Aunt Louisa and I. I kept calling her yesterday so we could talk. But she was dead."

"You've started my funeral!" says a woman from the door. "Frog Jaw, have you become a minister? I don't want ministry, I want music. I brought food."

A fashion plate, Garnet Williams, dressed in the top of New York style. She is carrying two brown paper grocery bags, which clank. The yellow-faced woman sits up. So does the dog. Behind Garnet the nighttime shadows of the neighborhood begin to arrive, a fat woman bringing a loudly-colored iced cake, a man with some kind of horn instrument, a dumpy white woman—he supposes she's white—and a fashionable white woman with an English accent.

The crowd spills out of the tiny apartment and into the hall. All of them look out of the corners of their eyes at Reisden, who gets himself against the wall out of the way.

To Perdita, they talk. How is she? How long's it been since she was in New York? That long? My land! A little one? Boy or girl? Does she have a picture? Reisden has a picture of Toby in his billfold. He passes it round. "Oh, isn't he a little prince."

The yellow woman fills bar-glasses of rum. Garnet Williams passes round champagne in unmatched glasses. "To the late great Garnet Williams!" she toasts. "To Nanette!" The yellow woman tastes the champagne, makes a face, mixes it with rum. There are dark tracks along the inside of her elbows. Williams puts his glass on the side table.

And Williams and Perdita begin to play.

They play a dirge, something slow with a dragging, hesitating rhythm. They're playing four-hands, and clearly they've played together before; they reach over and under each other's hands, throwing and catching each other's complex rhythms. She knows how to play this. She's comfortable here.

Don't you see we don't belong here, he wants to say to her; but he's only talking about himself. She belongs.

And why does she belong?

He's hearing why, music on a cheap piano.

What about Toby?

"Let's us play for your Aunt Louisa," the old man says.

"Your Aunt Louisa *died?*" Garnet says. "Was that why you weren't at the Strauses' service with us? That's awful."

"Garnet, she was murdered."

"And you're here? Grandpa, you play. Perdita and I need to talk."

The old man plays; Perdita slides off the bench and Garnet and she talk, crowded into a corner, hands clasped and heads together. The young man with the horn puffs his cheeks and begins to play. The yellow woman rolls cigarets, licks them closed with her purple tongue, and passes them round. Reisden shakes his head but he only has to breathe the smoke; the room grows smokier and the lights glow in colors.

In the crowd, the white Englishwoman is talking to Louis Johnson. "Paul's murderer?" she says. "Bring him to me, Louis, and I will shoot him with my own hands."

"You won't have to do that, ma'am," Louis Johnson says.

What is Johnson planning to do with Otis Church? Kill him himself?

Perdita comes back to the piano, sits down alone. "I played this for Aunt Louisa on Monday," she says, and begins to lure music out of the keys, stroking them softly and slow like the muzzle of a wary dog. He recognizes this music, one of her transcriptions.

Reisden has to deal with Gilbert, with Harry and Bucky, has to keep Perdita safe from murderous Otis, doesn't know how to do it all at once; all he wants to do is go to bed with her in New Jersey and comfort her while she comforts him, make her think how this will affect Toby; get her home, safe; and she's here instead, doing this.

What Harry would make of this scene he knows only too well.

Would it be easier if the music weren't good? The music is heart-wrenching. *I rock a little baby...* Why doesn't she do it, why does she play music about it?

He's not a jolly hashish smoker; the stuff makes him morbid. Many things do. He opens a window to keep his wits about him.

Garnet stands by the piano. She sings while Perdita accompanies her, *Bring on your rubber-tired hearses, bring on your rubber-tired hacks...*

"You the best granddaughter in the world, Garnet girl," the old man says, maudlin with hashish and whiskey.

"You're the best grandpa."

"How can you leave church, girl?" the fat woman says. "How can you leave walking down Broadway and talking to all your friends?"

"How can I leave your cake?" Garnet says, laughing, cutting herself a slice. "But I have to."

Louis Johnson makes his way out of the crowd into the hall.

Reisden follows him. Johnson is sitting on the stairs, halfway up to the next floor, elbows on his knees, head on his hands.

"It's like that?" Reisden says.

"If I were white I could have her," Johnson says. "I could give her New York." He looks up, realizing he's talking to the white man. There's enough awkwardness here for everyone.

"I give Perdita Paris and balls all she cares," Reisden says.

"D—n the women," Johnson says after a minute.

Reisden sits down on the stairs too. The two men sit in silence.

"What will you do with Otis once you have him?" Reisden asks.

"I don't know. Can't give him to the police."

The old man plays again. The music pulses out of the apartment, thicker, more complex, gnarls and blood-slicks of sound. Reisden stands up, watches from the door: Perdita's back on the piano bench, the two of them are playing again. It's nothing like she plays in Paris. It's— He has no word but *American.* The man with the horn adds another voice, crying in a wilderness of sound. The crowd quiets, listening to them. Someone laughs from pure pleasure.

The two pianists go silent; there's only the horn, murmuring out a complaint, and a death-slow thump from someone banging on a pan with a wooden spoon.

"Ashes to ashes," says the old man, "dust to dust. If the black folk don't get you, the white folk must."

The sallow woman throws back her head, moans, throat-heavy. *Yaaah,* the fat woman calls out.

"*Oh didn't she ramble, she ramble,*" Garnet sings. "*Ramble all around the town...* Come on, people, second-line me. Take me to the subway, people, and you're not a-going to bring me back, because I'm working for the House of Windsor now."

She stands up, swaying a little. She takes one last look around her, hugs her grandfather and buries her head on his shoulder, then takes a deep breath, gropes through the crowd for her coat and hat.

The procession makes its way down the swaying stairs, along the street toward Broadway. The horn player leads them, and behind them march the old man, his dog—and Perdita, walking with the family. People fall in line behind them; some of them clearly are in it just for the parade. A few go inside and bring out umbrellas, begin to twirl them as they dance along. Reisden stays toward the rear.

"Goodbye!" Garnet waves from the kiosk entrance. The light catches her, a pretty fashionable brunette, a white girl. She turns. She's gone.

❧❧❧

REISDEN AND PERDITA wait for the night ferry across the Hudson toward New Jersey. While they're waiting, Johnson takes Reisden aside. "You have a gun?"

It's back in Paris, in his locked middle drawer, where it's been for years.

"Take this," Johnson says.

It's, of all things, a semi-automatic Roth-Steyr with a sawed-off barrel and a cut-down grip. "You ever used one of those?" Johnson asks.

Yes, he's used a gun before.

He checks the charger clip. How did Johnson get an Austro-Hungarian army pistol? It's meant to stop a horse. The safety works; the trigger is stiff and pulls heavily, which means he won't shoot anyone except by choice.

He looks up at Johnson. "Where'd this come from?"

"Pawn shop."

"You have a pawn shop," Reisden guesses.

Johnson half-smiles.

"What will you do with Otis once you have him?"

"I don't know," Johnson says again.

"Do you have a gun?"

"I have this for me." Johnson pulls a gun out of his pocket. A lady's muff-pistol, meant to protect the fair sex around 1870. A .22. With any luck and a favorable wind, the bullet could actually get through a muff. Behind this assured businessman, there's a man who doesn't know guns.

"Have you ever shot a man?" he asks Johnson.

Johnson shakes his head.

"Otis has."

Johnson doesn't say anything.

"If you've never shot a man," Reisden says, "don't start."

❧❧❧

ONE FORGETS HOW CLOSE NEW YORK IS to places that aren't New York. On the ferry Reisden watches Perdita standing stiffly, holding the rail; he stands by her, her watchdog, her comfort if she'll take him. Her advisor, which she won't take. She holds hard to the rail and stares out over the river, alone.

New Jersey is another world.

A farmer picks them up in a creaking country wagon. They go up a long switchback road and out of the sleepy industrial town of Fort Lee into actual country, narrow unpaved lanes between hayfields.

They're spending the night in a spare room in a farmhouse. Their room has a spool bed with a featherbed, a red-and-white quilt, a kerosene lamp for the only light, and, on the bedside table next the lamp, a copy of *Photoplay*. Dorothy Gibson is on the cover. He frowns at her. Perdita is standing in the middle of the room, lost in a place she doesn't know. He puts his arms around her; she leans against him, rigid with mourning.

"Come to bed, love?" he asks.

"There must be something to do about Aunt Louisa and Mr. Otis," she says. "Otis cannot get away with it."

Johnson can shoot him. *Or I can*, Reisden thinks. He has the sense to say nothing. He stays there, just holding her. He has to talk to her about Gilbert too. He can't face it now, won't weigh her down with it.

Who he's protecting he doesn't know.

"You can't insist Toby is black," he says. "Don't do it to him."

"I cannot bear any of this," she says. "Garnet is abandoning her grandfather. Garnet has the new job and the new place and the new name, and that's right and she'll do it beautifully, but oh, Alexander, it'll be as if she's gone into the lifeboat and all she'll think about later is she left him behind. People don't know until too late."

He leads her toward the bed. They sit down together on the edge of it. The old, tired featherbed slumps around them.

"Williams called you his granddaughter?" he says. "Susan?"

"We needed a story. Once I heard him at John Brown's I wanted to learn from him, and Garnet said I should pretend to be his other grandchild, who went off to pass."

John Brown's. "So you've been saying you're Williams's granddaughter and meeting him for lessons" in the worst dive in New York "for how long?"

"Five years," she says, her chin a little raised. But she sounds relieved. She has deliberately not mentioned this and she doesn't like to lie. He remembers Dr. John and Perdita on *Titanic. To people being valued*, she said, and raised her chin. She has valued people she has not shared with him.

Five years. When he first knew her she didn't even drink coffee; apparently just months later she was frequenting Dickensian haunts of vice. To play the piano.

There are parts of her he doesn't know at all.

"We'll never be able to play together in public," she says. "Unless I play in places like the Tiger. Or on the TOBA circuit. The black music circuit. But we are good. Did you like the music?"

"I didn't understand it." What he understands is how she feels about it.

"We are good, though."

"Your Mr. Williams," he looks for a neutral word, "is— He has a human skull on his piano."

"You have a human skull in your bookcase. Don't be prejudiced."

"I am not prejudiced, I grew up in Africa. But Harry will be able to make a colorful story of him." And so will everyone else.

"Harry already thinks Mr. Williams is my grandfather."

Otis and Harry should shoot each other. It would solve so much.

"Blind Willie might as well be standing on the deck of *Titanic* as be taken care of by that Liddy Boswick," she says bitterly. "I will not let him be neglected, or Garnet have the guilt of it; neither of them wants me to do it but I will hire him a real housekeeper. Or give him enough money somehow so he can hire one himself. He could die!" she breaks out. "I won't let him die!"

"We'll keep him from dying."

"It's so stupid for Aunt Louisa to *die* when she would never have told! She never did tell! Everybody is *dying*."

Titanic, he thinks, and *dead.* "What happened on *Titanic?*" he asks at last.

"Dr. John wouldn't talk to me, he handed me into the boat. I should have stayed to make him talk to me. But I went." Her lips tighten; she grimaces, her shoulders bow, she puts her hands to her face. He puts his arms around her.

"What happened on *Titanic?*" he asks again, quietly, gently.

"Alexander," she says, "don't you know? They all died. *And I took a seat on a lifeboat and I left children on board.*"

HE LISTENS TO HER ALL NIGHT.

She talks about Aunt Louisa and Dr. John; and then she talks about the children.

Later she'll find out the names and memorize them, and he will because she does. Ebba Iris Andersson, six years old. Ella Andersson, two. Sigvard Andersson, four. Ingeborg Andersson, nine.... Children giggling at the luggage on the pier at Cherbourg. Carl and Clarence Asplund, five and nine. Boys playing soccer on the deck. There was a baby floating all alone on the ocean. Gilbert Danbom, four months. William Panula, one year. "They were screaming," Perdita says. "I heard them screaming." Ruby Ford, nine. Salli Rosblom, two.

He thinks of Toby.

"I could have taken a child on my lap," she says. Alfred Peacock, nine months. Treasteall Peacock, three. "I could have done *something.*"

You couldn't do anything, he tells her silently. You couldn't do enough. You weren't the captain, running the ship too fast. You weren't Bruce Ismay, encouraging him. You weren't the lookout who missed the iceberg until it was too late, or the officer who locked the binoculars in his cabin. You weren't the iceberg.

And he knows it means nothing to her at all. And not much to him, because in every child's name he hears Toby.

"You were too late to do the right thing," he says. "It was too late."

"What is the right thing *now?*" she says. "There must be a right thing *now* but I cannot find it!"

Go back to Paris. Make Toby safe. Make yourself safe. Do the best you can to make as if it had never happened. Forget the Churches, forget the music. Forget everything you know you did wrong.

The way he did?

There is no right thing left. *Titanic* has sunk.

He takes a deep breath. It's obscene to compare this to what he's been thinking about Richard.

"You think you should have been able to do something," he says. "You should have been heroic, rushed to the bridge with the ice warnings, waved them in Captain Smith's face, demanded that he stop. You should have got all those children safe off the ship."

"Yes," she says.

"I should have somehow avoided killing William. But what else was I going to do, die? Some choices one doesn't have."

Should he have chosen not to lie about it? He was eight years old.

"I didn't want to die," she says.

"Thank you for not dying."

"But I am so ashamed," she says. "I don't know myself any more. I can't stay as I was. I have to change."

"Some things one can't change."

"But I must."

Perdita

IT IS A TERRIBLE THING to say to him. But tonight it is as if they are standing on the deck together, with nothing left to say except the truth.

"I have always had people trying to stick me in a corner and have me do *nothing*," she dares to say to him. "Even you. Making me into something sweet and innocent and good and in need of protection. I'm not good. When I tried to do something for myself, I did everything wrong. I can't live the way I did or I'll do it again."

He listens. For a wonder he doesn't try to help her, or fix her; he just listens.

She tells him about Aunt Louisa taking her to lunch with the Villards, how she played well because she ran from *Titanic*. He asks about the Carnegie Hall concert and she tells him about NAWSA taking her off it. "They wanted survivors who were innocent victims. I'm not innocent."

It's getting cold. He wraps the quilt around her. She considers whether this is protection and decides not to worry about it now.

"I told a woman I feel like Bruce Ismay and she was shocked. Do you understand how I feel like that?"

"Yes," he says.

Bruce Ismay must have been on my boat, she realizes, and she has the sense not to say that to Alexander; not to talk about how low in the water the boat was, how the sea got in and soaked all their feet, so when she rowed and braced her feet, her boots sloshed freezing cold. Bruce Ismay, frightened like her. Trying not to think about it. Trying to stay numb. To stay alive.

She can't be numb her whole life.

"I can't have survived just to sit in a lifeboat. At Mr. Villard's?" she says. "I realized something about music. It's not *for* me, it's not about my being a famous musician and all, but it doesn't happen without me. I am responsible to it. All those children, all those people. They had things to do. They didn't get the chance. I'm still alive. So no matter what I have done, and how wrong and evil and inadequate I am, I have to do what I can. It's not about big audiences or Carnegie Hall; it's about the music.

"And finding out about Dr. John is the same thing. Oh, Alexander, I can't let Aunt Louisa just die, and I do nothing."

"Is it about us too? Is it about Toby?"

She wants to say *I will never leave you. I will always be everything you need.* She said that to Harry once.

"I love you," she says instead.

"And Toby? Are we going to hurt him? Are we going to let ourselves do that?"

"I love him. I don't want to hurt him. I want to keep him as safe as he is loved. But— Do you think the highest thing a person should aspire to is to be protected? I don't ever want to tell Toby that people don't like him for no good reason. But I don't want to have to tell him that I let Aunt Louisa's murderer get away because I wanted to protect him, that I lied about who he was because I wanted to protect him—"

"I do want to protect him. I want him to have a good life. I want him safe."

"But what happens when he finds out anyway? I don't want to tell him his mother was a coward, like Bruce Ismay. But what happens when he comes to me and says 'You took a place in the boat *and you didn't tell me* and we're black *and you didn't tell me?* You *let a murderer get away* because you didn't want to tell me?' If I'm going to have that conversation with him ever, and he's smart and understands things so he'll understand that someday, I have to act the right way now."

He doesn't say anything.

He doesn't say anything for so long that she reaches out from the quilt and finds his hand. "You're cold," she says.

"No," he says. "Thinking."

She gets up and wraps the quilt around them both. She puts her arms around him, lays her head on his shoulder. He leans his head on hers.

"Toby," he says. "Yes. I think the same thing. About me. About what I did. What happens when Toby learns Papa's a murderer?— And you know why, Perdita? Because being a murderer isn't what I want for me. This is all me. I want a family. A nice, pretty, innocent family, a better family than Richard had. Showing off to God, I suppose. 'Look, here's my son. His life is perfect.' He has a perfect father.

"Otherwise, what possible right way is there to be his father?"

She puts her hand over his heart and feels it beating hard and fast.

"And perhaps there isn't a way," he says.

It was self-defense, she thinks. She knows not to say anything.

"I've hurt people. Gilbert spent twenty years looking for Richard and he won't get much out of it. Harry's been Richard's substitute all his life. I treat you badly. I keep you from America, Perdita, where part of you belongs. And I want to keep on doing it. I love you for my own reasons, want you safe for my own reasons, try to protect you so you'll be around for me to love and you to love me. I use you. I try to love you, but I need you. I need you like I need air."

I thought you would come in and solve everything, she thinks, wondering, and I would resent you for it.

"I lie," he says, "but not even lying works. And I don't know what to do."

They sit with their arms around each other. It's late; it's cold. In the fields outside, the morning birds are beginning to cheep. She can hear them because she's not dead. And because she's not dead, she has obligations.

"Come to bed, love. We should get a bit of sleep if we can."

He kneels down in front of her, unties her shoes, eases them off, massages her feet. She thinks of her stockings, which she has had on for two days now. They must be awful. He tucks her into bed and lies down beside her, both of them still dressed.

There's something lumpy in the bed. "Do you have a book in your pocket, Alexander?"

He moves something to the bedside table, not one thing but two; one of them is heavy and sounds metallic.

"You do love us," she says. "You don't have to be innocent to love us."

He puts his arm round her and half-laughs. He sounds so sad.

What they'll tell Toby, what they won't and can't and must, hangs over them like the shadows of lifeboats.

After a bit Alexander says "Do you know the slayer rule?"

"What?" she says sleepily.

"A fairytale, love, for people who have never gone through anything. Enshrined in every legal code in Europe and America. 'A slayer cannot profit from his victim's death.'"

"As if we profit."

"We do. We lie. We re-tell the stories so we're innocent, and the dead people can't contradict us. Do you know," he says, "sometimes early, when I'm having coffee and the rest of you aren't up, I think *why am I alive?* And I push it away, not a healthy thought, not one I should indulge. I take Elphinstone out for a walk instead, I come back, William's still dead, the coffee's still warm, and I wonder: Do I deserve to have survived? I know what William did, but the answer's not yes. Still I get up in the morning and drink the coffee and take the dog out, and it's a good life really, and so I profit from my victim's death."

"I'm not just alive," she says. "I play better."

"And Richard is the center of Jouvet," he says. "I inherited from William. But, Perdita? Other people pay. Toby will pay if it's ever found out. Gilbert's paid. Harry's paid. You do. I try to protect Toby, and I can't. I drink the coffee and he'll be a murderer's son."

"Does it ever get better?" she asks.

It's Richard she's asking.

"It gets different," he says.

"Will I always regret it?"

He doesn't answer for a minute. No need. They both know.

"Yes."

Reisden

FORT LEE, THE MOVIE CITY. One main street, still with some private houses. A cottage with a white picket fence. A village store with two windows. A camera store that advertises CONTINUITY STILLS-ONE HOUR PROCESSING. At the end of the street, in front of a saloon that looks overmuch like a saloon, a gunfight is going on while a cameraman films it. On the other side of the street, a crowd of pirates and policemen are watching, and yawning actors are hurrying from the ferry toward the studios tucked away behind Main Street.

Miss Nisensohn meets them outside the Éclair Studios on Linwood Avenue. It's a big new building with tall glass windows. On the first floor the film assembly line is roaring full-speed, thousands of feet of film racing through immense developer machines and tint baths. The dye drips back into tanks in colors of disaster: scarlet for fire, blue for shipwreck at night. The film painters, girls in grey smocks, sit at long tables by the windows, dabbing more colors onto the dyed stock; tiny flecks of color, fairies' wings, dragon's breath, explosions.

"*Titanic*'s upstairs."

The movies are filmed on the upper floor. The entire ceiling is glass. There's not a shadow and it's oven-hot already. Every window that can be open is open, and ranks of electric fans beat the air behind every camera, but the place stinks of fresh paint, fresh-sawn wood, machine oil, and sweat. The sets are mounted on huge turntables so that they can be turned to catch the best light; two stagehands with long poles are rotating a scene.

Brocade walls, pink-shaded lights: the Ritz.

"It's nothing like *Titanic*," Perdita says. She sounds relieved.

"I like that," Miss Nisensohn says shakily, "when I've tried so hard."

Titanic surrounds them in fragments. To their right, a bit of Ritz, detailed down to the ranked spoons and forks at each place. *I will never have lobster,* he hears Miss Lady saying; *that is a Yankee dish.* To their left, a stateroom like theirs, but larger; a bed with a bed-rail. *Alexander,* Perdita asked him, *do you have a book in bed?* There should be flowers, he thinks; a bunch of lilacs, a basket from Gilbert with chocolate, crackers, a whistle, all the necessities for shipwreck.

"Uh oh," Miss Nisensohn says. "Here *she* comes."

"You're here!" says Dorothy Gibson.

She looks shockingly pale, her face swollen under thick cinema-yellow makeup. She's in an evening gown; a butterfly hair comb trembles above her haunted eyes.

"Cheekbones!" she says. "You're here! And Baroness! We're just doing the Verandah Café scene—"

There's the Verandah Café turning into the sunlight, rattan chairs and twined ivy.

"I can't be in the film," Perdita says. "My Aunt Louisa died. I've only come to sit with Miss Nisensohn."

"Oh noooo." Dorothy Gibson turns her eyes from Perdita to him.

"Sorry," he says. "My family too."

"That old lady, the one with the purple velvet coat. Is she with you?"

"She's dead," Reisden says. Dorothy Gibson's eyes turn drowned-black; she blinks.

Louis Johnson's operative, Fred Troutman, arrives. No change in Dr. John, he reports, and no one has seen Otis. Johnson is having St. Vincent's watched.

Perdita and Miss Nisensohn sit together to one side of the filming. This should be the moment when Reisden is free to work out some clever thing that will redeem them all, disarm Harry, get Gilbert back to Paris. He doesn't have anything. He goes downstairs, finds a phone, and calls the Waldorf again, trying to speak with Bucky Pelham; no luck. He and Perdita watch while Dorothy Gibson does a romantic scene with the actor playing her fiancé, holding hands in the Verandah Café.

"Will he drown?" he asks Miss Nisensohn.

"Nah, he's a hero. He's going to stay on board," Greta Nisensohn says. "She wants to stay too, because she's a heroine, but he makes her leave. When the ship sinks he rescues a baby in the water and hands the baby into her boat and they let him in too. So everyone lives happily ever after."

Perdita shivers. "They're going to *put a child in the water* just to *film* it?"

ॐॐॐ

NOT ALL THE SCENES are filmed in the studio. Following a bus full of actors, Johnson's operative Fred Troutman drives them in his car to a town near Newark, where the stairway of a bank stands in for *Titanic*'s Grand Staircase. A glass-and-iron dome flowers overhead; a balcony leads round the second floor. From the open windows in the second-floor offices comes a wind from the Hudson, the smell of the sea. The bank clock chimes the half-hour, but on the landing a too-familiar clock has its hands set at quarter of midnight: a hurried papier-maché copy of the clock on *Titanic,* Honor and Glory Crowning Time.

The director stands under the clock and shouts through a megaphone. "Half-hour break to eat, then we go into the scenes after the iceberg hits. Look at what you're wearing right now because that's what you're wearing tomorrow. Boys, tie your tie the same way. Girls, if you've got flowers in your hair, take 'em out. 'Cause just like *Titanic,* they won't last the night."

The caterer serves ham sandwiches, coffee, and pie on the bank front steps. The catering wagon advertises *Rambo's Hotel, Coytesville! Moving Picture Headquarters! Service to the Stars!* Reisden leaves Perdita with Miss Nisensohn and stands in line to get food for the three of them. The extra in front of him takes a sandwich and peers into it. "No mustard, and apple pie. What we always get when we got to keep our clothes clean. 'Cause apple pie stains don't show on the film, see? You new in town?"

He doesn't answer. He has just recognized a man waiting in line in front of them. A mustache, a finicky air.

"Is that Bruce Ismay?"

"Him? Ismay used to hire him to double at parties. Now he's gonna have to change his look and go back to vaudeville, 'cause no parties for Bruce."

"I saw Ismay. The real one."

"You were on *Titanic?*"

"Not when it sank."

The extra asks, as if it's something too personal, "Is this anything like *Titanic?*"

The Klieg lights, the camera on its spider legs; the extras eating their dinner off the bank tellers' windows. Actors are picking at their food, making nervous jokes.

"I wonder what I would have done," the extra says.

Reisden sees as if in a passing shadow what *Titanic* may mean someday even to those who weren't on her. The imagination of disaster; the desire to be a hero, the fear of not measuring up; sea-shadows on the staircase under the darkening dome; *Titanic* in dreams. *Titanic* remade for the living. A trolley car's brakes screech from the street. Ismay slips a sandwich into his pocket to take with him into the dark.

At the edge of the crowd, he sees Louis Johnson, who is supposed to be in New York. Johnson gestures to them.

"It's Dr. John," he says. "He's going. I've got the car. I'll take you to St Vincent's."

Perdita

THEY'RE ALMOST TOO LATE to say goodbye.

They hear the sound from the hall, an exhausted child trying to suck a last bit of liquid through a straw. The sound is terrible. It scratches and drags, stops and starts again. Perdita doesn't want to go inside; it's terrifying, that sound. She makes herself sit beside Miss Fan, smelling medicinal stinks that remind her of Aunt Louisa's apartment, menthol and eucalyptus and pharmaceutical smells. It is as if Aunt Louisa sits down beside her, more real than if she were alive.

She takes Dr. John's cold lax hand. Now, she thinks; now he is on the deck of *Titanic* and I am here with him. There is no boat for us.

She has only this chance, this one last moment where they can speak the truth.

"Dr. John," she says, hesitating. *I should not know. I must know. I already know.* She leans forward and whispers in his ear.

"Grandfather," she says so only he can hear.

There is a stirring, a groping, in the rattle of his breath.

"Miss Perdita, I think he hears you."

She doesn't want to know. Only if the answer is right. But if you stay on the deck of *Titanic* with someone, you have responsibilities. What you are is what you do. You tell the truth before you die.

There are no miraculous escapes from here.

Who are you? What a question to ask, as if it could be answered in one word?

She leans forward, down, near his ear. "Say yes if you are Dr. John."

His breath pauses. In the sudden blessed silence she can feel him gathering his forces. Enough breath to speak, to say one word, say yes, yes—

But he doesn't say it.

And that is her answer.

The silence goes on so long that she would think he had died if she didn't feel the faint engine-thrum of his pulse in her fingers.

"He can't speak because he can't breathe," Alexander says, low.

He can't speak because nobody speaks. Not on *Titanic,* not on the tilting, crowded, panicked deck at the very last; nobody speaks of passing or lying because people don't give each other away. They don't even give themselves away, because they'd give away their wives and children, their whole long struggle for the life they should have had.

Only one word do they say. *Freedom. Like life after death. Freedom.*

"Elevate his head or turn him to one side," Alexander says. "He can't swallow, he's drowning." He moves to help.

Dear Alexander, looking for something to fix. Because trying to fix is how he helps himself out of suffering. He is Dr. Reisden of Jouvet. And this man is Dr. John Rolfe Church of Fair Home. And they are not. And they are.

"Here, let me hold him up," Miss Fan says. "John, dear John, do not leave me—"

Perdita moves away so Miss Fan can lift Dr. John, so she can rest his body and head against hers.

Freedom.

What did Miss Lady do? Made Miss Fan marry Dr. John. Made her marry Isaac. But after that, kept Miss Fan to herself always, like a servant, so that Dr. John and Miss Fan could never be alone together, never for a moment be free to love, even to think it?

What do you say to another person, on the slanting deck, with all the lifeboats gone?

One word in him perhaps still, one word, and not to be wasted—

She turns toward Miss Fan.

"Miss Fan," she says, "do you take Dr. John to be your husband? Say yes if you do."

What if Miss Fan doesn't?

But "Yes, with all my heart," Miss Fan says. "Dear John, stay with me—"

"Dr. John, do you take Miss Fan to be your wife?"

They all hear it, one word, a sigh, a groan, almost laughter, but clear, clear as the last word in a story, *yes.*

Perdita moves back away from the bed, leaving Miss Fan to murmur to her husband. Perdita leans against her own husband. Alexander puts his arms around her. She almost hears Aunt Louisa's voice. *Have you been strong, dear?* Strong enough to lie with a clear conscience if she has to. Strong enough to tell the truth if she can. *I lied, dearest granddaughter. I didn't know better. But I was never ashamed, not for a minute.*

Neither will I be, she promises. And I'll make sure Toby isn't ashamed. Of himself. Of any of us. Whatever I have to do. If I have to change the whole world.

If I have to lie.

Or tell the truth.

She feels something go out of the room, like water rushing away into the sea. The room is very still, the only sound is Miss Fan murmuring *dear John, my dear John,* all the endearments she never said. The words pile up on his deathbed like flowers.

But he has stopped breathing.

Reisden

JOHNSON, IN HIS CHAUFFEUR'S JACKET and cap, drives them back up Broadway to Riverside Drive. The women sit in the enclosed passenger seats, crying. Reisden sits up front, out in the air, with Johnson. In the bustle of afternoon New York traffic, they can talk without being heard. Reisden slumps against the back of the seat.

"Otis Church?" he asks.

"No word of him."

"What do you think he'll do now?"

"We're lucky, he'll get out of the city."

Yes, let's be lucky. The book weighs down one of Reisden's pockets; the gun weights the other.

"How do you think he'll go? Penn Station and south?"

"Fourth largest building in the world, Penn Station. Easy to keep out of sight."

"Let him run," Reisden says.

"I don't know I can do that."

A policeman halts them. A Macy's auto-truck has broken down ahead of them on Broadway. Cars and wagons are trying to get past and onlookers are making it worse. Johnson inches his big car forward like the rest of them. The policeman raps on the windscreen frame with his baton. "Hold it, Blacky, didn't I say to stop?"

"Sure thing, Sir. Just trying to get these white ladies home, Sir."

"If they're meaning to get ahead of the traffic, have 'em hire an Irish chauffeur." The policeman gives the frame another tap, hard enough to shake the glass. "You stay right here."

The policeman gestures traffic in front of them. Reisden swears under his breath.

"I brought something for you," Johnson says. "Miss Perdita gave them to me, but don't you give them to her." He unbuttons a jacket button, reaches into his jacket and pulls out an envelope about the size of a pack of big cards. "This woman in New Jersey was taking pictures on *Titanic.* She gave the negatives to your wife because there's a picture of him that's dead in there, and I got them developed. Don't let her see them. A lot of them are pretty rough."

Reisden unwinds the string holding the envelope closed.

Titanic. Mailbags and trunks ready to be loaded aboard the tenders. A line of French porters, bent over, with trunks roped to their backs. A man in a porter's apron reading the *Racing Form.* The lights of *Titanic* over the water at Cherbourg. The Grand Staircase, the dining room. A boy spinning a top on deck. Diners at the Ritz. A steward exercising the dogs, a crewman adjusting an oil lamp. Bridge players in the smoking room. The Strauses on the promenade deck. A sentimental closeup of a pair of hands, his clasping hers.

Sunday service in the first class dining room, the tables moved aside, the seats in rows; passengers of all classes standing in the sunlight, singing, secure in God's love. There is no peril on the sea. They are safe.

And there are the Churches, a group on the sunny deck after service, four or five good pictures. Dr. John, a smiling Santa in a white suit, standing between his mother and his wife. Beside them, her coat-skirts blowing in the breeze, holding her wide hat on with one hand, is Perdita, smiling, innocent.

And then he goes on to the next pictures, to Sunday night.

All the pictures are taken by flash, jagged flattened light against shadows.

A group of men on deck kick something like broken glass. People are sitting in the lounge. Men are ordering drinks at the bar.

They all have the same expression. A stunned indignation, a dulled inwardness, a look of having just remembered something very important and needing to think it over: the look of death. Their mouths are drawn down, they have seen something or felt something, a sudden great inward wound. They have just been told that the pain is inoperable, their case is hopeless, they're going to die; that difficulty they have in recalling names and figures, that's not momentary; all they can do is endure the fear and the pain and the indignity of death.

A woman is sitting outside on the deck, on one of the benches. Her hands are clasped in her lap, her shoulders are hunched over. She knows what will happen to her. They all know.

Who are they? They are about to find out.

"All those heroic words on *Titanic*. 'We have dressed in our best and are prepared to go down like gentlemen.' The polite crowds. We thought they didn't understand the ship was going down. They understood exactly."

"You see what I mean, don't show them to her."

"Too late. She was there."

The policeman reluctantly waves them forward, turns it into an impatient gesture, *go along now.* Johnson eases the car into gear and moves forward carefully past the disabled truck.

蝥蝥蝥

JOHNSON ENTERS THE APARTMENT FIRST. Mrs. Daniels is there and hasn't seen Otis Church. Fred Troutman and another man, a black operative, are already on guard, one outside the front door, one at the alley entrance.

"I should sit with Miss Fan and Aunt Jane," Perdita says.

Reisden looks at Johnson; Johnson nods.

Perdita takes the Church women into the front room; Johnson stands by the front door, keeping an eye on the door and the women. Mrs. Daniels goes to the kitchen and wheels a tea-trolley into the front room. *Coffee?* Reisden asks her silently, miming a cup. She nods and brings him back some already made, steaming.

Reisden calls the Waldorf-Astoria and reaches Bucky.

"Harry has a story about my niece and Louisa," Bucky Pelham begins.

"Tomorrow, noon, you and Gilbert. 125th St. ferry slip on the New Jersey side. By the ship that's moored there. We'll talk then."

He hangs up on Bucky Pelham's objections.

Clementine Daniels offers him sandwiches. He takes one into their bedroom. They need clean clothes to take back to New Jersey. He opens Perdita's trunk of clothes. Cook's chocolate cake is on top, ominous in a taped metal box; at least it's not oozing. He takes it down the hall to Clementine Daniels, who is sitting in the kitchen with the daughter, Arbella.

They are picking the tape off the box when Fred Troutman's police whistle tweets from the back of the building. From the kitchen Reisden can see a square of the alley.

In the middle of the alley stands Otis Church.

❧❧❧

JOHNSON AND REISDEN burst out the front entrance together. Riverside Drive is busy with delivery vans, carriages, cars, and servants. Troutman is standing by the car, pointing. Church has outrun him and is at the corner. An iceman's cart is by the curb; the iceman is halfway down a tradesman's-entrance alley with a block of ice over his shoulder. Otis Church pulls something out of the pocket of his coat, *he has a gun,* but he doesn't; it's some kind of heavy curved knife. He slashes the cart harness; four quick cuts and the surprised horse is free. Otis throws himself across the horse's back, whips the horse into traffic with the loose ends of the reins, and lashes it into a canter, weaving expertly among the other horses and the cars.

"Look at him," Johnson says under his breath, "he was a jockey, wasn't he."

Johnson's car is too large. In this traffic it'll be like trying to chase the man with *Titanic.*

"Where do you think he's going?"

"The 125th St. Ferry."

At the very edge of the street, a ginger-haired boy in a flat cap, some clerk or lower servant, is wobbling carefully along on a two-wheeler.

"If I had that bicycle I could catch that horse," Johnson says.

Johnson can catch a horse on a bicycle?

"Do it. I'll drive," Reisden says.

The ginger-haired boy loans his bicycle for an exorbitant dollar. Johnson throws himself onto the bicycle and pumps out into the traffic, bent-backed like a skater, disappearing north. Johnson's men pile inside the car. Reisden pushes the car north, finding every hole in the traffic.

They pass the Strauses' home, swathed in black, the blinds drawn.

Almost to the 125th St. Ferry, a little north of Grant's Tomb, they catch up. The cart-horse is hitched to a tree, panting, blown. The bicycle is leaning against the next tree. Reisden parks the car hard against the curb. Troutman and the other man jump out of the car. Through the trees in back of Grant's Tomb, the land falls away almost vertically. Reisden can see Johnson standing by a small white monument behind a fence, holding onto the fence and looking down. They make their way cautiously toward him.

Manhattan Island is mostly bedrock, but on the West Side, the high point above the Hudson, it's crumbling sandstone. The tides of the Hudson saw through it, leaving drop-offs to match the Palisades across the river. Trees hang by slanted roots over the rock. The monument is the Tomb of the Amiable Child, who was killed by falling down the slope a hundred years ago. Reisden knows this because Perdita showed him it, back when he was finding excuses to visit New York and not-quite-courting her.

"He's down there," Johnson says. "Heading for the tracks."

The only way to get down is to slide, and Otis Church is scrambling downward, holding onto roots and spindly trunks, grabbing and reaching as his feet slide. Below by the river, the land flattens out again into a gravel railroad bed, the track of the Hudson Line.

One side-wheeled ferryboat is halfway across the Hudson to the ferry-slip at Fort Lee; the other is moored at the slip.

"He'll get away," Johnson says. "He'll run up the railroad tracks and get the ferry and be gone to New Jersey before we catch him."

"I'm not going down after him, though," Johnson's black operative says. "You can, Frog Jaw, but I'm not going to."

"Hold my coat if that's the way."

"I'll take the car and cut him off at the ferry," Reisden says.

❧❧❧

AT THE BOTTOM OF 125TH STREET, the ferry pier is a cluster of buildings: a couple of storage buildings, a ticket-taker's office, an open-sided shed. Under the shed roof a middle-aged woman is percolating coffee and heating buns and sausages.

"Did a black man just take the ferry?"

No, because here Otis comes.

He's made it down the hill. He runs high-stepping along the railway line, jumping from tie to tie. Far behind him Johnson slithers down the last of the slope, staggers, and comes after him, sliding on the gravel. Troutman is still inching down the slope, a hundred feet above them. It's Johnson and Reisden against Church.

Johnson has his lady pistol.

Reisden has the Roth-Steyr.

He pulls it out of his pocket. It's heavy.

All he has to do is what Richard did. He sights along the barrel, one hand cradling the grip, the other steadying the shot. One shot and Perdita won't need to say why Otis killed Aunt Louisa.

Someone begins screaming; he glances over his shoulder. The cook is shrieking and waving a long kitchen fork at him.

"Oh, murder, murder, murder!" she shouts.

"Stop that."

By the bar there's a green trash can with a lid. She grabs the lid by its handle and hides behind it, flourishing her fork at him like Don Quixote. He can see Otis Church's knife clearly by now. It's a hoof pick, the size of a horseshoe, a wicked heron-necked recurved thing, blacksmith-made, sharp as a scythe and heavy.

To get it away from Church, he'll have to shoot it out of his hand, or shoot him.

All he has to do is shoot him.

Shoot him and save everybody.

And do it now, because Otis Church is running forward as if he knows that Reisden won't.

Stupid fool, why not?

He looks around. A length of rebar, something long and heavy—There's only the cook's fork, maybe a foot long in all. Longer than Church's weapon but not heavy enough.

"Give me that," he says to her, "and hold this." He checks the safety and hands her the gun. "Do not point it at anyone. Especially me."

She stares at him.

If he's going to do this the only way that can work, there'll be a moment when he leaves himself completely undefended. "I need that too." He grabs the trash can lid, smelling yesterday's rancid garbage and hot dogs.

South of the storage buildings he positions himself on the track to meet Otis. Otis has been glancing backward as he runs. Johnson is slogging his way heavily through the gravel. Otis looks up and forward and sees Reisden waiting.

The cliff on one side, on the other the river. Johnson behind him, Reisden in front; Otis will attack one of them. Which will he choose? Will he run back and try for the black man who looks like a prizefighter, or forward, toward the ferry and the thin man with the trash can lid?

Stupid. Idiot. Fool.

And then the tracks begin to quiver underneath their feet. A train.

It's behind Reisden, southbound, going presumably to Penn Station, which means it's already slowing. At slow enough speeds, if you believe the thriller films, a man can board a moving train.

Otis has won. He'll jump on the train, get to Penn Station from the direction no one will expect, from the north. From Penn Station he can go anywhere.

He'll need to be on the river side of the tracks. Reisden steps off the tracks on the river side, onto the sliding gravel footing. Otis does too.

The train rips past them, belching coal-smoke into a cloud. Reisden can't see Otis, only shadows through the smoke. He runs forward into a steel wall of sound and grit. Otis appears suddenly in the smoke, too close, looking over his shoulder; a freight car roars past him, door half rolled open. Jump, pull himself up, and he'll be safe. They stare at each other. Otis snarls and lashes out with the hoof pick.

You don't need a sword to fence. You need a weapon an inch longer than the other man's. Reisden charges him with the can lid; steps out of the way of his slash, saber-cuts with all his weight behind the fork and knocks the hoof pick out of his hand. Otis dives after it, gets it, slashes out with it again; it rips against the lid and sends it spinning.

But the train is getting away, the freight car doors loll closed, the last car is past. Otis grabs at it with the hook of the hoof pick but misses, staggers; and then the caboose is swaying away from them down the track to Penn Station, leaving the coal smoke, the dust, the heat shimmering over the tracks; and Louis Johnson is behind Otis and Reisden is facing him; they have him between them.

"You're not catching me," Otis says and backs away from them, down the scrub and stones into the water.

"No, man," Johnson says, "don't go in that river. You'll drown."

"I don't drown."

Otis wades out into the water, wide comical strides, up to his knees or so, then launches himself forward and begins swimming.

The tides are less strong in the lee of the pier; his coat captures air at first and holds him up. He arrows out into the Hudson toward the Jersey shore, swimming slowly and methodically, head out of the water. Across the river, by the Fort Lee slip, is anchored Miss Gibson's *Titanic*, rusty aft as if dragged from the ocean, but gleaming with paint at her bow and with a brand-new white lifeboat hanging from a shining set of davits.

"Is he trying to swim to Jersey?" Troutman says, coming up beside them panting. "Why didn't you shoot him? I think he's going to get away. Why didn't you shoot?"

Perdita

IN THE CAR FROM ST. VINCENT'S, the women sob. Aunt Jane cries harder than Miss Fan.

Back at the apartment, "Arbella, honey?" Aunt Jane says. "Bring my picture of my boys. I need to see my boys."

Arbella does, weeping softly. Perdita asks both Church women to come into the front room. "Arbella? Go see Mrs. Daniels for a bit. Miss Fan and Aunt Jane and I must talk."

The door closes behind her. Aunt Jane sits down in a heap, a broken old lady. For a moment Perdita hesitates, trying to recall something she should do, something she's done for most of the past week every time she came near a phone. And then she remembers what it is; call St. Vincent's or Mr. Johnson to ask about Dr. John.

"I thank you for what you did this morning, Miss Perdita," Miss Fan says wearily. "Your aunt must have spoken with you by now. So you know that John's and my marriage was irregular. Your aunt, your grandmother, is John's wife. But I do thank you all the same for letting us say those words."

Perdita has spent the ride back considering how she can say this, and there is no good way.

"Miss Fan, you are truly married if those words can make you so. Aunt Louisa died yesterday."

"Oh no!" Miss Fan is shocked out of her own grief. "How could that be? Miss Perdita, I am so sorry."

"Oh, Miss Baroness," Aunt Jane says. "I am grieved for your loss."

"Oh my dear," Miss Fan says, "She was a generous woman and I would have liked to know her better. How did she die?"

Perdita isn't able to say anything. *Mr. Otis murdered her.*

I don't need to know why she died because I know already. Dr. John told me.

My grandfather, Isaac, told me.

It is too late to escape. She has heard the truth, the water is rising, and all the boats are gone; and Toby is left behind with her.

Miss Fan hiccups, almost a laugh, the way sometimes people are taken with fits of laughter in the midst of crying. "Miss Lady would be spinning in her grave that John and I are married."

She breaks off abruptly.

"Didn't she think you were married before?" Perdita says.

Did they lie about the marriage too? Did Miss Lady have Miss Fan *not* marry Dr. John? There is only one reason; Perdita knows it; Dr. John told her in his silence. Now she must say it.

"Dr. John," Perdita says, and swallows. "Dr. John was not her son, was he? He was yours, Aunt Jane; he was Isaac. Wasn't he? My grandmother married Isaac."

Miss Fan says nothing. Neither does Aunt Jane.

No one ever tells.

Every molecule of air in the room is silence.

"The real John Rolfe Church died in Paris," Perdita says. "Miss Lady didn't go to look at him, she didn't bother to see his dead face. I thought if she had been his mother, she would have; if she had been his mother, she would have been hunting for him forever; she would have taken no one else but him. If he were her son. So I thought he wasn't; I thought he was Isaac."

"John was her son," Miss Fan says, "of course; my John. Why would you want to think differently?"

Why would anyone want to think differently? No one wants to.

They can stop here. They can have a story instead, like the heroic dead of *Titanic*. But the heroic dead are dead, and she is alive and has responsibilities.

"But when we were on *Titanic*," Perdita continues, "Dr. John told me a story. He came back to Fair Home after the war. Everything was ruined. He said he was looking for 'Mamma' to find out if she was alive."

She turns away from Miss Fan, toward Aunt Jane.

"He was looking for you, Aunt Jane. Miss Fan, Aunt Jane, I can lie, I should and I will; no one will hear this but us in this room and someday my son. But I want to know what I'm lying about."

Aunt Jane lays down her photograph.

"Nobody has lied to you," Aunt Jane says.

Her voice is different suddenly, her manner is different, a woman who is talking to another woman, one of her own.

"Miss Fan, honey, let me talk a moment. Miss Perdita, tell me what my boy said on the ship."

My boy.

"He—" Perdita's voice trembles. It should not. She knows the story already. There are no miraculous rescues. She starts again. "The railroads were ruined, he said, the houses burned; he saw skulls in the fields. He came to Fair Home; the barns and the smithy were burned and the freedpeople had left. He wanted to leave; but he had to see you. And then he had to stay."

"Were we going to leave Fair Home?" Aunt Jane says softly. "It was our place."

"He stayed for you. But Aunt Jane, Miss Fan, why did Miss Lady ask him to be John? Why did she go so far with it? Why did she bring you into it, Miss Fan? A friend of mine said Miss Lady made him into a slave again, someone she could control; and once he agreed, she had a hold over him. Was it like that?"

"We were not legally married," Miss Fan says. "Miss Lady told John and me what to do. We stood up in the parlor and had the preacher in, but Miss Lady told me to cross my fingers in the folds of my skirt so it wouldn't be a true marriage."

Miss Lady made her do that?

"We pretended so Jeff could inherit, but I was so frightened. I used to lie awake shakin' every night," Miss Fan says, "considering what would happen if anyone ever found out about him. The White Camellia would have lynched us all up in a line, even Miss Lady. But she *had* to have John."

"Why?"

"Because John owned Fair Home."

"No," Perdita says, puzzled. "Miss Lady did."

"Until she *married*," Miss Fan says. Her voice breaks high. "Married women didn't keep their own property then. After Miss Lady married Mr. Charles, he owned Fair Home. And when he died, John owned it."

Oh. Oh.

"If John was dead it would have belonged to some cousins of Charlie Church's," Miss Fan says. "Awful people. They hung round like turkey buzzards, hopin' to know he was dead. And Miss Lady thought he was. But then Dr. John—then *Isaac* came back and he brought Whirlwind. So she took him for John. And Fair Home was safe."

"And he agreed, and you agreed."

"We all did."

"Nobody knew," Aunt Jane says. "Nobody knew what my Miss Lady did. She had courage."

"She made him cut his lip," Miss Fan says, "his own lip, cut it open and blame the Yankees, so his face would be ugly for a while and no one would look at him and see he was not who he had been. And he did it. It mended too clean for her liking."

"I sewed it up for him," Aunt Jane says. "I didn't want him ugly. He grew a beard."

"And he was my grandfather," Perdita says. "So my boy and I, my mother, all my brothers and sisters— We are all black people."

"Not if you don't care to be, ma'am," Aunt Jane says.

"I grew to *love* John," Miss Fan says as if she is confessing something. "That is the truth. And we had to do it."

We had to do it. For Fair Home and the livelihoods of everyone in it; for Dr. John's clients, who supported Fair Home, who had their teeth filled and their dentures made by a black man, who would have been disgusted that a *black* man had had his *fingers* in their *mouth*—

"You would have spoken of it on the deck of *Titanic,* Miss Fan, if we had not got off."

"I might have."

"I wanted to stay and talk with him."

Because on the deck of *Titanic* truth can be told for its own sake. But if you step into the lifeboats— You lie about yourself. You think you can control a lie, you can even call it truth. A better truth.

Freedom, Dr. John said. But he was never happy until he came home.

Can anybody dare to tell the truth? The truth is under no one's control.

So does everyone lie? Is that all there is?

"How did Miss Lady decide something so desperate?" What kept her at it, and kept her going so far that when the real John showed up, she denied him? Was it like stepping into the lifeboat, reaching thoughtlessly for safety? Across the field, up the drive to the house, Miss Lady saw the man riding toward him on her horse; she had only that long, from the fence at the end of the drive to the moment when he was close enough for her to see he was the wrong man.

And between one breath and the next, Miss Lady decided. To take Isaac for John; to make him cut his lip; to false-marry him to Miss Fan. To lie and take control. To choose the wrong man on the right horse.

"Wasn't there any truth she could have told?"

And between one breath and the next, Perdita knows why she told that one.

Why Miss Lady didn't even look at her own son John's dead face in Paris.

Why she thought she could get away with it.

What truth she was telling as she lied.

A bigger truth. A bigger lie.

Neither of the women speaks. Perdita does.

"I know why," Perdita says. "She'd done it before."

❧❧❧

AND THE SILENCE SAYS EVERYTHING.

"We did what we had to," Miss Fan says. "We women. Those suffragettes want the vote now. The vote! We didn't even have our lives. Our husbands owned our *clothes*. I know a man sold his wife's hair. One day Cousin Lady was heiress to Fair Home, the next day married to that Charlie Church who was a black-eyed villain. Fair Home was his. And of course, he wanted a boy out of her, to own *his* plantation when he was gone."

"Mr. Charles said," Aunt Jane says. "Mr. Charles said if she didn't give him a son he was going to put her aside."

Cast her off.

"He would have kept Fair Home," Miss Fan says. "And the horses. It would have broken her heart."

"Miss Lady, she started one baby after another, but she couldn't keep 'em." Their words are tumbling out as if the truth has been waiting to be said.

"She had to do something," Miss Fan says.

"My Mamma was one of fourteen children and we were all light," Aunt Jane says. "I went to Mister Charles and I say, Mist' Charles, I *know* Miss Lady going to have a baby, I *long* to have me a son to wait on Miss Lady's son, same way I wait on her. He did what I figured he would. So I knew the child would look like him.

"As soon as I knew I had a baby coming on, Miss Lady told him she had started a baby too and this time she was going to Washington where there were good doctors and she wasn't coming back till she had her baby in her arms.

"So we both went to Washington. She was padding her clothes out with cotton, eating herself fat, but there was only one baby. Mine.

"It took us a long time to say what we both intended, because Miss Lady liked to be the one having the ideas. All I could think is if Mister Charles knew I had a baby and Miss Lady didn't, he'd send that baby to the field, he'd take his angryness out on that baby and send it to the field. If things hadn't come out right I would've had to run. I'm praying, let my baby look white so I can give it to Miss Lady. She's saying *what'll I do, Jane, what'll I do,* and I'm saying we going to figure out something, the Lord will provide. But it took us both a long time to say what we intended.

"I was going to say I had lost my baby. But there wasn't a need."

"My brothers Al and Phil," Perdita says. "They're twins. They don't look just alike, they're not identical twins, but they were born at the same time. Twins run in our family."

Our family.

"I was big but I didn't know till the birthing. Miss Lady got me a doctor just like a white woman. I was saying to myself all through the birthing, it'll be all right, he'll be her son but I'll be his mammy, he won't know me but I'll know him. The doctor put the one boy in my arms, and I saw he was light as milk and I was praying *thank you Jesus,* and then the doctor say 'Whoo, you got another one.' It was the Good Lord providing for us both. Miss Lady says to me, 'Your son *never* be a field hand. Our sons live with each other all their lives like you and I do. One of 'em be called master, the other be called servant, but they both be our boys and I take care of you and them like you take care of me.'"

Nobody says anything for a minute.

Miss Fan lets out a long sigh like a moan. "She never told me. Back before the War, she would have got me to marry the other one and she never told me he was black."

Aunt Jane doesn't say anything.

"Oh, that—*woman*," Miss Fan says. "That *woman*."

"I guess she just had to put it out of her mind," Aunt Jane says.

"Aunt Jane, you took one baby and Miss Lady took the other." Who chose which one? Miss Lady did, of course. She would have taken the first one, the bigger, healthier baby. But Aunt Jane would have been Mammy Jane to both, the son she couldn't claim and the one she could.

"Did John, I mean the son Miss Lady took, know he was your son and not Miss Lady's?"

"No, ma'am," Aunt Jane says.

"And Isaac?"

"No, ma'am, they neither one of them knew."

"And Miss Lady didn't like Isaac?" Perdita says.

"Oh, no, ma'am. She liked him well."

"But wasn't she going to sell him?" No, it was John who had sold Isaac at Manassas—no, Isaac sold John—but hadn't it been Miss Lady's idea first? "How could you bear that? After what you'd done and what she'd promised? How could you bear *her*, when she was going to sell your child?"

"Ma'am," says Aunt Jane. "She wasn't."

"But she had the slave dealer in."

"No ma'am," Aunt Jane repeats. "Mr. John had the slave dealer in. It wasn't Miss Lady who wanted to sell my Isaac," Aunt Jane says. "It was her son."

Her son.

Your son.

No. Because they had decided on their story. Their lie. John was Miss Lady's son. Why be surprised he acted like it?

"Mr. John brought that Mr. Champ Strounge to Fair Home. He told Miss Lady, 'Mamma, I got to have those uniforms, I got to pay my muster fees.' Fair Home was his, he could do what he want. Miss Lady says no, you don't sell Isaac, I don't let you sell Isaac, you hear? You sell someone else. And they were fighting about it, with nothing decided.

"Then those Yankees started down toward Manassas, and I knew if my Zack went up there, he could walk North. The night before the battle, that night Mr. Fate marry Miss Fan, I saw John talking to that Mr. Champ on the verandah. When I tell my Isaac goodnight, I tell him to get up early with the horses, to have everything ready for the fight, to go off fast, I tell him go off, don't you let that Mr. Strounge keep you from the fight, go off. I can't say *you ought to run,* because I have my responsibilities, but John never treated Zack like Miss Lady treated me, so I say, you go off with the horses, you go.

"I knew he couldn't get me word where he was. I was afraid he'd died. We all went up to Manassas and there were dead men everywhere. I thought, what if he got shot in the fighting and I don't know his face.

"I prayed for four years. And then July 27, 1865, four years and five days after Manassas. A Thursday, near dusk. I saw him at the end of the avenue, coming up toward us. I wheeled Miss Lady out on the verandah, and we didn't know which of our boys had come home till he was right by the steps. And she did something, I will be proud of her till the day I die. Miss Lady said 'John, you have come home.' He just stared at her. She held up her hand and said, 'John, welcome home. John, you have come home.' She was the strongest woman. I guess she trampled on her feelings to take my boy for her own, and Miss Fan, I guess she trampled on yours. But we both knew what had to be done."

"She told me to stand up in front of the preacher with him," Miss Fan says. "And she told me to cross my fingers. It was that or we'd've all been out on the road."

It is almost heroic what they did. But Perdita thinks of Paul deMay.

"I used to dream I had married John for true," Miss Fan says. "I knew such a thing could never happen, but Aunt Jane, I want you to know that this morning," she pauses and swallows hard. "I am honored to have married such a man as your son. I am."

They were almost heroic, Perdita thinks, Miss Lady and Aunt Jane, Miss Fan too, Dr. John; all of them; but if they were heroic, what was Mr. Otis when Paul deMay came to visit Fair Home; what was Mr. Otis when Aunt Louisa came to meet Miss Fan? Was that heroism too? It was the same story.

"You are married to him," Perdita says, "because my Aunt Louisa, my grandmother, was *killed* early Tuesday morning, just after she saw you. The way that Paul deMay was killed. For the same reason. By the same person. To keep the same secret."

There is a silence that seems only puzzled, not guilty, and then—

Then the front door opens. Alexander and Mr. Johnson are talking together. Mrs. Daniels comes out from the kitchen and asks them something, not like a servant or a cook but like one of Mr. Johnson's operatives. Mr. Johnson says something about Otis.

"Paul?" Miss Fan says sharply. "No. He had nothing to do with us. He was shot by the White Camellia for consortin' with a white woman. They killed him nearby but—"

"He was killed because he knew Dr. John was Isaac," Perdita says. "You needed to survive, you did what you had to; I understand. But look what happened."

"Otis?" Aunt Jane says. "Where is Otis? *Where is my son?*"

Reisden

"LET'S GET OUT OF HERE," Reisden says.

The girl Arbella is screaming "Uncle Otis, Uncle Otis!" He and Perdita leave Johnson to give the horrible explanations; they just go, without luggage, without anything; they just leave. They walk in Riverside Park while Perdita explains to him.

"So," she says. "I am a black woman. Toby is black and my family is black."

"You'll lie about it?"

"I have to. Except to Toby. Someday."

It's getting toward dusk. They walk toward Broadway.

"Where shall we go?" Perdita asks him.

"Not anyplace Otis Church might think of." He explains about Otis Church, who's probably drowned. He doesn't explain why they're not sure of it; how he once again has protected no one.

They consider what hotels will take a couple without luggage. Not the Waldorf-Astoria. They try the Knickerbocker. The front lobby is full of potted palms and groups of chairs; add the sound of an engine and it would be the lounge of *Titanic*. On the wall is a black-festooned portrait of John Jacob Astor. The clerks and bellmen each have a bit of black ribbon pinned to their lapels. From the dining room they can smell dinner worthy of the Ritz and hear a string trio.

Sometime forever and ever
We'll be together again...

"Not here," Perdita says. She leads him out onto the street.

"We could go to the hotel where we waited for Mr. Johnson."

Where he feels uncomfortable, and where most of the people feel uncomfortable seeing them. There's no place for them in all of New York City.

"I'm calling Bucky Pelham," Reisden says.

This time they reach him.

⮾⮾⮾

THEY MEET BY THE LIONS in front of the big new library on Fifth Avenue, three people in dark clothes. The southernmost lion, Leo

Astor, is in mourning too, a black wide ribbon around its neck and a wreath between its paws for Astor and the victims of *Titanic*.

"Gilbert will go back to Boston," Bucky Pelham says. "And we are asking for the return of the money he gave you. We are asking that, on the grounds that he was unduly influenced to give it," Pelham continues. His cheeks are flushed. "Harry intends to have Gilbert's mental stability assessed if everything Gilbert gave you is not returned. Everything."

The book is weighing down Reisden's coat pocket.

"Harry means to say Uncle Gilbert is mad?" Perdita asks.

"Hardly mad, Niece—but not capable of handling his affairs—"

"Uncle Gilbert is perfectly capable!"

"He called you Richard," Pelham says to Reisden. "Twice."

"Don't you know who Alexander is?" Perdita asks Pelham.

"Don't you know why I won't go back?" Reisden asks.

Pelham hesitates. He looks up at the lion.

"I know why no right-thinking person would want the matter spoken of. Why anyone not lost to all shame—"

"Does Harry know why I won't go back?"

Pelham says "Yes" finally.

"So. Then what is he afraid of," Reisden says.

"If Harry has nothing to be afraid of," Pelham says, "why does he not have that book?"

"You know about the book."

"All he wants is to move the Knight Companies into this century, without *false assertions* and *loss of control* and *scandal*—"

"I'll trade the book for Gilbert."

"You will give us the book," Pelham says sharply. "Go back to Paris where you belong. Gilbert Knight belongs in Boston. You cannot hope for anything else."

"Uncle Bucky," Perdita interrupts, "do you know what happened with Aunt Louisa? Did you guess that too?"

"I know nothing," Pelham says sharply.

"It is as bad as you guessed," Perdita says. "Harry will learn it and he will create scandal. If you help him, Uncle Bucky, he will."

"I intend to tell Harry nothing from either of you!" Pelham says. "You must give him what he wants."

"Then Harry and I will have to talk in person," Reisden says. "Tomorrow noon, by the 125th Street ferry in Fort Lee. Bring Gilbert."

❧❧❧

THEY WALK UP FIFTH AVENUE, having nowhere else to go.

"Anyone not lost to all shame," she says, stopping on the sidewalk. "He was *counting* on your being ashamed of being Richard, and not talking, and not helping Uncle Gilbert."

A man jostles them. Reisden draws her out of the sidewalk traffic toward a window of women's fashions, walking suits in rose and black-and-white stripes.

"Why tell him about Louisa?" he asks her. "Why give him a weapon against you?"

"He was counting on my being ashamed too. I have things to be ashamed of; I will not be ashamed of that. May we go and check on Mr. Williams?"

"It's only been a day since Garnet left."

"He's playing at Holiness tonight. We can eat up in Harlem."

"We'll sleep in New Jersey."

"I want clean clothes—but oh, poor Miss Fan and poor Aunt Jane, I haven't the heart to face them. What did Uncle Bucky mean," she says, "about false evidence and a book?"

He's not going to talk about this on crowded Fifth Avenue. He hails one of the big new motor cabs with a privacy screen between the chauffeur and the passengers. He hands her in, gives the address of the church, and pulls the glass screen closed so no one but themselves can hear.

"I could prove I'm Richard," he says.

❧❧❧

SHE SIMPLY STARES AT HIM.

He takes the book out of his coat pocket and hands it over. He watches while she touches the crusted pages. He has to explain. "Those are fingerprints, which don't change. They're Richard's, and they're mine."

"So Uncle Bucky is expecting you not to use actual evidence you have, and to let Harry just kidnap Uncle Gilbert and say he's not capable?"

"He's expecting me to maintain a decent silence, love, and I'm trying to trade that for Gilbert. Pelham was saying they'd force me to sue them over whether or not this book is real. And the first question anyone would ask is 'Why did Richard leave?' I don't see a way to answer that without telling the rest."

"So what will you do?"

"Love, I don't know." Save you, save Toby, save Gilbert. How? "Harry has always said I'm not Richard. If there were proof I am, nothing else he says would be believed. Not about Gilbert. Not about you. But you'd be a murderer's wife and I'd be Richard."

"There has to be another way."

"I haven't found it."

The cab takes them no further than the southern end of the new black neighborhood; they have to walk the rest of the way. Servants, who work Friday and Saturday nights, are given their evening out on Thursday; the shops are open and the streets are full. Eyes follow them, curious or resentful. Among the restaurants and fruit stands and the dealers in secondhand clothing, musicians are playing in restaurants and on the street. They pass an accordionist and a singer making percussion with a pair of sticks. Perdita pauses, listening. *Blessed are the poor in spirit,* the man sings, and the sticks shimmy in his fingers, tapping like a vaudeville dancer's shoes.

In among the little shops, a storefront church is open for Thursday night services; blue-and-white cross painted on the window glass, HOLINESS CHURCH OF GOD'S REDEMPTION;

bright-lit through the windows and the open door, a room full of worshippers. They look inside the door for Williams sitting at a piano.

Piano, but no Williams. A black man in a white suit is standing at a lectern in front of a row of choristers robed in blue satin. The whole congregation is singing; the sound streams out into the street.

"Let's go in," Perdita says. "I don't like his not being here. He's usually here."

They stand at the back of the room. The preacher is singing in a sort of chant:

I love the Lord He heard my cry
I oh I love I oh my Lord—

It's the same strange American music that Perdita and Williams were playing. Perdita stands transfixed, listening, and Reisden watches her, the expression on her face. The preacher throws back his head and sings; every man and woman in the room is singing with him, standing, swaying, maids and butlers, janitors and street sweepers, an ocean of voices. In the congregation Reisden sees the woman with the cake, singing *Well...*

I may be dead and gone
Well, a bass sings. *Oh yes!* a woman calls.
Dead and gone...

Perdita stands listening with her whole body.

My brothers and sisters, I'm giving you the text tonight, Hell under the Water. There was a man by the name of Jonah...

Even here, Reisden thinks; here's *Titanic,* even here.

And Jonah paid his fare and got on the ol' ship... The wind blowed so hard until everybody on the ship got frightened and got scared...

Oh, well, the congregation sings, *all right now...*

He watches his wife.

Won't be no more rejoicing, won't be no more song—

Do you know what you're doing? he asks her silently. *Where are you going with this music in your life? What America are you going to?* Of course she doesn't know. No more than he did when he first discovered Jouvet, or ran from being Richard.

There may be no America in which she fits. No world in which they do.

If he claims to be Richard, if she claims music, they will lose the worlds they have.

And if they don't claim anything—

Jonah prayed, he prayed his prayer. Deliver me...

"What do they call this?" he whispers to her.

"Gospel."

She listens, they listen, until the sermon finishes and the congregation is singing and clapping, *Oh when the saints come marching in.* She shakes herself, pulls herself away from the music.

She consults with the pastor. Mr. Williams was supposed to play tonight, she reports back, but didn't show up.

"I hope he's all right," Perdita says.

They go to a couple of restaurants looking for Williams, but no one has seen him. They pick a restaurant by its music and eat chicken, cornbread, and anonymous greens.

Nothing could have happened to Perdita's piano partner. But, he reflects, nothing could have happened to *Titanic.*

"Let's try his apartment," he says, uneasy now himself.

They smell the smoke from two streets away.

Mr. Otis W. Church

THE FISHING SKIFF THAT RESCUES OTIS picks him up almost at the end of Manhattan. By then he's lost his overcoat, his shoes, his hat. The white man who picks him up asks him how much money he has in his pocket and charges him a dollar to take him to the shore.

What was the fool going to do if he didn't have money? Throw him back?

It's Thursday night; there's a Sally Army meeting down by the docks. He spins them a story: Southern man, visiting here from Georgia (fools don't know the difference between Virginia accent and Georgia). Got mugged, got dropped in the river, nearly drowned, Sah. Not a drinker, no Sah. They give him dry clothes and shoes that pretty much fit and ask him if he's accepted Jesus.

"Oh, yes, Sah. I am obleeged to you, yes, Sah."

"We are all equal in Jesus."

No we ain't, Otis thinks; you're some poor-ass Jesus-drummer and I got Fair Home.

But I got to earn it. Again.

The girl's not dead. Her man saved her off the tracks.

She's going to talk.

She'll be telling it all over: Fair Home is run by blacks.

Miss Arbella told him the girl was in New Jersey yesterday, at the boat where they making the movie.

They making it again tomorrow. She'll maybe be there.

The Sally Army dressed him like an Irishman, little flat cap and a wool jacket all out at the elbows; he don't look like himself. White folk don't recognize a black man anyway. She won't. She's blind.

He's got his hoof pick. And, blind woman? She can't swim. He's got the river.

He'll cut her or drown her.

Reisden

PEOPLE HE RECOGNIZES from Garnet Williams's party are standing aimless, bewildered, staring at the building where they used to live. It's a charred, stinking ruin, dripping with water. The woman with the purple tongue is sitting on the curb, moaning, holding her arm.

"Sturgis!" Williams is calling, his voice full of tears.

"Oh, Mr. Williams!" Perdita gropes her way toward him and hugs him.

"D—n, girl, you was right, Liddy was smoking and she set the couch afire. Oh, G-d, Sturgie, don't you be dead, dog."

In this sort of disaster, in Paris, Jouvet would provide sandwiches and comfort. Here— "I'll call Johnson."

There is no telephone in the nearest bar or drugstore. He has to send a boy to Johnson with a message. Johnson arrives in five minutes, with a car and a man whom Reisden recognizes as the pastor of "Holiness."

"Come on, folks, Pastor's putting everybody up in the church." Johnson will transport them, women and children first.

"Take me to the hospital," the purple-tongued woman is saying. "I think my arm broke; I got to have it set."

"Sturgis!" Williams is calling out. "I got to find my dog."

"You go with Williams," he tells Perdita; Otis won't find her in the middle of a Negro church. "I'll hunt for the dog."

He doesn't expect to find the dog; but he does, a pathetic heap of fur at the mouth of the nearest alley. It's lying on its side, its mouth open, its legs stretched out. Can't anything go right? Come on, did the blind man's dog have to die?

Across the dog's cheek is a burned gash.

It's still oozing.

Oxygen, no. Adrenaline, no. "Do any of you have smelling salts?" The last thing the dog needs is to breathe ammonia, but— He holds the smelling salts under Sturgis's muzzle and pounds on its ribs. "Come on, breathe. Stir, you bastard. Don't be dead."

He and another man haul the dog vertical, thump its chest and sides, and are rewarded with a smoky cough and retching. They bully the beast into some approximation of consciousness. By the time Johnson returns with the car, Sturgis is slumped against Reisden's legs, head down, moaning and shaking and stinking of burned beer.

"Sturgis!" Johnson says. He takes off his own coat and lets the dog lie on it, in the front seat.

Johnson must love Garnet Williams.

⧉⧉⧉

BACK AT HOLINESS CHURCH, people are settling down with blankets and pillows in the pews. Williams weeps with joy over his rescued dog. Perdita and Reisden go outside and sit on the steps.

"What'll happen to Williams?" Reisden asks.

"Garnet *can't* come back and take care of him. Not now she has her chance—" Perdita broods, leaning against his shoulder, then sits up and turns to face him. "And I can't leave him on the street with nothing but that dog."

"Johnson will take him."

"As charity! Because he thinks Garnet will like him better for it, which she won't! Mr. Williams deserves more. Alexander, he's a musician. His piano just burned."

"Do you want to take him on?" Williams? And the dog? Just pray the skull burned.

"I want to offer him a tour," Perdita says.

"Yes?" he says when she hesitates.

"The two of us together, playing double piano or four-hands. We'd have to do it in France. You'll like that, me being in France."

He would. But he hears *have to do it in France.* It's a moment before he asks, because he wants her in France, safe; but he loves her. "Will you like it?"

She hesitates for almost as long, which tells him everything he doesn't want to know. "At least I'll have the music. I've missed that as much as anything."

His heart is a house of cards. He lays the last card on top and asks her to knock it down. "What would you do," he asks gently, "if you could do what you wanted?"

And her face changes. She sits up, she smiles the way she did when she got them in to see the kitchens and the engines of *Titanic. Watch me be more pathetic than Miss Williams,* she said. *Watch me.* "We'd play in America," she says. "There's so much nonsense about black people and white people being separated. But we're good together. We would be all political and insist on open audiences, we would let anybody buy any seat and sit next to anyone. We would play classical and jazz, we'd both play both, the way we do practicing, so no one would know what to expect from us. We could even play in the dark, a bit; people would have to guess which one of us was playing. And we would make every one of them glad they came.— That's what I'd do if I had the nerve."

Her jacket is smeared with ash; the neck of her blouse is crumpled and a lock of her hair has come loose. She looks wild and happy; she's never been more beautiful. "You do have the nerve," he says.

"Toby?"

"Toby will be proud of you."

"There aren't hotels where black people and white people can both stay; there aren't restaurants where we can eat. I'd have to call myself ivory. Black but looking white. And how could I rob Toby of America? And what would I say to my mother and sisters and brothers? They are as much affected as Toby and I. Alexander, I said I'd lie, and I must."

"Your America, my darling, is a prejudiced place, it's not the prize you think it is. But if it's ever to change so Toby belongs in it, someone will have to do something."

"America needs two people playing pianos in the dark?"

"Needs what you can give it."

She leans against him and closes her eyes. "I can't," she says. "It's not only Toby. My mother and my brothers and sisters. It's their secret too. I can't give them away."

❧❧❧

THEY SIT ON THE STOOP IN SILENCE, holding hands. He wraps her in his overcoat. She falls asleep on the stoop, leaning against the balustrade. When he tries to lead her inside, she protests; so there they stay, him awake, her asleep, huddled against each other in the early morning chill. He thinks of the deck chair where they spent the last of their one night on *Titanic*.

She's right. She can't.

He can.

He's got the book.

It is the way to shut up Harry. *You're accusing me of pretending to be Richard and Gilbert of believing me? I am Richard and here's the proof. Talk and see who believes you, because I'm the millionaire Knight heir now.*

It sickens him.

It would be suicide. He'd have Perdita and Gilbert and Toby. But not Jouvet. He'd have to be Richard. And everyone in the world would know what Richard did.

It comes to him, sitting there beside her, how profound a privilege it has been to be Alexander Reisden. It wasn't a lie or a disguise. It wasn't only getting away with murder. It has been a good life. It brought him his family.

The only way to keep it good is to give it up for them.

And it will be his death to do it.

He sits beside his wife, wraps his overcoat around both of them, sits with her, his arms around her, until it's time to go back to *Titanic.*

❧❧❧

FOUR HOURS until they meet Harry. They take the 125th St. ferry to New Jersey. The sun is just rising; gulls cry over the water; the surface of the river looks like hammered bronze. Three hours as the actors gather by the pier. The cinematographer is placing lights, pale in the morning sun. They wait in the crowd with Miss Nisensohn.

Fred Troutman arrives. Otis Church's body still hasn't surfaced. Troutman thinks the man made it across the river. Reisden leaves him guarding Perdita and walks up to Main Street.

The Kodak store advertises one-hour developing. He gets the book pages and Daugherty's report photographed and copied. The walls of the store are covered with film stills. On the way back he passes the village store again. One window is still stacked with cans, but the other has been turned into a movie set, a milliner's shop. A girl in ringlets peers longingly through the window at a monstrous hat while a cameraman films her.

He gives the book to Fred Troutman. "Ask Johnson to keep this for me."

They mingle with the extras. Everyone is dressed in clothes from yesterday. A wardrobe assistant steams wrinkled jackets. Perdita brushes her hair. Reisden has bought a new Gillette safety razor on Main St.; he tries to use it waterless, then stands in line for an outdoor barber.

At quarter to ten, they are all asked to go aboard the boat.

"I've got to," Miss Nisensohn says. "You don't."

"I want to be there," Perdita says. "I won't be filmed, but I want to stand on the deck."

All three of them, Miss Nisensohn, Reisden, and Perdita, go up the jouncing gangplank together, back on *Titanic*, into the last moments of the ship.

For this last scene, hundreds of extras have crowded the deck. Ismay stands at the front of the crowd. Most of the extras are dressed as first class. There are no children. The ship has been winched downward; the deck is tilting.

Miss Nisensohn is shaking with nerves. "Is this right?" the set dressers ask her. A bench there, she says, underneath the windows; ice on the deck.

"I picked up a piece of ice for you," Perdita says to Reisden. "From the iceberg. It's at the apartment."

The director is setting up Dorothy Gibson and her leading man to replicate the drawing that's been in all the papers, "The Final Farewell." Women in the lifeboats, men on the deck of *Titanic*; in the foreground, a woman clings to a man; she doesn't want to leave him. The cinematographer complains about the light.

"Quiet on the set!" the director interrupts. "OK, Hero, you come over here, and Jerry, I want that Cooper-Hewitt— Right. Yeah. Fill light on both of them, back light on Dorothy. It's the deck of the ship, two o'clock in the morning. The last lifeboat is leaving. Ismay gets in the boat, but Girl won't get in. Dorothy, you shake your head and hold on to Hero."

"Alexander," Perdita whispers. "Let me talk first."

"It's all right, love."

"No, let me talk to Harry. I have an idea."

"Now," the director turns a page, "Officer drags Girl toward the lifeboat. She resists, but Hero says, 'Be brave, little girl! See you in New York!' Got that? Three, two, one—"

The actor playing Ismay bullies his way into the boat, pushing women aside. Dorothy Gibson clings to her hero. The Officer approaches Dorothy Gibson from camera left. The hero spans Miss Gibson's waist with both hands, lifts her toward the Officer's arms.

"'Be brave, little girl—'"

Dorothy Gibson stretches one hand back toward the hero. He stretches his toward her.

"And hold it, hold it— OK. Now we got to get the shots on the lifeboat or the tide's gonna start going out."

"Where's the baby? Jerry, you got a baby?"

"What baby? I don't got a baby in the prop list, Boss."

"Alexander," Perdita says. "Don't say you're Richard."

"It's what we have. It's all right."

"Let me speak first, though. I want to tell Harry to do something." She holds up her hand. "Don't ask what. If you ask, I'll realize it's stupid. I just have to do *something*—"

They move to the rail of *Titanic,* carefully out of shot, and watch Dorothy Gibson and the extras dangling in the overcrowded lifeboat along the side of the ship. Miss Nisensohn looks over the tilted railing with them, her fists over her mouth, her knuckles white. "It was like that," she says. "The bow was so far down."

Down below, over the rail, a camera has already been set up at the end of the pier. Tied to the pilings is a River Patrol motor-launch, in case someone falls in the Hudson. In case someone is about to drown.

"Get me a baby! Jerry, I need you down there to get the shot from below, 'cause we're only going to lower the lifeboat once."

The lifeboat inches down raggedly, one side lower, then the other. It looks authentic. Reisden's imagination conjures the lifeboat tipping, victims spilling into the sea.

"Who's got a baby?" the prop man calls to the onlookers.

There are actually children on the shore, farmers' children hooked from school for the day to watch the famous movie being made. One woman has brought a baby, but when the prop man advances on her with a dollar bill, she clutches her child to her.

"Come on, we'll use a rolled-up blanket or something."

"Blanket's gonna sink, Boss."

"Get me a dwarf!"

The lifeboat has reached the water. It's secured to the pier by three ropes, weighted to keep them under the water's surface.

Reisden pulls out his watch to check the time.

Five minutes to noon.

The prop man is going round to the onlookers on the pier, talking with the shortest people—

Harry and Bucky Pelham are standing in the crowd.

And Gilbert.

"They're here, love."

"Oh Alexander," she says. "I'm so scared."

❧❧❧

OTIS HAS COME ABOARD THE SHIP in the early morning. He's hiding toward the stern, thinking of Fair Home. The green pasture down by the horse-pond. Those Italian foals with their velvet muzzles. Miss Arbella sitting in the office with Miss Lady, going through the breeding-books.

Oh, the colts: how they hop and rear, how their little tails broom and flick. How they take to running, and then trot round nuzzling their mothers, and say "See me? Look at me, a fine thing!"

The girl. Zack's grandchild. Things had been different, she might have been at Fair Home too, growing up like Miss Arbella. They might all have been there, him and Zack. Family.

Sure. Starving together, thrown out on the road.

What was I after you lit out, Zack? Your body servant. Starving all through the War. Your jockey, your stable hand. You lit out but I stayed. When you were learning to make those shiny white false teeth, learning to be shiny white, I stayed at Fair Home, I was out there mucking the stables. Times I was so hungry I could have eat the straw.

I saved Fair Home.

You be proud of me. You be proud of everything I done.

He sees the girl.

❧❧❧

THEY ALL MEET toward the stern of the ship, inside: he and Perdita, Pelham and Harry, and Gilbert. The space might have been a dining room once, an entryway, a lounge, but the ship-breakers have stripped everything away for salvage. Now it's rusted walls and worn wooden floor and two portholes to light the shaded space. Rust bloodies the rail as if the ship has been raised from underwater, and the deck is tilted downward, unsteady to walk on.

Gilbert is still wearing the same clothes he wore on the boat on Tuesday. That tells its own story. Reisden smiles across at him, trying to look encouraging. Gilbert smiles back as if he were looking up at a scaffold.

Harry's a shock. Six years ago he was a burly college football player. Now: late hours, cocktails after work; his collar's tight on him, his mouth discontented. But he's more muscular than ever, aggressively muscular. Harry works out.

"You have a book for us," Bucky Pelham begins.

"I have something to say to you first," Perdita says. "Uncle Bucky, Harry, I want you to say I am a black woman."

What? Reisden stops himself from saying anything.

"Niece!"

"Mr. Williams is not my grandfather, of course," she says. "He's my teacher. But I'm hoping to tour with him, so, Harry, if you will, please, *please* say I am a black woman. You know it's dangerous for a black man and a white woman to tour together, so I must say I am a black woman, at least while I'm on tour."

"Niece, you cannot do that," Pelham says. "Think of the family!"

"Then say nothing, Uncle Bucky," Perdita says. "But I am asking all my friends to do it, and telling them why they must."

They wait. She takes Reisden's hand again. *I'm so scared,* she said. No wonder. Reisden watches Harry's stout displeased face. Gilbert is watching him too.

"Your husband is hiding behind you, Pet," Harry says finally. "He thinks I don't have anything on him, but I do—"

"This is nothing to do with Alexander."

"You don't have an idea he didn't give you," Harry says.

"Hardly," Reisden says. "Let her husband speak for himself."

He holds Perdita's hand, kisses it, lets it go. "You tried," he murmurs to her. "Good try too."

"Don't do it," she murmurs back.

Too late. Now.

"We believe it is time for Gilbert to return home," Pelham starts.

"I want that book," Harry says.

"I will go back to Boston," Gilbert says steadily.

"You will do that if you will, Gilbert, but not for me," Reisden says. Now; here we are; he crosses the line between himself and Richard. It is as if Richard takes the envelopes out of his jacket, a man more uncomplicated than he. One envelope to Bucky Pelham, one to Harry. Reisden still does not know what Richard will say.

"Gilbert, you know what's in this."

Bucky Pelham fingers his envelope open.

"This is a photograph of two pages out of the book you want," Reisden says, as outwardly calm as if he were giving a deposition. "It was Richard's." He should say, it was mine. "Roy Daugherty had my fingerprints compared with those. His report shows the result of those tests and establishes the book's provenance and the chain of custody."

Bucky's mouth drops a little open; he sucks his lips closed. He looks at Harry.

"This is a forgery," says Harry. "I'll prove it and send you to prison."

"Do you really want to fight me in court?"

"The two of you," Pelham says. "My niece saying *she* is— And *you* saying— In *court*— Do you have no shame?"

"I have a right to the Knight Companies," Harry says. "You're not taking advantage of a crazy old man to grab everything I've worked for. Do you know how much he's spent on you? We're not made of money."

For a moment, at just the wrong time, he's reminded of William. *Do you think I am made of money, that you ruin your books?* "Be careful."

"Or what? Or you'll shoot me?"

Or I'll ruin you. "I want Gilbert free to do as he wants, with any restrictions you and he make about how he spends his money. I want you to stop saying he's incompetent and stop slandering me. About Perdita, you say whatever she asks you to."

"Good luck."

"Or I will sue you for slandering my investor and we'll compare stories in court. You'll say the prints are forged, which is impossible as far as I know." Now. Say it now. "We prove the prints match. I'm Richard."

There. Said. He's expected it to give him some relief at least; he's told the truth. It tastes of lies. Who is he?

He doesn't know, but whoever he is, that man is here.

"They're a forgery and you're a crook."

He keeps his voice steady, a man giving evidence. "Gilbert knew about the fingerprints—how long have you known, Gilbert? Gilbert has known for some time. He also knew I don't want the Knight Companies and you do, and he chose to say nothing. He told me only last week when I had to come to America."

Then you bloody well kidnapped him. Or he went willingly, but he hasn't changed clothes in two days.

Harry looks at Bucky Pelham. Pelham is still turning over the pages, turning them back and forth, as if something invisible is written on the back.

Gilbert clears his throat. Reisden goes over and stands beside him. Gilbert smiles at him tentatively.

"Ate you all right?" he asks Gilbert under his breath.

"Oh, fairly well, dear boy. Are you?"

Oh, fairly well.

"What do you want?" says Pelham. "You're dead. You were declared dead."

"What do you mean, *you*?" Harry says.

"I didn't have proof then," Reisden says. "I do now. Don't make me use it."

"We will fight you if you do," Bucky Pelham says.

"Richard had the money and you want the money," Harry says. "That's what you want."

And, between one second and another, Reisden knows the rest of what he's going to say. He never wanted the money. Now he knows why and he knows what he wants. It surprises him. He moves away from Gilbert, from Perdita, stands in the light between them and Harry. Standing in the light, taking up attention: that's something he learned from Reisden. Who he is in this moment, he does not know.

"I think," he says, "I want to tell the truth, so that I can say something more afterward."

"The truth!" Harry jeers.

"I sympathize. But there is a truth here. This is a confession. From that child who left the fingerprints. Richard was terrified. It was too late for any right thing to happen. He shot William. I don't remember but perhaps by then he meant to. I know he was glad he did.

"I don't entirely blame him for that.

"But then he ran. Gilbert, he left you to wonder for years what had happened to him. Pelham, he made you worry about who would inherit the Knight Companies. Harry, he left you to be his replacement. Sometime during then he turned into me. If he had known what it would do to any of you, I would have done differently. I am sorry for what I caused.

"I apologize to you all.

"Now I have a chance to do something about it.

"I don't want to be Richard. I don't want the Knight Companies.

"I don't want my son to be a murderer's son.

"But some of that is going to happen now.

"I intend to confess I committed murder. If Toby's going to know that, I want it to be something he grows up knowing. I want him to ask me about it when he's five, and I want to be able to tell him that it happened and I'm sorry. That I would never have done it if I'd known about him.

"What I do after that? Harry, that's your choice."

"You give up this bullshit or—"

"Harry. Listen. I will confess to murder; you don't have a choice about that. I don't intend to do it in the *New York Times* or in sackcloth in front of Notre-Dame, but I mean to let it get out.

"Your choice is whom I say I killed."

"What the—?"

"If you make me, I'll say I shot William Knight and I am Richard. If we can come to terms, I'll say I shot someone else, someone anonymous; someone in the wars in South Africa, when I was young; someone I had to kill or he would have killed me. Someone

I didn't know. I shall make it as uninteresting a story as murder can be.

"Your choice. Yours to control what comes next.

"Run the Knight Companies. Be a better Richard than Richard would have been. Let Gilbert do what he wants. Say about Perdita whatever she wants you to say.

"Or drive us into a corner and we all lose."

"This is about the money," Harry says.

"Actually, it is, Harry." He feels as if he hasn't taken a breath in minutes; he pauses for a moment and breathes in. Here goes the rest of it.

"Pelham, do you know the slayer rule?"

Pelham nods.

"Explain it to him."

Pelham's eyes widen.

"A slayer cannot inherit from his victim," Reisden says finally.

"It doesn't count!" Pelham says. "'Willfully and with malice aforethought—A slayer *willfully and with malice aforethought* cannot inherit—'"

"I will not take the money. I'll take what Gilbert has invested in Jouvet; Richard would have got that much from his father, there's no blood on it. But as for William, if I am going to be notorious for murdering him, I'll be notorious for being sorry. I will not take his money."

"I don't care for it either," Gilbert says. "I never have."

"Please do not speak," Pelham says to Gilbert. "It belongs to you, Reisden, unless you killed him *willfully and with malice aforethought—*"

"God save us, Pelham, do you think that matters? Did Ismay mean to kill fifteen hundred people willfully and with malice aforethought? He thought the ship would look better with fewer lifeboats. He saw a chance to live and he took it. Did anyone mean to do what they did? But in the end the lifeboats were gone and there was no right thing to do and people died. I'm not taking the money."

"Sure," Harry says, "you say that today, and tomorrow—"

"No, Harry. You control this. Either you take up the job of being Richard and be properly grateful to Gilbert for it, or none of us gets the money. If I am forced to be Richard I will formally renounce any claim to it; and Pelham, would you like to remind Harry whom Gilbert inherited from?"

"I will renounce it too," Gilbert says. "It has been nothing but trouble."

Pelham holds up his hands. "Quiet! Be quiet for once. You!" he says to Harry. "And you! And you! Shut up, all of you! I will not be a victim of your nonsense any longer. Twenty-five years, Dr. Reisden! I have spent twenty-five years trying to establish a legal heir for the Knight Companies! You will not give that up. Neither will you, Harry! I will not let you! Don't you all understand? *Richard was William's heir!* You," he stabs his finger at Gilbert, "you inherited from Richard, not from William! And you," he points at Harry, "you inherit from Gilbert! If Richard doesn't inherit, Gilbert doesn't, and, Harry, you don't; and nobody inherits anything; and twenty-five years of my life will have been wasted and I will not have it!" He is red-faced and trembling.

"Then we had better be astonishingly kind to each other," Reisden says.

∂~∂~∂~

HE SWEEPS UP GILBERT AND PERDITA and takes them out onto the deck. From here they can see the scene, still being filmed. The lifeboat is in the water. The tide has turned. Somewhere the filmmakers have found a child, or some equivalent. Out on the Hudson, the river water is riffling past the pier, pulling the lifeboat and the "child" downstream toward the harbor.

Miss Gibson leans over the side of the boat, but can't reach the child. Two of the prop men pull on the ropes. Oh, get the scene done, Reisden thinks; let everyone be safe.

Harry and Bucky Pelham head down the gangplank, shouting at each other.

Here we are, he thinks, on the deck of *Titanic,* and the last boat has left. And what I just said, I suppose, is what I had to say.

"Someday," he says, "Toby's going to find out about this and realize I've given millions of dollars away from him for the sake of my tender conscience. I can't imagine he'll take it well. And I've potentially given the money away from you too, Gilbert."

"I shall get a job," Gilbert says. "I really don't mind, Alexander. I can sell books."

"We do have books to spare."

"And I shall have some money from Aunt Louisa, I expect," Perdita says. "It'll be all right."

From the shore, Pelham gestures to them; come down. Harry is heading away toward the pier. Who, Reisden gestures to Pelham; Gilbert, me, both? Both, Pelham gestures.

"That's encouraging," Reisden decides. "Gilbert, will you go down to him? I want a moment with Perdita."

"Of course, dear boy."

He watches as Gilbert makes his way carefully down the gangplank, staggering a bit on the tilting deck, clutching the rope handrail.

"Perdita, I've committed to confessing to murder; oh G-d. Am I doing the right thing for Toby?"

Perdita takes his hand. "I don't know. Am I?"

"'Toby, your father committed murder.'"

"'And your mother's a black person. And Uncle Gilbert is going to live with us, but this is Mr. Williams, who's going to live with us too, at least until he finds someplace.'"

"'Don't smoke anything he gives you.'"

"'Don't give beer to his dog.' Oh, Alexander, two dogs! Elphinstone and Sturgis! Toby will be in heaven. I want a dog like Sturgis. *Three* dogs."

"I wanted to protect him. And I didn't."

They hold hands, fingers interlaced on the rough railing.

"I wanted to stay on the deck of *Titanic*," Perdita says. "To hear the truth. And I did."

From below, Pelham gestures to him again: come here. "I'm being asked to negotiate. Want to come?"

"Uncle Bucky doesn't want to see me. I'll stay here."

"That really was ingenious about asking your friends to say you're black."

"We'll see if they still want to go to a restaurant with me."

"Your friends will. The rest don't count."

"What they think of me," she says, "that's their problem."

He goes forward toward the gangway, then turns back, looking at her. Perdita is leaning on the rail, carefully because of the tilt, looking down at whatever she can see of the women in the boat. Oh my love, he thinks. Oh my shameless, clever, astonishing woman.

Two-twenty in the morning; the *Titanic* is going down. And they are all still on the boat. Their fate is in the hands of Harry, an angry, disappointed man who is as likely to drive them into the iceberg as steer away.

Harry is standing by the rescue boat as though he wants nothing more than to jump in it and sail off. Reisden told him, *be Richard:* that will be as hard for him as Reisden's being a murderer.

"Look up!" the director shouts through a megaphone. "Her stern is rising!" The extras in the boat all look up, toward him. "She's going under! Scream!" The ship creaks frighteningly. The extras gape with terror. The undertow of the Hudson pulls at the boat like the sinking *Titanic* itself. "OK, cue the waves!" Two men are standing on the dock with a railroad tie on ropes. They let it go and it hits the water like a giant hammer; even with three ropes holding it, the lifeboat tosses wildly.

The "child" is bobbing on the end of a fishing line. Miss Gibson reaches out her hands gracefully, like a heroine.

The extras in the boat are still looking up, some of them are pointing, and they are screaming now, pointing at the ship.

Reisden looks back, toward Perdita, and sees Otis Church.

❧❧❧

"YOU AIN'T LETTING OUT OUR SECRETS," that's all he says.

He grabs her. She twists away from him, stomping at his feet, kicking at his legs. Something hard jabs her, *a book* she thinks, then *the hoof pick.* A line of fire scrapes along her side.

Otis lifts her up, over the railing, and tosses her. But there's no boat this time, no lifeboat, and she is falling and falling. She grabs for the rail but there is no rail and she is lost.

The fall takes forever and there's a crash that jars her in every bone, and it's so cold in the water, and she thinks lifeboats, *I want a lifeboat,* but the water fills her mouth and nose and the current grabs her. Alexander taught her to swim. She kicks out against her waterlogged enveloping skirt and tries to find the surface and the air. But she can't.

REISDEN DOESN'T EVEN THINK. Otis Church jumps with her and he throws himself after them; he hits the water as if it were pavement. For a moment he's stunned. He is looking up from cold darkness, water stinging his nose and eyes, seeing his own last breath streaming in pebbles of air toward the light; then he kicks upward, hits the surface with a gasp. Somewhere, far away, people are screaming.

He sees her. The flow of the Hudson is frighteningly fast, impossible to swim against. She's being carried down toward the ferry pier. Past the pier the tide will be stronger, and the piers are too large to catch onto.

The three ropes holding the lifeboat are their only chance.

He looks up and sees the river patrol's rescue boat casting off from the pier. If he can get to the ropes with her and hold on long enough—

Reisden reaches Perdita and catches her by her tangled skirt as the tide pulls her out into the current. He grabs at one of the ropes, but can't hold her and it too; he has to let it go or let go of her. The two of them are being carried past the ropes.

Otis Church sweeps past them, caught in the current too.

Something underwater grabs them; part of the rope, creaking, bucking, trying to roll up over them and push them underwater, and he manages momentarily to hook his right arm around the rope and hold on to her. But the current is pulling them away.

The rescue boat comes at them from behind, engine choking. He and she bump against the hull, then spin away again. Someone in the bow of the boat reaches down and grabs Perdita. Reisden pushes her forward, toward the reaching hand, toward safety.

And as she is pulled to safety, he loses hold of the rope and the current takes him.

It is not true that your life flashes before you in an instant, only the important parts. Toby is building a rampart of blocks around Elphinstone. Elphinstone sniffs at the blocks and pokes part of the wall down with his muzzle, and Toby laughs.

Toby laughs.

Dear boy. My son.

The boat slams into his side, and for a moment he's caught between the hull and the current, being pushed under, drowning. Before he can be pulled under, some man in the boat reaches down, over the side of the boat. Reisden catches hold, almost pulls the man in, struggles over the side, sprawls at the bottom of the boat, coughs water painfully out of his nose and mouth and lungs. Gasping, he looks up at the sky he never thought he'd see again, takes what feels like the first ragged breath after the end of his life.

And sees the man who rescued him. The two of them stare horrified at each other.

Because it's Harry.

❧❧❧

OTIS CHURCH jumps in with the girl; he can swim; he'll get away, down the river and back to Fair Home, but something goes wrong, there's a cracking stabbing pain in his neck and suddenly all he can feel is his head whirling around in the water, twisting, his arms and legs gone. There is a tide, there is a race, there is a river. Paul's face is framed between the stalks of corn. Miss Arbella is sitting on the steps outside the kitchen.

This is death.

I saved Fair Home, he thinks, but I died doing it and I'll get all the blame.

Oatie, a voice says in his ears.

Otis is in the stables, just about to give up, a ten-year-old boy starving in the hay, Fair Home is too big for him, he's got to let go; but down the path from the house, Zack is coming, Zack is coming back from the dead; and he is leading a bay horse, the only horse in the world.

Whirlwind? says Otis Church. *Whirlwind*?

Zack says, You kept Fair Home going?

And Zack puts the reins in his hand.

Oatie, Zack says, then I brought him back for you.

❧❧❧

ON THE PIER, Reisden and Perdita cling together; someone throws a blanket around them. They're both shaking like half-drowned dogs. "Are you all right?" he asks Perdita.

"I hurt everywhere." He does too, jarred in every bone. There's a long scrape along her side, still bleeding; he sends someone off for antiseptic and bandages.

Out in the river, the patrol boat is searching for Otis. From the deck of Miss Gibson's *Titanic*, extras are pointing. "He jumped off the ship!" Miss Nisensohn says, stunned. The patrol boat circles around a bit of flotsam in the water.

"My dear—" Gilbert is standing by Perdita. They all embrace each other. Gilbert's being drenched.

"That was amazing!" Dorothy Gibson is saying. "Can you do it again?"

Oh, shut up, woman.

"My dears, you must get off your wet clothes, you will get a chill, and the river is full of *unspeakable* things, you must bathe—"

"That man jumped off the *ship* and *he never came up!*" Miss Nisensohn is crying hysterically. Reisden sends Gilbert to find her sandwiches and hot tea from the catering wagon. It's what Jouvet does.

Perdita and he lean against each other, under the one blanket.

Reisden knows two things, one of which he doesn't want to know. Richard's father and mother, he thinks. In a rowboat, on a lake, one day in summer. It was a beautiful day. She fell in the water. He jumped in after her. Neither of them could swim and they both drowned.

And Reisden jumped in after Perdita today. Not thinking of his son, not thinking at all of Toby.

Richard's father didn't have a will; Reisden does. Tom and Sophie couldn't swim; Reisden learned to swim and taught Perdita.

None of that would have been enough.

Did he think that Toby would blame him for giving away money? Nothing to how Toby would've felt if they'd drowned.

But he didn't think of Toby, any more than Richard's father thought of Richard.

He thinks of Toby now. Toby dear, one doesn't choose between loves. No; one does one's best. And then things go wrong. Love isn't safety.

Maybe my mother and father cared about me, he thinks, which is a bit of a shock because he has never consciously thought they didn't.

Everything went wrong, but maybe they cared about me.

And dear boy, no matter how imperfectly we'll protect you, dearest Toby, know this. We care about you.

❧❧❧

SHIVERING UNDER THE BLANKET, with Alexander beside her, Perdita comes to the end of one story. Once upon a time she loved Harry for himself, or thought she did.

Now she loves him because he saved Alexander from drowning. Uncle Gilbert will love him too for that; and that is cruel. Harry deserves better.

"We must say thank you to him at least," she tells Alexander.

"Let me tell him," Alexander says.

"You think?"

"I have something to say to him."

She nods. Alexander tucks the blanket around her. She feels for a moment the fog-damp warmth of a steamer blanket on *Titanic,* the two of them cuddling together in a deck chair, and then the crowded tilting deck, the weight of the oar, blood in her mouth, and her hands burning in the icy sea, reaching out, finding no child to save.

Harry must know one thing.

"Tell him it's a good thing to rescue people," she says.

❧❧❧

GOING TOWARD HARRY, Reisden is waylaid by reporters from the *Times,* the *Evening Post,* the *Jersey Journal*; he waves them away and tells them to interview Dorothy Gibson.

Harry is at the end of the pier, all by himself, his jacket soaked to the shoulders. No one's interviewing Harry.

He stands in front of Harry. "We would have drowned but for you," Reisden says. "Thank you."

"I should have let you drown," Harry says. "Next time I will."

There won't be a next time, Reisden thinks, but for once he says something else. "No," he says, "you won't. I was there. You reached out for both of us without thinking an instant. You did it because you're a good man. Never regret it."

"Screw you," Harry says.

Reisden just sketches a salute and moves away.

Someday Harry will hear from someone else, someone he believes, his wife, his child, that he is a hero and he is loved. Harry will always be able to remember reaching out and pulling them to safety. He will never know, if he is lucky, how great a triumph that is.

The most uncomfortable of connections, to be an occasion of virtue for Harry.

A connection still.

战战战

THIS IS HOW IT WILL BE WITH ALL OF THEM:

Nanette Williams, one of the first supermodels, the beautiful face of the House of Windsor, will become a staple of the fashion pages, but just past the end of the First World War she will drop out of sight.

About the same time, Louis Johnson will leave New York. He never thought of Brazil before he heard about John Rolfe Church; but what he knows about Brazil now is that the color line is different there.

Bruce Ismay will die twenty-five years after *Titanic*. Every film ever made of the disaster will portray him as a villain. But Ismay is not his reputation, nor entirely what *Titanic* did to him. He will be endlessly charitable to shipwrecked sailors and their families. His grave in London will be inscribed with a phrase from Psalm 107: "They that go down to the sea in ships and occupy their business in great waters, these see the works of the Lord, and His wonders in the deep." One would like to hope that in the end, Ismay found wonders.

Charles Lightoller will never make captain with the White Star line, or anywhere else; *Titanic* overshadows his career. At the time of the Dunkirk evacuation in World War II, he'll be a retired weekend sailor with a small and elderly yacht. He'll sail his yacht to Dunkirk to rescue troops. On the *Sundowner*'s single trip, Lightoller will cram her cabin, her hold, her deck, even her cabin roof with soldiers. He will save enough of them to have filled two of *Titanic*'s lifeboats. Perhaps he'll think of that.

Dorothy Gibson will get her wish to be famous from the movies—but not from her movies. She'll marry her Jules, then divorce him; move to Paris; become a singer. In the 1930s she'll sympathize with the Nazis, then, politically aware too late, she'll become an anti-Fascist spy. She will be jailed in Italy, and Indro Montanelli, a fellow prisoner, will write her into his classic *General della Rovere*.

Miss Lady's body will never be found. Aunt Jane and Arbella will look for her in every battered face, every rescued body brought to Halifax, but she will never return to Fair Home.

Otis will. His broken-necked body will be found in New York Harbor and sent back to Fair Home, and (it's Perdita and Reisden who arrange it) the other John Rolfe Church's body will be returned from Paris to Fair Home. John Rolfe Church, Isaac Church, and Otis Church are buried together under a single stone in the family graveyard, all with the death-date 1912. Now, a hundred years later, unless a passerby knows the story—and no one does—there's no way to tell who was white and who black, or even which body is whose. All you can tell from the stone is they were brothers.

Jouvet exists still, a discreet, legendary company well into its third century. The apartment where the ninth Dr. Jouvet now lives is still full of pictures of Reisden and Perdita—photographs, concert posters of the scandalous dual-piano team Ivory and Ebony, a portrait of Reisden and Perdita and their children. Deep in a storage closet, in an unused bedroom, there is an unmarked box of souvenirs. A tin toy boat. A passenger list. A little boy's grubby scrap of stuffed animal, barely recognizable as Puppy Lumpkin. An ink-bottle with a chipped stopper, still with some water in it. A pin of a little brass bird flying through a lifesaver. A telegram, SAFE CARPATHIA. A postcard showing *Titanic* triumphantly entering New York.

Titanic exists too. Broken in half, covered in rusticles, she stretches for a half-mile across the Atlantic seabed. Since the wreck was discovered the roof of the gym has fallen in; part of the boat deck has collapsed onto the prom deck. In a hundred years there'll be nothing left.

Except for stories. A hundred years from her wreck, the three most recognizable names in the English language will be Jesus, Shakespeare, and *Titanic.*

But now, in this spring of 1912, *Titanic* drops off the front pages and life goes on.

❧❧❧

REISDEN AND PERDITA bring Williams home to their apartment: Williams and Sturgis and the skull, rescued from the fire by dubious miracle. Perdita sits Williams at the kitchen table and negotiates. The TOBA circuit, she says, and concerts in France; she can't do it without him; how will they ever get to play Schubert otherwise? She talks percentages with him while Reisden scrambles eggs at the stove, his only culinary trick, and silently loves his wife, and feels a little sad. He will never have as much of her as he wants; she will always be called away by music. That is the way he wants it, almost. Richard would need her there all the time. He is not Richard.

Harry isn't speaking to Reisden and apparently barely speaking to Pelham; it's Reisden and Pelham who work things out. Gilbert will be allowed to go back to Paris. Gilbert says not a word against Harry, but something has happened to him in those two days when he was in Harry's hands. "I believe I shall not be back to Boston in some while," he says, and goes to Boston and packs all his books to take with him. An unfinished story, Gilbert and Harry.

As a silent promise to Perdita, Reisden and Gilbert will travel on the same ship.

Reisden writes to Patrice de Varenne: step one of his life as a confessed murderer. He does about fifteen versions of the letter, spends two days at it, covers the floor with crumpled paper. Finally he writes *You may have heard that I killed a man a long time ago. I'm sorry I didn't say so before. I know about wanting the rope I didn't cut. Let's talk when I get back.*

He writes to Dotty, three pages of carefully considered confession, and she writes back, utterly ignoring everything he said.

Patrice de Varenne telegraphs. HOW DID YOU SURVIVE, he writes. TELL ME.

Someone may get some good from this.

Reisden delivers letters. All those letters to all those grieving widows and orphans. Philadelphia, Connecticut, Washington; Springfield, Massachusetts. He comes back from these trips shaken. We are lucky, he says to Perdita, standing in the hall, his hat on the hall table, his coat not even off, his arms around her. They take each other to bed. We are lucky, they say.

They are survivors.

సాసాసా

THE DAY BEFORE HER NAACP CONCERT, Perdita gets an envelope from Fair Home. She takes it downtown where she is to meet Alexander by the Chelsea Piers. Alexander wants to see the huge pier that was to have berthed *Titanic*.

"You were on *Titanic*?" the guard asks. "Yeah, go on in."

They walk through the faded velvet light of the huge customs shed, the long areas for passenger cargo, and out onto the pier itself. Up and down the river, great shadows of cranes are swinging cargo into holds, immense shadowy stacks and hulls loom up and down the Hudson; but on the longest pier in the world, there's only the river and blue sky and emptiness.

They walk out onto the enormous promenade, which smells of tar and the sea.

"*Carpathia* left the lifeboats here," Perdita says.

At the end of the pier, the salt breezes from the Hudson tug her hair. It's like being on deck. She remembers Dr. John's rough overcoat; feels Dr. John swinging her over the rail to save her; Otis Church grabbing her around the waist and swinging her out over the rail, the falling, the freezing Hudson water and her skirt wrapped round her legs. She remembers the wooden lifeboats knocking together on the water, the crowds of reporters shouting *Tell us your story!*

My story is I survived.

My story is—

She takes out the envelope from Fair Home and hands it to Alexander. "What does this say?"

She hears him unfolding the paper. "Two letters. One from Miss Fan, thanking you."

Perdita has made an investment: some of Aunt Louisa's money will help Arbella. Arbella will come to New York, where Garnet will dress her and Mrs. deMay will make her sound like a lady, and then she will go to Signor Tesio's trainers' program in Italy. Arbella will have her chance.

"And one from Jane Church." Alexander hesitates.

"What does she say?"

"She's telling you who you are," he says in an odd voice.

"Who I am? Read it."

"She says you're white."

"No."

"Yes. She's giving you your genealogy. 'My great-great-great grandmother, Enjany, came from Africa. Her master, Mr. Isaac Stanhope, favored her with a daughter, Excellent—' Do you want them all?"

"Yes."

"Excellent had a daughter with Robert Thornton. Her daughter, Maria, had a daughter with James Burrell. That daughter, Clarissa, with Edward Thornton— 'My grandmother Clarissa was seven-eighth white, which made her white in Virginia.'"

But— The first thing Perdita thinks is, oddly, *But.* As if she means to object.

"No?" he says. "You believe in the one-drop rule?"

"What else does she say?"

"'By Virginia law, my mother was a white woman; I am a white woman; Isaac and John; your mother; you; your son— We are all white. I hope this may reassure you.' You're white," he says. "They're all white. After all this."

For a moment she is tempted. A simple story would be so much easier to live with.

"But whiteness is a story," she says. "Garnet says white is just a convenience for white people and they change the law whenever they want to. Aunt Jane is white? She was still enslaved. I can see, but people call me blind and then decide I can't see. It's a story that everyone knows except the people who are in it. Someday," she says, and stops; there are wishes so personal that they are hard to speak.

"Someday," she says, "there won't be stories like that. People will be to each other what they must have been on the deck of *Titanic,* with all the lifeboats gone. They'll listen to each other and say only what they mean and not judge." There is no word to say what she means; she cups her hands together as if she is holding something precious between them. *Freedom.* "Someday it won't be a problem that Mr. Williams and I play music together. Someday people will just sit next each other in the audience, and people's stories will be what they make them."

"Someday you and Toby will be at home in America. May it come."

She holds out her hands. "I think it will, and I think people will like it. At least," she stretches her fingers, all healed now. "I bet they'll like the music."

ߪߪߪ

THAT GESTURE, hands outstretched to the future. *Better stories. Better music.* Schubert, Reisden thinks, and jazz and gospel. And what else?

He knows what love is. It's not a simple story, but it'll do.

"Dr. John said something to me," he says. "That night aboard *Titanic.* 'Let them value themselves and know themselves, and they will be known for who they are.'"

"That's what he might have told me," she says, wondering. "I heard it after all."

"We should have brought champagne," he says. "To toast him."

"To my grandfather," she says, lifting up an invisible glass, and thinks of Aunt Jane, saying that sometimes you're given so big a gift you have to take it. A holy gift.

"To your grandfather, love. To you."

She thinks of champagne on the deck of *Titanic* and Dr. John talking about Uncle Otis. She thinks of Aunt Louisa.

She raises an invisible glass to Aunt Louisa, to all the dead; she hesitates, looking outward into the featureless light, as if the empty dock is some great stage.

"We were on *Titanic,*" she says finally. She knows what she wants to say, but not how to say it, not even whether she is being honest or callous.

"We were on *Titanic* and it was beautiful. Just to be aboard was grand and special. Do you remember how enormous the dining-room was and how the engines roared? Everything went wrong later— But *Titanic* was beautiful. And now here we are going somewhere else new. Women asking for the vote. People not being all black or all white. Such new things." She puts out her hands as if to play some keyboard in the air. "I hope those ships go better, but oh, Alexander, whatever happens, it is good to be aboard; it is beautiful."

She looks up, as if she is seeing something in this empty stretch of water, and he follows her eyes and sees it too. What ship? For a moment it is *Titanic,* that magnificent ghost; he sees her as she might have been, steaming up the Hudson toward her New York home. *Titanic:* Six thousand lightbulbs, a drawerful of ship's-wheel pins, a giant potato masher, a room inlaid with mother of pearl, vast clashing engines, rows of deck chairs; a world. The New York tugs nudge her toward her berth. Here she is, *Titanic* in New York, looming above them, still streaming with water from the fireboats that greeted her; her white decks, her four great caramel-and-black funnels; the largest, safest ship in the world.

From every deck the passengers are waving. Gangways reach out from the shore, living sailors secure them to *Titanic's* side, and here the living passengers come. The richest men in America. The Strauses. Bruce Ismay, honored chairman of the White Star Line, showing off his glorious new ship. Dr. John Church, plantation owner, Santa in a white hat, and his wife, and his mother in her purple coat and her fan with the ivory sticks, returning to Fair Home. The dogs: the little bulldog, the Poms, Astor's Airedale Kitty, sniffing and wagging. Wallace Hartley coming down the gangway carrying his violin, a greater musician than he'll ever know.

And here come the third-class children, herded toward the Ellis Island ferry, at the beginning of their American lives. Rossmore Abbott and his brother Eugene. Lillian Asplund and her brothers. Little girls who played on deck: Salli Rosblom, Margrit Skoog, Ida Lefebvre. Boys with a soccer ball.

He stands with Perdita. They lean against each other's warmth.

If *Titanic* had made that perfect voyage she was expected to; if she hadn't almost collided with another ship in Southampton; if Captain Smith had stopped *Titanic* in Iceberg Alley, waited the night, and missed the iceberg. If –

The ship changes. Rust drips off her. She shatters into lifeboats. Bodies slump in the water. The musicians; the waiters at the Ritz; the engineers; the mothers and fathers and children. Wallace Hartley, Captain Smith, Astor and Straus and Guggenheim, Thomas Andrews—

What can we say to you?

You died.

We survive.

Some of us live with an iceberg.

Some of us found lifeboats, or made them, board by board.

You had two hours to make your lives count. You kept the lights on as the water rose above your heads. You stayed on the boat and comforted each other. You played music after the last boat had gone.

We have a lifetime; we have this living unfinished moment. We are each other's lifeboats. We are sailing. Not knowing where we're going, what iceberg waits for us, what wreck or rescue. But here we are.

He looks up at *Titanic*; he has only one thing to offer, and he offers it to Perdita.

"It's all one story. I was ashamed of my own wreck. But—" He holds Perdita. "Richard, Gilbert, you, Toby, Jouvet. It's the same story." It is as if he and Richard fit together; Richard is a key that opens a door.

"A good story?" she says.

Who knew he would ever think so? "Yes."

Leave them there then, holding hands, kissing on the dock, in the breezes off the Hudson; leave the passing tug that whistles at them, leave them laughing and fading back into the shadows of the pier. She whispers something to him, wanting him to say yes, and he murmurs back, "Oh my shameless woman," and if the guard at the entrance thinks he hears laughter, he looks the other way. All too soon this time will end, this year of 1912, this century. The great pier will dissolve away like *Titanic* and every survivor now living will be dead. He and she will not always live happily ever after; no one does; they will live adventurously, lovingly, all that can be asked for in any voyage.

At the other end of the building, the guard smiles out onto Eleventh Avenue. Through the bustle and dust of the traffic, he smells spring.

All stories end.

But not yet.

Acknowledgments

"THE THING ABOUT...HISTORY is that the truth is so much more complex than anything you could make up," says Henry Louis Gates, Jr. The missing word is "black," but it could be so many others. American. *Titanic*.

Titanic's story has drawn me since I was a child. I'd like to acknowledge some other people whose lives have been touched by *Titanic* and whose work has inspired mine:

- Always to be remembered: the 1500 who died and the 700 who lived.
- Edward Kamuda, founder of the Titanic Historical Society, his wife Karen Kamuda, and his sister Betty Kamuda. As a teenager, Ed Kamuda began writing to survivors of *Titanic*. He became friends with many of them, and because of him and Karen, a huge part of the history of *Titanic* and her survivors has been preserved, not least in the pages of the excellent THS magazine, *The Titanic Commutator*. I had the pleasure of talking to Ed at many Titanic Historical Society conventions, including the 100th. To my lasting regret, Ed died before this book was finished. To you, Ed. May you walk on her deck and may your voyage be long.
- Walter Lord, whose *A Night to Remember* inspired both Ed and me.
- James Cameron, filmmaker, inventor, explorer of the deepest ocean, an inspiration to us all.
- Robert Ballard, who, when asked to do a secret project for the Navy, suggested he could use as a cover story that he was searching for *Titanic*—and found her.

- Steven Biel, author of *Down with the Old Canoe,* with whom I first talked about writing "a different version of the story." Thanks for steering me past the first of many icebergs, Steve.
- Connie Willis, for being Connie Willis, you dear woman, and for *Passage,* the best and most original novel ever written about *Titanic.*
- Jack and Françoise Little, dear traveling companions on many trips to Indian Orchard.
- Don Lynch, Ken Marschall, Tom McCluskie, Judith Geller, Wyn Craig Wade, George Behe, Jonathan Smith, the contributors to the *Encyclopedia Titanica,* and others too many to mention, all the many dedicated *Titanic* writers and researchers who have written about the ship and the stories around her. I'm honored to count many of you as friends.
- Friends in the Titanic Historical Society and other Titanic societies who have shared their interest, knowledge, and enthusiasm. A special shout-out to the Titanic gathering in New York, 2018, and to our knowledgeable tour guide Dave Gardner.
- Paul Kurzman, great-grandson of Isidor and Ida Straus, and Joan Adler, Executive Director of the Straus Historical Society, whom I had the pleasure of meeting at the THS 100th.
- *Titanic*-era historians including Lawrence Beesley, Archibald Gracie, Filson Young, and the staff of *The Shipbuilder.*
- Frances Wilson, author of the Bruce Ismay biography, *How to Survive the Titanic.* Thanks also to John and Malcolm Cheape, members of the Ismay family, who have eloquently defended Bruce Ismay.
- Randy Bryan Bigham, author of *Finding Dorothy*— whose biography of Dorothy Gibson has absolutely

nothing to do with the way I treated her. I tried mightily to get a copy of *Finding Dorothy*, which was a limited-edition book at that point; I sent letters through several channels to get in touch with Randy directly; but though I'm pretty good at these things, I got nowhere. Obviously, God was telling me to make a story up. So I did. *Saved from the Titanic* was made in Fort Lee two weeks after *Titanic* sank, and, bizarrely, it apparently did use a full-size wreck to stand in for *Titanic*. Otherwise it's a different story. Read the excellent *Finding Dorothy* for more. Randy, it's good to be friends now!

- For the sake of the story, I occasionally bent other facts. For instance, passengers were on the tenders before *Titanic* arrived in Cherbourg, but I wanted Reisden and Gilbert together to see it arrive. Wouldn't you? And the *Bremen* sailed exactly when and where I wanted her to. She actually did encounter a field of the *Titanic* dead.

- Was the ice cream on *Titanic* brought on board, or was it made fresh? Fresh ice cream is so much better, and it lets the cook offer Perdita some. Was all the ivy in the Verandah Café real? Probably not, but don't trust me on it.

- How did Irene/René/Renée Harris spell her name? Different ways at different times. In 1912, usually "René," but that's weird. I used the spelling she chose for her tombstone.

- There were actually (at least) four black people aboard *Titanic:* passenger Joseph Laroche, his two daughters, and Ben Guggenheim's valet, Victor Giglio, whose mother was Ethiopian. (In the Cameron *Titanic,* the role is played by a white actor because the single existing picture of Giglio hadn't yet been found.) Given the open racism of America in 1912, it's rather nice that when

Ben Guggenheim said "We have dressed in our best and are prepared to go down like gentlemen," he was referring to himself and a black man.

- There are no recordings of singing preachers as early as 1912, though they clearly did exist. The man Perdita and Reisden listen to in Holiness Church is the brilliant Rev. E.D. Campbell, who recorded his sermons in 1927. On the street Perdita and Reisden listen to another favorite of mine, Luther Magby's "Blessed Are the Poor in Spirit," from about the same time. You can hear them and my whole *Titanic* playlist on the *Titanic* pages at www.sarahsmith.com .

- The survivors lived more complex lives than the simplification I've shown here. Everybody does. Some experienced the lifelong darkness I've cast over them, but not all. Millvina Dean enjoyed flirting and had a good man friend, and other survivors actually enjoyed their late-in-life fame.

And thanks to the following:

- My dear former agent Christopher Schelling of Selectric Artists, who provided splendid editorial suggestions, especially for the middle of the book. Christopher, you are a genius. If I had known what book I was writing, it'd have been easier to get there… Now you know how sausages are made.

- My brilliant current agent, Esmond Harmsworth of Aevitas Creative.

- Kate Miciak of Ballantine Books, who provided the right dose of narrative dynamite at the right moment.

- Maggie Topkis of Felony & Mayhem, who gave the book its opening and so much more. I owe you, Maggie.

- The members of the Cambridge Speculative Fiction Workshop: Steve Popkes, Heather Albano, Brett Cox, Jim Cambias, Gillian Daniels, Alex Jablokov, James

Patrick Kelly, Ken Schneyer, and Cadwell Turnbull. Steve and Heather did helpful last-minute reviews. Thanks for the ending fix, Steve.

- Ellen Kushner and Delia Sherman, who loaned their beautiful New York apartment to Reisden and Perdita. Thanks twice to Delia, who gave me my mantra for this whole book: "If there's a problem, I want to be part of the problem." Thanks for years of friendship, dear ones, and here's to years of friendship to come.

- K. Tempest Bradford, for African-American New York, sensitivity reading, and critical acumen. You were *so* right, Tempest.

- The Tuesday night gang: You know why. Thank you, survivors.

- Gordon Linzner and Veronica Schanoes, for help with historical New York.

- For Fort Lee, Richard Koszarski and the gang at the Fort Lee Historical Society.

- In Virginia, thanks for hospitality to Katherine Neville, and for research help to the African-American Historical Society of Fauquier County, the Fauquier County Historical Society, the owners of Neptune Lodge and Brentmoor (the Mosby Museum), and the National Park Service, administrators of Manassas National Battlefield Park.

- For Sturgis: Nobody who knows Susanna Sturgis should be surprised that she let me use her name for a dog. Thanks, Susanna.

- For Miss Nisensohn and Miss Fan: Thanks to Greta Nisensohn Kahn and Frances Shedd Fisher, whose generous donations to worthy causes got them onto *Titanic*. One of Frances Fisher's Civil War-era relatives was actually named Fate deMay; who could resist?

Thanks, Frances, for lending your name to the complicated Miss Fan, and a shout-out to Jessica too. Jessica, keep writing!

- From the WPA collections of narratives of previously enslaved people comes the story of the black man who sold his white master, as well as some aspects of Otis Church's story. The real analogue of Otis Church did something so outrageous that Tempest Bradford told me no one would believe it, so you'll have to look it up yourself, or ask me.
- For how places that black people didn't own became "our places": Carolyn Finney's magisterial and pioneering *Black Faces, White Spaces*, and Black/Land.
- Before you ask: Yes, it was considered impossible to forge fingerprints in 1912. Thank you, Google Books.
- For downtown whites and "voluntary Negroes": among many sources, I found particular help in Mary White Ovington's *Half a Man* (1912), Willard Gatewood's *Aristocrats of Color*, and Louis H. Patterson's *Life and Works of a Negro Detective* (1918). Thanks to all of the staff at the Schomburg Library (and please, Schomburg or Google Books, republish Louis Patterson!).
- "Downtown whites" are really too good not to do more with. I don't have plans currently. So I'm releasing Garnet Williams and Louis Johnson into the world (and Clementine Daniels too). If you would like to write stories about them, please do.
- Thanks to friends in the writing and Facebook communities and former and current colleagues at my day job, Pearson; you are too many to count, but particular thanks to Lewis Costas, Pamela Mayne, and Ram Kelath.

There's more about *Titanic* at my Web site, www.sarahsmith.com, including more *Titanic* stories, a library of free *Titanic* books, links to Pinterest boards on *Titanic* and 1912 New York, and that playlist of music used in the book (including a really evil do-wop version of "My Heart Will Go On"—you *do* want to hear this thing). To talk and hang out, contact me through my site or friend me on Facebook; I'm sarahwriter and Sarah Smith's Books on FB, sarahwriter on Twitter and occasionally Instagram, and swrs on Pinterest.

Thank you for reading.

The stories are nothing without you.

—Sarah Smith

Made in the USA
Columbia, SC
15 June 2020